FANTASY NELSON

MY RUNNING NIGHTMARE

iUniverse books may be ordered through booksellers or by contacting:

iUniverse
1663 Liberty Drive
Bloomington, IN 47403
www.iuniverse.com
844-349-9409

Because of the dynamic nature of the Internet, any web addresses or links contained in this book may have changed since publication and may no longer be valid. The views expressed in this work are solely those of the author and do not necessarily reflect the views of the publisher, and the publisher hereby disclaims any responsibility for them.

Any people depicted in stock imagery provided by Getty Images are models, and such images are being used for illustrative purposes only. Certain stock imagery © Getty Images.

ISBN: 978-1-6632-3806-1 (sc)
ISBN: 978-1-6632-3805-4 (e)

Library of Congress Control Number: 2022911313

Print information available on the last page.

iUniverse rev. date: 06/16/2022

PROLOGUE

The man sat down at the bar and looked around. There were so many people here tonight. He ordered a drink and just sat and watched them come and go and flirt with each other. After a while, a beautiful woman walked up and sat beside him.

"Care to order me a drink?" she asked with a purr.

"Who can resist a request from such a beautiful woman?" he asked as he smiled at her.

He ordered her a drink, and they sat there talking for an hour before she asked him to dance. What he didn't know was what he was getting into with this woman. He didn't know that she had a psychotic stalker. Not until halfway through the dance.

"What the hell do you think you're doing with my woman?" a harsh voice asked.

Kevin turned toward the voice. There stood a man almost his height and well-muscled. Kevin wasn't worried, however. He knew he could take him as he was in great shape, and this guy looked drunk. However, he was hoping it didn't go that far.

"I'm sorry. I didn't know she was taken," Kevin answered.

"Billy, I'm not your woman. You're drunk, and I have told you repeatedly that I'm not yours. We broke up six months ago. It's time for you to move on. I'm tired of this. Now go away."

"We didn't break up. You just decided to give it some time and never came back. I have been here. You belong to me, and I refuse to let a punk like this get his hands on you."

Kevin let go of her and started to walk off when Billy grabbed his arm and stopped him.

"Where do you think you're going, punk? We aren't done talking yet."

Kevin looked at him and said, "We're done, and you will let go of my arm. I'm not going to fight you over anyone. It isn't worth it. The lady doesn't want you and has said as much. However, on top of that, I didn't know she was with anyone in the first place."

"You think using some big words on me will stop me from pounding your face into the ground? Come on outside, Mr. Bigshot, so we can settle this," Billy said.

Kevin just shook his head and knocked the guy's hand away. Then, he walked toward the bar and paid his tab. Then, he proceeded to leave the bar with the man and woman arguing. He thought it was over until a few minutes later when he was unlocking his car, he felt a blow to the back of his head. He fell to the ground, feeling his head spinning. When he was rolled over, he saw Billy over top of him with a knife in his hand.

"I told you we were going to settle this, punk. I meant it. You can fight like a man, or I can cut you up right now," Billy said as he snickered.

Kevin kicked out and landed his foot square in Billy's knee. Billy cried out in pain and crashed to the ground. He dropped the knife and Kevin dove for it. But Billy grabbed his leg and pulled him back. The man flipped him over and started punching him in the face and gut. Kevin fought back and landed a good blow to the man's gut. He rolled off, and Kevin saw him grab the knife from where he landed.

Kevin got up and turned to punch the guy, but the guy was there slashing with the knife. It caught Kevin's arm, and he felt a sharp, hot pain go through his arm. The man slashed out again, and Kevin dodged it. Then, he punched the guy in the chest and went for another blow when the guy kicked his feet out from under him and rode Kevin down to the ground. The knife came up, and Kevin grabbed his wrist with both hands. He managed to turn the guy's wrist, so the knife wasn't pointing toward him. At the same time, the guy thrust his body down to shove the knife into Kevin's chest.

Kevin heard the guy make a shocked sound. He shoved him off and looked at him. The blade was sticking out of Billy's chest, and blood was gushing out. Kevin took off his shirt and started packing it around Billy's wound. He screamed for help. A man came running, and when he saw the blood, he started screaming at Kevin.

"You son of a bitch! That's my brother! You killed him! You killed him!"

"I didn't do this on purpose. He attacked me, and I tried to stop him from killing me. Stay here with him. I'll go get help," Kevin stammered.

Kevin ran back into the bar and told the bartender to call for help. The lady saw the blood on his hands and ran outside, hollering Billy's name. The bartender called the police, and Kevin slumped against the bar in shock.

When the police got there, Billy had already died. The ambulance carted him off. Billy's brother came into the bar escorted by the police. The minute he saw Kevin, he flew into a rage and tried to get to him, but the police held him back. Finally, they took Kevin's statement and took him to jail, where he was held overnight.

The next day he was arraigned, and a trial date was set. In one month, he would know if he was still a free man or not. What was he supposed to do? Was he supposed to let that man kill him? And over some woman he had just met? Kevin was afraid for his life. That man's brother had threatened to find him and kill him as revenge. He had threatened to torture him in ways that he couldn't even imagine. All he could do was wait.

CHAPTER 1

Renee walked into the living room with popcorn in hand. She sat down beside Kevin and set the bowl in her lap. She looked at him and smiled. Today was their second anniversary. She had fallen madly in love with him as he was the perfect man for her. He was six-foot, blonde-haired, and green-eyed. She loved his eyes the most as she got lost in their bright green color all the time. He would ask her what she was looking at so intently, and she would laugh.

Kevin smiled back as he leaned in and kissed her softly. He had something special planned for tonight. This woman was the one he planned on being with forever. Kevin just hoped she felt the same. He was found innocent and met Renee a year after that. He was surprised she had not heard of the incident or him. So, he had never told her about it. He hoped she never found out because he loved her. He was afraid he would lose her if she ever found out about what he had done, what he had been capable of doing.

"So, what did you pick out for us to watch?" Renee asked him.

"I picked The Lucky One because that's how I feel about you," Kevin replied.

"Aw. You are just too sweet. I love you so much," Renee said.

"I love you, too. So, do you want to watch the movie, or maybe we can skip it and…." Kevin trailed off, winking at her.

"Kevin, you are terrible. I would love to see this movie first. And then I will do things you can make a movie out of," Renee laughed as she ran her hand over his thigh.

Kevin felt an immediate thrill run through him. Everything she did was a turn-on for him. He leaned in and kissed her deeply. She leaned back, and he moved forward, pressing against her. She wrapped her arms and legs around him, pressing herself against him as hard as she could, and pulled his hair out of the ponytail. She ran her hands through his hair and kissed him harder. Kevin knew Renee liked the feeling of his hair running over her body.

He broke the kiss to move down her neck and let the hair run across her neck and chest. She moaned, and he ground himself into her. Renee tugged on the bottom of her shirt, and he moved back and watched as she removed her shirt and bra. Kevin removed his shirt and started to kiss her breasts. They kissed and caressed each other until a noise came from the kitchen.

Kevin sat back and looked at Renee. He put his finger over his lips, and she nodded. He got up and moved slowly towards the kitchen. Renee sat up and waited, but when she heard the noises of a struggle, she went running to the kitchen. Kevin had a man sitting on top of him, punching him. Kevin was fighting back, but the man had the upper hand. Renee ran over and tried to grab the man off of Kevin. He elbowed her in the chest, and she fell back, trying to catch her breath. Then, he started slamming Kevin's head into the floor, which knocked him out. He then turned towards her, and she tried to slide away.

He grabbed her and dragged her over to a chair. Then, he took the rope sitting on the table, tied her to the chair, and started touching her breasts

2

while he did. After that, he grabbed Kevin and tied him to a chair. Then, he came toward her. She had finally caught her breath, and she screamed.

He laughed and said, "Scream for me, baby. No one is going to hear you. The good thing about the house you chose to live in is that its miles from anyone else. Thanks for that, by the way."

The man continued petting her bare breasts as she hadn't thought to put her shirt back on when she had heard the commotion in the kitchen. He unbuttoned her pants, and she tried to kick out, but he merely sat in her lap, so she couldn't. She wouldn't give him the satisfaction of screaming again. He undid the rope around the chair and jerked her up, where he tied her hands behind her back. She struggled, but it wasn't much use. It just made the rope pull even tighter.

He pulled her pants down and sat her back in the chair. Next, he tied her upper half to the chair. Finally, he pulled the pants completely off and tied her ankles.

When Kevin woke up, his head was pounding, and he wasn't sure where he was. He groaned and looked around. His eyes sprung open as he saw Jesse sitting in his kitchen. He looked around and saw Renee sitting naked and tied in another chair. She had bruises setting in on her face and breasts.

"Welcome back to the world of the conscious, Romeo. We've been having some fun while waiting for you to wake up. Now it's time for the real fun," Jesse said as he untied Renee's hands from the chair.

Kevin saw her hands were still tied behind her back. There was a rope around her ankles, but it was loose, so there was space for her feet to move apart. Her head was lolling back and forth as the blows to her face had probably knocked her almost unconscious.

"Jesse, don't do this. She has nothing to do with what happened," Kevin pleaded.

"An eye for an eye, you bastard. You took what I loved, so I'm just returning the favor."

"Kevin, what's going on?" Renee asked, pleading for him to help her with her eyes.

"So, you haven't even told your precious woman who you are? She doesn't know you're a murderer, does she?"

"I'm sorry, baby. I moved and thought that had been left in the past. I'm not a murderer. Jesse's brother was psychotic and wouldn't leave his ex-girlfriend alone. I wound up meeting her one night at a bar. Billy didn't like that I was spending time with her. I tried to walk away, but he followed me to the parking lot. The psycho pulled a knife on me. I wound up turning it on him, and he died. I was acquitted."

"My brother wasn't psychotic. You were messing with his woman!" Jesse yelled.

"A woman who didn't want him," Kevin spat back.

Jesse punched Kevin. Renee tried to shove Jesse with her shoulder, but he just slapped her. She fell back and hit the floor. There was no way to brace herself as her hands were tied. She twisted, so she hit her side. Her head hit the floor, and she saw stars.

Renee was being dragged across the floor. Renee tried digging her nails into the floor, but it made them bleed. She started to cry. Her hands were pinned under her, and blood from her broken nails got on her back.

She pulled her legs up so she could kick Jesse. He moved to the side and grabbed her ankles, pulling them down. He lay on top of her. She knew what he would do as soon as his hand reached in between them. She heard him unzip his pants. She struggled, but he was too heavy, and she couldn't get any leverage with her hands pinned under her.

"I like it when you struggle," he said, his hot breath in her face.

She felt him pressing against her, and she screamed in his face as she head-butted him. However, that just made her dizzier and him angry.

"You'll pay for that, bitch."

"Leave her alone!" Kevin yelled. "It's me you want to hurt. Not her."

"But this will hurt you, and I don't like men," he laughed.

He pushed himself inside Renee, and she bit her lip until she drew blood again, trying not to scream. Then, she turned her head and saw Kevin struggling against the ropes tying him to the chair. He was screaming obscenities at Jesse and threatening to kill him.

Jesse didn't slack up but instead laughed at the pain and anger he saw on Kevin's face. Kevin wound up toppling the chair and couldn't get himself back up. He was trying to use his toes and the side of his arm to push himself, but he wasn't getting very far.

Renee couldn't stop herself from crying, but she would be damned if she gave him the satisfaction of screaming from the pain she felt at him ripping her apart. Finally, she grew tired from crying and where her head had been hit so much. The last sound heard was him groaning in her ear as he came inside her. She wanted to die.

"I like her. She doesn't scream, but she still struggles," Jesse said as he zipped his pants back up.

"You bastard! I will make you pay for this. I've seen you, so it's not like you can deny it's you." Kevin said, seething with anger.

"To what crime? I think your girl is coming with me. She won't be saying anything. I would kill you both and run, but I think this is better. I waited three damn years to plot out your murder, but you gave me the perfect revenge. Rape and kill your girl in front of you and then kill you. It would have been an eye for an eye, the person you love for the person I loved. However, I think it'll hurt you even more if I keep her, and you won't know if I have killed her or not," Jesse said as he smiled.

"No!" Kevin yelled as Jesse picked Renee up and slung her over his shoulder.

He heard some rustling throughout the house. Then he heard the door open and shut. He kept pushing himself, and it took hours, but he finally got to the wall with the phone on it. He kept trying to rock himself, and he finally got to his knees.

He threw himself backward onto the floor, and he felt the chair crack. After a few more hours, he'd finally broken it enough to get his hands loose. He pushed himself onto his side and got onto his knees. He scooted himself over to a counter and awkwardly pushed himself into a doubled-over position. Knocking the phone off with his chin, he sat back on the floor and felt for the numbers. He dialed 911. He gave them all the information they asked for and just sat there, feeling defeated.

He hadn't been able to help the love of his life when she had needed it the most. What kind of man was he? When the police came, they cut the ropes from around him. They questioned him about what had happened.

He was getting irritated because they weren't looking for Renee. Jesse could have killed her. The police had roped off the crime scene and were taking pictures and evidence, while all he could do was sit there and wonder what was happening to Renee.

* * *

Jesse picked the girl up off the floor and took her to the living room. She had passed out. He grabbed the shirt that was lying on the floor. He'd see if he could find a skirt to pull over the ropes. He put the shirt over her head and pulled it down. He wasn't too worried about Kevin getting to him anytime soon, so he could take his time.

He went through the house looking for anything valuable and took it. He was going to kill the girl after he'd raped her, but he figured it would hurt that jackass more for him to take her. So, he'd keep her, and he could fuck her anytime he wanted until he grew tired of her. So, he would take some of her things and head out. Since he hadn't originally planned on taking the girl with him, he would need extra stuff now.

He had money saved up from the robberies over the past three years, but was it enough for two people? He had patiently waited to go through with his plan just to get so angry at the last minute. He was too impulsive sometimes, and it got him into trouble. So now he was going to take a prisoner, too? At least she would be a bit of fun for a little while.

Once he had everything he would take stuffed into some pillowcases, he went downstairs. He heard Kevin yelling and cussing. A sick smile curved his lips as he threw the girl over his shoulder and left. Hell, this wasn't his first rodeo with the police. He knew how to hide.

He drove for hours before taking a break to run in a store. He had to ditch the car and get some fake identification for the woman in the trunk. He already had his, right down to a birth certificate. At one point, he pulled over on a deserted road to get her out of the trunk. He had heard her start kicking the trunk.

She'd tried to run, but he'd overpowered her, and she couldn't do much with her ankles still tied. He put her in the passenger seat and threatened to kill her if she tried anything. She had finally settled down, but she kept crying, which was getting on his nerves.

Once they had left the state, he rented a hotel room with his fake ID and returned to the car. He told her that he would kill her and return for Kevin if she didn't keep quiet. She was to do everything he said from then on. She nodded. He untied her hands and loosened the rope around her ankles. She spat on him when he took the duct tape off her mouth. He slapped her and then yanked her out of the car and into the room.

"I'm going to let you get cleaned up. I'm right outside the door, so don't think of doing anything stupid, ok?"

Renee nodded. Jesse sat her on the bed, took the rope off her ankles, and then stood up. He watched her for a minute and then stood back. She looked at her ankles and saw the blood on them where she had struggled against the rope. She slowly stood up and walked over to the bathroom. She tried to close the door, but Jesse shook his head.

"At least give me a little privacy to go to the bathroom. Where am I going to go?" Renee queried.

"Leave it open just a crack then. Just enough so I know you aren't trying anything stupid."

"Like what? What am I going to do besides try to kill myself? You only took me to upset Kevin. Moreover, you've threatened several times to kill me. So, what difference would it make if I did kill myself? You'd be rid of me, and you could run without a burden."

"Nah. Then they'd find you, and Kevin wouldn't suffer anymore not knowing what happened to you."

"Then dump my body somewhere they won't find it. It's better than being with you," Renee spat.

"I like you. You're spunky. I think I'm going to keep you for a while first. Now go take a shower," Jesse said as he took his shoes off and sat back on the bed.

Renee had to figure out a way to get out of this. She got in the shower, turning the water to the highest level of heat she could stand. She slumped onto the bathtub floor, letting the hot water hit her as she cried. Her body was bruised, and her lower half was hurting from the assault. She saw blood running down the drain from between her thighs. She couldn't live like this.

Why was he keeping her? Was he going to continue to beat and rape her every day? He couldn't keep her tied up all the time, so how would he stop her from trying to run or scream? If she went docile, would he let her go then? Her being her usual self was something he liked.

CHAPTER 2

A month later, Jesse had gotten a fake ID for her. He had sold his car, and they had taken a bus to another state. The whole ride, he'd kept a knife pressed into her side. He had tied her up every time he left and duct-taped her mouth. He wouldn't stay gone long, but she had tried everything to get out of the ropes each time. He hadn't beat on her like he did the first time.

He would come for her, and she would struggle, but all he would do was slap her around or choke her almost to the point of passing out. She tried to refuse to eat, but he made her. When she had missed her period, she thought it was due to the stress. Now, she was worried it was because of something else.

She bit her lip as she thought about the possibility of the monster getting her pregnant. She looked over where he was sitting on the couch in the small cabin he had rented. She had learned not to speak because that turned his attention to her, and she didn't like it when he looked at her. He came for her then.

However, she had to know the truth. It was going to gnaw away at her if she didn't. What was she going to do if she was pregnant? Moreover, what if she was pregnant by Kevin? They hadn't used protection when they were together. If it belonged to Kevin, there was a possibility of Jesse hurting the baby. But could she keep the baby if it belonged to the monster? Or would he beat her so severely that she lost it? She finally cleared her throat to get his attention. She cringed when he looked at her.

"What?"

"I, um, I missed my period."

"So? What do you want me to do about it?"

"I'm usually pretty regular. I, I need a pre-pregnancy test," Renee stammered.

Jesse looked at her for a few minutes and then stood up. He left her tied to the chair she was in but checked to ensure the ropes were tight. Then, he grabbed his keys and left. He didn't even bother gagging her this time. She screamed for all she was worth, but there was no one around the cabin to save her. She cried until she heard the car pull up.

Jesse walked in and untied her. He dragged her to the bathroom and took the pregnancy tests out of the bag. He handed them to her, and she just looked at him. Was he expecting her to pee on them right in front of him?

"What are you waiting for?"

"For one, I don't have to pee right now. For another, there is no way I'm peeing on those things with you standing here. If you truly intend to keep me hostage, you will have to slack up on this watch everything I do crap. If I am truly pregnant, I'm not going to do anything to harm my baby. You have kept me tied up for over a month. My wrists and ankles are raw and hurting. I need some relief. I can't even sleep because you have me tied to the bed, so I can't move. I'm too tired to try to run. Either kill me or give me some space."

"Who the hell do you think you're talking to? You don't get to make demands. You do what I say."

"Whatever. I'm beyond caring what you think or say. You have beaten and raped me every day, several times a day. My life isn't worth a damn, so maybe if I piss you off enough, you'll just go ahead and kill me," Renee said and leaned against the sink.

"No, I'm not going to kill you. Keeping you is a lot more fun. You're feisty, and I love it. Killing Kevin would control you better. If you are pregnant, I won't put my hands on you anymore, but you will have to get with the program on the sex. I'll leave you untied as long as you don't try anything. I want my baby to be healthy."

"So, let me get this straight. My attitude problem is a turn-on for you. Furthermore, you won't beat me, but you expect me to have sex with you willingly? You are crazy. I'm not going to give my body to you willingly. You do not turn me on. I hate you. I hate it when you touch me. It makes me cringe. I'll never willingly give myself to you. As for being untied, I already told you I wouldn't do anything to harm my baby. It disgusts me to think you got me pregnant, but it's still my baby."

Jesse pressed against her. She tried to get away from him, but he put his arms on either side of her. His face was right in front of hers. Her body tensed as she waited for the blows to come. Instead, he just continued to look at her, and she shivered as his expression was dark and brooding. She couldn't do anything but look at his face.

"Keep running your mouth, and I will put it to good use. I don't care if you like me or not. I'm still going to do what I want with you, and you can either learn to enjoy it or continue to squirm. It makes no difference to me. I'm on the run for life, so why not have a sex slave? Eventually, I'm going to have to get a job. So, you'll have to be by yourself. You'll get with the program if you don't want to stay tied up while I'm gone. Believe me when I say that the first stop I'm making is to kill your precious Kevin if

I get any hint of trouble. I'll leave you alive so you can see his mutilated body. Then when you least expect it, I'll come for you, too," Jesse sneered.

Renee felt a shiver go down her spine as a picture sprang to mind that made tears well in her eyes. She knew he meant what he said, but there was no way she could give herself over willingly. She felt dead inside. He had told her that she was his sex slave, so he would never let her leave. He may have killed her before if she pushed hard enough but thinking she was pregnant just ended that.

"I need to go to the bathroom now. Can you please leave the bathroom?" Renee asked politely.

"Since you asked so nicely, I'll wait outside," Jesse said and kissed her, crushing her lips under his.

She didn't kiss him back, but she didn't fight him either. When she felt his tongue running across her lower lip, she opened her mouth so he could stick his tongue inside. She closed her eyes and imagined Kevin. Jesse was about Kevin's height, maybe an inch or two shorter. She imagined Kevin's body pressing against hers while he kissed her passionately. If she could at least let her imagination run away with her, she could forget that this horrible man was touching her.

When Jesse finally stepped back from her, she opened her eyes. She found him smirking at her before he left the bathroom. She frowned. He didn't think she had enjoyed that kiss, did he? She took the pregnancy tests out of the boxes. Once she had used them, she placed them on the counter. She leaned against the counter, not even wanting to look at the tests. Instead, she tried to figure out what had happened between her and Jesse.

When he knocked on the door, she said, "I'm done."

It shocked her that he had knocked. Jesse came in and looked at her for a second, and then walked over to the tests. He looked at both of them and then at her. She showed him the boxes and how to read the tests. Truthfully, she didn't want to know, but the look on his face told it all. He was grinning from ear to ear.

"Well, I will be damned. I'm going to be a Daddy."

Renee burst into tears. She didn't want to be pregnant with this monster's baby. Jesse surprised her when he wiped her tears away. She initially jerked when she felt his hand on her face, thinking he was about to hit her.

"Hey, I told you, no more hitting. Stop crying. A baby is a blessing."

"Not when it belongs to a monster. I'll be damned if my child will grow up to be a rapist, abuser, or all-around asshole," Renee yelled.

She stormed past him, but he grabbed her and yanked her back against him. She was angry and scared all at the same time. Her whole body was shaking with it. Jesse squeezed her hard when she started trying to get away.

"Do you want to be tied back up? If so, keep this up. If not, calm your ass down. I like your fire, but I'm only going to tolerate so much disrespect before I get nasty," Jesse whispered in her ear.

"I don't care. I'm a human being, and I have a right to be angry and hurt by someone who constantly hurts me physically and mentally. You will be the person you already are no matter what I do!" Renee yelled while still squirming to get away.

Jesse walked out to the bedroom with her still struggling in his arms. He threw her on the bed, and she tried to get away, but he grabbed her ankles. He lay on top of her, and she began to cry again, knowing what was coming. He took her off guard by just laying there, restraining her. When she finally grew tired of trying to get away, Jesse moved and pulled her onto her side against him.

"Now, we can make this work if you just get with the program. Stop fighting me. I'm the bad guy. I know. However, you are having my baby. That changes things. I may be a bad guy who has done some truly fucked up shit to you, but I will never treat my kid like my father treated my brother and me. The man did us just like I've done you."

"Then you would think you wouldn't want to do that to someone else," Renee whispered, feeling exhausted.

"It's what made me the bastard I am today. Your boyfriend did the rest by killing my brother."

"That doesn't have anything to do with me. You brought me into this situation to hurt Kevin. All you're doing is hurting me."

"Then don't make me hurt you anymore. I like your fire, as I said before. Truth be told, it's a turn on, but my temper won't tolerate it too much depending on what you say. I'll raise the baby with you, and I will treat you well if you just stop fighting."

Renee knew that no matter what, she had to protect her baby. What if it wasn't his? Would he kill her if it wasn't? She had no money, no car, no phone, no way to run without him being able to catch up to her. He was a light sleeper and woke up every time she moved. She started to cry again, but Jesse held her until she fell asleep this time.

*   *   *

She was not tied to the bed when she woke up like she usually was. She rolled over and found Jesse was sitting in the chair in the room. He was watching her. She sighed and rolled back over, acting like she was still asleep. Unfortunately, he had seen her look at him. He stood up and grabbed her arm. He pulled her up and off the bed. She was too tired to fight. He took her into the kitchen and sat her on a chair. He then proceeded to put hair dye in her hair. She just sat there and let him.

"It's unfortunate that I have to cover your real color. It is pretty to look at with the gold tones in it. But we can't be too careful if you have to go out. We have already been here for a week. Time to get going again."

"Jesse, we can't keep running. It's not going to be healthy for the baby. I need to start seeing a doctor to get prenatal care. And when the baby is born, it will need regular checkups, too."

"We have some time. We'll just start staying in hotels for a night or two until we get far enough away. I'm thinking of Canada. I know someone there that can get us fake citizenship."

"You are truly planning on keeping me hostage, aren't you?"

"You are going to have my baby. I can always take the baby and run, but until you have it, you stay."

"I'm not letting you take my baby from me!"

"Then, I guess you are no longer my hostage but are willingly staying," Jesse said as he smirked.

Renee was taken aback by his suggestion that she would willingly stay with him, but when looking at it that way, she supposed she was. There was no way she would let him kidnap her baby and take off with it. Was he planning on taking the baby and ditching her? She had to know.

"What are you going to do after the baby is born?"

"What do you mean?" Jesse asked.

"Are you going to kill me, ditch me, what?"

"I'm not going to kill you. I told you and that boyfriend of yours, I'm keeping you. You belong to me now. Plus, a baby needs its mother. We will raise the baby together, in Canada. Eventually, you will become complacent, and we can have a nice, normal routine," Jesse said.

After the dye sat long enough, Jesse took her over to the sink and began to pour water over her head to get it out. Once it was done, he shampooed and conditioned it. Renee hated to admit that it felt good to have him wash her hair. After the month and a half he'd beat on and raped her, she was surprised to have some feeling besides hate. Jesse dried her hair and then brushed it.

Renee tried to take the brush from him and do it herself, but he held it where she couldn't. She closed her eyes and imagined Kevin brushing her hair. He used to do it every night. By the time Jesse was finished, she felt very relaxed. She didn't even realize she had made a few little noises of pleasure. She tensed as she felt his hands run over her shoulders and down her back slowly.

"Relax. You were just enjoying what I was doing. Just stay with that thought," Jesse whispered in her ear.

Renee knew what was coming as soon as he started touching her. Telling her to relax wasn't helping the situation. She tried to release the tension in her body, but she couldn't. The more he touched her, the tenser she got. He had taken her off guard by being kind instead of rough when he had dyed her hair. He had even been sweet in brushing her hair. Usually, he didn't touch her first when he forced himself on her. He would just take what he wanted. When she struggled, he got really rough with it.

Had her being pregnant changed him that much? Was it because he had something else to threaten her with now so he could do whatever he wanted? She knew he didn't actually want her. She was just a way to torture Kevin. Maybe if she played along, he would allow her some more freedom, and she could escape. But where would she go? He never left his car keys out where she could get them. She didn't have any money to go anywhere or even a phone to call from.

How could she tell anyone he had physically abused her or raped her since there would be no evidence by the time she got away? He had already told her that he'd run from the police once and was capable of hiding and getting away with murder. Because he knew someone who could get him fake IDs and citizenship, there was no way to catch him that she could see. So, if she got away, how long would it be before he caught up to her?

What would he do to her and the baby? Or Kevin, for that matter? It wouldn't matter if she never saw Kevin again. Jesse would kill him, and not in a quick manner either. If he had waited years to plot this type of revenge on Kevin, what would he do if she managed to get away? She shivered as images flashed through her mind.

Jesse stood her up and sat on the chair. He pulled her into his lap and kissed her. Renee tried her best to play along, but she couldn't find it in her to kiss him back. She felt him run his hands up her back and under her shirt. It was taking everything she had not to struggle. Finally, he broke the kiss, took her shirt off, and unhooked her bra. He took it off and threw it in the direction of her shirt.

Renee hissed when his hands ran over some of the still bruised and tender places. She saw him frown as he lightly ran his fingers over them. Was he feeling bad about beating on her now? He sure hadn't felt bad about it while he was doing it. He stood her up and took her pants and panties off. He lightly touched all the bruises and then placed feather-light kisses on them. Renee kept her eyes down, so all she could see was his feet as he undressed and stood there.

"Look at me. I want you to actually see me."

Renee felt her face get hot as she slowly looked up, her eyes seeing all of him. He had a great body. There were several tattoos on his arms and chest. He even had a big one going up his side. You could tell he worked out. When she got to his face, she noticed he had red, full lips. They were kissable lips. His nose was a little crooked, like it had been broken before and not healed right. His gray-blue eyes were beautiful. His jet-black hair was hanging right below his ears, just this side of shaggy.

"Do you think I'm ugly? Or do you like what you see?"

"It doesn't matter what you look like. A person's personality is what has always mattered to me, and yours is not good. If you think that telling me to go along to get along will work, you're wrong. I don't love you. I don't want to be in a relationship with you. I want my life back!" Renee cried.

"This is your life now," Jesse said as he picked her up and carried her to the bedroom.

His touch was no longer gentle. He took what he wanted while Renee cried silently. She had made the mistake of telling him that she didn't want him and never would. She didn't fight him so it would be over sooner. He didn't put his hands on her, so at least she wouldn't be hurting all over this time. Once he was finished, he got up and left the room. Renee curled up into a ball and cried herself to sleep.

CHAPTER 3

Over the next month, Renee and Jesse made their way across the country. Jesse had changed his mind about Canada as he said it would be easier to stay under the radar if a new citizenship didn't pop up somewhere. So, they traveled from Florida to Washington state, stopping every night to get a room and sleep. Jesse always held her at night, so she couldn't move without waking him up. Since they were backtracking now, Jesse made sure to keep away from North Carolina.

What they didn't know was that Kevin was looking for Renee. He had grown tired of waiting for the police to do anything. They had told him that they didn't have any new leads about what had happened to Renee. They hadn't found any evidence of Jesse killing her in his apartment. They eventually found his car in Georgia. The police had issued the report to the Georgia police, and they had searched, but no one had seen Renee.

Kevin wasn't going to give up hope. He wouldn't stop looking for her until he found Jesse or found Renee, dead or alive. It was his fault that she was even in this mess. He quit his job, took all of his savings, and traveled from state to state. He would work odd jobs just to make a living and eat, but he never stopped. Once he had searched a city, he moved on to another until he had worked the entire state.

When they finally got to Washington state, Jesse found a house in the country that he put a down payment on. He began to look for a job. He put locks on the doors to lock her in when he left. She had no phone service or internet. He had hooked up the cable so she could watch TV when he wasn't there. He hadn't been kind to her since the first time he had tried, and she had rejected him.

He had kept his promise and not put his hands on her again, but he still took her whenever he wanted. He no longer tied her up. She had been allowed to walk around freely with his ever-watchful eye on her. She hadn't bothered to start a conversation with him as she didn't want to get to know him. Every night, he would hold her as he slept. She wasn't sure if it was because he wanted to or if it was a way to keep her from running.

When she was three or four months along, she asked him about finding a doctor for her. He looked them up on the phone and checked into them with her. At least he was allowing her to decide which one she wanted. When the appointment was set, she talked him out of going into the room with her as she was uncomfortable with being examined while he watched. She came on to him to make him think she was complacent and wouldn't try to get help from the doctor.

Jesse was taken by surprise, but he did agree to it. He rather liked the fact that she had come to him. Perhaps he could begin again by trying to be nice. He let her undress him, and then he made her look him over. She didn't look disgusted when she looked at him. Maybe it was a good sign.

"Do you like what you see?" Jesse asked.

"You're a handsome man," Renee responded.

"That's not what I asked you."

Jesse watched as she looked him over again. Finally, she closed her eyes and took a deep breath. When she opened her eyes, she smiled at him.

"Yes, I like what I see. You are very attractive," Renee whispered as she walked up to him.

Jesse smiled and wrapped her in his arms. He kissed her softly. Renee responded and kissed him back. He ran his fingers through her hair and over her back. He didn't know that she had imagined Kevin the whole time.

Jesse lay her on the bed after undressing her. He began to kiss down her neck and make his way to her breasts. He began to pay special attention to them as his hand roamed over her stomach. When he lay his hand on her stomach, her heart skipped a beat. He felt her body tense. When Jesse began to kiss his way down to her stomach, she relaxed. Then, he felt her push her fingers through his hair.

Jesse continued to kiss his way down until he found her sweet spot. He slowly ran his hand down her leg and back until he caressed between her thighs. His tongue was making slow circles over her. She gasped as he pushed his fingers inside of her. He stopped and moved back up. He ran his hand across her cheek.

"Open your eyes and look at me."

Renee slowly opened her eyes, and Jesse said, "Why are you crying?"

"I'm sorry. I didn't mean to," Renee whispered.

Jesse frowned and moved his hand back down her body. Her body tensed as his hand caressed in between her thighs. She squeezed her eyes shut as he slipped his fingers back inside her.

"This is hurting you, isn't it?"

"Yes," Renee blurted out.

Jesse withdrew his hand and moved back down her body. He settled between her thighs and began to use his mouth on her. She wasn't responding, but he kept going. Finally, her body started to react to what he was doing.

Jesse moved back up and pressed against her. Her body tensed, and he waited for her to open her eyes. Her hands shook as she put them on his chest. She pushed him off her and onto his back. He felt angry until she crawled on top of him.

She began to kiss his neck and chest. What he didn't realize was that her eyes were still closed. She kissed her way down his body until she could place her mouth around him. She took care of his problem for him.

When she was finished, she slowly crawled back up the bed and lay down on the bed. Jesse watched her. He moved his arm, inviting her to come over. She slowly moved close to him and rested her head on his shoulder. She put her arm over his stomach and pressed her body against his side. His arm went around her shoulders, and his hand rested on her back.

Jesse put his hand over hers. He felt the baby bump she had pressed into his side. It made him smile. If she was hurting when he tried to take her, she wouldn't be able to see the doctor. She had to heal up. If he let her heal and then tried to take her, perhaps she would react differently to him, just like she had today.

*   *   *

Renee walked into the doctor's office and felt nervous. She had to remember her name. The fake ID she had said her name was Tabitha Morgan. Jesse had it made to match his fake ID. She had hoped that he was not using the ploy of them being married, but she quickly found out that is what he had done. She couldn't act strangely, or people would know something was happening. She sat down in a chair and waited for Jesse to get the paperwork.

He handed it to her, and she just looked at it. She had to remember information that she didn't know. She bit her lip, and Jesse took it from her and started filling it out. He put her fake name on it and the address they were living at. She hadn't even known what that was. However, when it came to things about her health, she put down the truth.

When they called her back to the room, she stood up and looked at Jesse. He was staying sat down. She kissed his lips and said she would be back. This was just a routine checkup where a wife left her husband in the waiting room. She took a deep breath and let it out slowly. She walked into the room, and the nurse had her change into a gown. Jesse hadn't forced himself on her in a month. She felt good, but she was still worried that the doctor would hurt her with his examination and then ask questions that she wasn't sure she could answer.

What happened if she told him what was going on and he called the police? Would people act strangely and tip Jesse off? Could she get away from him without him being able to run? She felt fear as she thought about him getting away and coming after her. She lost her nerve to try.

"Mrs. Morgan, I'm Doctor Gilly. It's nice to meet you. I understand you are here for your first checkup in your pregnancy?"

"Yes, that's correct."

"Why did you wait so long to seek medical care for your pregnancy?"

"Honestly, we were in the process of moving and I didn't want to start with one doctor and then have to switch to another. And, well, promise you won't tell my husband?" Renee asked, nervous.

"Yes. Patient/Doctor confidentiality is in play here."

"I don't think it's his baby. I, well, I slept with someone else right before we got back together from our separation. I have been too nervous to find out because I don't want him to know if it isn't his. Is there a way to find out and not mention it again?" Renee asked.

"I think you should tell him, but that is none of my business. We can do an ultrasound and find out exactly how far along you are."

"Ok. That would be great."

The doctor asked her a few more questions and then had her lay back. He called his nurse in, and she assisted him with the examination. Renee had never liked having pelvic exams anyway. She felt a slight pinch when he started, but it wasn't too uncomfortable. Renee thought back to the last time she and Kevin had been together. If the baby was Kevin's, she estimated she was five months. If it were Jesse's, she would be around four to four and a half months.

When the nurse brought in the ultrasound machine, Renee was interested. They put the gel on her belly and started taking pictures of her baby. Finally, the nurse pointed at a spot and showed her the baby. It was about the length of a banana, and Renee began to cry as she listened to its heartbeat. The nurse left the room after the examination, and the doctor came back in a little later.

26

"You are approximately twenty-one weeks. That puts you a little over five months pregnant. May I ask if it is your husband's?"

"No," Renee said as she closed her eyes.

"Ok. What happens if you go into labor? Won't he realize it's too early?"

"Can we just say that happens sometimes? It does, doesn't it?"

"Yes, it can happen. Are you ok with your husband coming in now?"

"Yes, he can come in now. He will most likely be at every appointment after this. I wasn't really comfortable with him being here for the initial examination."

"Mrs. Morgan, can I call you Tabitha?"

"Yes," Renee replied.

"When I did your pelvic exam, I noticed some scarring like you recently healed from some trauma. Is something else going on besides this not being your husband's baby?"

Renee felt her face pale, but she quickly lied and said, "My husband likes it a little, um, rough. We had to stop doing that as I got farther along."

"Are you sure that's all there is? The damage looks more like forced sex or some sharp objects were used."

Renee felt a blush creep up her face as she lied again and said, "We like to use certain, well, certain things in the bedroom. Has it caused a lot of damage?"

"It's a fair amount. I would suggest not continuing with the role play in the bedroom with whatever you are using. If you stop now, you should be ok as the scarring won't be too bad. If you continue with that behavior, you may never enjoy sex again. It can also lead to you not being able to have any more children."

"I understand. Do you want to tell my husband that when he comes in? I'm not much for that type of role-playing anyway. I only did it to make him happy, but frankly, it hurts," Renee said, trying to get the doctor to make Jesse understand how badly he was hurting her.

"I can talk to you both about it while he is in here. That's not a problem. Let me get a nurse to go get him."

The doctor walked out of the room, and a few minutes later, a nurse brought Jesse in. He walked over and kissed her cheek. Then, he sat down in the chair against the wall. Renee bit her lip as the doctor returned to the room after a few minutes. Then, he held out his hand to Jesse, and Jesse shook it.

"Mr. Morgan, I brought you in here as I've already talked to your wife about this. I noticed your wife has quite a bit of damage internally. Now, she has told me that you guys' role play and use a lot of things as she calls them in the bedroom. I have told her and I am going to tell you, that if you guys continue with the toys or whatever it is that you are using, she will most likely wind up not being able to enjoy sex ever again. The scarring isn't too extensive right now, but it can definitely get worse and it could cause her not to be able to have any more children as well."

Renee watched Jesse's face as the doctor talked. To her surprise, he didn't look angry. He looked thoughtful. He had looked at her when the doctor had said she had told him the damage was from the use of other things, but he hadn't looked angry.

"Now that's out of the way, do you two want to know the sex of the baby?"

Renee looked at Jesse and then said, "Yes."

"Doesn't matter to me as long as the baby is healthy."

"Alright. I'll take that as a yes. You are having a boy. Congratulations."

"Thank you," Renee said.

"Do you two have any more questions for me?"

"I think we're good," Jesse replied.

The doctor nodded and left the room with instructions for her to get dressed. Jesse stood up and came over to help her up. He put his hand on her back and pulled her up to a sitting position. She slowly stood up, and he handed her her clothes.

"You didn't tell the doctor the truth," Jesse said.

"No. What would have happened if I did?"

"You already know what would have happened if I had seen anything suspicious. And it wouldn't have been pretty. You are learning. How about a reward?"

"What kind of reward?" Renee asked, suspicious.

"You need some new clothes. The ones you have don't fit anymore. I bought a few but you have outgrown those, too."

"That tends to happen when you are pregnant. Your belly gets bigger and sometimes you put on weight elsewhere. What are you going to do if I stay fat after the pregnancy?"

"Nothing. You still aren't going anywhere. I told you before, you belong to me now."

Renee continued to put her clothes on as her mind raced to figure out what to say. She didn't want to stay with Jesse. Even getting fat and ugly wouldn't work with him. She sighed. He cupped her chin and made her look at him.

"Stop trying to figure out ways to get away. That's going backwards, not forwards. You're mine. The baby is mine. Make it work. You have been doing pretty good so far. Have I treated you badly this past month?"

"No," Renee admitted.

"We can keep it that way as long as you keep it as it has been."

"I need something from you, then. If you want me to move forward and go along with this fake marriage, I need you to stop locking me into the house. I need a phone, too. What happens if I fall or if I go into early labor? I have no way to get help."

"I'll think about what you want. Show me you aren't going to do anything stupid, and we'll see. Show you are truly going to go along with this fake marriage as you called it."

"How am I supposed to do that?"

"Act like my wife. Do everything a wife does."

Renee knew what he meant by that, and sex was the one thing she didn't want to do with him. She had been doing things for him so he wouldn't try to have sex with her. But she knew he hadn't forced himself on her because he wanted her to heal up so the doctor wouldn't find evidence of the rape. He had regardless, but she'd been able to play it off. She took a deep breath and let it out slowly.

"Ok. If that's what it takes, I will do it. I can't take the risk that something may happen to the baby and I can't do anything about it."

"Alright. You can start today. Let's go shopping."

CHAPTER 4

They went shopping. Jesse took her hand as she got out of the car. He held her hand through the store like they were an actual couple. She picked out a few items and tried them on. Jesse had her come out and show him everything she tried on. He picked out the ones he liked and paid for them.

When they returned to the house, he dropped her off and left. She sighed and sat on the bed, looking at the clothes. At least he hadn't come in and tried to sleep with her. She put her things in the dresser and went into the kitchen. She noticed the back door was ajar. She walked over to it and pushed it open. The backyard was pretty big.

Jesse had done this on purpose to see if she would try and escape. Nevertheless, the urge to just sit in the sunlight was too great to resist. She had been cooped up in the house for months except for today. So, she walked out onto the back porch and sat down, just enjoying the sun.

Jesse had moved the car and walked back to the house. He was in the woods, watching, waiting to see what she would do. He watched her as she sat on the porch and turned her face up to the sun. She was a pretty woman. When she didn't think he was watching, she would let her guard down and let her feelings out.

He watched her as she stood up and walked around the yard. There were flower beds that were dying as he hadn't taken care of them. He could care less about flowers, but she seemed to be interested in them. She got on her knees and started pulling weeds. He watched her a little longer before he walked back to his car. Just because she hadn't tried to run this time didn't mean much. She might have been suspicious of the open door. She had covered up what had happened at the doctor's office.

He'd give her a little freedom and see what she did with it. Maybe he could get her a burner phone that only allowed her to call him and 911. That way, if something did happen, she could get help. He hadn't thought about something happening while he was gone. Perhaps his threat had worked. He pulled into the driveway and went into the house. She hadn't come back inside. Maybe she hadn't heard the car. He walked out the back door and saw her sit back and wipe the sweat from her face. When she looked up, he saw fear on her face. She quickly pushed herself up off the ground.

"You didn't try to run," Jesse said as he walked over.

"N-no," she stuttered, wringing her hands.

"It's alright. I left the door unlocked on purpose, but I'm sure you already figured that out. You like flowers?"

"Yes. I've never been good at keeping a garden, but it gave me something to do other than being cooped up inside," Renee said as she walked up to the house.

Jesse reached out to pull her to him, and she flinched. He wrapped his arms around her and kissed her. She never kissed him back, but she had let him kiss her whenever he wanted. He didn't want her to flinch or pull back when he touched her. If he could break her of that habit, perhaps he could take her out more. Maybe over time, she would respond to his touch. He had noticed that her eyes were closed the only time she responded to him trying anything with her. Maybe she imagined someone else, or she couldn't look at him because of what he had done before. However, he wanted to keep her around for himself now instead of only keeping her because of Kevin.

She sometimes pushed her limits with the things she said, but he couldn't deny he liked it. He didn't like docile women. When he broke the kiss, he wrapped his arm around her shoulders and walked her back inside. Maybe he could buy some flowers for her, and she could do something with the flower beds. It might even score him some brownie points with her. It couldn't hurt.

*   *   *

A few months went by, and Renee had been able to go outside more when Jesse was home. He had left the back door unlocked a couple of times, and she had gone out and tended the flowers. Sometimes, he would bring flowers home for her to plant. The flower beds were weeded and watered. She would sit outside sometimes and just enjoy the smell of them. Jesse had bought a couple of chairs to sit outside. He sat out there with her often. Renee never really felt comfortable, but she was starting to get into a daily routine. When she had a doctor's appointment, he would drive her to it and go in with her.

Jesse took her with him to the store after one appointment. She had looked at some of the baby items. She found a baby book that she liked, but she returned it. She had also picked up a tiny frame for the baby's first picture that would be perfect for the pictures she'd been given. She would have bought so many things to make memories with for the baby, but she had no way of doing that now. She sighed and started to walk away.

"Is there something you want?"

Renee stopped and asked, "Does it matter? It's not like I have a way of getting anything."

"Maybe you should just ask. I'm sure we can work something out."

"By working something out, do you mean me sleep with you for it? I'd rather get a job and earn my own money."

"You can't work while being pregnant anyway. You can do other things for the money. It doesn't always have to be sex."

"I already clean the house and cook. It's not like I have anything else to do all day. I tend to the flowers. What else is there?"

"Sometimes a person likes a good old fashion back or foot rub. Maybe you could draw me a bath," Jesse grinned.

"A back rub? And what would that earn me?"

Jesse shrugged and said, "Depends."

Renee shook her head and walked away. She would like a back and foot rub, too, but there was no way she was asking him for one. Her feet were swollen, and her back hurt from the pregnancy. Her belly was big now. It wouldn't be much longer, and the baby would be here. What happens if the baby needs something? Would she have to barter for that, too?

"You don't seem too interested."

"I'm not. I shouldn't have to barter for anything," Renee snapped as she turned towards him.

She moved close to his ear and whispered, "You kidnapped me. You raped me and got me pregnant. So now you want me to either screw you or do something else for you for me to be able to get anything at all. Who in their right mind would do that?"

Renee started to walk off, but Jesse grabbed her arm and pulled her back to him. He had a look on his face that used to scare her, but now she was just bored. He wasn't going to hit her while she was pregnant, and they both knew it, so that threat was out the window. She still had a couple of months of freedom on that end.

"That mouth of yours will get you into trouble one of these days. You won't be pregnant forever, and when you aren't anymore, all of these times will be remembered," Jesse whispered threateningly.

"Yeah, I figured as much, but I just don't care anymore. You're going to do whatever you want whether I like it or not. I'm not running away because I believe you will do what you said you would, but other than that, I don't have to care what else you do. You're going to hurt me, so what? You were going to do that anyway. The doctor already said if you keep going with it that I won't be able to enjoy sex. Hell, I'm just hoping it makes me numb to it all together so I can't feel anything at all. No pain or pleasure. So, go ahead and keep going with it. It makes no difference to me because frankly, I'm tired of the threat of it."

"Have you ever heard the expression that you catch more bees with honey than vinegar? You keep saying you want me to be more compliant, but you give me no reason to be. Honestly, I never will be. I am who I am, and no matter how much you try, you won't beat it out of me," Renee snarled as she jerked her arm away from him.

He smiled as he grabbed her hand and laced his fingers through hers.

"Alright. Let's go baby shopping," Jesse said as he chuckled at the shocked look on Renee's face.

He watched her tentatively pick out a few things for the baby. It was all clothes and diapers. Things the baby would need, not the things she wanted. He took her back over to the aisle she had initially been on and picked up the baby book and photo frame. He put them in the buggy, and she looked at it and then back down at the floor with a slight smile.

They went home, and she took the baby book and the picture frame out. He watched her as she placed one of the photos in the frame and the other in the baby book. She had a smile on her face as she lovingly put the frame on the nightstand beside the bed. She was a completely different person when it came to the baby. He found that he was a little bit jealous. He wanted her to treat him that way, too.

She had said something in the store that had attracted his attention, the old expression of attracting more bees with honey than vinegar. If he continued to threaten her to keep her in line, she was more likely to lash out. On the other hand, if he were nice to her, she would be nice to him. That was what he had gotten out of it. He had bought her the things she wanted, and she had been nice on the way home. He had talked to her, and they had a conversation.

He watched her as she picked up a pen and started writing in the baby book. No doubt filling it up with everything that had happened before. He watched as she flipped back to the beginning of the book and bit her lip. She was deep in thought as he walked over to look at what she was looking at. It was the first page where you put the baby's name. He hadn't even thought about naming the baby. He hated that the baby would have to take on the fake last name they had.

"Do you know what you want to name the baby?"

Renee looked up, startled by his question. "Yes. I would like to name him Christian Alexander."

"Sounds good."

"Are you going to let me name him?" Renee asked, surprised.

"Honestly, I hadn't even thought about names. That name sounds like a good, strong one. You have to remember to put your other name on the birth certificate."

Jesse watched as her face fell. She closed the baby book and put it aside. She lay on the bed and placed her hand on her stomach, closing her eyes. He sighed and walked out of the room as he heard her begin to cry. One step forward, three steps back. She'd come around eventually. He'd bought her a phone with his number programmed into it and blocked all others. He'd give it to her later tonight. Maybe that would cheer her up a little.

*   *   *

Renee walked out to the kitchen and began to fix dinner. She felt terrible as she'd had Braxton Hicks for a few weeks. Jesse didn't know she was now 39 weeks. He thought she was at 36 weeks. Today had been one of the worst days. The cramps had been so bad that she could barely stand up. Every time she moved, she felt pain.

She started taking everything out and setting it on the table when she had a cramp shoot through her stomach and into her back. She gasped and grabbed the chair. It felt like she had peed on herself. She looked at the puddle on the floor. Had her water just broken? She was hurting and scared to move. She needed to get to the phone. She slowly moved around the table and to the counter where she had set it. She picked it up and dialed the number Jesse had programmed into it.

"Hello?" Jesse answered.

"Water just broke," Renee said, trying to control her breathing.

"Shit. I'll be there as quickly as I can."

Renee hung up the phone, dropping it onto the table. She slowly tried to make her way into the living room. Another contraction hit her, and she grabbed onto the wall to steady herself. She finally made it into the bedroom and grabbed the little bag she had thrown together to take to the hospital. She sat on the bed against the pillows. The contractions were hitting harder and faster now. Jesse's job was roughly twenty minutes away. She didn't even know how far away the hospital was. Would she make it in time?

Jesse came running into the bedroom and grabbed the bag off the bed. He then took her hand, and she stood up. She cried out in pain as another contraction hit. She leaned against Jesse's chest, and he rubbed his hands up and down her back, slightly rubbing it through the contraction. She tried to control her breathing through it.

"Isn't it too early for labor?"

"No. I'm nine months. It's not premature. We need to go. I don't know how far the hospital is," Renee said in between her breathing.

"It's at least thirty minutes away. How long have you been in labor?" Jesse asked as he started walking her out of the bedroom.

"I don't know. I've been feeling bad all day. The cramps have been hitting since nine am, I guess. They have been steadily getting worse until my water broke. Of course, I called you immediately after it happened."

"Damn, Renee. You have been in labor all day. You should have called me earlier. I'm going to have to fly down the road and hope I make it," Jesse said as he slung the bag over his shoulder.

He bent down and put his arm behind her knees and picked her up in his arms. She cried out in pain as another contraction hit. She buried her face in his neck. Jesse reached out and opened the door and yanked it shut behind him. He didn't even bother locking it. Instead, he ran out to the car and set her down. Once he had her in the car, he hooked her seat belt and ran around to his side. He got in and hooked his seat belt, and hauled ass to the hospital.

He was going at least a hundred miles an hour, and a cop got behind him. He cursed and pulled over. Once the cop got up to the window and saw Renee grabbing her stomach and crying in the passenger seat, he escorted them to the hospital. He called dispatch to let them know that they were on the way. A nurse came out with a wheelchair and got Renee onto it. They stopped Jesse and made him fill out forms while they got Renee into the room.

Once he filled them out, the nurse took him into the room. Renee had already been put into a gown and prepped for delivery. The doctor was on the way into the room as he was being escorted in. A nurse was sitting in front of Renee and telling her to push. Jesse walked over to her, and she held out her hand to him.

He took her hand and smiled at her. He pushed her hair off her face and squeezed her hand as she squeezed his. The doctor took over the nurse's place and told Renee to push one final time. Renee sat up and bore down. She fell back against the pillows, and Jesse heard the baby cry. He looked at the baby in his hands.

The nurse took him and cleaned him up. Once they had done everything they needed, they brought him over and placed him on Renee's chest. She burst into tears as she looked at Christian. He had a head full of blonde hair and bright green eyes, just like Kevin's. Renee prayed that Jesse wouldn't connect the two since he had dark hair and gray-blue eyes. She had red-gold hair and hazel eyes.

Jesse didn't seem to notice. Instead, he had a massive grin on his face as he looked at Christian. Renee couldn't help but notice how he looked like a completely different person than the one she had known for the past nine months. Although he had been nicer the past few months, she still hadn't been able to get past the fact that he had abused her. But, here and now, he just looked like a brand-new father beaming with pride over his son.

Jesse looked at Renee and was surprised when he found she was looking at him, too. There was a soft look on her face, one he had never seen before when she looked at him. He had hoped to win her over if he was nicer to her, but it hadn't worked. Maybe now she was starting to see him in a different light? He would continue to treat her well, and hopefully, she would come around.

He would be a good father, something his own had never been. He wanted Christian to know that he was loved and never had to worry about anything. He wouldn't do anything to Renee to make her leave. Now that she had the baby, maybe it would be better because he could show her what he was like as a father and a man in a relationship.

He leaned down and whispered in her ear, "Thank you. You have made me very happy."

He kissed her lips and to his surprise, she kissed him back. It was just a soft kiss, but he would take it. It was an improvement. He picked Christian up and held him in his arms. He touched his tiny little hand and was amazed at how small he was. He didn't know you could love another person like this. He would do everything with him that his father had never done.

"You will always be loved and protected, little man. I'm going to make sure of it," Jesse whispered to Christian.

The nurse helped Renee sit up. Jesse reluctantly handed Christian back to Renee. Jesse watched as Renee lowered the hospital gown to expose one of her breasts and put Christian up to it. To his surprise, Christian did latch on and began to suck. He watched as Renee breastfed their baby.

It hit Jesse that he liked Renee. He didn't just want her for sex. He liked her for the spunk, the fire she possessed. He wanted to be with her, not just keep her because he had kidnapped her. He wanted to build an actual future with her. Jesse had never liked a woman enough to want to have a future with her. Was he falling in love with this woman? That thought terrified him.

CHAPTER 5

Over the next few months, Renee was utterly exhausted. She was up all night with Christian. She would get a few hours of sleep in between feedings. So, it surprised her when Jesse got up in the middle of the night and changed him. He would bring him over to her after he was done as he couldn't feed him. He had offered several times to get a formula, but Renee refused to give Christian formula.

Jesse had been sweet like a real husband would be towards his wife. He kissed her goodbye before he left for work. He kissed her when he came home. He would bring her flowers occasionally. He never locked the doors when he left anymore. He had helped clean up the house and take care of Christian even though he was tired from work. Sometimes he even gave her a break and let her take a little nap while watching Christian. She didn't even bother to go lay down. She would just lay back on the couch and pass out.

Today they were heading to Christian's checkup. Afterward, she had an appointment to get checked. She would talk to the doctor about being put on birth control. She didn't want any more children. She had gotten lucky that Christian was Kevin's baby. Of course, Jesse didn't know that, and she didn't plan on letting him find out. She wasn't sure what had gotten into him, but she wasn't going to complain as he was being nice and not hitting her or sexually abusing her.

Once the doctor released her to have sex again, she knew that it would start back up, so she would at least protect herself from having his kids. She wouldn't fight him when it came to sex because it hurt too much. Maybe if she just laid there, he would lose interest. That hadn't worked for her before as it had usually made him more aggressive. Then again, he hadn't been acting like he was now.

"What are you thinking about?" Jesse asked, taking Renee off guard.

"Birth control," Renee answered.

"What?" Jesse asked.

"I want the doctor to put me on birth control. I don't want any more kids," Renee answered honestly.

She looked at Jesse to see if he was angry, but his expression was thoughtful. Maybe he didn't want kids in the first place? He'd said he had only wanted a sex slave since he was on the run. Having kids would be a burden if he had to pack up and run again.

"If you are thinking about birth control, then that means you are thinking about having sex," Jesse suddenly said as he grinned.

Renee frowned as she said, "That wasn't exactly what I was thinking about when I mentioned it. I said I didn't want more kids."

"You have to have sex to have more kids."

"That's true and you have made it clear before that no matter what I want you are going to have sex with me."

Jesse sighed and said, "Haven't I been nice to you lately?"

"You've been nicer than you were, but at what cost? Are you just waiting until I heal up from having Christian before you force yourself back on me? I'm not really sure why you are being nice."

"I like you. You are the mother of my son. I've already told you that you belong to me now, so we might as well get along. I can be a nice guy. Would you rather me continue to treat you the way I am now or go back to the way I was before?"

"I'd rather you stay this way, but you can't actually expect me to develop feelings for you. This isn't a real relationship. I'm your prisoner. I know it pisses you off when I say it, but it's true. All I can do is pretend in public and try to be nice at the house."

"Being nice at the house is a good start. You might just find that after some time, your feelings will change."

Had he lost his mind? Her feelings were not going to change. She tolerated him so that he didn't go crazy and do something insane like kill her, Christian, or Kevin. Her heart ached every time she thought about Kevin. Had he given up on her? Was he going to move on with his life without her? Even though it broke her heart, she hoped he would move on and find someone else to love. It wasn't fair to him to live alone because she was no longer in his life.

He couldn't wonder if she was dead or alive and wait for her to come back when she never would. She prayed that he found someone to make him happy even though she never would be. Her eyes filled with tears as she thought about him loving someone else. She turned her face towards the window, so Jesse didn't see that she was about to cry.

They took Christian to his appointment, and the doctor said he was in good health. So Jesse took her to her appointment, and they all went in. The doctor did his pelvic exam while Jesse was in the room, and Renee couldn't help but feel uncomfortable. Jesse watched everything the doctor did and watched her face. Was he trying to see if she was enjoying it?

He would know that it was not enjoyable if he'd ever had a pelvic exam. Once the doctor had told her that everything looked fine and she was completely healed, they discussed birth control. He set her up for an implant in her arm. The doctor had told them to use condoms until she had the implant in, and it had time to take effect.

He also told her that the scarring was minimal now. He warned them to stay away from the items they had been using before. He had looked right at Jesse when he had said it. Jesse's face hadn't changed. The doctor had to suspect something, or he wouldn't have kept bringing it up, but Renee never spoke up about the rape out of fear. Jesse had been good about covering his tracks. Not once but twice. He would be able to do it again, and who knew what he would do the third time with nothing to lose.

*   *   *

Later that night, Jesse surprised her when he made dinner for them. He had her relax as he cooked. When she went into the kitchen, there was a candle on the table. The table was set with their food already on the plates. Renee's eyebrows shot up as she saw this. Jesse pulled out a chair and waved at it. She slowly moved towards it but stopped short, wondering what he was planning. She looked at the chair and then up at him, but he just raised an eyebrow, obviously waiting on her to sit down. She sat down, and he pushed the chair up to the table. He sat in the other chair and poured some wine into a cup for her.

"You know I can't drink wine. I'm breastfeeding."

"You can have a glass. You just have to pump before you feed again. You have some stored for when you go out with Christian. I can feed him next go-round," Jesse said as he smiled at her.

"At the risk of pissing you off and winding up getting hurt because of it, why are you doing this?"

"I told you already. I like you. I'm making an effort to be nice. I listen more than you think I do. And you told me something months ago that I heard. You seem to be responding well to me being like this."

Renee sat back in the chair, shocked. Was he talking about catching bees with honey over vinegar? Was he trying to catch her? It had been a little over a year since he kidnapped her, and she still cringed at his touch. She still hated it when he kissed or hugged her. She felt like she was being suffocated when he wrapped her up in his arms and fell asleep. How could he think she would like him, let alone love him? For the better part of the year that he had her, he had beat on and raped her! Being nice now wasn't changing that fact.

"What do you mean by you like me? I've done nothing but be a bitch to you. I've fought you tooth and nail on everything. I've only been complacent because I don't want you to go back and harm Kevin or Christian. I told you before that I would never develop feelings for you. I can't care for someone who has beaten and raped me. That will always be there no matter what you do now or in the future. Do you not understand that?"

"I like you. I can't believe you don't know what I mean by that. I like you like a man who likes a woman. I have watched you everyday for over a year. At first, it was the fact that you did defy me at every turn. It pissed me off but turned me on. Then, when you found out you were pregnant, it was the way you looked at your stomach and talked to it. It was the love on your face when you thought about Christian or talked to him in your belly. It was the way you took care of the damn flowers. I want you to look at me that way! I know what I did, dammit! I know I was a bastard and nothing I do will ever change the fact that I did it, but you won't even try to let me make up for it!" Jesse shouted as he pushed back from the table and stormed outside.

Renee sighed as she closed her eyes. What was she supposed to do? Just forget that she was this man's prisoner? Was she just supposed to forget that he had tormented her? Was she supposed to forget that he would not allow her to leave and be with the man she loved? Would she pay for this later if she didn't try to bring peace now? She rubbed her temples, trying to stop the headache that was forming.

She stood up and walked over to the door, staying inside the doorframe. Jesse had his hands on the rails and his face towards the sky. It had started to rain, and he was just standing in it. She didn't want to go back to the old Jesse who tormented her. Could she find it in herself to have a relationship with him? She tried to step outside of herself and look at him as a woman would who hadn't been abused by him.

Jesse was tall. He was muscular but not too much, sort of lean. His jet-black hair almost looked like a raven's feathers when the sunlight hit it. It was gorgeous. His gray-blue eyes were beautiful to look at. She knew his lips were full but just enough to be deliciously kissable. The man was handsome. His tattoos gave him a bad boy look about him. If he treated a woman the way he had been treating her for months now, it would be highly likely that she would have had a relationship with him.

However, she couldn't get past what he had done. Or the fact that she was in love with Kevin and always would be. But, at the same time, she had to make the best of her life now because it wasn't going to change. Jesse had already told her that she belonged to him, and she wasn't going anywhere. She knew in her heart that she would never love him, but could she find it in herself to at least like him? Would he allow her to have a life if she had a relationship with him? One where she could go out by herself and have friends, maybe even a job?

Renee shivered as she walked out into the cold rain. She walked up to him and slipped under his arm, and stood in front of him. He looked down at her, and she saw a sadness in his eyes. She was taken aback that she had hurt him. She never intentionally hurt people. She wrapped her arms around him and placed her head on his chest. All she could do was make her life work the way it was now since it would never change, even though it broke her heart.

Jesse wrapped his arms around her. He walked her back into the house, closing the door behind them. They walked into the bedroom, and he started to take off her wet clothes. His hands touched parts of her as he removed the clothing.

Renee stood there and let Jesse touch her. She had already decided that she wouldn't fight him. She closed her eyes and tried to fight the urge to tense up or cringe away from his touch. Jesse's hands stopped on her hips and stayed there. She slowly opened her eyes. She looked at him and found he was watching her face. She lowered her eyes, not able to look him straight in the eye.

"Why do you close your eyes every time I touch you?"

"Do you want me to answer that honestly?"

"Of course, I do. I wouldn't have asked if I didn't."

Renee sighed and said, "Because I'm trying not to jerk away from you. I'm trying to forget who it is that's touching me."

"Are you imagining someone else is touching you?"

"No. All I can think about is what comes with your touch, and it's never a good feeling. So, I just try to disconnect my mind. You wanted to know the truth; there it is," Renee said as she crossed her arms over her breasts.

"Fine. Close your eyes, but don't disconnect yourself. Just let yourself feel a touch. Don't think of me touching you. Allow yourself to participate and see where it goes."

"I can't. It's all I can do not to jerk away as soon as I see you coming towards me."

When Renee looked at him, he saw the fear in her eyes. She had never intentionally let him see it before. No matter how much he had hurt her, she had remained defiant. Instead, she had bottled up her pain and turned it into hatred. Showing him vulnerability was new for her. It struck something profound inside of him. He slowly wrapped his arms around her and moved his face close to hers.

He felt her body tense as she waited for him to get angry and hit her. When he didn't, her eyes widened in surprise. He brushed his lips lightly against hers and moved his hands around so he could grab hers. He placed them on his chest as he moved back slightly.

"I know what I did to you and I know it's hard for you to move past. I know you expect me to hit you or do worse to you every time I touch you. I can understand your dislike of me, but I am trying to do better. Look at me, really look at me, while I touch you. I want you to touch me, too. If it gets to be too much for you, then I will stop."

Renee bit her lip. Jesse let go of her hands and moved back from her. She watched him as he slowly undressed. Jesse stepped up to her, and he ran his hands up her arms and over her collarbone. His hands moved up her neck and into her hair. He began to play with it, running his fingers through it. When she felt his fingers massaging her scalp, her eyes closed. He wanted her to look at him, but he didn't tell her to open her eyes back up. He knew she was enjoying what he was doing. He leaned in and kissed her as his fingers massaged her scalp.

He lightly ran his tongue across her bottom lip. Her lips parted, and he moved his tongue inside her mouth. Renee placed her hands on his chest and began to kiss him back as her body relaxed into him.

Jesse moved his fingertips slowly down her back. He felt her start to shake, and he knew she was feeling fear, but she didn't stop him. He broke the kiss and moved back just enough to have a little space between them. He began to kiss down her neck to her collarbone as his hands lightly trailed down her back to her butt. He felt her hands slowly move up his chest to his shoulders.

He lifted her, and she quickly wrapped her legs around him as her arms slid around his neck. She yelped as he moved towards the bed. He made little soothing noises in her ear as he slowly lay her down on the bed, following behind. She released her grip on him, and he went to work on making her feel good. His touch was light on her body as his lips placed feather-light kisses where his hands had been.

"Look at me, Renee. I'm not going to hurt you. See me for who I really am," Jesse pleaded as he placed another kiss on her lips.

Her breathing had quickened, but he knew it was from fear. She hadn't told him to stop, so he kept going. He would keep his word to her and leave her be if she did. He kissed and sucked her breasts as his hand slowly went down her thigh. He felt her body tense back up as his fingers brushed her folds. Jesse looked at her and saw her eyes were open.

He moved, so she looked directly into his eyes when he moved his fingers back and forth over her. Her breathing started to slow from the erratic pace it had. Finally, her fingers loosened their tight grip on his shoulders and explored his back. Jesse took his hand from her, and he saw her eyes flick to his hand as he placed his fingers in his mouth.

"Don't tense up," Jesse said as he slowly pushed his fingers inside her.

He saw her eyes close and felt her body tense slightly, and he knew she was fighting her own body. He continued to go slow with her as his fingers moved slowly in and out. She wasn't as wet as he would like, but she was somewhat wet. Her body had responded to his touch, even if it was only slightly. He kissed his way down her neck to her breasts, and her back arched as he began to suck her nipple. He had to force his hand to slow back down as her reaction had excited him.

Jesse felt Renee jerk when he nipped her side, but her reaction was different when she jerked this time. She tightened around his fingers. When he began to lick her hip, he felt her pussy get wet and tighter. He replaced his thumb with his tongue and listened as her breathing sped up, but it sounded different than it had before. She wasn't scared but enjoyed what he was doing. It spurred him on to move a little faster. He was wondering if she was imagining someone else doing this as she only responded after she had closed her eyes, but at this point, he would take it.

Maybe over time, she would get used to it being him and come around. She moved her fingers into his hair as he moved his fingers and tongue faster. She gasped, and her fingers gripped his hair as he started to suck on her little nub. Her hips arched off the bed as she pressed his head tighter into her.

Jesse liked her reaction, and his fingers sped up more than he had planned, but she still didn't stop him. Instead, her body responded, and he felt her grow wetter. He pushed his luck and started to go even faster until he heard her cry out. His body jerked in response. He quickly moved up her body and pressed himself against her.

Her eyes flew open, and he felt her body tense again. He had hoped that she would be in a good mood and react differently this time with her just getting off. He watched as she bit her lip, and she opened her mouth like she was going to tell him to stop, but she quickly shut it. She closed her eyes again and tried to relax her body. However, he could feel it wasn't working.

"Open your eyes, Renee. I want you to see me while I take you. I want you to know that I'm not going to hurt you. I told you that you can tell me to stop at any point."

Renee shook her head no. He gripped her chin, stopping her from moving her head back and forth. He kissed her lips and then moved back slightly. She opened her eyes and looked at him. Jesse moved against her and started to push himself inside her just a little bit. Renee closed her eyes, and he stopped, waiting for her to open them again. When she finally did, he moved a little bit more.

"Stop. I can't do this," Renee panted.

Jesse saw her eyes were full of panic, and her breathing had become ragged like she was about to hyperventilate. He pulled out of her and put his head on her chest. He was trying to control himself from taking her regardless. He had promised her that he would stop, and he'd keep that promise. He didn't want to take her by force anymore. He liked her reaction to him just now. He wanted her to want him. He rolled off of her and onto his back. He closed his eyes and groaned as he was still hard as a rock, causing him some discomfort.

After a few minutes, he felt her weight shift, but he didn't even bother to look at her. She had asked him to stop, so he had. She was probably getting off the bed, away from him since he had allowed her to run. When he felt her throw her leg over him, his eyes shot open, and he moved his arm.

He watched her as she moved over him and her hand moved between them. He felt her grip him, and he couldn't hold back his groan. Her eyes shot up to his. He looked into her eyes as she squeezed him, holding him in place as she lowered onto him. He wanted to touch her, but he was worried that she would move away if he did. This was her show. Maybe she had been afraid of what he would do if he took her, but she wouldn't get hurt if she controlled the pace.

Her body was shaking as she lowered herself down on him. She stopped moving as his arms moved. He put his hands up, palms facing her as he moved his hands behind his head, letting her know that he had no plans of touching her. Instead, he would stop his instinct to touch her and just lay back and enjoy what she would do. She finished sliding down on him, and he groaned as he felt her surrounding him.

She started slowly moving as she got comfortable with what she was doing. Jesse watched her and tried not to move so he wouldn't spook her, but he found it very hard to do as his natural urge was to thrust up and grab her hips and breasts. Her eyes were glued to his. He found he enjoyed that she was watching him. When she started to pick up the pace, he rolled his hips under her and thrust up just a little.

Her eyes widened, and her lips parted. A slow grin spread across his face. So, she did enjoy that move. He did it again, but he thrust up harder as her body came down on his. She moaned as her eyes closed. He took the chance, moved his hands from behind his head, and placed them on her thighs, sliding them towards her hips. He mentally cursed himself as her body stopped moving. She looked at his hands, and suddenly she had them pinned above his head.

"Don't do that again," Renee said as she slowly began to move again.

"Whatever you say, Darlin'," Jesse drawled as he leaned his head up and took one of her breasts in his mouth.

He couldn't resist anymore. With breastfeeding, it was different trying to play with her breasts. He got a mouth full of milk. She laughed as he sputtered. He nipped her breast for laughing at him, but that just made her laugh harder. It was a genuine laugh, and it made him smile. She leaned down and kissed his lips as she slid back and forth on him, never letting him move his hands. He laced his fingers through hers as he continued to roll his hips and thrust up.

Renee broke the kiss and sat up as she picked up the pace. Jesse felt her tightening around him, and he wanted to grab her hips and start slamming himself into her, but he knew he couldn't. Instead, his grip on her hands tightened, and she looked at him again, her eyes never leaving his. It was incredibly intimate. Renee moved their hands and placed his on her waist. Hers was on top of his just in case he got too rough.

He gripped her and thrust up hard and fast, trying to keep himself somewhat under control. Renee tightened around him, and he groaned as she gripped him. Then, she started grinding on him fast. It took Jesse by

55

surprise when she came. He could tell it surprised her, too. Jesse gripped her and slammed himself upwards as he released as well.

He pulled Renee down onto the bed. She lay down against his side, and he wrapped his arm around her. Jesse grabbed her hand and put her arm over him, lacing his fingers through hers. He kissed the top of her head and closed his eyes, content with what had happened. They lay there until Jesse got up and heated their supper.

Renee lay there after Jesse left. Had she just given in to her tormentor? She had imagined being with Kevin, but that didn't change the fact that she'd had sex with Jesse and enjoyed it. What was wrong with her?

CHAPTER 6

Renee picked up Christian's to-go bag and got him ready to go. Today was his birthday, and Jesse had said he had something planned for him. Jesse had relaxed his grip on her after the night they'd had sex. Since then, he had gotten her a different phone. He'd also allowed her to go to a mommy and me group.

Renee had made a couple of friends there. Jesse had done a complete 180 with his behavior. He was sweet and caring. She still couldn't find it in herself to feel anything for him, and she knew he had to know that. He had told her he loved her so many times and all she had ever been able to do was smile at him.

It had surprised her to find that she was pleased when she saw how he was with Christian. He was a good dad. He spent all of his free time with him. Jesse didn't go out and spend time with buddies. He had made friends with a couple of guys at work that were married. He never hung out with them unless it was at their house, and she was invited. So, she hung out with their wives and Christian while they were there.

Jesse would always find her and kiss her or hug her. The other wives would always tell her how lucky she was that he did that. Their husbands weren't that affectionate anymore. Renee would always politely smile and say she knew but inside, she wanted to scream at them. They didn't know the truth of her situation. They didn't know that what she truly craved was for Kevin to walk into the room and take her into his arms. The life she had now with a baby and a husband was what she had wanted with

Kevin. It had been almost two years since she had seen Kevin, and she still longed for him.

She had finally been able to move past the situation of sex with Jesse. She drifted away into her thoughts and imagined Kevin most of the time. She had gotten better at doing it with her eyes open, so Jesse didn't think she was doing it. She didn't have much of a problem if she let herself think of Jesse as just a hot guy she was sleeping with. He always took his time with her now and made sure she enjoyed it. If she were too tired or not feeling well, he would leave her alone. That one always took her off guard.

Renee smiled as she watched Christian crawl around the floor. He came over and pulled up on her leg. She cooed at him as she picked him up. He was what she was living for now. He giggled as she blew on his belly, and she couldn't help but smile as he wrapped his arms around her neck and said, Mama.

Jesse had walked in just as Christian had wrapped his arms around Renee's neck. He watched the smile cross her lips. She was beautiful, and the look she got on her face when it came to Christian made her all the more beautiful to him. He had fallen for her. The woman he had only taken to get revenge on someone he hated, he had fallen head over heels for. However, he knew she didn't feel the same about him, and she had let him know so many times. She never hugged or kissed him. She never touched him unless he touched her first. She had finally been able to sleep with him regularly, but there again, he had to come on to her first.

He wanted her to look at him like she looked at Christian so badly. He had slacked up on her going out. She had a few women she would hang out with that had babies Christian's age. He had planned a birthday party for Christian today with all of the women from her mommy and me group. He hoped that the nice gestures would change her mind about him one of these days.

He walked up and kissed Christian's head and then kissed Renee's lips. She smiled at him, but it was a fake smile, and he knew it. It wasn't the genuine smile she had just had on her face. Christian reached out for him, and he took him from Renee.

"Hey, bud! I have something special planned for you. Let me take a quick shower and we can go, ok?" Jesse said as he handed Christian back to Renee.

He jumped in the shower, and Renee was in the bedroom when he got out. She was in the process of changing her clothes. When she saw him come out of the bathroom, she noticed he didn't have the towel on him but was drying his hair with it. It still surprised her that her body responded to him being naked. She didn't want him to know that she enjoyed how he looked. The less power he had over her, the better. But, he noticed her looking at him. He smiled as he walked over and wrapped his arms around her.

"Where's Christian?" Jesse asked.

"He's in his playpen, so I thought I would change into something nicer."

"This is nicer in my opinion."

Renee rolled her eyes as she said, "You're getting me all wet."

"I can take care of that for you," Jesse murmured.

"I meant from the water you still have on you," Renee said as she pushed on his chest.

"Way to hurt a guy's ego," Jesse said as he stepped back and began to dry off.

"As big as your ego is, it could stand to be deflated some."

Jesse walked up and slid his hand down her body as his arm wrapped around her. He slid his hand into her underwear, and his finger slid along her folds. She sucked in her breath, and he felt she was wet. He grinned and then kissed her lips. He played with her just enough to get her frustrated and then stepped back.

"Never mind. It's re-inflated," Jesse said as he stepped to his dresser to grab his clothes.

Renee's eyes narrowed. That egotistical bastard knew what he was doing and how to get to her. Two could play that game. She walked up and tapped him on the shoulder. He turned towards her, and she stood on tiptoe and kissed him as she pressed against him. Her hand went between them, and she gripped him and began to stroke his length. Once she was satisfied that he enjoyed what she was doing enough to cause issues, she broke the kiss and stopped stroking him. She backed away and grabbed her clothes off the bed.

Jesse was stunned by what had just happened. She never came onto him, and the one time she did, she was doing it just to leave him wanting more. He was not going to let this happen. He threw his clothes down and walked up behind her. He wrapped his arms around her and pressed into her. She had her pants on by this point, but her shirt wasn't on. Renee stiffened as he kissed her neck.

"Oh no. We don't have time for this now. You told your son that you had a surprise for him, remember?"

Jesse groaned as he said, "You are a frigging tease. You will pay for this later."

He realized he had chosen the wrong words when he felt Renee go still and her body stiffen in his arms. Her breathing had sped up like she was about to have a panic attack. He turned her towards him and saw that panicked look in her eyes that he had not seen in a long time. He sighed.

"I was just teasing you, Renee," Jesse said as he reached up to touch her face.

She jerked, and he dropped his hand. He stepped away from her and went to grab his clothes off the floor. He started getting dressed while he watched her. She closed her eyes and started trying to control her breathing. The one time, she had done something to tease him as a normal couple would, and he had screwed it up. He was a complete idiot. He watched her as she picked up her shirt and noticed her hands were shaking. He wanted to comfort her, but he knew that it would make things worse if he touched her.

Renee finished getting dressed and walked out of the room. She should not have taunted Jesse. She knew better than to do that. He could do whatever he wanted, but she couldn't. He could say he was just teasing, but she knew his threats. As long as she was complacent, she was fine, but the minute she wasn't, he would get angry and go back to the way he was before. He had relapsed a few times with his anger. He had not hit her again. However, there were times when he had been too rough with sex and had hurt her.

She picked Christian up and put him in his car seat. Then, she picked up his bag and headed out to the car. Jesse came out right behind her and saw her going through the motions. He had just ruined a perfect evening. He drove them to the park where the ladies he had spoken to had set up the party for Christian. When Renee got out and saw everyone, she plastered her fake smile on her face. Jesse hated it. He came around to take Christian so that he could speak to her before they went up to everyone.

"Please, don't let earlier ruin this evening. I planned this surprise out for you more than Christian. He isn't going to remember this, but you will. Can we please just have a nice time?"

Renee responded with a simple, "Ok."

They walked up to the party, and everyone greeted them. Renee sat with the other moms from her group. They had put together a nice little party. They had a little cookout while the men threw back a few beers. She ignored Jesse for the rest of the night, deciding to do what he asked her to. She had a great time talking to everyone but him.

She looked around and saw everyone laughing and joking and felt out of place. She liked a few women here, but she didn't know any of them. None of them knew the real her. She had to hide who she was out of fear of letting something slip. She claimed a husband she didn't have and didn't even have a fake ring to wear. She was claiming a life that she had never lived and was having an all-around hard time remembering to respond when people called her by Tabitha. Finally, she sighed and saw Jesse looking at her as he continued to throw back the beers. She shifted, uncomfortable with the way he was looking at her.

Was he a mean drunk? The way he was putting them down, she wondered if he would be able to drive them home. He hadn't allowed her to drive the entire time he had kept her, even though she had a valid driver's license under her fake name. If he continued like he was now, she would insist on driving them. No way would she let him drive her and Christian while being drunk.

She stood up and walked over to the park. No one was talking to her anyway, as they had all gathered into their groups. Lisa watched all the babies, so she would take a few minutes to herself. She started walking through the trees and enjoying the park itself. It was beautiful. The only time she ever got to go out was when Jesse took her somewhere. Even meeting the other women required him to drop her off and pick her back up. She took a deep breath and exhaled it slowly, breathing in the flowers and scents from the trees.

She jumped when she felt arms slide around her waist. She smelled beer, and her nose wrinkled. However, when she turned, it wasn't Jesse that had wrapped his arms around her. Instead, it was Patrick, Rebecca's husband. He smiled at her, and she frowned. What the hell was he doing?

"So, I was talking to Rebecca, and I don't know if you know this or not, but we are swingers. I think you are a gorgeous woman and wanted to know if you might be interested? Rebecca is ok with hooking up with Mark," Patrick said, smiling at her.

"Um, thanks for the offer, I think, but no," Renee said as she pushed on Patrick's chest.

"Oh, come on. At least think about it?"

"I'm a one-man kind of woman, Patrick. So, again, thanks for the offer, but no."

With that, Renee pushed on his chest hard, breaking his hold on her. She walked back up to the party, feeling shaken by what had happened. She didn't know that Jesse had seen Patrick walk up and put his arms around her. He hadn't moved close enough to hear what was said, but he didn't like Patrick's being with Renee. Were the two of them hooking up behind his back? His anger blinded him, and it took everything in him not to make a scene. Instead, he vowed to find out the truth later that night.

He went back up to the party, and everyone had gathered to watch Christian blow out his candle. Renee had him in her lap and blew out his little candle after everyone had sung Happy Birthday to him. Jesse watched her as she unwrapped Christian's gifts and let him see them all. He noticed that Patrick was standing closer to her now. He didn't know Patrick as he was married to one of the women in Renee's group, but he was damn sure going to find out about him.

Throughout the remainder of the party, Jesse watched Patrick as he touched Renee here and there. She would always pull back from him and smile politely, but she didn't look comfortable. She hadn't said anything to him about it, however.

Once the party was over and everyone had packed up, Renee put Christian in his car seat and headed to the car. She put Christian in the car and walked over to the driver's side. Jesse moved towards her, but she didn't budge. Instead, she held out her hand, and he just looked at her.

"Keys, please. You've had way too much to drink."

"I'm fine to drive. I'm not drunk."

"I'm not letting you drive me and Christian with that much alcohol in your system. If you want to possibly kill yourself, then so be it, but you won't take us with you."

Jesse stepped forward and pressed against her, pushing her body back into the car. He was trying to intimidate her, but she wasn't having it. She stood her ground, and he saw defiance in her eyes. What had made her so bold all of a sudden? Had she planned an escape with Patrick so she thought she could do whatever she wanted now?

"Either get out of the way or I will move you out of the way."

"Then move me out of the way. And you had better make sure I'm dead when you're done because you are not driving off with my son in the car," Renee said, pushing her body back into his.

"You're awfully bold all of a sudden. You planning something behind my back?"

Renee looked confused as she said, "What?"

"You heard me. You can tell me now or later, but if I find out about it later, there are going to be consequences," Jesse threatened.

He watched as fear flashed across her eyes. The alcohol he had consumed and his anger from seeing her with Patrick were hitting him. He smiled as he saw the fear. He knew better than to drink this much because of his temper. He had been letting himself wallow in self-pity because of what happened at the house. Also, Renee ignored him the whole party when he had set this up for her to be able to socialize.

"There is nothing for you to find out," Renee said as she stood straight.

He watched the flash of fear turn into anger and then hatred. In one night, he had managed to ruin any progress he had made with her. He smashed his fist into the car right beside her, and Renee jumped.

"Please, just give me the keys. Let me drive us home so that we all get there in one piece, ok?"

"Aw, you worried about my safety now?"

"You want me to lie or tell you the truth?" Renee asked with cold eyes.

"Neither one. I already know you hate me," Jesse said as he handed her the keys.

Jesse had to give her directions back to the house. Once they were at the house, she took Christian into his room and tucked him away for the night. Jesse was sitting on the bed waiting for her when she entered the bedroom. He stood up and walked over to the door, closing it. He turned towards her, and she backed up as she saw the look on his face. He grabbed her and yanked her against him.

"Jesse, you're drunk. Let's just go to sleep and discuss whatever is bothering you tomorrow."

"Oh, no. You got me all hot and bothered earlier and decided to take off on me. You ignored me all night long when I planned this whole thing for you to be able to hang out with people and socialize. Then, you decided to get snappy with me. And you are going to tell me about what I saw earlier one way or another," Jesse said as he started yanking her clothes off.

"I don't know what you're talking about," Renee said as he pushed her onto the bed.

"Oh, I think you do," Jesse said as he undressed and lay on her.

"You're drunk. Please, don't do this."

Jesse started kissing and touching her body. She wasn't into it, and he knew it. His touch started getting rougher and started to hurt. She just lay there and tried not to tense up, which would make this worse.

"Guess I'm not doing it for you now. Does Patrick do it for you? Does he touch you like this?" Jesse asked as he started touching her again.

"Or kiss you like this?" he asked as he kissed her neck, made his way down to her breast, and bit it.

"I haven't done anything with Patrick," Renee said as the pain hit her from his bite.

"Don't lie to me!" Jesse yelled as he took her.

Renee cried out in pain and yelled, "I'm not lying to you!"

Jesse was too far gone in his anger. He punished her body with his. The more he thought about Patrick touching her, the angrier he got. She was lying to him, and he knew it.

"I saw you two together! I saw how he touched you. You are mine. I will kill him before he touches you again," Jesse sneered as he moved faster and harder.

"Please, stop! I haven't done anything with Patrick. I don't like him and don't want anything to do with him. He asked about us switching with him and Rebecca and I told him no!"

However, Jesse was no longer listening. The alcohol and his rage had taken over. He went into a blackout rage, thinking about Renee being with Patrick. He no longer heard her cries or what she was saying. He took what he wanted until he finished. Then, he rolled off of her, and she tried to get away from him. He jerked her back against him and wrapped his arms around her, holding her, so her back was tight to his chest.

He fell asleep as she cried, hurting from what he had just done. Renee didn't dare to move for fear that she would wake Jesse and he would start all over again with his torture. He hadn't forced himself on her in a very long time. She didn't understand what had happened. Had he seen Patrick come on to her? Why would he think she had anything going on with Patrick? Was he going to continue to brutalize her body every night until she told him what he wanted to hear? If she lied and said she had been with Patrick, what would he do?

Hours later, she finally dared to move. She bit her lip to keep from crying out as the pain hit her when she went to throw her legs over the bed. She crept into the bathroom and looked in the mirror. She saw bite marks on her breasts and minor bruises from his rough touches. She felt rather than saw what he had done in between her legs. She slid down onto the floor and sat there until she passed out on the bathroom floor.

CHAPTER 7

When Jesse woke up to Christian crying the following day, he felt the bed beside him. Renee wasn't there. His head was pounding. He hadn't drunk like that in a long time. He slowly got up and threw on his boxers. He went into Christian's room and got him out of his crib. He changed him and then took him to the kitchen. He had yet to see Renee. Where was she? Had she run away? He felt anger take him over. He couldn't remember last night beyond where she had taken the keys from him.

He walked into the bedroom and noticed the light was on in the bathroom. He walked over and saw Renee lying on the floor, naked. He frowned. Why in the hell was she on the floor naked? He set Christian down and went to shake Renee. He started seeing the bite marks and bruises on her when he did. Shit. What had he done last night?

Renee jerked up, and when she saw him, she jerked away from him. She moaned. She saw Christian and covered herself as best as she could.

"Renee, what happened last night?"

He watched as her eyes narrowed, and she said, "You know perfectly well what happened."

She slowly stood up, and he saw her entire body. In between her legs was swollen. There was bruising all around the area. The bite marks were more profound than he had initially thought they were. The bruising wasn't bad, but it was in many different places. He frowned. He'd had a lot to drink yesterday as he had been upset about Renee's reaction to him. He remembered seeing Patrick with Renee, which triggered his anger again. He looked up at her and saw her visibly shrink in on herself.

Was that it? Had his anger and the drinking caused him to blackout? It wasn't the first time, but he had never done that with Renee. He had been trying hard to make her feel something for him, but hatred hadn't been it. His anger about Patrick touching her was something he couldn't hide. He stepped towards her, and she backed up, hitting the bathtub. He quickly grabbed her as she started to fall backward. She screamed the minute he touched her. That caused Christian to start crying.

He must have thought he had done something to hurt Renee. He let go of her and picked up Christian. He tried to soothe him, but Renee had burst into tears. That upset Christian further as he reached out to Renee. She took Christian out of his arms and tried to stop crying as she soothed Christian.

"It's ok, baby. Mama's alright. I'm going to be ok. You're fine, baby," Renee said as she tried to walk out to the bedroom.

Jesse stepped out of her way as she refused to walk past him. He watched her walk over to the bed. He'd done a number on her. She was ambling and making little pain sounds with every step she took. She opened her drawer and took out a long shirt that buttoned and set Christian on the bed. She slid it over her head and gingerly sat down. She pulled the shirt aside and let Christian latch on.

She had been weaning him off the breast, but she always fed him first thing in the morning. Today, she was hurting so badly that she burst into tears as he latched on. Christian released and started crying again. She cuddled him and tried to calm herself down.

"I'm sorry, baby. Mama's not feeling well. You can have a regular breakfast today," Renee said as she slowly got up.

"Sit down. I'll fix breakfast. Afterward, we need to talk about what happened last night."

"Why? Are you going to continue to torture me until I tell you what you want to hear?"

Jesse frowned as he said, "I remember seeing you with Patrick. I don't remember what happened after you took the keys. You being upset is upsetting Christian. We will talk once he takes a nap or he is busy playing."

After Jesse walked out, Renee let out the breath she had been holding. She hated that she had upset Christian. No matter what Jesse did to her, she couldn't let Christian see it. As he grew, he would think what Jesse was doing to her was ok, and it wasn't. She would not let him grow up to treat a woman like this.

Once Renee got Christian calmed down, she put him in the playpen so she could try to take a shower. The hot water stung the bites on her body. She was tired of crying. She bit her lip until she tasted blood, holding back the tears. She scrubbed her body, trying to get rid of the feel of Jesse's touch, but it was useless. She got out and dried off.

Christian wasn't in his playpen when she walked out to the living room. Her heart skipped a beat. She went to the kitchen and found Jesse feeding Christian. He was so sweet and caring to Christian. If he could control his anger, they wouldn't have these problems. She knew by what he had said last night that he had seen Patrick come on to her.

She sat in the chair next to Christian's high chair and reached for the bowl of oatmeal Jesse was feeding him. Jesse pulled it away from her, and she dropped her hand. She had always fed Christian. He took the bowl with him as he went over to the stove and fixed a plate. He sat it down in front of her and went back to feeding Christian.

The food smelled good, but she didn't have an appetite. She went to get up and get some juice, but Jesse reached out for her. She withdrew from his hand, shrinking into the chair. He sighed and got up. He poured a glass of juice for her and brought it to her.

"You need to eat."

Fearing what else he may do, Renee pushed the food around on the plate, taking a bite here and there. She ate about half the plate before she couldn't force herself to eat anymore. Jesse fixed himself a plate, and once he was done eating, he cleaned everything up. Then, he took Christian into the living room and put him in his playpen. Then, he came back for her.

"Now, tell me what's going on between you and Patrick."

"I already told you last night. I told you there was nothing going on between us. You didn't believe me then, so what difference does it make now?" Renee said as she looked at Jesse with a cold stare.

"Why did he keep touching you? Why did you take off in the park? He left after you did and I saw you two together. Did you do that to meet up with him?"

"You never let me go out without you. I just wanted to walk around and have a few minutes to myself. I didn't know it was Patrick that had grabbed me until I turned around. I told you all of this. Why are you acting like you don't know? I told you that he wanted us to switch with him and Rebecca. I told him no. I was uncomfortable at the party, but I didn't want to ruin it. It doesn't matter, because you don't believe me anyway. The more I tried to tell you that I didn't do anything wrong, the more you raped me," Renee said as the tears stung her eyes again.

Jesse stood up and pulled her out of the chair. She wouldn't scream, but her body tensed. She was waiting for the blows to come or for him to force himself on her again. He wrapped his arms around her instead and pulled her against him. He stroked her hair.

"I'm sorry. I haven't had a blackout rage in a very long time. Seeing you with someone else enraged me. The alcohol just fueled that rage. I know you aren't happy with me and I just thought you had found a way around leaving but could still be with someone else."

Renee was taken off guard by Jesse apologizing. He had never apologized to her before when he did something like this. She didn't relax. It made her angry. Did he think that apologizing to her was going to fix this? Her hatred for him came back in full force. She couldn't live like this.

Jesse pulled back and looked at her. She wouldn't even look at him, and her body was still tense. Her hands were balled into fists. He cupped her chin and made her look up. The look he saw in her eyes was pure hatred. He ran his thumb across her lips, and she turned her face away from him.

"So, we are back to square one, I guess."

"We were never away from square one. I hate you and that has never changed. I hate it when you touch me. I hate that you keep me here. If it weren't for Christian, I think I would have taken my own life a long time ago. Anything is better than being here with you," Renee spat.

Jesse felt his anger rise. His temper had always been his biggest downfall. He had tried changing for Renee as he had come to love her. Finally, he let go of her and walked away so he could get his anger in check. He didn't think she would kill herself because she wouldn't leave Christian. However, he wondered if she would if he kept going the way he was. She might not have cared for him before, but at least she had responded to his touch. Now, even that was gone.

For the rest of the day, Renee felt like she was just going through the motions of what she usually did. However, she found her body ached worse when she moved in specific ways. Jesse kept trying to help her, but when she jerked away from his touch or tensed up when he came in the room, he would stop trying to help her.

When her phone went off, she ignored it, but Jesse didn't. He picked it up and looked at the message. She had not been able to lock her phone, so he could look at it whenever he wanted. She saw his face grow dark as she had turned to put a dish in the cabinet. Unsure of what he was reading, she tried to act like nothing was wrong. He brought the phone over and set it on the counter, pressing his body into her back.

"Either you get rid of this guy or I will," Jesse said, his breath tickling her ear.

Renee was confused. She picked up her phone and saw Rebecca's number on her text message, but she knew the message wasn't from her.

It read, '*I hope you have thought about my offer. I really would love to slip myself inside of you. I think we could have a lot of fun together.*'

Renee shivered as she thought about what could happen because of that text.

"Does the thought of that turn you on, Renee?" Jesse whispered.

Renee turned towards him, and he pressed his body fully against hers, pressing her into the counter. He placed his hands on either side of her body so she couldn't go anywhere. She had been here before, and she didn't like it. She had been pretty compliant for almost a year. She started going to the mommy and me classes about four months ago. She'd made friends with some of the moms in the group, but Rebecca hadn't been one of them. She had only met Patrick twice when he had picked Rebecca up.

"No, it doesn't turn me on. For one, Patrick is married. I would never go after a married man. For two, you and I are not in a damn relationship. I'm your prisoner, but if you and I were actually together, I would not cheat. I'm not that type of person. For three, Patrick and Rebecca are swingers. That's what Patrick told me when he grabbed me in the park yesterday. He said Rebecca was ok with being with you while he was with me. Frankly, that disgusts me. And four, Patrick is not really good looking. You look better than he does and I don't even want to sleep with you. You don't even turn me on, so no, Patrick is definitely not going to."

"Whether you like it or not, we are in a relationship. You belong to me and no one else. I don't want anyone else and I'm damn sure not letting anyone else touch you. And you can say I don't turn you on all you want, but I know I do. I've seen the way you look at me when you think I'm not looking. You like the way I look. If I didn't turn you on, then you wouldn't get wet for me."

"Maybe I just got better at faking it," Renee lashed out.

"Nah. You couldn't cum if you didn't enjoy it," Jesse said with an evil smile.

"You can if you aren't thinking about the person you are fucking," Renee said sweetly, with a fake smile.

Jesse's hands gripped the counter so hard that his knuckles turned white. She had imagined someone else the whole time they had been together. It hadn't been him that had done things for her, but her imagination. Had she been thinking about Kevin the whole time? His fist banged down on the counter, and she jumped.

"It doesn't feel good to have someone hurt you, does it?" Renee whispered as she looked down.

Had she been taunting him with her words yet again? He couldn't tell if she had just said it to be cruel to him or not, but he could feel the tremble in her body. He knew she was afraid of what he would do next. She was trying to be defiant, but she was terrified of him this close to her. His anger was almost palpable. He gripped her chin and lifted her head. She kept her eyes down as he crushed her lips under his. He broke the kiss when he felt moisture on his face and realized it was her tears. He licked the cut on her lip that he felt.

"Your words don't hurt me, but if you aren't careful, they will hurt you. I've tried to be nice. That clearly isn't working. So, since you want to choose me being the bad guy, so be it. When you are ready for me to start being nice to you again, you let me know. Until then, I'll just take you like I used to. You will understand one day that you belong to me. Once you do, and you come to me willingly, I'll treat you nice again."

With that, Jesse moved back from her. His anger taking over had already fucked things up so severely between them that she was back to hating him. He still wanted her to want him, but was he going to be able to settle for her coming to him out of fear? Would she come to him willingly even if he was hurting her? She hadn't before. The only time she had willingly fucked him was when he had told her she could tell him to stop. He picked up her phone and handed it to her.

"Take care of this now."

Renee texted Rebecca's number and told Patrick that she didn't want anything to do with him. She told him that her husband didn't appreciate him coming on to her, and she didn't want to hear from him again. She also blocked Rebecca's number so he couldn't text her anymore. Then, she showed it to Jesse.

"I don't want you going back to that group anymore. I don't trust that he will stop just because you blocked her number. If you act right, maybe you can find something else to do."

Renee felt empty. He was taking the little bit of freedom he had given her away. She had worked hard to gain that freedom, and now, because of someone else, she was losing it. She became angry. She always knew this ploy of his was just to toy with her so he could hurt her worse once she had started to relax.

She shoved his chest and screamed, "I hate you!"

"You'll get over it," Jesse said as he walked away.

Renee slid down to the floor and pulled her knees up to her chest. She placed her head on them and cried. There was no way she could go back to him brutalizing her every night. But, she couldn't bring herself to give in to him willingly. She didn't want him, and he knew it. If this was his sick, twisted way of getting her to fall in love with him, he was crazier than she had initially thought. If being nice to her hadn't made her fall for him, why would he think going back to the way it had been would?

She got up, went into the bedroom, and then lay on the bed. She had already been suffering from depression, but now it was hitting her hard. The pain in her body, crying, and thoughts took a toll on her. Finally, she fell into a restless sleep, and nightmares took her over.

CHAPTER 8

Weeks went by, with Jesse keeping a closer eye on Renee. She didn't try to harm herself, but she was closed off. He had stopped taking her to the mommy and me group each week. She rarely smiled anymore. He had been checking her phone and the usage to see who she had been messaging. So far, she hadn't deleted any of them off the phone. There were messages from the other women in the group asking her where she was and was everything ok. She never answered them.

When he touched her, she tensed up or shrunk away from him. She didn't fight him, but she was no longer responsive. Instead, she would cry at night when she thought he was asleep. Even Christian couldn't get her to smile most of the time. He sighed as he sat on the couch, watching her play with Christian on the floor. She had a slight smile on her face, but you could tell it was only there for the sake of Christian, not because she was happy.

There was a knock on the door, and Jesse quickly looked at Renee. No one had ever come to their house before. Who even had this address? Renee just looked at him, and he knew she wasn't expecting anyone. He went to the door and looked out of the peephole. It was Rebecca. He opened the door as he frowned.

"Hey, Mark. Is Tabitha home?"

"She is. Why are you here?"

"I, um, I think she may have stopped coming to the mommy and me group because of my husband. So I wanted to apologize to both of you and see if I could talk her into coming back. We all miss seeing her."

"Why would you need to apologize to both of us?"

Rebecca looked at him with a slight tilt of her head and said, "You don't know what Patrick did? I'm pretty sure you do with the way you were looking at him and Renee at the party. Did she tell you anything?"

"Yeah, I know what happened. I wasn't happy about it either. I don't care what you two do, but you should know better than to approach someone like that. At least gauge what type of person they are first or the type of person they are with."

"Is Tabitha ok?" Rebecca asked, suddenly looking worried.

"She's fine. She just doesn't want to be around you and your husband," Jesse replied, trying to close the door on Rebecca.

Rebecca stepped inside the door, so he couldn't, and said, "I would like to see her for just a few minutes so I can apologize."

Jesse felt a hand on his arm. He turned and saw Renee standing beside him. She looked at him with those dead eyes, and he frowned again. There was no emotion about anything she did lately. He crossed his arms and stood there just looking at her, waiting to hear what she said.

"I'm fine, Rebecca. I'm not comfortable being around Patrick anymore. I told him no at the party and he used your phone to text me. Needless to say that Mark wasn't happy about it. I can't say as I blame him. I was rather upset myself. So, I have decided not to come back to the group. Please tell everyone I'm fine and that I didn't mean to hurt anyone's feelings."

"Oh, Tabitha. I'm so sorry. I never wanted you to feel uncomfortable. And I don't want you and Christian to quit coming to mommy and me. So I hope you'll reconsider," Rebecca said as she hugged Renee.

Jesse watched as Renee slowly patted Rebecca on the back. When Rebecca pulled back, she put a small smile on her face, but yet again, Jesse could tell it was not her genuine smile. Rebecca must have known, too, as she frowned. Finally, she told them goodbye, and Jesse closed the door. Renee turned to go back into the living room, her fake smile gone already and the blank face now back in place. He grabbed her arm and felt her tense.

"You handled that very well. I'll find another group for you and Christian, ok?"

"Don't bother. I don't care anymore," Renee said as she tried to walk away.

Jesse held on to her arm and said, "You act like you don't care, but I know you do. You wouldn't be this sad if you didn't."

"I'm depressed because I'm stuck here. I'm your prisoner and no matter what I do, that isn't going to change. You hurt me over and over and don't care that you do it. You could care less about what I want or even what I like. You say you love me, but I know that's a lie. You don't hurt someone you love. At least not intentionally, but everything you do is done intentionally. You wanted me to be compliant. You have that now. I won't fight you anymore. I won't ask to go out. I won't fight you when it comes to sex. I won't ask you for anything. Just don't expect me to be happy when I'm not," Renee said as she jerked her arm away from him and walked away.

Jesse punched the wall, trying to control his anger. He busted his knuckles open and cursed at himself for being so stupid. How could she say he didn't love her? He had done so much to prove he cared and all she had done was throw it back in his face. His anger had gotten the better of him more than once, which had set them back, but none of it had been this bad. He had to try to fix things, but how?

* * *

Months went by, and Jesse had still not been able to bring Renee around. She hadn't been sleeping well. She would have bad dreams at night and lash out. Sometimes she hit him, but he didn't do anything out of the way because of it. Instead, he wrapped her in his arms and held her tight. She would wake up terrified, and her body would shake for a long time before she would finally fall back asleep. Her eyes had dark circles under them, and she was barely eating. He would have to force her to eat at dinner, or she would just wind up pushing the food around on her plate.

Summertime had hit, and the flowerbeds she had tended to the past two years were starting to bloom. She hadn't been outside to tend to them even once. He'd tried to get her to come out and help him with them, but she had told him no every time. So instead of getting angry or forcing the issue, he had let it be. He watched the flowers die as Renee sunk further into a shell, almost like it was symbolizing her dying.

He had wanted her to be compliant at first, but now, he just wanted the defiance back. He had liked the way she was before. He kept trying to do nice things for her, but all she saw was him trying to trick her like he had the first time. She had even stopped talking to the women she'd made friends with in the group. He hadn't told her that she had to cut all of them off. He didn't want her in the group because of Patrick.

He started looking for other things she could do. He found a few groups that she could go to with Christian. One night he took her to one, but she had come out and told him she didn't want to go back. He had made her go back a few times, but she didn't seem to lighten up. He'd had enough.

"Renee, you have got to stop this. I don't want you to be like this. You are going to start going to that group and talking to the women there. Make friends with a few. Also, I am planning a surprise for you."

"Why? Why plan a surprise for me? I won't care about it anyway. And, I told you that I'm not going back to that group. I'm not going to make friends with anyone. What's the point? I don't have a normal life. It's not like I can go out whenever I want or have friends that I can hang out with. You have made it very clear that even when I don't do anything wrong, you are going to find something wrong with it. What happens if I make friends and then something happens you don't like? Something beyond my control? It will be like last time. I will get punished. No. You may force me to go to that group, but I don't have to talk to anyone while I'm there. If you are going to hurt me because of it, then so be it. I won't do it no matter what you do to me."

"I don't want to hurt you. I want you to have friends and be happy. I want you to be happy with me."

"What don't you understand about I'm not going to be happy with you? I don't want to be with you! You don't love me. You don't know what love is. If you did, then you wouldn't keep hurting me. You would control your anger and learn to deal with situations that come up without hurting me. If you knew what a true relationship was, then you would know you have to talk through things, not force things on people. You should never raise your hand in anger. Or in your case, force yourself on someone. And you would let me go!"

"You're right. I don't know what a true relationship is. I've never had one. The only relationship I ever saw was my parents. My dad beat on my mother all the time. He raped her every night. We heard her screams. That's the relationship I'm used to. And my anger stems from all of that. It comes from watching my mother die as I shielded my brother from seeing it. I've never been with a woman longer than a couple of nights for this reason."

"So, you were, what, worried about becoming your father? So, you did exactly that? You didn't even try to break the pattern. I can see why no woman would mind you not wanting to stay with them."

Jesse clenched his fists but didn't make a move to hit her. She was daring him to hit her as she yelled at him. He had stopped that a long time ago, however. Now, he just abused her body when he got angry. To her, it was all the same as he bruised her when he did it. She stepped close to him as she continued.

"You say what your father did messed you up. So, are you going to mess your own son up the same way? Are you going to make me scream every night so he can hear it? Are you going to beat me to death in front of him? I can only assume your father went to jail and you went into foster care. Is that what you want for your own son?"

"No!" Jesse yelled as he jerked Renee against him.

Renee tensed, but she didn't try to pull away as Jesse continued, "We didn't go into foster care. We hit the streets as my father ran. I've gotten good at hiding. I've stolen from stores and beat grown men as I robbed them. Everything I did was to keep my brother out of foster care. I was fifteen. He was only ten. That bastard killed him when he was 21. It's been 5 years and I still can't move past it."

As much as Renee hated Jesse, she felt sorry for him. He'd had a rough life, but he should've tried to change his life instead of making someone else's miserable. Jesse was 31 now, and she wondered if he could change at this point. He had been doing better with the way he treated her. He still messed up, but it wasn't all the time. Then, a thought suddenly occurred to her.

"I'm the same age as your brother would have been. He would be 27 now. Would you want him to see you like this knowing what he also went through as a child?" Renee asked as she put her hand on his arm.

Jesse looked at her hand on his arm and thought about what she had just said. His anger wasn't towards her. It was towards Kevin. If he hurt her, then he could hurt Kevin. However, Kevin didn't know about any of it. So, he was just hurting her and putting her into the same life his mother had. The difference was that Renee truly cared about her son. She loved him and gave everything of herself to him, whereas his mother could have cared less about her two children. Billy would have been upset at him for treating his woman this way, as Billy had never mistreated a woman.

The last girlfriend he had left him. He was not cruel to her or hit her, but because he was too clingy. Billy had always been worried that he wasn't good enough for anyone. Being that clingy posed a problem for many people simply because they don't like it. Billy had always shown up where Clarissa was, but not to stalk her. He simply wanted her back. His jealousy had won out in the end, and he had picked a fight with Kevin. Jesse closed his eyes as he thought of that night. Yes, Billy had been wrong, but Kevin had always acted like Billy was psychotic. Jesse couldn't find it in himself to believe his sweet baby brother would ever kill someone. He had never done anything like that before.

Jesse tensed as he felt Renee's arms slip around him. It took him by surprise as she never touched him, let alone hugged him. He wrapped his arms around her and took a deep breath. He felt her fingertips run across his cheek, realizing he had been crying. She was wiping away his tears. He opened his eyes and looked at her. She looked confused and was frowning.

Jesse pulled her against him, and she rested her head on his chest. He inhaled her scent and felt his anger and tension slip away. Could this woman change him? He wanted her and had for a long time, but she didn't want him. Could she finally come to care for him if he could get rid of his anger? He had never talked to anyone about his past, but she was drawing it out of him without even trying.

Renee was shocked to see Jesse crying. He was always so tough around her, even when he told her he loved her. She had never expected to see him cry. Talking about his brother struck him. She wasn't sure if she should console him or walk away, but she felt the urge to hug him and make him feel better. She wasn't sure why she felt like she should comfort him after everything he had done to her, but she did. She wiped the tears from his face as he looked at her. She hated him, but she had never seen this part of him. She found it shocking to think he had real emotions, but here they were.

Renee listened to Jesse's heartbeat. It was starting to beat faster and faster. His body was no longer tense like he would hit her, but why was his heart beating so fast? It was almost like he was scared of something. She went to pull back, but Jesse's arms tightened around her. She didn't feel threatened and was surprised that she didn't tense up. She let him hold her until he finally pulled back on his own due to Christian crying. Then, he lightly kissed her lips and let her go.

Confusion had set in Renee's heart. She felt like she was dead inside for so long that she didn't know how to take what she was feeling now. She took care of Christian while her mind raced. What had just happened between her and Jesse? He had opened up just now, even if it was initially out of anger. He had said he didn't know what a genuine relationship was. She believed that completely. But could he change and improve who he was at his age? Most people developed as a person in their teens and usually didn't change from that point on.

Once she finished changing Christian, she returned to the living room. Jesse was sitting on the couch, leaning over with his elbows on his knees. He looked deep in thought, so she left him alone. She could feel him staring at her and Christian, and she couldn't help but wonder what he would do next. When he suddenly stood up, she tensed, waiting for him to do something to her. Instead, he took Christian out of her lap. He stood her up and kissed her while holding Christian on his hip. Christian put his hands on their faces, and Renee smiled at him as Jesse broke the kiss.

"I've been talking to someone about watching Christian. She's agreed to watch him tonight. We are going to go to the store first and get some things," Jesse said.

"Um, ok. I'll go get Christian's bag," Renee said as she walked into the bedroom.

Renee was feeling even more confused now. After everything that was just said, Jesse was still going ahead with his surprise. Furthermore, he was getting someone to babysit Christian. She wasn't sure how she felt about leaving her son with someone she didn't know. She also felt something about him talking to another woman behind her back. She wasn't sure what emotion it was and didn't want to dive into an analysis of it. He could be with whomever he wanted. Maybe it would save her from him if he found someone else.

They went to the store, and Renee noticed the store was full of beautiful dresses and shoes. It looked more like a boutique. Why had Jesse brought her here? She didn't need a dress or dress shoes. She never went anywhere fancy to need these things. She was more comfortable in her jeans and shirts anyway. That way, if he bruised her, she could cover it up.

She looked at Jesse and said, "Why are we here?"

"This is part of the surprise. I would like you to pick out a dress and shoes. Please, try them on and let me see them, ok?"

"Do I really have to? I don't go anywhere that requires a dress."

"Well, maybe you will. But, please, just find some dresses and try them on. I'll be here with Christian, waiting for you to come out and show them to me," Jesse said as he sat down on the chair outside the changing room.

Renee sighed and walked around the store, looking at the dresses. She found a couple that she liked but didn't think would look good on her. A woman came over and asked her if she could help. Renee told her she was just looking, but the woman insisted on helping her. She picked up a dress, and the woman told her whether it worked on her or not. After finding five different dresses and shoes to go with them, she went to the changing room.

She put the first one on and looked at herself in the mirror. It didn't look bad, but she wasn't used to wearing a dress anymore. Would Jesse let her go out in it and not cause a scene? When he knocked on the door, she nervously opened it. It was just a simple blue dress with a sweetheart neckline that she had on. It had roses embroidered down the sides and a cinched waist.

Renee stepped out of the dressing room and felt extremely self-conscious. The dress wasn't revealing except for her legs from the knees down. It covered her breasts nicely. Jesse smiled. He liked the way it looked on her.

"It's nice. Do you have any others to try on?"

"Yes. I have four more," Renee said.

"Ok. I want to see them all."

Renee went back into the changing room, tried the dresses on, and let Jesse look at them one by one. The attendant had her put the less revealing dresses on first. The fourth one had a Queen Elizabeth neckline showing her breasts, and the last one was the most revealing. She also found it beautiful, but she realized just how much the Décolleté neckline showed once she put it on.

It went past her breasts and didn't leave much to the imagination. It was a deep purple color, and it stopped right above her knees. It had lace flower appliqués on the top and going around the bottom of the skirt. She turned to the side and saw the back of the dress was right above the small of her back. This dress was way too revealing. Jesse would never allow her to wear this out in public. She stepped out of the dressing room with her head hung down.

Jesse looked up as he heard Renee open the door. When he saw her, her head was hung down as if she was scared. He looked over the dress and how it fit her, and his mouth began to water. He had the urge to set Christian down and push her back into the dressing room and take her right then and there. The front was barely covering her breasts. It fit her body like a glove. She slowly turned without even looking up to see if he was looking. The back of the dress showed off her back right down to the small of it. It stopped right above her knees, and he saw a split going up one side to her hip.

He put Christian in his car seat and buckled him in so he couldn't go crawling away. He walked up to Renee and turned her to face him. When he lifted her head, he saw fear flash in her eyes. He wrapped his arms around her, not understanding the fear he saw there. He kissed her lips with all of the passion he was feeling. When he broke the kiss, he saw she was still looking down and not at him.

"What's wrong? Do you not like the dress? I mean, I'm having a hard time not pushing you back into that dressing room and taking you. You look gorgeous in it. Why do you look scared?"

Renee bit her lip and finally answered honestly, "I know how you are. If someone sees me in this dress and says something you feel is out of the way, I will get the punishment for it."

"I promise you that I will not say or do anything out of the way if a man says something to you as long as you can promise me that you won't respond back in kind."

Renee looked at him then and saw no dishonesty in his eyes. All she saw was lust. She blushed and finally agreed to the terms. She took the dress off, and Jesse had the clerk ring up the last two dresses and the shoes. Renee was surprised by this but didn't say anything. She was trying to figure out why she would need one dress, let alone two. Once they left the store, Jesse drove her to another store. This one was full of makeup, hair supplies, and anything you would need to make yourself look fancy.

She tentatively looked at some things. She was worried about his reaction to her buying something expensive or a lot of stuff. She would pick something up she liked but put it back immediately when she saw how much it cost. Jesse hadn't said anything about the things she was looking at. When she made it out of the makeup section, she casually looked at the jewelry. They had an extensive selection of beautiful things, but she knew all of them would be too expensive.

When she turned around, she saw Jesse had things in the buggy. She looked at it and noticed all of the makeup she had picked up and put back was in it. She slowly lifted her eyes to find him looking at the jewelry. He was looking at the necklace she had looked at the longest. It was a beautiful silver necklace with tiny diamonds set into it. It had a genuine gold chain on it. She knew it was expensive just because of the tiny diamonds and was surprised when he asked the clerk for it.

She slowly walked away, acting like she hadn't seen him do it. What was he planning? This was a costly outing, from what she could tell. Just the dresses and shoes were hundreds of dollars. Now the makeup and jewelry? She knew he made good money at his job and could take care of them, but how much was he willing to spend? She was looking at the rings when he walked over.

"See something you like?"

"I was just looking. I don't have a need for jewelry."

"That's not what I asked. Do you see something you like? Do you like the wedding sets or just the regular rings?"

"I was looking at all of them. I'm not married so I don't see a need for a wedding set."

"Well, technically we are married," Jesse whispered.

CHAPTER 9

Renee had thought about Jesse's comment all the way back to the house. She knew their fake IDs had them listed as a married couple, but they weren't married. So why would she need a wedding ring after all this time? She had to admit that she would have liked to have married one day, but now, she knew she wouldn't. She had hoped that one day Kevin would propose, but he hadn't. She had seriously thought he would do it on their anniversary, but Jesse had ruined that. She sighed and started putting away all of the things she bought today.

"I got you all of this stuff as part of the surprise. I'd like you to wear that dress you had on earlier. Use the other stuff, too. We are going to drop Christian off on the way out. I'll get ready to go and then watch Christian while you get ready."

"Um, ok," Renee said as she lay the dress on the bed.

She got in the shower and then sat on the bed for a few minutes, looking at everything. She would doll herself up for the first time in over two years. She bit her lip as she looked at the dress and thought about what makeup to wear. She finally decided to wear a deep blue color and a smoky-looking gray on her eyes. First, she applied eyeliner and mascara. Then she looked at the two lipsticks she had. She finally settled on the red wine color and applied it.

She took her hair, twisted it, and then clipped it. A few tendrils were hanging down on her neck. The rest was hanging over the clip, so it looked wavy as it dried. She looked at herself in the mirror and was shocked. She looked like a completely different person. She didn't know why, but she felt nervous as she stepped out of the bedroom and into the living room, where Jesse played with Christian.

Jesse looked up when he heard Renee come into the living room. He leaned back against the couch as he sat on the floor with Christian. He started at her feet and made his way up to her face, and then he made his way back down again. When his eyes returned to her face, he saw she was blushing, but she also had a small but embarrassed smile. It was cute, and he liked that him looking at her had made her do it. He found he didn't want to go out tonight but stay in and slowly strip her of the dress.

Jesse stood up, and Renee got to see what he was wearing. He had on a navy-blue dress shirt and navy-blue slacks. His hair was slicked back. The navy blue set off the blue in his eyes, making it more pronounced. He walked up to her and went to kiss her. She put her hand up in front of his face to stop him.

"You'll ruin my lipstick."

"I don't care. You can reapply it," Jesse said as he kissed her long and deep.

A little bit of lipstick got on his lips, and Renee wiped it off and went and reapplied her lipstick, making sure that it wasn't smeared. Jesse came up, and she saw him in the mirror as his hands came around the sides of her face. She wondered what he was doing at first until she felt the necklace settle on her chest. She looked down and saw the cross she had been eyeing earlier. Jesse kissed her neck as his hands slid around her waist. Renee felt a blush creep up her neck as she saw the look in his eyes in the mirror.

She cleared her throat and said, "We should get going."

Jesse sighed and said, "Yeah, if I actually want to carry through with your surprise instead of undressing you here and now, we should."

He kissed her cheek and walked out of the room, gathering Christian. As they rode down the road, Renee started to recognize the area. They were going to Nancy and Greg's house. Jesse worked with Greg, and Renee got along with Nancy. They had two kids, aged eight and five. Nancy had an affection for Christian and always spoiled him when they were over.

When Jesse pulled into their driveway, Renee realized whom the woman was watching Christian for them. They walked up to the door, and Jesse knocked on it. Nancy answered the door and smiled when she saw them. Renee was nervous about leaving Christian with Nancy and Greg. It wasn't that she thought they would mistreat him, but she had never left him anywhere before.

"Hey, guys! You finally came to drop Christian off," Nancy smiled.

"Yes," Jesse said as he handed Christian's car seat to Nancy.

"Wait. I need to tell him bye first," Renee said as she took Christian out of his car seat.

"You poor thing. Is this the first time you have left him with someone?" Nancy asked.

"Yes. How did you know?"

"I remember that look. I had the exact same one the first time I dropped Matthew off with a babysitter. I was nervous the whole night and kept calling the sitter. I drove her nuts, but I promise you that Christian won't want for anything tonight."

Renee held Christian in her arms as he played with her necklace. She smiled at him and kissed his head. Her heart felt like it was being squeezed as she handed him over to Nancy. Jesse placed his hand on the small of her back and turned her to leave as he thanked Nancy. He opened the car door for her, and she got in, still looking at the door as Nancy waved bye to them.

"Christian is going to be fine, Renee. Don't worry. Tonight is about having a good time with no worries."

"Easy for you to say. A mother never stops worrying about her kids, no matter how old they are. I've never been away from him. This is harder than I thought it would be," Renee said as she sighed.

"At least try to have a good time."

"I'll try," Renee said as they pulled off.

Renee was quiet as Jesse drove them to a nice restaurant. She wondered if she could have a good time knowing that she was out with Jesse. She had felt nothing for so long that she wasn't sure she could feel anything anymore. She hadn't even been pleased when she was with Christian. She had faked her way through the days, and she was always exhausted by the end. Jesse had been playing the nice card for a while now, but she knew it wouldn't last. He always lost his temper and took it out on her when he did. It was just a matter of time, and she knew it.

The max he could go was six months, and he was hitting that time frame now. Furthermore, they were going out, and she was all dressed up. She wondered what was going to happen tonight to set him off. Moreover, how bad would it be when they got back home? She shuddered as that thought ran through her mind. She tried to relax her body as Jesse came around and opened her door. He helped her out, and she tried her best not to jerk away from him. She wasn't going to give him any reason to be abusive.

When they walked into the restaurant, Renee gasped. It was gorgeous. Some tables were set with stained glass. The windows were also stained glass with pictures of flowers and angels. There were little vases with flowers in them on the tables. The Maître D sat them at a table in the corner, and Jesse pulled her chair out for her. Renee sat and just looked at everything, taking it in. This was a pricey place, and she knew it before seeing the menus.

"This place is beautiful."

"Yes, it is," Jesse said.

Renee noticed he wasn't looking at the restaurant but directly at her when he said it. She found herself blushing. What was happening to her today? She had felt bad for Jesse earlier and then had felt a twinge of something when he said he had been talking to a woman. Now, she was blushing because of a compliment. She was losing her mind. When the waiter came over, Jesse ordered a bottle of wine. Renee was no longer breastfeeding, so she could drink wine without worrying about it.

"Do you see anything on the menu that you would like?"

"Um, it's all really expensive. I think I'm just going to get a salad."

"Nonsense. I brought you here knowing what the cost would be. I'm not worried about it. Order whatever you want, or I can order for you. Whatever you'd like."

Renee bit her lip and looked over the menu again. She finally picked out a steak with baked potato and a salad. She took a sip of her wine and peeked at Jesse as he looked at the menu. Something was different about him since they had their fight earlier. He seemed more relaxed. He was more affectionate today than he had ever been. She had never believed him when he told her that he loved her. How can you love someone and terrorize them at the same time?

"Penny for your thoughts," Jesse said as he brushed his fingertips over the top of her hand.

"Have you ever been on a date before?"

"Honestly, no. I told you that I don't date women. I have sex with them and that's it. I never saw the point of dating one when I could just have some fun and leave. I didn't want a relationship with anyone so it worked for me."

"Then why are you doing all of this?" Renee asked as she waved her hand towards the restaurant and herself.

"Do you really want to know? If so, we will talk later. This isn't the place for this conversation and you know why."

"Yes, I want to know, but I don't want to wait until later. You don't have to go into specifics. Do you consider this a date?"

"Yeah, I consider it a date."

"Then, talk. People get to know each other when they go on dates. That's how it works. You ask someone out and you two go and get to know each other better."

"Fine," Jesse said as he lowered his voice. "I wasn't planning on keeping you. You know that. When you found out you were pregnant, I found I was actually happy. I never wanted kids because of my past but I couldn't seem to give up my kid. I started watching you with the flowers and with Christian while he was still growing inside of you. It hit me that I wanted that, too. I wanted someone to look at me that way and care about me the way you did those stupid flowers. I'd never had that before. I told you this."

"So, you just decided to try to make me like you since you wanted someone to like you?"

"No, not exactly. I liked you, the real you. I liked the way you were and how you cared. I liked the fact that no matter what I did, you didn't break. You were strong and still caring. I still like all of those things. I love all of that about you. It took me off guard, too, when I came to realize I liked you. That was something that I wasn't expecting. So, when I felt that I loved you, I didn't know how to handle it. I tried to get rid of that feeling because I didn't want to love a woman. It was already too much that I liked you in the sense that I wanted to date you. But, the more I tried to get rid of the feeling, the more I hurt you in the long run. So, eventually, I just stopped fighting it."

"So, tonight *is* about trying to make me like you, too?"

"Not exactly. Tonight is about trying to make up for all the bullshit. I want you to like me, but that isn't going to happen if I can't control myself with you. I'm not even sure if you can like me, but I'm trying my best to be nice and make this work. Tonight is my first date ever, but it's our first date together. If everything goes well, I hope to have more dates. Everything from us leaving the house to going home will lead up to something later, but for now, I just want us to have a good night."

Renee was stunned to hear Jesse admit this to her. He was trying to date her now. He'd always tried to make her submit to him and force her to like him. She wasn't sure how she was supposed to respond. What if she said something she shouldn't, and it caused issues for her later? She shuffled in her seat, uncomfortable with the idea of dating Jesse.

"Don't overthink it, Renee. Let's just talk and have a real date. I want to get to know more about you. Let's just start off with something simple, ok?" Jesse asked.

"Ok," Renee whispered as she felt her gut wrench from thinking about all the things that could go wrong to land her in punishment.

"What's your favorite color?" Jesse asked.

"Purple. And yours?"

"Blue. What's your favorite flower?"

"Um, I have two that I can never decide between. I love roses and lilies," Renee replied.

"So, you liked the flowers I bought you for the garden before?"

"Yes. They were beautiful and they smelled wonderful when they bloomed," Renee said as she thought about the flowers she had been neglecting lately.

"What are some of your hobbies?" Jesse asked.

"I don't have hobbies anymore, but I used to like going to the movies before. I also..." Renee trailed off, embarrassed about her hobby.

"What? What was it?" Jesse asked, genuinely interested in her answer.

"I used to like going four-wheeling. I loved to go through the mud and kick it up. I loved the feel of the four-wheeler under me. I loved the feel of the wind whipping my face when I went fast. I'd come home dirty as all get out, but I didn't care. I had a blast," Renee said as excitement crept into her voice.

Jesse sat back and smiled. She had a wild streak. He had never seen that from her before. Of course, he hadn't seen any of her different sides as she had never let loose around him. He found her more intriguing now and wanted to know all of her. He liked the little smile she had on her face as she thought about when she went mudding.

"So, you are a country girl?"

"Oh yeah. I loved to camp and go four-wheeling. I love a good bonfire. Good old fashioned country nights are always the best. You go four-wheeling, build a bonfire, camp out at night and wake up the next morning to fresh country air. It's even better to wake up next to someone in that tent."

Renee's mind had drifted, and she had started thinking about all the nights that she and Kevin had camped in the mountains. When she looked at Jesse, she knew she had said or done something she shouldn't have. He was frowning. She cleared her throat and tried to change the subject.

"What are your hobbies?"

"Did you often go camping with someone else? Is that what you were thinking about just now?"

"Yes," Renee whispered, biting her lip.

"I'm not mad, Renee. I just noticed you drifted away as you talked about it. You had a life before me and Christian. I can't help but feel jealous as you can't think back on anything with me and have that fondness. I would like to change that. I also don't want to have to keep fighting you know who's ghost. Will you at least try to be happy with me?"

Renee knew if she said no, there would be trouble, so she answered, "Yes, I'll try."

"Thank you. I know I have no right to ask that, but I find myself wanting a future with you. That's something I have never wanted before. I've also never talked to anyone about my past. Today was a real first for me. And I never really had any hobbies. I was good at shooting pool. It was a side hustle for me to make extra cash. That's all I ever did. I played pool and drank. I've always had a bad temper, so I stayed in trouble all the time. I didn't have friends that I hung out with. The only person I was ever around was Billy."

"That sounds like a really lonely existence. Didn't you meet anyone that you thought you wanted to be friends with?"

"No. I was too busy just trying to survive. I had a hard time holding a normal job because I would get angry and start a fight at the drop of a hat. Having people I talk to on the job and hang out with outside of work here actually surprised me. I don't think any of that would have happened if it hadn't been for you and Christian."

"Oh," Renee responded.

The waiter brought their food, and they ate in silence for a little bit. Renee ate most of her food, but she didn't finish it. Jesse had watched her as she ate. He could tell by the look on her face that she enjoyed it.

"Would you like to split a dessert with me?"

"I'm pretty full. I don't know if I can eat anything else."

"Ok. If you're sure. I would like to try this chocolate cake they have. You might change your mind once it gets here."

The waiter brought the cake, and Renee had to admit that it looked delicious. Jesse tried it and found it delicious. He put a piece on the fork and held it out to Renee. She slowly moved forward and took the fork into her mouth. She closed her eyes. Jesse found her reaction sexy as hell. She even let out a little moan of appreciation. He would eat a piece and then offer her a piece.

Renee wasn't sure how to take Jesse feeding her. She also wasn't sure about her emotions about this night. His whole attitude had changed, and she could only hope the rest of the night went this well and there wouldn't be some change of events that ended with brutality. Being on a date with her tormentor was giving her a slight headache. It was confusing her because of his sudden change of personality. Was this what Jesse was like? He had tried being cruel and then nice to her, but she hadn't responded well either way. If she came around, would he continue to try to woo her? Or was he just going to go back to his usual cruel self if she didn't come around to the idea of being in a relationship with him?

CHAPTER 10

Jesse paid for the meal when they finished eating, and they left. He kept his hand on the small of her back the whole way out to the car. Finally, he opened her car door for her and shut it, too. He got in and started driving. She wondered where they were going now. She also hoped that half a bottle of wine was all he would drink because she had already figured out he was a horrible person when he was drunk due to the blackout rages.

"So, where are we going now?" Renee asked casually.

"Well, you said you liked going to the movies, so how about we go there?"

"Um, well, we can go do something you like instead. I like to play pool. I'm not the greatest at it, but you can show me how to play," Renee offered.

Jesse thought about it. Showing her how to play would require him to be all over her all night. That thought alone made him want to go. He smiled as her suggestion sunk in. She had suggested it, so maybe she wouldn't jerk away from his touch. She had been looking at him all night with such confusion on her face. He wanted this night to go smoothly in hopes that the look on her face would change to something else.

"Alright. I know where there's a pool hall. It's close to my job."

"Have you been there before?" Renee asked.

"No. I've never actually been in it. I've always come straight home after work. Worried I did something there?"

"No. I was just curious," Renee said, shifting uncomfortably.

She hoped he hadn't taken her question wrong. She wondered if he had come straight back to the house after work like he had told her he had. But he could do whatever he wanted, and she couldn't, so it's not like it mattered. At the same time, she found that it did bother her to think about him being with someone else and then coming home and sleeping with her. Even though she didn't like sleeping with him, she didn't want to know that he was with someone else at the same time as her.

She felt Jesse lace his fingers through hers, and she peeked at him out of the corner of her eye. He was smiling. He wasn't squeezing her hand or hurting her, so she relaxed into the seat. After a few minutes, she felt Jesse's thumb rubbing circles on her hand. She closed her eyes as the sensation tickled her hand, but it was also causing a slight reaction in her body.

When they got to the pool hall, they walked inside and found a table. Renee sat down, and Jesse got them a drink. When a table opened, Jesse grabbed it and racked the balls. He handed Renee a pool stick and offered to let her break. As they played, he watched her. She wasn't as bad at playing as she claimed.

When it came to the shots where she had to angle them, she wasn't that good. He walked up behind her and slid his hands over hers. Renee didn't tense up when she felt him press against her. They were having a good time, and Jesse had laughed and joked with her. She didn't want to ruin it by tensing up. One of his hands moved to her hips and down to her thigh, where he moved her legs apart. Then, he pushed on her back slightly, so she was bending lower on the table.

"Bending lower allows you to see your angle better," Jesse whispered in her ear.

Renee felt a shiver run through her body as his hand traced her back and around her waist. He showed her how to point the stick, and he drew it back and thrust it forward so she could feel how hard to strike the cue ball. He continued to do this as he showed her different shots throughout the game. He would not only show her how to shoot, but he also took advantage of touching her in a way that was sexual. Renee found that being shown how to play was a very intimate thing.

After the game, Jesse left her with the table to get them another drink. She started racking the balls when a guy came up to the table. She ignored him when he smiled at her. She looked towards the bar and found Jesse was still there. She was surprised that she hoped he would come back soon as the guy moved closer to her.

"I can't help but notice there's no one else around. Would you care to dance?" The man asked.

"No. I'm actually waiting on someone."

"Oh. You got a man?" He asked.

"Yes. I'm married," Renee replied as she finished racking.

"Really? I don't see a ring on that finger. I would have put a ring on a pretty thing like you if you belonged to me. What's your name, sweetheart?" The man asked as he leaned against the table beside her.

"She's taken," Jesse said as he handed her the drink he'd gotten for her.

"You the husband?" The man asked as he arched an eyebrow.

"So, she told you that she was married and you are still hitting on her?" Jesse asked, fuming.

"I don't see a ring on it, so I think she's single. Can't blame a brother for trying."

Jesse's hand balled into a fist. Renee put her hand on his, and he looked at her. She smiled at him and shook her head no. He unclenched his fist, and she gave him a genuine smile. She drank her drink quickly and then laced her fingers through his. She pulled him away from the guy and onto the dance floor.

"Come on. Dance with me," Renee said.

"Are you just trying to get me away from the guy so I don't knock his lights out?"

"Yes. There's no need for that. You let him know I was taken as did I. It's over. Now, dance with me," Renee said as she felt the alcohol hitting her head.

She had never really been a big drinker, and it had been a long time since she had drunk this much in one night. Plus, she had just downed the drink he'd brought her. Her head felt like it was swimming and she felt her body completely relax. She had always gotten a little crazy when she drank too much. She wrapped her arms around Jesse's neck and pressed her body against his.

Jesse wrapped his arms around her. Renee started to move her body against him. She put her hand on the back of his neck and pulled his head down. She placed her face beside his head to whisper in his ear.

"Dancing is just like sex. You just move your bodies to the rhythm of the music and to the rhythm of each other."

Jesse's hands moved down, and he grabbed her hips, grinding himself into her. She gasped and rolled her hips as she ground into him. Suddenly, she turned, so her back and butt were pressed against him. She ground her backside into him and swayed her hips from side to side. She slid partway down him and then back up again.

"I'm not sure how long I can take you doing this before we will have to leave."

Renee laughed and continued grinding on him until the song was over. When a slow song came on, she turned back around and wrapped her arms around his neck. Jesse looked into her eyes and knew she was drunk. Her pupils were dilated. Nevertheless, he wasn't going to complain. He put one hand on her back and one hand on her hip and pulled her against him as he started to sway them to the music. Renee put her head on his shoulder and just danced.

"I think I should give you your surprise now. I was going to wait until we got back home, but after that guy said something about not seeing a ring on your finger, well, I think it's better to do it now."

Renee pulled back a little bit, and Jesse reached into his pocket. He pulled out a ring box and opened it, revealing a beautiful set of rings. Renee's heart sped up. So, he had planned on marking her as his for real. This had been his surprise. No wonder he had made that comment about them being married. Her mouth went dry as he took her hand and put the rings on her finger. The engagement ring was a medium-sized band with tiny diamonds clustered around a sapphire. The wedding band was gold with small diamonds going around it. She noticed another ring in the box and knew it was a man's wedding band. Jesse took it out and put it on his finger.

"There. Now you truly are mine. There won't be anyone else thinking you are single. Do you like them?"

Renee wasn't sure how to answer. While they were beautiful, she didn't want them. This was his way of saying she belonged to him forever, and she didn't want to belong to him. Even though he had been nice tonight and was wooing her, she was waiting for the other side of him to appear. He had started slow dancing with her again as she looked at the rings.

"Are you not going to answer me?"

"I'm not sure how I feel about them," Renee said as she peeked at Jesse's face from under her eyelashes.

She noticed the frown on Jesse's face and sighed. He was definitely angry even though he was trying to hide it.

"They are beautiful, but I know that this means you are marking me. I'm trying not to say the wrong thing and piss you off. This night has been great so far, to my surprise. I don't want that to change. But, I also feel like if you want me to come around, making me your possession is not the way to do it. Are you marking me because you plan on taking me out more often and you want everyone to know that I belong to you?"

Jesse looked at her face as she pulled back from his ear. She had a look of confusion on her face. So, this was just another way for him to own her in her mind. He had thought she would like them since they were technically married on their fake IDs. He sighed as he pushed his anger aside. She had said that this night was good so far. He didn't want to ruin that.

"Yes, I plan on taking you out more. You are my wife on that marriage certificate I have. And I plan on letting everyone we meet know it. I don't want any more misunderstandings when it comes to that. I'm still trying to woo you as you put it, but you are mine no matter what. That isn't going to change so you might as well get used to it."

Renee just nodded and put her head on his shoulder. She didn't want him to see the frown on her face. Her mood had just gone downhill. She wasn't used to the weight of the rings on her finger, and she kept twisting it with her other finger.

"I'd like another drink," Renee suddenly said.

"Ok. I'll get you one. Wait for me at the table."

"Ok," Renee said as she went and sat down.

She was going to need more alcohol to get through the night. She wondered if she had made Jesse mad and what would happen when they returned home. She kept staring at the rings. They were beautiful, but she kept thinking that this was Jesse's way of making her his possession. She was no one's possession. If he had waited and given her time to adjust to the idea of him wooing her, it might be different. But, this was just too sudden for her. It was too much of a change for her to get used to in one night, and she couldn't help but think that this wouldn't last.

Jesse brought her a drink, and she gulped it down. He handed her the second one he had brought her, and she slowed down a little bit on that one. She noticed Jesse was frowning now.

"Tell me what you're thinking," Jesse said as he leaned close.

"If I tell you, then you will just get mad and punish me later."

"I promise I will not let my anger get the best of me. Talk to me."

Renee watched his face, and when she saw no anger, she replied, "This is too much for me in one night. You have been nice before and then went back to being horrible. These make me think you are trying to turn me into a possession. I'm not your possession. I'm a person, and like any other sane person, I want to feel like you want me, not to own me. This was just too much, too quick, I guess. Are you going to start treating me like you own me and can do whatever you want all over again?"

Jesse sat back in the chair and watched her. She was wringing her hands, and she had a look of fear on her face. She was terrified to tell him what she thought. He took her hand in his so that their rings were side by side. She was his, and that wasn't going to change, but he was trying hard to win her over. Her thinking like that would get them nowhere. He wanted her to think of him as her husband and come to care for him.

"I gave you the rings so I didn't have to worry about anyone hitting on you. You are mine. You are with me and it's that simple, but I also bought a wedding band for myself. You are mine, and I am yours. So, if you are looking at it that way, wouldn't I be your possession?"

Renee's head snapped up. She looked at Jesse's face to see if he was lying, but there was no sign of it. So was he actually saying he belonged to her? If that was the case, shouldn't she be able to have some say in her own life? She decided to push her luck and ask.

"If you truly belong to me and I belong to you, does that mean you are going to slack up on letting me go out? Are you going to let me have a normal life?"

"Tonight is the start of a normal life. Show me that you are taking this seriously and yes, I will allow you to start going out. If you can prove to me that you are my wife and that you won't do anything stupid while you are out, then I see no reason why I can't trust you to do what you want."

Renee sat back and thought about it. So, she had to act as his wife. That required her to have a relationship with him, and she just couldn't bring herself to do it. She didn't love him and wasn't even sure if she could do what he wanted. The alcohol made her head swim, and she was no longer thinking clearly. She would have to put this train of thought off before she said something idiotic and set him off.

"All I can do is try."

"I'll take it for now. Shall we continue to dance or would you like to play pool?"

"I think I'd like to go back to playing pool."

"All right. Let me grab a table," Jesse said as he stood up.

Renee downed the rest of her drink. When she stood up to go over to Jesse, she swayed and grabbed the table. She had drunk too much. Her thoughts were pushed back into the fog as she went and played pool.

Over the next couple of hours, Jesse got her drinks, and she drank them. She was completely drunk and messed up all of her shots, but she laughed at herself. Jesse would have to help steady her and help her shoot. Sometimes, she would press her body back into his when he was close to her. At one point, she turned her head, so her face was close to his, and he kissed her. It took him by surprise when she kissed him back. He had stopped drinking to keep an eye on her as he could tell she was completely plastered.

"I want to go dance," Renee said when the game was over.

"Alright," Jesse said and led them to the dance floor.

The way Renee was grinding on him, he wasn't sure how much longer they would be there. She had a wild side when she was drunk. He had to admit that he liked this side of her. He grabbed her hips as she ground herself into him, and he made sure she felt him as he ground himself in between her thighs.

"Somebody's happy to see me," Renee said with a laugh in Jesse's ear.

"You're going to find out how happy later," Jesse whispered back.

Usually, she would have tensed up at that comment, but she didn't. Instead, she took Jesse off guard and kissed him. The alcohol was flowing through her, and she was in a good mood. Drinking had always made her horny, and tonight was no different. It had been a long time since she had felt this way. She hadn't felt the urge to have sex or felt like she needed it since Jesse had taken her. But, tonight, she felt the craving for it. She felt like her body was on fire, and she needed that fire to be put out.

"Let's get out of here," Renee whispered into Jesse's ear and then started nibbling on it.

Jesse felt a jolt of excitement run through him. He knew it was the fact that Renee was drunk that she was coming on to him, but he liked it. He was hoping that this night would be a turning point for them. If she could just get over the fear of being with him, they could move forward. In her current state, she was feeling no fear, and he would take full advantage of that. He led her outside and to the car.

Before he could even open the door, she turned and kissed him. She pressed her body into his and pushed her fingers into his hair. He groaned into her mouth as she ground herself into him. He licked her lip, and she parted hers for him. He thrust his tongue inside her mouth, and she met it with her own. Pressing her into the side of the car, his hands traveled down her body. He felt her shudder, but he knew it wasn't out of fear this time.

He broke the kiss and leaned against her for a minute, trying to gather himself to take her home. But she wasn't stopping. Instead, she kissed his neck, and her hands massaged his shoulders.

"Renee, I can't take us home if you continue this," Jesse said in a barely audible whisper.

"You've never had a problem taking me before. What's the problem now?" Renee asked as she continued her assault on his neck.

Jesse's body jerked in response as she bit his neck. He was practically panting from need. He pulled her hands off of him and stepped back. Renee moved forward, but he pushed her back from him. He opened the door and pushed her inside the car.

Renee was pouting, and he almost yanked her out of the car and took her. Instead, he quickly went to the driver's side and got in. It took everything in him not to fly down the road to get to the house before she changed her mind. The whole way there, she kept running her hand over his thigh and across the crotch of his pants. Occasionally, she would squeeze him through his slacks, and he almost went off the side of the road. She giggled when he did that.

When they got to the house, she didn't even wait for him to come around and open her door. Instead, she got out, and Jesse grabbed her immediately. He kissed her again as she pressed into him.

"You are driving me crazy," Jesse said, breaking the kiss.

"Then do something about it," Renee taunted him as she walked up to the door.

CHAPTER 11

Jesse didn't wait to take her into the bedroom. As soon as he unlocked the door and pulled Renee inside, he pressed her against the door. He kissed her again as his hands went to her shoulders, moving the dress off them. He felt Renee's hands move to the buttons of his shirt. At first, she fumbled with them and got frustrated when she couldn't get them undone. Finally, he felt her grab his shirt near the buttons and yank. The buttons went flying, and her hands were on his chest.

That was a major turn-on for him. He quickly pushed the dress off her and broke the kiss as he moved back. He pulled the shirt off and threw it. Renee was already working on his pants. He pushed her hands away and pushed his pants and boxers down. Renee pulled him against her and started kissing his chest. Jesse wanted to slow this down. He wanted to take his time and enjoy her coming on to him. He gently pushed her back so he could take his clothes completely off.

When he looked up, she was taking her bra off. He watched as she took off her panties and kicked off her shoes. She reached out for him, but he gently pushed her hands away. She let out a sound of frustration, but he just looked at her. He wanted to see all of her. He liked that she was looking at him, too. She clearly wasn't waiting anymore as she pressed her naked body against his.

He kissed her gently this time and moved his hands over her. He played with her breasts as she deepened their kiss. Her hands went in between them, and she moved her fingertips over his chest and stomach.

Her hand went further, and she gripped him. He groaned into her mouth. His hand traveled down to her hip, gently moving it between her thighs.

Her body jerked against his hand, and he slowly moved his fingers inside of her. He broke the kiss and moved his mouth to her breasts. He kissed and sucked them as he moved his fingers inside of her. Her body started riding his hand as her hand squeezed him tighter.

"Please," Renee whispered.

"Please, what? Tell me what you want, Renee," Jesse said as his body jerked in response to her saying please.

"Stop torturing me," Renee said as her hips jerked forward against his hand.

"Tell me what you want. I want to hear you say it," Jesse said and started licking circles over her nipple.

"I want you to fuck me. I need, I need release," Renee said as he felt her tighten around him.

He hadn't even touched her when they had arrived, and she had been so damn wet for him. Now, she was soaking wet and so tight and hot. Hearing her tell him to fuck her excited him. He pulled his fingers out of her and grabbed her ass. He lifted her slightly, and she instantly wrapped her legs around him. She started grinding on his dick, wanting him to take her. He shoved himself as deep as he could inside of her. Renee cried out her pleasure as he began to fuck her against the door.

He started kissing her neck, and Renee leaned her head to the side to give him better access. Her hands were all over his shoulders, back, and chest. He felt her tightening around him, and it was driving him insane.

"Faster," Renee urged as her fingers dug into his shoulders.

Jesse started thrusting in and out of her as fast as possible, going in as deep as he could, no longer wanting to go slow. Renee was moaning and whimpering in his ear, turning him on even more. The faster he went, the more Renee was slammed into the door. She wriggled her hips to grind against him as he slammed into her. She pushed her fingers into his hair and gripped it as he nipped along her collarbone. He kissed his way up to her ear.

"Is this what you want, Renee?" Jesse said as he slammed himself into her even harder.

"Yes! Yes! Don't stop!" Renee yelled.

"God, you are driving me crazy!" Jesse said as he claimed her lips.

Renee felt the tension in her body building, and she couldn't take it. Her fingernails dug into Jesse's back as she felt him pounding into her. Finally, he broke the kiss and bent to take her breast into his mouth. When he started sucking on her nipple and nipping it, it pushed her over the edge. She cried out as she felt that rush of warmth between her thighs. Jesse continued to pump in and out of her until he released. He only slowed slightly. This only heightened Renee's orgasm. She felt the tiny shockwaves of pleasure continue to crash through her body until Jesse finally stopped. She rested her head on his shoulder, trying to stop herself from panting.

Jesse put his hand on the wall beside her head to steady himself. Slowly, he controlled his breathing and walked to the bedroom with her still wrapped around him. He wasn't ready for this night to end. He lay on the bed and began to kiss and touch Renee slowly. Now that the urgency was over, he wanted to take his time with her.

Renee didn't jerk or cringe away from him as he touched and kissed her. On the contrary, her reaction to him had even taken her off guard. She couldn't remember the last time she had been that wanton. Now that her lust had been somewhat sated, she thought she would go back to not wanting him to touch her. However, she found he was still bringing her pleasure. She touched him as he touched her. She liked the feel of his skin pressed against hers.

She liked his reaction to her when she touched him. He was moving so slowly and taking his time to make her feel good. She jerked when she felt his mouth on her nub. It was still sensitive. He worked her with his tongue until she was crying out with pleasure. But he didn't stop there. He began stroking her, letting her hand take hold of him.

She stroked him until he could take it no longer. He wanted to feel himself buried inside of her again. He moved to take her, but she suddenly pushed him away. She moved so he couldn't get on top of her. He couldn't believe she was pushing him away after everything they had done. However, he was pleasantly surprised when she got on top of him. At first, she was just kissing his chest as she rubbed herself back and forth over him.

Then, she sat up and said, "My turn."

She slid down on him and ground herself back and forth on him. He watched her face as her lips parted and her eyes closed. The look of pleasure on her face made him want to take control, but he held back. He wanted to see what she would do on her own as she never did this. Finally, she opened her eyes and looked at him. He smiled at her.

She gave him a shy smile back and reached for his hands. She placed them on her breasts and squeezed her breasts with his hands. She let him know what she liked, and his dick jerked inside of her in response.

She moaned, and her eyes closed as she began to pick up the pace of her grinding on him.

Jesse began to play with her breasts just like she had shown him. He pinched and rolled her nipples. He squeezed her breasts, and when he couldn't take it anymore, he sat up so he could take them in his mouth. Renee pushed her fingers into his hair and arched her back, pushing her breast further into his mouth.

She started bouncing on him as she rolled her hips. He moved his mouth off her breast and pushed his face between them, feeling them bounce on his face. Her grip on his hair tightened as he felt her tighten around him. His hands grabbed her hips as he moved his hips up so he was entirely inside of her as she ground against him.

"I want to feel you cum for me, Renee."

He felt a shudder run through Renee's body at his words. Did she like having someone talk dirty to her? He started saying all kinds of things about what he wanted her to do and what he wanted to do to her. Her body tightened so much that he felt like she was strangling his dick. But, at the same time, he loved it. He looked into her eyes. He loved the look he saw there.

He felt his release, but she kept going until she came for him. It was almost as if feeling him go had also caused her orgasm. He sat there with her on top of him, wrapped around him for a long time. He held her tight. He didn't want this night to end and things to go back to the way they were before. Would she only do this if she was drunk? He hoped she would stay like this in the morning when they woke up.

They had sex multiple times throughout the night and into the early morning hours. When Renee finally passed out, she felt a little sore, but in a good way. Jesse wrapped her up in his arms and pressed her back against his chest. For the first time since she had been here with him, she felt like he wouldn't hurt her.

He kissed her shoulder and whispered, "I love you."

*　　*　　*

When Renee woke up, she had a shooting pain go through her head. She moaned as she tried to open her eyes and the pain hit even harder. She'd had way too much to drink the night before. She felt like her head was going to split open. She tried to move but felt Jesse's arm over her and his body curled around hers. When she went to lift his arm, he tightened his grip on her. She felt her body tense as she waited for him to do something to her.

"Good morning," Jesse whispered as he held her tight.

"Not so good," Renee whispered back, feeling that stabbing pain in her head as she talked.

Jesse propped himself up on his elbow and looked at Renee's face. He felt hurt that she said it wasn't a good morning. After everything that had happened, he was feeling great. He noticed she had a look of pain on her face. He frowned.

"What's wrong? I didn't hurt you, did I?"

"Um, no, I don't think. I haven't really tried to move yet. My head is pounding. How much did I drink last night?"

"You don't remember?"

Renee thought about it. She was getting flashes of what had happened. She had come on to Jesse. She felt heat creep up her neck and into her face. She stretched her body to see if anything was hurt. She was sore but not from abuse. From the flashes of what had happened last night, they'd had sex a lot. She slowly opened her eyes and looked over her shoulder at Jesse. He was frowning.

"Are you telling me that you don't remember what happened between us?"

She traced the frown on his lips and said, "I'm getting flashes of it. I can't say I remember in great detail, but I know we had sex. A lot of it, but my head is hurting really bad."

"I'll get you something to help with the pain."

He stood up, and Renee saw scratch marks on his back. She gasped as she saw them, knowing that she had done that. There were several bite marks on his neck. She'd never felt the way she did last night. Was it because it had been so long since she had craved being with a man? Or was it because it had been so long since she had drunk that much?

Jesse brought her a glass of water and some aspirin. She sat up and felt like she was going to throw up. She took shallow breaths, and when her stomach stopped rolling, she took the aspirin. Jesse sat the glass on the nightstand and crawled onto the bed. He wrapped his arm around her shoulders and pulled her head onto his chest. His fingers went into her hair, and she felt him start massaging her scalp. She cuddled into him.

After a while, he asked, "Are you feeling any better?"

"Yes, thank you," Renee responded.

"Do you fully remember what happened last night?" Jesse asked, feeling himself tensing up.

Renee was unsure why his body was tense, and she worried that she would anger him if she said no. She felt her body tense in response to his and bit her lip. Then, she slowly lifted her head and looked at him. His eyes didn't hold anger, but that didn't lessen her fear.

"I can't say that I do remember all of it. I was really drunk. I remember enough to know what happened last night. Well, at least part of it. I didn't know I had done all of this," Renee said as she touched the bite marks on Jesse's neck.

"Are you upset because you marked me or fucked me?" Jesse asked, feeling his anger rise.

"Because I marked you," Renee squeezed out.

She couldn't find it in herself to regret what she had done. She had been drunk and had let herself go. She'd had a perfect time. However, now, Jesse was angry again, and she didn't want to provoke him further. She wondered if he would continue with what he had told her last night. Was he actually going to woo her? If so, he couldn't keep getting angry at every little thing and hurting her, could he?

"If you really don't regret what happened last night, then kiss me."

Renee felt a blush creep up her face. She wasn't drunk now and wasn't as carefree as before. She still wasn't comfortable with the thought of dating Jesse and being with him. But she didn't want to make him angry either. She slowly moved and sat on his lap. Her body was shaking slightly, but she would do this one way or another. She was not going back to being hurt all the time.

Jesse watched her as she moved and sat in his lap. She was shaking. He could tell by the look in her eyes that she was scared. He'd thought they had made some progress, but she was still terrified of what he would do. He guessed he couldn't blame her as he always wound up hurting her when he was angry. He was angry at the moment, but he was trying to push it aside. Of course, she regretted what she had done since she had fought him this entire time. She closed her eyes as she got close to his face. He grabbed her hair, pulled her into him, and claimed her lips. Her naked body pressing against his was causing him to want her again. It didn't matter how much sex they'd had; he was still craving her.

Renee gasped into his mouth as he stirred under her. She kissed him harder as she pressed her body into his. His hands began to trail down her back and around her sides to her stomach. They moved up to her breasts, and she began to shake a little more. He broke the kiss.

"Why are you shaking?"

"You're mad. I, I know what happens when you're mad."

Jesse shifted and said, "I'm trying. Can't you at least give me a chance?"

"I'm sorry," Renee said as she looked down.

"I don't want you to be sorry. I want you to stop being afraid."

Jesse pulled her into him and kissed her again. He began to touch her as he broke the kiss and started to kiss down her neck. He moved slowly so that he wouldn't scare her. He caressed her as his mouth trailed kisses from her neck to her collarbone and to her breasts.

Now that she wasn't drunk, she was nervous and scared about being with him. He hadn't hurt her last night. He had only done what she had asked him to. Her body slowly stopped shaking. She gasped as his hand brushed between her thighs. She slowly began to run her fingers over his shoulders and down his chest. He groaned as she shifted over him. Finally, she felt him push his fingers inside of her.

"You're already wet for me," Jesse whispered.

Renee felt a shiver go down her spine as his breath brushed her ear, and his lips followed behind. His fingers worked her into a frenzy, and she moaned as he pulled them out of her. He shifted her on top of him and positioned himself at her entrance. Renee looked at him and found he was looking at her, waiting on something. Was he waiting to see if she would say no?

"Are you ready for me?"

"Yes," Renee whispered.

Jesse thrust into her. She closed her eyes and slowly began to rock herself back and forth on him. Jesse wanted her to open her eyes, but he didn't want to push his luck. Right now, she was still responding to his touch. She wasn't afraid, and she was enjoying the sex. So it surprised him when she pushed her fingers in his hair and kissed him. She nipped his lower lip and then pushed her tongue into his mouth. He growled against her lips and grabbed a handful of her hair, taking over the kiss.

He wrapped his arm around her waist and moved on to his knees. He lay her back on the bed and broke the kiss. He yanked her off the bed, so her bottom half was in his lap, and he began to take her hard and fast. She didn't tell him to stop. Her eyes had flown open, and she was watching him. She wrapped her legs around him, holding herself in place. The position he was in allowed him to go deeper than before. He grabbed her hips and drove himself inside her as hard and fast as possible.

"Do you like this? Or do you want me to slow down? Tell me what you want, just like you did last night."

"Don't slow down. I like it when you roll your hips," Renee whispered.

Jesse smiled and began to roll his hips as he thrust in and up. His hands trailed over her stomach and up to her breasts. Her body jerked as he began to squeeze them and her hands gripped the sheets. He felt her grow tight around him. He picked up his speed in reaction.

"Damn, you are getting so tight. I love the way you are responding."

Renee's face grew hot as she felt herself blushing from his words. She wasn't used to being talked to during sex, but she found she didn't mind it. She found it sensual. Jesse suddenly jerked her up and against his body. She gasped as it scared her, but it also felt good at the same time as he began moving her up and down on him. She felt emboldened by the look in his eyes and began to kiss his neck. She ran her tongue over the bite marks she had left.

Jesse grabbed her hair, jerked her head back, and claimed her lips with his. She wrapped her arms around him and pushed her fingers in his hair as she picked up the pace and ground into him even faster. She felt that pressure building inside her as he rolled his hips under her and thrust up as he did. He moved his hand between them and moved his fingers over that sensitive spot. It was too much. She cried out into his mouth, and he suddenly moved, so he was on top of her. He took her hard and fast until she felt him release inside her.

He lay on top of her, putting his head on her breasts. She ran her fingers through his hair as they lay there catching their breath. Jesse felt good as she held him. He wrapped his arms around her and held her tight. He'd never held a woman like this after sex. It was a new experience and one he found he didn't want to lose. He liked that she was playing with his hair and letting him hold her.

"Thank you," Jesse said as he looked at Renee.

"For what?" Renee asked, looking confused.

"For allowing me to hold you and not jerking away from me."

"Oh," Renee said as a frown formed.

She had given into Jesse. She just hoped this wasn't a new form of torture. Make her feel good and get her guard down, and then he would start the abuse all over again. Jesse traced the frown on her lips and then kissed her softly.

CHAPTER 12

Jesse and Renee went to pick Christian up and hung out with Greg and Nancy. When they showed up, Nancy gasped as she saw Jesse's neck, but she got that knowing look on her face. Renee's face had been so hot that she got dizzy. She'd heard Greg ribbing Jesse about the love bites. She was embarrassed, but Jesse loved it. He was proud that she had marked him.

"So, I guess things went well on your first date out after having Christian," Nancy said, smiling at her.

"Yes. I had a little too much to drink."

"Nothing wrong with that. Anytime you two want to go out, you know who to call. Christian was an angel."

"Thank you, Nancy. I appreciate you keeping him."

"Yeah, no problem. Enjoy the moments you have alone. Once you have kids, they are few and far in between. I love my kids, but I treasure my little shopping trips as it gives me some time alone," Nancy laughed.

"Oh, I never go to the store alone. I always go with, Je, uh, Mark," Renee stammered.

She had almost messed up and called Jesse by his actual name. She bit her lip as Nancy looked at her with an odd expression. How could she have been so stupid? She felt like she needed to come up with a lie to cover her tracks, but what was she supposed to say?

"Tabitha, are you having an affair?" Nancy asked.

"No! Why would you ask that?"

"Well, you started to say another name besides your husband's. It's none of my business, but curious minds do wonder."

Renee thought quickly and lied by saying, "Mark and I were role-playing last night. I guess the name I used was still on my mind."

"Oh!" Nancy laughed.

Renee felt the blush creep up her neck as she thought about what Nancy was probably thinking had happened between her and Jesse. If she only knew what Renee had been going through for over two years now. If she only knew that she couldn't say or do anything out of the way without being punished. She sighed. Hopefully, things will get better. Then, all she had to do was go along with whatever Jesse wanted.

They talked for a bit longer before joining Jesse and Greg in the living room. They all sat around talking and joking for a few hours before Jesse and Renee left with Christian. For the first time in a long time, Renee had a good time. It was comfortable, and she didn't feel like she had done anything to get punished for later. When they got home, Jesse got Christian out of the car, and they all went inside.

Jesse put Christian in his crib as he had fallen asleep on the ride home. He went looking for Renee. She was putting Christian's dirty clothes in the wash. He wrapped his arms around her and felt her tense. He frowned. He hadn't done anything to make her afraid. How long was she going to do this?

"You did really well today. Keep this up and I think we'll be just fine," Jesse said as he kissed her cheek.

He felt Renee's body relax. He turned her towards him and kissed her softly. At first, she just stood there, but she finally kissed him back. She was still fighting him. He was going to wear her down eventually. He just knew it. He broke the kiss and let her go.

"Would you like to watch a movie with me? You can pick it out if you want," Jesse said.

"Um, sure," Renee said, a little shocked as she had never done anything with him before.

She searched through the movies and found a comedy. She put it in and went to sit on the chair she always sat in. Jesse quickly got off the couch and moved toward her. She cringed as he reached out for her; fear set in. He sighed and moved her towards the couch. He sat down, so his legs were lying on the couch. He then pulled her down so her back was to him, and she was sitting between his legs. He wrapped his arms around her and pulled her completely against him.

She slowly relaxed as he didn't try to hurt her. Sitting up stiffly hurt her back, so she lay back against him. Jesse kissed her cheek and continued watching the movie. Renee watched the movie, and for the first time in a long time, she enjoyed watching something. She laughed at the movie and enjoyed the time of not being in constant fear.

Jesse heard Renee laugh at the movie, and it surprised him. She had laughed and joked with him last night, but she had been drunk. Even when she was laughing at something someone said, he could always tell it was a fake laugh. This was her genuine laugh, and she wasn't drunk. He liked its sound and wanted to hear it all the time. He wrapped her tighter in his arms and laid his head on her shoulder. Renee didn't try to move away. He watched as she slowly placed her hands on his arms. Hopefully, this was a good sign.

*   *   *

Months continued to go by, with Jesse continuing to be nice. Renee couldn't believe it. She had gone back to tending her flowers until the winter had set back in. Now, she was cooped up in the house all of the time. She was going stir crazy. This had always been a problem for her before, too, but she had never said anything because she feared what Jesse would do. He had promised her that she could start having a normal life if she had acted as his wife.

So far, all she had been able to do was go out with him or go to the new group he had taken her to. However, she still had to be taken and picked up by him. She wanted to go out whenever she wanted and go wherever she wanted. He never left her any money because he didn't allow her to go out without him. She wasn't fighting him about sex, but she wasn't coming on to him, either. She also didn't touch him during sex. She could tell that it frustrated Jesse that she didn't.

She had been drunk and had a hangover when she could do that. When she had all her wits about her, she found that she couldn't bring herself to touch him. She knew that he wanted her to greet him when he got home or tell him goodbye when he left. He wanted her to act like she was in a relationship with him.

It scared her to think about Jesse now. His opening up and showing her the human side of himself confused her. He'd had a sad life. There had been no one there for him when he needed it. With being raped and beaten by his father, she could understand his anger. He had always protected his brother, so his father had always come for him.

She had shuddered when he had told her about it. He had stopped coming for Jesse when he had become a teenager, but Jesse still wouldn't let him near his brother. He had taken many a beating to keep his father from touching Billy. Billy had been the only person who cared about Jesse, but Jesse had never really let him be there for him because he was the older brother. He wasn't supposed to tell him that everything would be all right. That was Jesse's job as his older brother and only family.

Jesse had told her about the night he had killed a man. He had been 17. He had grabbed Billy, and they had gone on the run. They finally stopped in North Carolina. He had thrown the gun into a river along the way. Texas was far enough away to where he didn't think they would ever find him, and he had been right. But unfortunately, North Carolina had been a bad place to wind up as it had caused him to lose his brother. Renee found her heart felt like it was breaking when she saw Jesse's eyes fill with tears every time he mentioned his brother. What was happening to her? She shouldn't feel anything for him.

She knew for a fact that she didn't love him. But was she coming to care for him? Every time he showed her the parts of himself that he had never shown anyone but his brother, she was curious to know more. She hadn't been jerking away from him or tensing up as much. She sighed and took the baby monitor with her to the kitchen, where she fixed herself a cup of hot cocoa.

She grabbed her jacket and gloves. She put them on as she went outside and sat on the back porch. It got frigid in Washington. She sat outside, sipping her hot cocoa for a while. She was restless, and looking at the snow was helping to relax her. They got snow in North Carolina, but it was nothing like this. She started shivering as the cold seeped in. She sighed and went back in. She sat her cup on the counter and started taking her gloves off when she heard the front door open.

She frowned. It was too early for Jesse to be home. She took her coat off and hung it up. She started walking to the living room when Jesse came into the kitchen. He looked like he was angry, and she stopped dead. He looked at her, and she could tell he was angry but also upset. Slowly, she walked up to him and hugged him. She was still shivering from outside but hoped he wouldn't take it the wrong way and get angrier.

"Are you ok? You're never home this early."

"I had to leave before I lost my job. Someone messed up and blamed it on me. They watched the cameras and found it wasn't me, but it set me off. So, I took the rest of the day off."

"Oh," Renee said as she tried to pull away from him.

"Why are you trying to pull away?" Jesse asked, tightening his arms around her so she couldn't.

"You're angry again," Renee whispered.

"Dammit, Renee. Yes, I'm angry, but not at you. Well, I wasn't mad at you. I am now because I'm tired of this. No matter what I do, you always go back to the same old thing. Get over the shit," Jesse said as he let go of her and walked away.

Renee sighed. If he stayed angry, then she knew what would happen later. She forced herself to find him. He was in the bedroom taking his shoes off. He always showered and changed when he first got home. She slowly walked over as he stood up to take his clothes off. She walked over and stood before him as he pulled his shirt off.

"What do you want, Renee? It's been a messed up day and I just want to get in the shower and then relax."

"I'm sorry. I didn't mean to make you mad. I'm still nervous when you get mad, even if it isn't at me."

Renee moved forward and wrapped her arms around him. She put her head on his chest and listened to his heartbeat. Her hands began to stroke his back, and she heard his heartbeat get faster. She felt his skin ripple under her fingers. He wrapped his arms around her and held her for a few minutes. She slowly pulled back from him and moved her hands around his sides and down to his pants. She unbuttoned them as he watched her. She shied away, not able to bring herself to go any further.

"I'll let you get in the shower now," Renee said and pulled back.

Jesse let her go. He had been hoping she would start something with him, but all she did was touch him a little. He sighed and pushed his pants and boxers down. He stepped out of them and walked into the bathroom. He knew Renee was watching him, which brought a little smile to his face. He stood in the shower for a while, letting the hot water hit him. He was frustrated about what had happened at work and was further frustrated by Renee still being scared of him. What more did he have to do to win her over?

When he got out of the shower, he wrapped a towel around his waist. He walked out into the bedroom and found Renee was sitting on the bed. He watched her face as he walked toward her. She wasn't looking away, but instead, she was looking at him like she wanted him. Sometimes she got that look after the first date they had gone on, but she never looked at him long when it was there. It was more that she was craving sex and not craving him. Now that she was looking straight at him, he felt more like she was craving him for sex.

He wanted her to touch him, to come on to him, but he wasn't going to force it. Instead, he simply went around the bed and headed to his dresser. He already knew that if he said something, she would not start anything because she wanted it. She would only touch him a little bit because she feared what he would do if she didn't.

Renee watched as Jesse came into the bedroom. She could smell the soap he used. She had always liked the musk scent and something about it did something for her. She watched him as he walked toward the bed. He was still wet from the shower, and she tracked the water dripping down his chest to the towel. She was expecting him to come over to her, but he suddenly went toward his dresser. Usually, he would have tried to take her. He must be irate, and she knew she had to get him out of that before he did something she didn't want. However, he didn't look angry. Instead, he looked......disappointed, which surprised her.

She stood up and walked over to him, feeling herself shake from being nervous. She still hadn't come to terms with herself on being with Jesse as his wife. She walked up behind him and tugged the towel off of him. Jesse stopped what he was doing and just stood there. Renee dropped the towel on the floor and put her hands on his hips. She slowly slid them up his back and down his arms.

Jesse waited to see what she was going to do. As she started moving her hands on him, he felt her hands shaking. Even though he tried not to, he felt anger rise in him. He wanted her to want him, not fear him. He had purposely not touched her or said anything out of the way so she wouldn't come on to him out of fear. He closed his eyes and let her touch calm his anger down before turning towards her.

Renee blushed as Jesse turned toward her. She pressed against him as she looked into his eyes. Sliding her hands over his chest and neck, she pulled his head down and kissed him. It was a gentle kiss at first, but then she began to nip and suck on his bottom lip. Jesse kissed her back, but he did not attempt to touch her. She wasn't sure what was wrong as he usually never held back. Finally, she broke the kiss and took his hand, pulling him over to the bed and sitting on it.

"Lay on your stomach, please."

Jesse did as she asked. Renee stripped to her underwear and crawled on top of Jesse, sitting on his hips. He groaned as she massaged his shoulders. She massaged all the way down to his legs. She moved back up and gently pushed him until he flipped over. She straddled his hips again.

Jesse watched her as she started rubbing his chest. She blushed, and her hands started shaking again. Jesse put his hands behind his head. He wasn't going to do anything even though he wanted to touch her. He wanted to see how far she would go. She leaned down and kissed him as her hands moved down to his stomach. She broke the kiss and started trailing kisses from his jaw to his chest.

She sat up and took her bra off. Then she moved off him and took her panties off. She threw them off the bed and looked at Jesse. His eyes traveled down her body and then back up to her face. His eyes were filled with lust, but he had no expression on his face. Renee frowned, but she moved back on top of him and began to kiss and touch him. She kept glancing up, but Jesse's expression never changed, and he didn't try to touch her at all.

Renee found it frustrated her that he wasn't doing anything. Why? She never cared before if he touched her or not. She had been happy when he didn't, but now, her frustration was building. He groaned and thrust his hips up when she took him in her mouth. Finally, a reaction. She worked him with her mouth until he finally stopped her.

"Come up here, Renee," Jesse said, his voice hoarse.

Renee moved up, so she was straddling him. She thought that's what he wanted her to do. However, she wasn't wet enough. She'd liked his reaction, and it had done something for her, but she knew it wasn't enough. Jesse still didn't attempt to do anything for her, however. So, she wet her hand and began to move it over herself. She felt Jesse jerk against her and knew he enjoyed watching her play with herself.

She started rubbing herself on him at the same time. When she felt ready, she grabbed him and slid down on him. He was thick enough to give her the feeling of being filled but not stretching her. She began to move slowly, and as the pressure built, she moved faster. She felt Jesse start thrusting his hips up as she came down on him.

"Jesse, I want you to, to," Renee stuttered and stopped.

"What do you want, Renee? Tell me what you want and it'll be yours," Jesse replied, waiting.

"I want you to touch me. Now," Renee said, still frustrated that he hadn't touched her.

Jesse was more than happy to comply. His hands went over every part of her body that he could reach. He pulled her down so he could kiss and lick her breasts. She tightened around him, and he lost his control completely. He grabbed her hips and started moving his hips from side to side as he thrust up. He felt his release, but he kept going until she cried out as she came. He pushed his fingers in her hair, pulling her head down. He claimed her lips with his.

"If I had known not touching you would get you to do this, I would've stopped touching you long ago."

Renee blushed as she realized what Jesse had done. He'd gotten her frustrated by not having anything to do with her. That made her want him to touch her. She had come onto him and had her way with him instead of lying there while he did whatever he wanted. He had made her come to terms with the fact that she wanted to have sex. She was angry that she had come to want her tormentor.

CHAPTER 13

Renee decided she would ask Jesse about going out on her own since she had done what he wanted her to. She was tired of being cooped up in the house all the time. She gathered her courage and walked into the living room. He played with Christian, and she watched him for a few minutes. He did love Christian. It was sweet to see him just playing trains like it was no big deal. She smiled and sat in the chair.

"Jesse, I want to talk to you about something."

"Yeah, sure," Jesse said, not looking up.

"You said if I acted like your wife, that you would allow me to live a normal life. So far, I haven't been able to do that. I'm restless being cooped up in the house all of the time."

Jesse's head snapped up, and he looked at her. Renee felt herself cringing into the chair. Damn. She had hoped that she would be able to keep her courage up as she demanded he allows her to go out. But, here she was cringing away from him just because he was looking at her.

"Yeah, I did say that. So far, you have managed to do something with me once without me asking you to or demanding it. Other than that, you won't have anything to do with me unless I take you out on a date. It makes me wonder if you are still trying to figure out a way to get away. If you want to go out, I will take you out."

"You aren't home most of the time. I would like to go out on my own. Even if it's just window shopping, it would get me out of the house," Renee whispered.

"No. Until you show me that you are actually with me and not going anywhere, you go out with me only. If you want to go somewhere, just ask," Jesse said as he went back to playing with Christian.

Renee frowned. He wasn't going to hold up on his promise, and she knew it, but it still disappointed her to think that she had believed he would. She felt tears prick her eyes, and she got up to leave. Jesse looked up at her as she was getting ready to leave the room.

"Where are you going?"

"Outside," Renee said.

"Come here," Jesse said.

Renee sighed and stood her ground. She balled her hands into fists, feeling her nails bite into her palms. She was fighting back the tears as she wouldn't give him the satisfaction of seeing her cry. He stood up, grabbed her chin, and lifted her face. She kept her eyes down, hoping to hide the tears.

"If you want me to hold up on my end of the deal, then you have to hold up on yours."

Renee's head snapped up as she said, "How do you expect me to act like your wife when I'm not and I don't love you? I don't know what you want from me."

Jesse felt his anger rise. He had controlled himself for so long. He couldn't let it get the best of him now and ruin what little progress he had made with her. Renee was staring at him with anger in her eyes, but there were also tears that she was trying not to shed.

"I don't expect you to love me, Renee. I just want you to act as my wife would. Touch me, talk to me, be with me. Why is this so hard? Haven't I kept up my end and not hurt you in any way? Haven't I been nice? Why can't you be nice in return? Why can't you at least let yourself like me?"

"Because I'm still your prisoner. I can't bring myself to love you because I'm still in love with someone else. I can't bring myself to like you because you took everything away from me!" Renee shouted.

"I haven't taken everything from you," Jesse said as he moved closer to her, so his face was just a breath away.

Renee saw Jesse's eyes flick to Christian. She looked at him in horror as her train of thought went to him hurting Christian. She shoved him away and picked Christian up.

"You wouldn't hurt your own son," Renee said as she held Christian.

"No. I will never hurt my son, but you will no longer be around him. Hurting you doesn't get me what I want and if I can't have it, then I will simply leave with Christian. You won't be a prisoner anymore, but you won't have your son either."

"You wouldn't do that. You wouldn't make your son have the same life you had."

"I don't want that. I want you. I want us to be a family. Why can't you understand that?"

"Why can't you understand that I can't give you what you want? You can give me what I want, but you choose not to. You say you love me, but you don't. You love that I'm your possession. You dangle freedom in my face just to rip it away. If you truly love me, you will stop treating me like I'm your possession, your prisoner. If you truly want me, us as a family, then show me that side of you. You show me that side of you only when we go out and talk. Treat me like a wife who is allowed to live her own life. Maybe then I can give you what you want. You keep telling me to tell you what I want. There it is—my freedom. I want to be able to live my life. Not just sit in this house day in and day out and wonder if I'm going to die here slowly," Renee said as she broke down in tears.

Jesse walked up and wrapped his arms around Renee and Christian. Christian had started crying at the sound of their arguing. He kissed Christian on the forehead and tried to soothe him. He put his hand in Renee's hair and pulled her head onto his chest, trying to soothe her.

"I'm sorry, Renee. I lost my temper again. I'm trying, but you push my buttons and I lose it. You finally told me what you wanted and I like that. I'll think about what you said. Ok?"

Renee shook her head and started to pull back from Jesse. He held her tight, and she felt like she was suffocating. When was this running nightmare going to end? When could she finally have a life and not worry about being afraid all of the time? Even now, he wouldn't let her move away or be on her own for even a few minutes. Jesse finally stepped back and took Christian from her.

"Go get cleaned up and take a few minutes. I'm going to call Nancy and see if she'll watch Christian. We need to talk about all of this," Jesse said as he kissed her forehead.

Renee went into the bedroom and cried some more. She was sick of this. She couldn't love Jesse. She loved Kevin, and she didn't see that changing. She analyzed her feelings for Jesse. She found that she cared about the part of him that was a father. She cared about the part of him that he showed when they were on a date, the vulnerable part. But, in the same instance, she hated him for keeping her prisoner, for not allowing her to be able to do what she wanted. She wasn't going to go anywhere. She knew the consequences of that. With that always in her mind, she had difficulty bringing herself to like Jesse.

She stood up and walked into the bathroom. She put a cool cloth over her eyes for a few minutes. When she took it away, her eyes were not as puffy. She put on some makeup to cover the puffiness that she couldn't get to go away. Then, she walked out of the bedroom to find Jesse and Christian were gone. She walked around the entire house and then ran to the door. She flung it open and found the car was gone.

Renee freaked out. Had Jesse taken Christian and left? No. He wouldn't do that. He'd said he was going to call Nancy. She sat in the chair and grabbed her phone. She called Jesse, but then she heard his phone ring. She looked over to the end table and saw it. She began to pace the floor as she waited to find out if Jesse was coming back or not.

When the front door opened, Renee ran to it. Jesse walked in, but he didn't have Christian. Her breathing sped up, and she felt like she would pass out. What had he done? He hadn't taken off with Christian like he said he would, but had he hurt him?

"What did you do to Christian?" Renee yelled.

Jesse's brows furrowed as he said, "I didn't do anything to him. What's wrong with you? Why are you breathing so heavily?"

"I came out of the room and you were both gone. And right after you said you were going to take him away from me. I tried calling your damn phone, but you left it here. Now, you're here and he isn't."

"Hey. Calm down. I told you I was going to see if Nancy would watch him so that we could talk," Jesse said as he put his hands on the sides of Renee's face.

"Calm your breathing. It's ok."

Jesse wrapped his arms around Renee and felt her shaking. He'd done an excellent job scaring her about taking Christian away. Her body was tense in his arms. She was back to tensing up or cringing at his touch. She hadn't done that in so long that he hoped she had finally stopped doing it. He sighed and pulled back. He slowly kissed her lips. When he broke the kiss, he looked into her eyes. There was terror there.

"I'm sorry. I shouldn't have scared you like that. I figured it would save some time to just drop Christian off and come back while you were getting yourself together. I figured this way, we could talk and not have to worry about upsetting Christian. Come on. Let's go sit in the living room."

He sat on the couch and pulled her down into his lap. She sat there, stiff and not looking at him. Finally, Jesse cupped her chin and lifted her face.

"Let's talk. You say you want your freedom. I say that I want you to be in a relationship with me, a real one. Neither one of us is going to get what we want unless we compromise. I told you what I wanted from you in order to start letting you go out on your own. You refuse to do it. I've tried everything I can think of, but you still won't do what I ask."

"No, you haven't tried everything. You just switch one form of torture for another. Yeah, you stopped hitting me, but you kept abusing me sexually. You finally stopped doing that for longer than 6 months. I'll give you that one, but you still torture me by holding me in this house. We're too far out for me to walk to anything, especially with Christian. But, I can't drive anywhere. I can't call a cab. I can't do anything without having your supervision over it. It's always in the back of my mind that you are going to hurt Kevin if I do something wrong. I am constantly worrying about you losing your temper because of something I said or did. There's a constant fear there. You did it again tonight. Because you didn't get what you wanted, you threw out another threat. How can you expect me to ever like you when you continue to do things like that?"

Jesse didn't say anything to her for a long time, and she kept shifting in his lap, worried that she had said something wrong. Finally, he grabbed her hips and made her sit still. She peeked up at him to see if he was angry or not. He was looking at her, but he wasn't seeing her. His hands idly moved up and down her hips. She shifted again, and Jesse's hands gripped her hips. He really looked at her then, but his eyes didn't hold anger. They held lust.

"I can't think when you are shifting on me like that."

"I'm sorry," Renee whispered as she looked at her hands in her lap.

"I'm not. I just can't think about what you said when you are doing that. My mind has gone to someplace else. Someplace that involves you shifting on me while you're naked."

"I thought you said you wanted to talk?"

"We did talk. I was thinking about what you said, but you kept shifting. Why are you so uncomfortable?"

"I'm not uncomfortable. I'm nervous that I said something you didn't like. I'm afraid that you will do something to hurt me."

"I'm thinking of something to do to you, but it's not hurt you. However, I was serious when I said I wanted us to talk. So, I guess I'll have to let that go for now," Jesse said as he wriggled his hips under her, pressing into her.

Renee felt heat creep up her neck and into her face. She felt even more nervous and shifted again to get away from him pressing into her. She slid back, but Jesse pulled her hips forward again. Then, he wrapped his arms around her and kissed her slowly. He broke the kiss and started trailing kisses down her throat.

"What am I going to do with you?" Jesse whispered in her ear and then nibbled on it.

"Talk to me and work things out," Renee whispered as Jesse's hands slid up her sides.

Jesse sighed and put his head on her chest. He was trying to get himself under control, but she had gotten him all hot and bothered by sliding around all over his crotch. He heard her heart beating fast. Was it from fear or desire? He slid his hand up and began to rub his thumb over her nipple through her bra. He heard her heartbeat get even faster as he felt the nub harden.

"How about this? I'll add you to my bank account. You will have your own debit card. I can see how you spend the money and where. I would rather you go out with someone else at first and see what happens," Jesse said as he slid her shirt up.

He started sucking her nipple through her bra. Renee sucked her breath in through her teeth. His hands started to roam over her sides and down to her hips.

"How about you let me have the debit card and let me go out by myself. In return, I will try my best to be in a real relationship with you."

Jesse looked up at her. She was looking at him intently. She really wanted to go out by herself. Why wasn't she willing to go out with someone else if she wasn't trying to run away? The debit card would allow him to see where she spent money, but she could easily return things and get cash for it if she went out alone. She would need cash to get a cab into town.

"How about you do your best to be in a real relationship with me and go out with me or Nancy at first? Then, after a month or so, we will reevaluate the situation. Are you willing to compromise and do that?" Jesse asked as he went back to sucking on her breast through her bra.

Renee chewed her bottom lip as she tried to ignore what he was doing. Then, she felt his fingers slide along the waistband of her pants. She shifted again, trying to get away from him, but all that did was make Jesse groan as she pressed against him. Next, he slid his hand under her pants and rubbed over her panties.

"If you stop this, I'll compromise and go out with someone for the first month," Renee said as she felt him apply pressure between her thighs.

"You want me to stop rubbing on you? Or do you want me to stop rubbing on you through your clothes?" Jesse asked as he slid his finger along the side of her panties.

"Yes," Renee gasped as his finger slid further in and along her folds.

"Yes, what? You want me to stop or you want me to take your clothes off? Tell me what you want, Renee."

"I told you. If you stop what you are doing, I'll compromise and do what you want."

Jesse sighed and removed his hands from her. He didn't want to stop, but he wanted her to compromise. He fell back against the couch and looked at her. If she was willing to compromise and be in a relationship with him, why did she want him to stop? She looked at him and got a shy smile on her face.

"You actually stopped," Renee said, feeling surprised.

"Yes. You wanted compromise. If I want a relationship with you and want you to do as I ask, then I guess I should do the same."

"Thank you. It means a lot that you actually did something I asked," Renee said as she leaned forward.

She pressed her lips on his and kissed him lightly. Her heart was still beating fast, but it was from being nervous this time. She knew Jesse wanted her, so why was she still nervous about touching him? If anything, shouldn't she be angry at herself for actually wanting to touch him? She had been trying to make the best of her situation, but it still surprised her that she felt pleasure from his touch. She had only made him stop because she was still trying to suppress that she felt good when he caressed her, but she knew he already knew. Nevertheless, his stopping when asked, even though he wanted to have sex, did mean a lot to her.

She slowly slid her hands up his thighs and under his shirt to his stomach. Jesse tried to deepen the kiss, but she pulled back. How far could she push it before he wouldn't stop anymore? She looked into his eyes and saw a hunger there, but he didn't try to press the issue. If she was going to hold up on her end of the compromise, she supposed that meant being involved in instigating sex. However, she was still struggling with it. She was, after all, still his prisoner.

Her hands moved down his stomach and then moved from under his shirt. He was watching her intently. She grasped his shirt and lifted it as Jesse raised his arms, allowing her to take it off. She tossed it and began to run her fingertips over his chest and stomach. Jesse reached out toward her, and she moved back. He dropped his hands, and his face showed pure frustration. She was teasing him, and he didn't like it.

She leaned down and began to kiss his neck, and slowly made her way down to his chest. He groaned as she ran her tongue across his nipple while her hand continued blazing heat trails on his skin. She moved back and unbuttoned his jeans. She moved off him, and he grabbed her pants and yanked them down. She stepped away from him and took her pants off but left her panties on.

"Can you lift up and push your clothes down?"

Jesse looked at her as he lifted and pushed his pants and boxers down. Renee finished taking them off. He reached out for her again, but she moved away. His frustration was rising, and so was his anger. He had to keep himself in check and let this play out.

Renee came back and blazed a trail of kisses over his chest and stomach. Her fingers wrapped around him and began to squeeze and caress him as her mouth found its way down to the tip of him. She flicked her tongue over his tip, and he groaned. She worked him with her mouth until he was about to explode, and she stopped.

She slid her hands up his body until she was on her knees in front of him. He reached for her shirt, and she moved back. Jesse was extremely frustrated. He wasn't going to keep stopping himself from touching her. Finally, she stood up, and her waist was level with his face. She slid her panties down and then grabbed his hair.

She pulled his head close to her body, and he grinned. His mouth went directly in between her thighs to her folds. He rolled his eyes to look at her, but she wasn't happy with him not moving. She moved her hips forward, urging him to use his mouth on her. His tongue darted out, and he slid it up and down her folds until she was wet enough for him to move it inside to her nub. He reached up to grab her ass, but she pushed his hands away.

"No touching," Renee said as she pressed his face tighter to her body.

Jesse obediently obeyed as he dropped his hands and continued using his mouth on her. She was being aggressive and commanding him. He had never really seen this side of her. She had told him things she wanted him to do, but only after he had talked shit to her and made her tell him. Now, she wasn't telling him what to do so much as making him do it.

She pulled his head back as she got close to cumming. Then, she went back to using her mouth and tongue on him. Every time he got close to finishing, she stopped what she was doing. He found what she was doing erotic and frustrating as hell. He didn't know what type of game she was playing, but he was losing his patience with it. He was hurting from all the blood that had rushed into his dick.

She stopped again as he felt like he was about to explode. He was about to yank her up and take her when she got back onto the couch. She threw her leg over him and moved back and forth over him so his tip was the only thing being touched. He felt how wet she was as she glided back and forth over him. He kept trying to touch her, but every time he did, she told him no.

He figured out she was trying to see how far she could go with telling him no and before he finally didn't stop. That had to be her game. He would show her that he could stop himself even though he was having a tough time doing it. She kept gliding back and forth over him as she slowly lowered her body a little more, so he was going in slowly. When she finally surrounded all of him, it took everything in him not to take her the way he wanted.

Renee took her shirt and bra off and pulled his head down to her breasts. Jesse decided two could play this game and just rested his head on her breasts. She stopped moving and clenched her muscles around him. She sat like that for a minute until he finally began to suck on her breast as his hand found the other one. She began to move again, but it was at a faster pace this time.

So, he was only allowed to touch her when she wanted him to. Other than that, it was a torture game. He was so hard and ready to explode, but she made sure she didn't go fast enough for him to finish. He could tell by how wet she was that she was enjoying this.

"Is this what you wanted from me, Jesse?" Renee whispered in his ear.

"I want to do so many things to you right now, but you already know that. You're torturing me for the fun of it, aren't you?"

"Oh, this is torturing you? I'll just stop then," Renee said as she started to slide off of him.

"Oh, hell no," Jesse said as he went to grab her hips.

"No touching!" Renee said as she slammed herself back down on him.

Jesse groaned and moved his hands away. Renee put her hands on his shoulders and pushed him back into the couch. She wrapped her arms around his neck and kissed him as her body pressed into his. His tongue went to war with hers as she started moving faster on top of him. She broke the kiss as he was about to cum and stood up. He was pissed.

"Alright. You can fuck me now," Renee said as she got on her hands and knees on the floor.

Jesse quickly got off the couch and slammed into her so hard that her body rocked forward. He grabbed her shoulders and began to pound himself into her as hard as possible. He'd thoroughly enjoyed what she had done as it had him harder than he'd ever been before, but it had also frustrated him to the point of anger. He could hear his body slapping into hers as he fucked her. He was rock hard, and her muscles were clenching all around him. He moved faster and faster until she cried out, and he felt her cum shoot out on him. He growled as he slammed into her until he came deep inside her.

CHAPTER 14

"So, I was thinking we could go out tonight to celebrate the first month of our compromise. You interested?"

"Sure," Renee responded as she finished putting the clothes away.

"Do you have anything in particular you would like to do?"

"Whatever you want to do is fine," Renee responded absentmindedly.

Her thoughts were on Kevin. Jesse might not realize it, but today was her and Kevin's anniversary. Unfortunately, it was also the day her life had turned into hell. Today made three years that she had been held prisoner. She had done everything she could to keep her mind off it, but it kept going back to those thoughts. She wondered what Kevin was doing now. Had he moved on yet? Was he happy now?

She hadn't moved on from loving him, but she knew she never would. She had managed to make her life now work. She was getting better about showing Jesse some affection. She still wasn't where he wanted her to be, but he would just have to deal with it. It would take time for her to come to terms with being his 'wife'.

"Renee. Earth to Renee. Renee!" Jesse shouted.

"Sorry. What were you saying?"

"Did you hear anything I said at all? Where were you at just now? Your mind is obviously somewhere else."

Renee blushed. She couldn't tell Jesse where her mind had been. She knew it would piss him off and probably lead to some type of punishment. He turned her towards him, but she didn't look at him.

"Are you going to tell me?"

"Are you going to get mad?" Renee whispered.

"I can't promise not to. Depends on what it is, but if you have to ask, then it must be something you know will piss me off."

"Will you promise not to hit or punish me in any way?"

"Alright. I promise I won't do anything to hurt you."

"Do you know what today is?" Renee asked.

"It's Friday. Why?"

"No. I don't mean what day it is. Do you know what the significance of today is?"

"Just spit it out, Renee. You know I don't like guessing games."

"You ruined my life three years ago. You caused me to lose the love of my life. Because of what you did, my dreams were shattered," Renee said, not daring to look up out of fear.

Jesse stood there for a minute. What she had said had angered him, but he couldn't blame her for thinking it. He'd hoped that she was coming around as she showed him affection and was with him more and more every day. His hands balled into fists, and he had to walk away before he said or did something to ruin the progress they had made. He wanted today to be special, not a disaster.

He had to do something special tonight so she would stop associating this day with what he had done to her all that time. He was trying his best to change for her. He wasn't even sure if he could completely change, but he had kept his anger in check for the most part. Of course, it had only been a month. Who knew what could happen later on? Jesse paced around the living room until he calmed down and went back into the bedroom.

Renee quickly stood up as he came back in. He saw the fear in her eyes before she looked away. He sighed. No matter what he did, she would always go back to being afraid of him. He'd given her no reason not to. With her being his first real relationship, he wanted it to work. He still couldn't figure out how in the hell he'd fallen in love with her when his only intention had been to use and then kill her.

He knew that she would never love him because she was still in love with that prick, and he had tormented her for too long. He was just hoping that she could at least learn to like him at this point. He walked and hugged her. Renee didn't hug him back. Instead, she tensed up, and her breathing sped up. He pulled back so he could look at her.

"I'm not planning on hurting you, Renee. Believe it or not, I really am trying to change for you. I was hoping that one day you would be able to come to love me, but I guess that's just wishful thinking. Does it piss me off that you are still stuck on him? Yes. Does it make me hate him more? Hell yes! But, am I going to hurt you because of it? No. If I continue to hurt you, then you will never want to be with me."

Renee looked at Jesse. She tried to relax her body, but the adrenaline from the fear was still there. She took in a deep breath and let it out slowly. This was progress. Even though she felt like she was crazy for it, she had come to care for Jesse.

When he had started opening up and showing her the part of himself that he didn't show anyone else, she couldn't help but feel something. He had been hurt so much that it had made him into a real bastard. Of course, that wasn't an excuse for what he had done to her. But she understood more than before. Then again, she could have turned into a bitch with all he had done to her, but she hadn't.

"Ok, Jesse. I believe you. I'll be ok eventually, just not right now. Today is just a bad day. It will pass and be better tomorrow."

"I still want to make tonight good. You said you didn't mind us going out. Let me make some calls and see what we can get into tonight, ok?"

"Ok," Renee replied.

*   *   *

"Alright, Renee. Are you ready to go?" Jesse called out.

"Yes," Renee said as she came out of the bedroom.

Jesse smiled as he saw her. He had told her to dress down, but he wasn't expecting her to still look so good. She had braided her hair and wore jeans that fit her just right. She was wearing a button-down shirt that was a light gray. It was tight across her breasts, which enhanced how her voluptuous breasts looked. He watched as she bent over to pick Christian up from his playpen. The jeans were tight on her ass, and he felt his mouth water.

He had promised her a good night. But, he couldn't do what he wanted to because of the snow, so he had another plan. First, they drove to Greg and Nancy's and dropped Christian off. Then, he took her to a little shack in the woods. He stopped the car on the road. Jesse got out of the car, came around, and opened her door for her.

"Did you bring gloves like I asked you to?"

"Yes," Renee said as she slipped on her jacket and gloves.

They walked up to the little shack, and Jesse spoke to the man inside. She heard him agreeing to a price and taking his wallet out. She watched as he handed the guy a $100 bill. Jesse turned to her after he had signed some paperwork. His lips turned into a big grin as he held up keys.

Renee's eyebrows shot up as she tried to figure out what he was up to. He took her hand and led her outside. They walked over to the building with the tarps. Jesse pulled one of the tarps back, and Renee saw a snowmobile. She was definitely curious now. Jesse pulled another tarp and revealed a second snowmobile. He put the keys into the ignition of both and cranked them. Then, he walked back over to her.

"I know this isn't the same thing as a four-wheeler, but with it being wintertime, I couldn't find anywhere to rent those. So, I figured we could do this instead. Are you surprised?"

"Very," Renee said as a grin spread across her face.

She walked up to one of the snowmobiles and sat on it. She looked it over and realized it was like a four-wheeler to control it and make it move and stop. Jesse got on the other snowmobile and looked at her. Renee smiled, her face slightly flushed from excitement.

"I haven't been on a four-wheeler or snowmobile. Mind showing me how to use it?"

"Sure. How about you get on this one with me and watch what I'm doing. Then, you can try it with me sitting behind you. If I think you are getting ready to do something wrong, I will tell you. Sound good?"

"Yeah, that sounds good."

He climbed off the snowmobile and climbed on behind Renee. He pulled some things out of his pocket and wrapped his arms around her. He held up a pair of goggles and a bandanna. Renee took them and put them on. She had him tie the bandanna for her. He put his own on and wrapped himself around Renee. He rested his head on her shoulder and watched as she put the snowmobile into gear with her foot. She accelerated it, and he watched as she guided it out of the building. They rode around for a few minutes, and he noticed that she would push the clutch with her foot when she got to a certain speed.

She hit the clutch as they slowed down and returned to the building. When she climbed onto the back of his snowmobile, she wrapped her arms around his waist, pressing into his back. He loved the feeling of it. She watched him as he shifted the snowmobile into gear and moved forward. Then, when he got to the point of changing gears, she leaned forward so she could speak directly into his ear.

"Do you hear how it's starting to make that revving sound?"

"Yeah," Jesse shouted over his shoulder.

"That's telling you that you need to shift gears. When you hear it, change gears, ok?"

"Ok," Jesse replied.

He did what she told him to do, and they rode around until he got it up to speed to go through all the gears. She watched him as he shifted the gears, and when they came back to the building, she watched him shift when the motor whined. He had learned rather quickly.

"Do you know how to drive a stick shift?"

"Yeah. It was the first vehicle I ever learned on. I stole it."

Renee shook her head and got onto her snowmobile. She sat there for a minute, just listening to the engine. She loved the way the snowmobile felt under her. It was a machine with so much power, and if you didn't control it, you could quickly get yourself killed. She revved the engine and smiled as she listened to it. She had missed four-wheeling. She was a country girl, and country girls didn't have snowmobiles, but she could get used to it.

Renee guided the snowmobile towards the trees. She went slow at first as she didn't know the terrain. Once they had circled at least once, she saw some clear trails that they could go on and open the snowmobiles up, which is precisely what she did. She felt the exhilaration of the cold air hitting her face and the power beneath her. She pulled a few donuts and laughed as the snow kicked up at Jesse.

Jesse had stopped his snowmobile and was now just watching Renee. She was having fun. When she had seen him just sitting there, she had come by and done a donut which had thrown snow on him. He shook his head to get it off his face and revved the snowmobile's engine. Renee came close and hollered at him that he was no fun. He smiled and gave chase to her. When he started to get close, she sped up. As he was about to catch up to her, she veered off into the woods.

He had to whip back around, and when he went into the woods, he didn't see her. So he slowed down and started looking for tracks in the snow. He found the snowmobile, but it was turned off, and Renee was nowhere in sight. He frowned and cut his off. When he didn't hear anything, he got off the snowmobile and looked around.

"Renee!" Jesse shouted.

No answer.

"Renee, where are you?"

Still no answer. She couldn't have been thrown because the snowmobile would have kept going and crashed. It definitely wouldn't have been turned off. Suddenly, he felt something hit him in the back. It was cold, and fell off his jacket. He turned around to see what it was right as a snowball hit him in the chest. He looked up and saw Renee run behind a tree. So, she wanted to play. He could do that. He hid behind his snowmobile and made some snowballs.

He heard her moving in the snow and popped up with snowball in hand. He threw it at her and hit her shoulder. He kept throwing the snowballs as she ran around to dodge them. While throwing them, he was moving toward her. When he ran out of snowballs, he ran after her. He heard a throaty laugh come from her, making him speed up to catch her. He did catch her and wrapped his arms around her, pulling her back against him.

He turned her around, facing him and saying, "Gotcha."

He pressed his lips against hers and deepened the kiss when she opened her mouth. When he broke the kiss, she pulled out of his arms. He watched as she lay down in the snow and moved her arms and legs. She was making a snow angel, but she was the angel to him. He lay down beside her and made a snow angel with her. He turned his head and saw her head was turned towards him. Their eyes met, and he saw happiness in hers. Her smile actually reached her eyes. It was the first time she had ever looked at him like that. He couldn't help but smile back.

They played in the snow for a little while and then got back on the snowmobiles. They rode at a slow pace back to the building. Once they had returned the keys, Jesse opened the car door for her. He got in and drove to a local restaurant. It was home cooking, so the way they were dressed was just fine.

Renee's thoughts were jumbled. Jesse had managed to make this a good day. If she put what he had done to her out of her mind, she found that she could enjoy spending time with him. How messed up was that? He had taken everything she cared about away from her. He had tortured and hurt her repeatedly. He had been nice and then done something else to torment her. She still lived in fear of what he would do next, but she felt happy when there were days like today. How twisted had her mind gotten in the past three years?

Today could have gone so differently when she told him that Kevin was the love of her life, but it hadn't. Things were just so confusing now. How can you possibly give a damn about someone like Jesse when you were the one he killed on the inside with torture?

CHAPTER 15

Jesse pulled the chair out at the restaurant for Renee. He would give her a gift tonight since she had come around so much over the past five months. He knew she still didn't love him, but she acted as if she cared at least. She would kiss him goodbye and hug him when he came home. She would even initiate sex now. She still got embarrassed when she first started, but she was aggressive once she got into it. He smiled as he thought about it. He liked the aggressive side of her. She'd even gone out with Nancy and been talked into buying sexy lingerie to make her husband happy. He still owed Nancy for that one.

He sat across from Renee and watched her as she looked at the menu. She was no longer afraid to order what she wanted. They had at least one date night a month now. Sometimes, she would even pick the places they went to. Renee smiled at him when she caught him staring at her. He cherished that smile. It wasn't the fake one she used to have. It was the real deal, and it lit up her whole face. He knew at first she wasn't into the relationship, and there were only a few times she was happy with him, but now, things were different. They talked about everything now. He even asked her when her birthday was.

At first, she had told him it didn't matter as it hadn't been celebrated in three years, but he had finally worn her down. When she asked him what his was, he had told her. He'd also told her that he had only celebrated his birthday five times. And that was after Billy had gotten a job at sixteen. It had never been anything significant, just a cake and maybe a movie. His parents never celebrated their birthdays.

That part seemed to sadden Renee. It had been the reason she had told him about her birthday. She probably thought that he'd forgotten, but he hadn't. Renee hadn't even mentioned it being her birthday this morning before he'd left. He'd kept quiet, so she thought he'd forgotten about it. He'd asked her to go out to dinner with him and Christian as a family so they could spend time together.

Now, here they all sat. Renee ordered for herself and Christian. Jesse ordered and sat back, just enjoying watching her talk to Christian. They had never taken Christian out to eat before. He was pretty good for a toddler. Jesse realized it made him extremely happy to do things as a typical family. Since his family had never been typical, it was a nice change to see that he could have that.

"You still with us, Jesse? You look like you're a million miles away."

"Yeah, was just thinking about some things."

"Wanna share?"

"I was just enjoying this, my family. I never thought I'd have one. And as messed up as my childhood was, I never even thought I'd have a normal life. I'm actually happy which in a way feels strange to me. I know that sounds crazy, but there it is."

"It doesn't sound crazy. You've been through a lot in your life. Having some type of normalcy is good and if it makes you feel happy, then that's even better. Everyone deserves to be happy."

"Are you happy?"

"Right now, yes, I'm happy. It's been a good day and so far, a good night."

"But, you aren't always happy. I get that. I'm not always happy. That wasn't really what I was asking you though. Are you happy with this?" Jesse asked as he spread his hands out to include him and Christian.

"Yes, I'm happy," Renee said as she looked at Christian, trying to hide what she was truly feeling.

"I feel like there is something you aren't telling me. Are you happy with me? Don't worry. I know you don't love me and I can't really ask for that after everything, but are you at least happy with me? Are you happy with the changes I've made?"

"Yes. I'm happy with the changes you've made. I just...never mind."

"What is it? You can tell me what's on your mind. I won't do anything," Jesse replied.

"That's just it. I shouldn't have to worry about saying what I think or feel. I shouldn't feel scared all the time, but I do. You have been nice and loving, and I appreciate that. But, we've been here before. Something I say or do eventually sets you off. And I have it in the back of my mind all of the time. That thought of 'when is he going to snap and hurt me' is always there," Renee whispered.

Jesse started to say something as the waiter brought their food. He stopped and waited until he was gone. Renee was no longer looking at him, but instead, she was shifting uncomfortably and playing with her food. Jesse placed his hand over hers and stopped her from fidgeting.

"Look at me, Renee."

When she looked up, Jesse said, "I know what I've done. I know I've been a bastard. But, I am trying my best to be better for you. I think things have been going well. I want that to continue. I'm not expecting you to fall in love with me, but I can't help but hope that you do eventually. I never wanted a family because I just knew it would end badly. I never wanted a relationship because I knew how I was. But, you have made me want all of that. You've made me realize that I need all of that. I know it's going to be hard, but I want you to stop thinking the way that you are. I love you and I'm going to do my best every day to prove that to you. I want you to be happy that you are with me. I want you to be happy that we are a family."

"I can't promise any of that," Renee sighed.

"I know, but will you at least promise me that you will try?"

"I'll try."

"Thank you. That's all I can ask of you," Jesse said as he kissed her hand.

Renee gave him a shy smile, and he couldn't help but grin back at her. They talked while they were eating, and Renee fed Christian. He noticed that while Renee was talking to him, it almost seemed as if she was sad. When they finished eating, Jesse excused himself.

Renee was surprised he had left her and Christian alone in the restaurant. She looked around and didn't see him anywhere. She picked Christian up out of the high chair and got ready to stand up when she saw their waiter heading her way with a birthday cake in his hands. She turned back towards the table as she saw Jesse right behind him. She had been down all day today because it was yet another birthday she wouldn't celebrate with her loved ones.

Renee was surprised when the waiter brought the cake to the table. Jesse sat in his seat across from her, but he had a funny look. Did he know she was thinking about trying to run? Other waiters and waitresses came over and sang Happy Birthday to her along with Jesse. Renee felt a blush creep up her face from everyone's attention being on her. Tears stung her eyes as she realized Jesse hadn't forgotten about her birthday but had set all of this up just for her.

She blew out the candles as everyone left. Christian was busy trying to reach the cake as she looked up at Jesse. The look on his face softened as he saw the tears.

"You didn't forget. You did all of this just for me?" Renee asked, a tear falling down her cheek.

"Yes. I wanted you to think I'd forgotten so I could surprise you. You looked really sad up until now."

"I was. I always spent my birthday with the people who loved me, the people I loved. I haven't been able to see them, and it hurts. I miss them."

"Well, I can't bring them back in, but Christian and I are here, and we love you. I do have a question, though. Were you planning on trying to make a run for it while I was gone? That's the first time I've left you alone in public."

"No. I need to take Christian to the bathroom. If you don't mind, I'd like to do that before we enjoy the cake."

"Ok. I'll be right here."

"Ok. Be right back."

Renee stood up and grabbed the diaper bag. With Christian on her hip, she found the bathroom. Her body shook as she entered the bathroom and leaned against the wall. She'd almost got caught trying to make a run for it. She should have known that Jesse wouldn't leave her alone in public. Yet another test. He was never going to let her have her freedom. He monitored everywhere she went. His account was set up to alert him every time his card was used, so it wasn't like she could just skip out by using it.

She sighed and placed Christian on the changing table. He did need a diaper, so at least that hadn't been a lie. Christian laughed as she wiped him clean. He could always make her feel better. He was almost three now. Time to start trying to potty train. She used the bathroom and washed her hands.

As she crossed the restaurant back to the table, she saw Jesse watching every step she took. Was he ever going to give her freedom? It was the one thing she craved the most and the one thing it seemed he would never give her. She had tried to find a way to leave so many times, but he caught her every time she even remotely got the courage to leave.

"Ok. Do you want a piece of cake now?" Renee said as she sat back down.

"Yeah. Let me cut us a piece off."

They ate their cake in silence. Once they were finished, Jesse loaded up the cake, and Renee took Christian. They drove home in silence as well. Once they were home, Jesse took the cake in, and Renee grabbed Christian. They went into the house and played with Christian until he fell asleep. Once Renee had put him to bed, Jesse pulled her down on the couch with him.

"I got you a present for your birthday. I hope you like it," Jesse said as he pulled something out of his pocket.

Renee felt disappointed as she saw a small box. It was probably just jewelry. She took it but didn't open it. Jesse watched her as she just held the box, staring at it.

"Aren't you going to open it?"

"Jesse, you know there is only one thing that I want and it's free."

"Please open the gift. You might find that you like it."

Renee sighed and looked at the small box. Nothing in that box could hold something as big as her freedom. She unwrapped the box and took the lid off. Removing the tissue paper, she frowned. It wasn't jewelry as she thought it would be, and she wasn't sure what it meant. She looked at Jesse.

"What's this supposed to mean?"

Jesse stood up and held out his hand. Renee took it, and he pulled her up. He walked to the front door and opened it. He walked her outside and then went back in, closing the door. What the hell? She heard the bolt being locked. Had he locked her out? Realization dawned on her, and she looked back at the box in her hand. With shaking hands, she picked up the keys. She put the first one in, and it turned, unlocking the deadbolt. She slipped the other one in and turned the doorknob. When she opened the door back up, Jesse was no longer in the hall.

He'd given her keys to the house. Did that mean she would be able to go out by herself? She'd only been able to go out with Nancy when Jesse had been home to watch Christian. She walked into the house, shut the door, and leaned against it. Her heart was racing. With a smile on her face, she walked into the living room. Jesse wasn't there either.

She walked into the bedroom and found that he was lying on the bed. His eyes were closed, and he had his hands behind his head. Her eyes roamed his body as he was in nothing but his boxers. He was trying to play it off like the gift had been no big deal. Shaking her head, she went over to her dresser. He wanted to play that game; then she could too. She grabbed a couple of things and went into the bathroom.

Jesse opened his eyes and watched her go into the bathroom. She hadn't even said thank you. He had thought the present would get more of a reaction out of her than that. Instead, she hadn't acted excited to get what she had asked him for. He leaned against the headboard while waiting for her to come out of the bathroom. Her lack of excitement had irritated him.

When the bathroom door opened and Renee stepped out, his irritation quickly dissipated. There she stood in the sexiest lingerie he'd ever seen. The top was an ocean blue, see-through bra. It had a tiny lace rose over each nipple, which was the only part of her breast it was hiding. She had a garter belt hooked to black fishnet hose. The panties she wore were also ocean blue, and it was nothing but straps. The only part that covered anything was the small rose covering her folds. The stem of the rose went down and turned into enough material to cover the bottom of her folds. She slowly turned to show him the back. The bra's straps crisscrossed twice, and that's all there was. His eyes roamed down her back to the panties. He felt a shiver of desire go through him. The panties were a thong. The lingerie covered just enough to make you want to see what little was covered.

"Come here," Jesse said, his voice sounding gruff.

Renee walked over to the bed, her hips swaying seductively. Jesse felt like it was his birthday instead of hers. She stopped beside the bed. Jesse swung his legs over, pushing his boxers down as he did, and pulled her towards him. He began kissing her stomach as his hands roamed down to her butt. He slid his hands back up and under the panties. He pushed them down and pulled her onto his lap. He kissed her as he ground his hips into her. Breaking the kiss, he lay back and grabbed her thighs.

She moved up, and he positioned her right over his face. Renee's eyes closed, and her hips bucked. His tongue slid in and out of her as his hands squeezed her butt. Her fingers tangled in his hair as she rode his face. He sucked her clit, and her fingers gripped his hair as she moaned. Jesse lapped her up as she orgasmed.

Jesse moved his hands, so they were on her back, and his arms were surrounding her. He sat up, so she went back on his hands and arms. Renee let out a yelp of surprise. Her body was now lying on his legs, which he spread, so she lay between them. His hands slid over her breasts, and he found a clasp at the front of the bra. He unhooked it and began playing with her breasts. Her legs were still up in the air, held in place by his arms.

Jesse slowly let her legs down as his hands started caressing her body. He ended with his hand sliding over her just enough to make her moan for more. His fingers began to squeeze her thighs, and then he made his way back up. His hand slid up, so his thumb grazed along her slit. He pushed it inside her folds and slowly circled her nub before applying pressure to it.

"Beautiful," Jesse said as he watched Renee's face.

He slid the other hand down and pushed two fingers inside of her. He went from watching the pleasure on her face to watching his fingers slide in and out of her. When Renee started to ride his fingers, he increased the pressure on her clit and the speed of his fingers. Jesse stopped messing with her just as she was about to cum again. He grabbed her hips and yanked her against him, rubbing his dick along her folds, so its head rubbed over her clit. Her hips bucked up, and Jesse groaned as he felt the tip of his dick slide down to her entrance. He quickly jerked her body towards his, thrusting his dick into her.

Renee wrapped her legs around his hips and began to ride him as she rolled and lifted her hips. Jesse began to move his thumb over her clit again. When he felt her getting tight, he grabbed her hips and made her stop riding him. She moaned in complaint.

"Not yet," Jesse panted as he slid back away from her.

He pulled her up and then flipped her over onto her stomach. He straddled her butt and gave it a hard slap. She jerked as she moaned. He rubbed his dick against her as he slapped her butt again. She tried lifting so he would push inside of her when he moved forward.

"Do you want my dick inside of you, baby? You want to feel it filling up that tight, wet pussy?"

"Yes," came out, sounding strangled.

Jesse slowly slid his dick into her. Then, he pulled out and rammed it in. He fucked her slowly, pulled out, rammed back in, and fucked her hard. Each time he felt her about to cum, he stopped.

Renee felt like she would scream from the tension in her body, crying out for release. She knew this game. He wanted her to talk to him. She felt him shove his dick inside her, lay on her, and move his lips close to her ear. His hand wrapped her hair around it, and he yanked it, pulling her head to the side, exposing her neck. She looked at him out of the corner of her eye. He was watching her face. She turned her head enough to kiss him.

He started rolling his hips in response, sliding his dick around her walls. His hand slid under her as he began to play with her breast. His grip on her hair tightened as he broke the kiss and trailed kisses down her neck. He bit her shoulder, and her body tightened from the pleasure/pain sensation. His hand slid down until she felt him massaging her clit while rolling his hips. Her insides were quivering from the need to release.

"Jesse, I need to cum."

Jesse stopped moving again, and she screamed into the bed. His mouth and tongue blazed a trail from her shoulder back up to her ear. He started nibbling on her ear as he pressed his lower body into hers, causing pressure but not the friction she needed to release.

"All you have to do is tell me, baby."

"I need you to fuck me. Fuck me hard, and don't stop until I cum all over you!"

Jesse sat up, and his hands gripped her ass, pushing forward on her cheeks, which made her pussy even tighter. He slammed his dick into her, becoming more aggressive as his body slapping against hers got louder. He felt her getting so tight that it made her whole body shake.

"That's right, baby. Cum for me. I want to feel your juices cover my stiff dick," Jesse said as he slapped her ass again.

Renee cried out as Jesse felt her pussy sucking his dick with her orgasm. She sucked his orgasm out of him, too. He shuddered as he pulled out of her and came all over her ass and pussy. Fucking her would never get old. He loved how she was shy and reserved one minute and then aggressive the next. He'd never get enough of her.

CHAPTER 16

Renee was packing Christian's bag to go out. She had started going out by herself. At first, she was cautious when she went out, still worried that this was some sort of trick from Jesse. She would set up an Uber, which was charged to Jesse's card. This way, he always knew where she was. Next, she started window shopping. Then, she would go out for groceries. Today, she was going to go to the library. It would be the first time in years she'd gone to one.

It was always boring in the house just watching TV. Christian was four now and liked to look at the picture books she'd bought him. So why not get a library card and get books for both of them? Renee was excited about this outing. She loved to read, and the library had computers. Internet that Jesse couldn't trace.

When Renee got to the library, she signed up for a library card. She immediately found a book for Christian to look at while she got on the computer. She nervously looked around to see if anyone was watching her. She didn't think Jesse would send someone out to spy on her, but she couldn't be too sure. Once she had thoroughly looked around and didn't see anyone looking in her direction, she logged onto the computer.

She went to her old social media account and tried logging in. She immediately set it so it wouldn't show that she was online. There was a message from Kevin. Of course, she couldn't pull it up as it would show that she had read it. But what she could see of it showed that it was recent. Her eyes welled up with tears. She went to his page. The main picture had a "Have you seen me?" picture, one of the last pictures he had taken of her. She scrolled through his page. He hadn't posted much over the last few years.

She went back to her page and scrolled through it. Kevin had posted several things on there that were messages to her. He had shared memories of them and mentioned how much he missed her. She felt ashamed of living her life with Jesse while Kevin was still being tormented by her being taken. She still didn't understand how she had even come to like having sex with Jesse, let alone come to care for him. She still didn't love him, but everything else was a betrayal to Kevin, and she knew it. She wiped the tear away that slid down her cheek and logged out.

She bit her lower lip as she contemplated contacting Kevin. Could it be that easy? Could she just log back in and message him? No. That would be a mistake. Perhaps she could do something else. She brought up another internet tab and created an email address. Then, she went back to the site and created a new page. Was it a good idea? If Kevin figured out who she was and came for her, would he get hurt? She wanted to talk to him so badly. She would just have to be careful.

Using her middle name and fake last name, Marie Morgan was created. She sent a message to Kevin, telling him that she understood his pain. She clicked on the button to send him a friend request. She figured he wouldn't respond right away, if at all, so she logged off and started going around the library, looking at books. She ordered an Uber and logged back onto the computer while she waited. There was a message from Kevin. Renee felt her heart race.

*   *   *

Kevin heard his phone go off as he got ready for work. He picked it up and looked at it. There was a friend request from a woman he didn't know. He went to the profile and saw there were no posts on it. No friends. No picture on it either. Nothing. They had to be a scammer. Finally, he saw there was a message and clicked to open it. It was also from her. The message spoke of a deep pain that resonated within him.

"My friend, I see you have lost someone, too. I can see she means a great deal to you, as your whole profile is all about the life you had together. I lost the man I love. I still love him with all of my heart, even though we will never be together again. I did not choose to leave him or have him leave me, but life happened. You can't stop what you can't control. I can only imagine your pain as everyone is different. The man I love is good and cares for everyone above himself. He loved me with everything he had in him. When he was ripped away from me, I felt dead inside. It took me years to come back from that. As you can tell, I'm still not completely there. Time does not always heal all wounds. It only bandages them, and sometimes they still bleed. I would give anything to have him back."

"Seeing the picture on your profile struck a chord in me because of the date it said she went missing. How you have held onto hope, this long is beyond me. You must still love her a great deal to have kept looking all this time and never given up. Looking at the rest of your profile, I felt you needed someone to talk to—someone who will understand your pain. I don't know that for sure as you may have moved on with your life and be with someone else, but I can't see you doing that with everything you have on your profile. If you would like someone to talk to to get your pain, anger, frustration, or anything else out, I would be more than willing to do that. I am not always available to talk as I can only get online at certain times, but I would be more than happy to respond."

Kevin went back to the profile. He stared at the name. Marie. That was Renee's middle name. How had this woman who had just joined Stratus found his page? He felt his chest tighten as the thought crossed his mind that this was Renee. But why would she wait so long to reach out, and why wouldn't she just tell him who she was so he could come to get her? He shook it off, responded to the message, and accepted her request.

"Hello. I appreciate your offer to talk. No, I have not given up on Renee or moved on with my life. I honestly don't think I could be with someone else. I have moved from state to state to find her. She didn't just run away. She was taken from me by an evil man to punish me. His brother and I got into an altercation where his brother pulled a knife on me. I defended myself, and the man got killed. His brother plotted out revenge, but instead of physically harming or killing me, he took my fiancée instead. I have never forgiven myself for the situation I unknowingly put her in. It would be nice to have someone to talk to about all of this, as I've kept it all bottled up for so long. But you have already said you can only get online at certain times. May I ask why?"

"I don't have the internet at home. The man I live with thinks it rots your brain. Even my phone is just a basic one. I come to the library every once in a while to check out books. I decided to start an account and surf the site. That's when I stumbled upon the picture. Hence, why I said I may not always be able to reply right away. Now, if it was a scheduled day and time, I could talk for the hour it will allow me on the computer. But I have to go now. My ride is on the way to get us."

"Alright, Marie. I can understand if you have to use the library to communicate back and forth. Maybe if we get to know each other better, we can talk on the phone sometime, or text. Having a basic phone doesn't stop you from doing that. I have to work day shift the rest of this week, but I am off next Tuesday. Would you like to talk then? Say around 10? By the way, the man you live with, is he your boyfriend? Would he get mad about you speaking to me? I would hate to cause any trouble for you. I don't know if he is there with you or not as you said that you were waiting on a ride to come get us like he was there with you."

"My ride is almost here, so I don't have time to explain everything. I will come here on Tuesday and log back on at ten, so we can chat. But, no, he is not here with me. My son is. The man I live with was not originally my boyfriend. I have moved on with my life, and I am trying to live it the best I can. However, we can discuss all of that next time. Until Tuesday, Marie."

Kevin felt even more confused as he read the message. Why had this woman all of a sudden appeared? Was this a sign that he was supposed to move on with his life, too? Over the years, he'd never had anyone message him because of that picture. His family and friends would occasionally text him to check up on him, but that was it. His profile had only become public once Renee was taken, and he had started posting the "Have you seen me?" pictures all over his page. He shoved his phone into his pocket and went to work, feeling dazed.

*   *   *

Renee walked into the house and put everything down that she had gotten today. It had been a busy day. She'd even gotten some things for Jesse's birthday. She had gotten lucky, and it had fallen on a Saturday this year. She was planning on making him a cake and a homemade meal. Jesse had yet to see some of the lingerie Nancy had talked her into buying. That would be for later that night. She was planning Jesse's birthday party right after messaging Kevin pretending to be someone else. Yeah, she was screwed up in the head.

Once she had put everything away, she started making dinner. Jesse would be home soon. She tried to make sure that dinner was waiting on him, so he didn't get mad at her. She liked the newfound freedom she had, and she planned on keeping it. Moreover, now that she had established a connection with Kevin, she had to double down on keeping her freedom. Marie was her only link to Kevin.

Renee was finishing up supper when Jesse got home. She jumped as she heard the door slam. She had barely turned around as Jesse came into the kitchen. He looked mad. She shrunk into herself as he headed straight for her. He put his hands on the counter, effectively trapping her between his body and the counter. She had been here before. She'd be damned if he was going to punish her when she hadn't done anything.

"Why were you at the library? I never told you that you could go there," Jesse said as he pressed further into her.

"I-I went to check out books for Christian and me. You never said I couldn't go. I just thought it would be something to do when I was at home. There's nothing to do here but watch TV. And Christian likes to look at picture books. If nothing else, I figured I could start teaching him the basics of learning. They have books there for that," Renee stammered.

"Is that all you did at the library?"

"Yes. What else am I going to do at the library? Find a date?"

"Don't even joke about that," Jesse said in a low, threatening voice.

"I didn't do anything wrong. I just went to the library. I checked out books. I even got us a movie," Renee whispered as her eyes filled with tears.

No matter what, Jesse was always going to be this way. Why in the hell did she keep falling for this? It had been so long since he'd even lost his temper that she had thought he had changed. Now, here they were. He was pissed all because she went to the library. True, she did do something she wasn't supposed to, but he didn't know that.

Furthermore, she had no plans of telling him about it. So why couldn't he just let her leave? He supposedly loved her. Didn't that mean he should want her to be happy? She tried to keep her head down as Jesse cupped her chin, but he forced her head up.

"Look at me, Renee."

"No," Renee whispered, determined not to let him see that she was upset by his behavior.

"Look at me, Renee. We already know what happens when I lose my temper because you don't do what I ask."

Renee jerked her face out of his hand and looked at him; her eyes narrowed, and the tears disappeared. Now she was angry, not upset. Jesse's face showed anger, and her anger quickly fizzled out into resignation. She was tired of this game that Jesse played. She had done everything he had asked and he had acted as a loving human being for over a year. Why did something so trivial always set him off?

"Yeah, we all know what you do when you are mad. Go ahead. I don't care. I'm too tired to play this game anymore. I can't keep up with the bipolar side of you that goes from loving to asshole in less than sixty seconds. You promised me freedom. You gave me freedom, and now you want to take it back because I went to the freaking library. You want to beat or rape me, fine. Just make sure you don't leave bruises where Christian can see them. I won't scream so he won't hear anything. I'll be damned if he learns those behaviors."

Jesse looked into Renee's eyes and sighed. He reached out to push her hair behind her ear, and she jerked. He stepped back from her and sat down at the table. Renee sighed and grabbed some plates from the cabinet and put them on the counter. She would ignore Jesse if she could, but he wouldn't allow that.

"Come here, Renee, please."

Renee turned and looked at him. He patted his thigh, signaling her to sit on his lap. She slowly walked over to him and stood there. How could he expect her to just come around after what he had done? He grabbed her hips and pulled her into his lap, so she was straddling him. He wrapped his arms around her, holding her in place. One hand moved up her back and pushed into her hair, pushing her head towards him as he kissed her.

He broke the kiss and said, "I'm sorry. I really didn't think the whole freedom thing through. I'm not taking it away from you. You came back home to me. I have to trust that you will do that or I'm going to drive myself crazy and push you away from me for good. And I'm not bipolar. I'm possessive and you are mine."

"I don't belong to you. I'm not your possession. I'm a person. I thought we already went through this. You say you don't want to push me away but you don't seem to understand that you have always done that. I'm trying to do what you want, but you already know I don't love you. I have come to care for you even though I don't know why. But then you do or say something to make me regret even caring about you. You either trust me or you don't. I mean, if you did trust me, then you would allow me to live my life and not keep doing stupid shit like this. I want to get a job. I want to be able to go out on my own and not have to be tracked. I'm tired of always being in this house. I want the life that I used to have. I used to have friends and was able to make plans whenever I wanted. I didn't have to run them by someone else."

"We talked and I already told you, you belong to me. I belong to you. You don't have to keep throwing it into my face that you don't love me. But, you have come to care about me and you said you never would. It's an improvement and maybe, someday, you will come to love me, too. I'm trying really hard to let you have a normal life, but I can't let you go. At first, it was because of what I'd done, but now I can't live without you. You and Christian are my whole world. I don't want you to leave me."

Renee sighed. The one thing she wanted the most was a life with Kevin. But, she was being denied that. So why should she stay with Jesse other than the fact that she knew what he was capable of? She looked at Jesse and saw something like desperation in his eyes. Was he desperate not to lose her? She didn't care enough about him not to want to leave. She did, however, fear him enough not to.

"Then don't make me feel like I'm still your prisoner. Feeling trapped makes you do anything and everything to be free. You have to stop doing this. Either trust me or don't. It can't be in between. Stop threatening me. Every time you do that, I start to hate you all over again. Is that really what you want?"

"You know it isn't. You know what I want. It's what I've been wanting for a long time now."

"And it's the one thing I can't give you. I can't give you something that already belongs to someone else. I've tried to move on, but I can't make my heart move on. I know I risk making you mad and bringing on a beating or worse, but I can't help how I feel."

"I know you don't believe me because I can feel you shaking, but I'm not going to hurt you. My anger does get the best of me and I do say things I shouldn't. I'm not perfect by any means, but I have been trying. I really am trying to be a good man. I've never let anyone in, and I'm scared to death that you are going to leave me. For the first time in my life, I am actually scared of something. I wasn't scared of my father and all of the things he did to me. I wasn't scared of living on the streets or having to rob people for money, but you, well, you terrify me."

Renee felt her heart speed up. She felt terrible about what she had said after hearing him confess that he was scared for the first time in his life. He ran his thumb across her cheek as she searched his eyes to see if he was lying. He had a slight tremble in his hand. He was telling the truth; he was scared. She was scared of him, but for different reasons. She cared about the scared little boy inside of him, begging to be loved. That little boy deserved to be loved by someone, but could she be that person for him?

She just didn't know. Maybe if he'd had someone to show him what love truly was, he wouldn't have turned out the way he did. He said he was possessive, but he had never really had anything besides his brother that mattered to him before. He didn't want to lose the one thing he had always wanted but never had: someone to love and care for him.

There wasn't much she could do to ease the pain of never having someone love him, but she could be there for him as comfort, at least. So, she did the only thing she could think of and gently kissed his lips and then hugged him. She held him tight as she pressed her body into his, letting him know she was there. He wrapped his arms around her and buried his face in her neck. It took her off guard when she felt moisture soaking through her shirt. She tightened her grip on Jesse as he cried.

CHAPTER 17

Renee had been trying to forget about the other night when Jesse had come home angry. After their talk, he seemed to agree with her going out to certain places. She had been genuinely surprised to find she had hurt him with her words. He'd told her many times that he loved her, but she had never really believed him. He was scared to lose her. She didn't know why, but she felt terrible about not being able to love him. She had indeed gone crazy. She shook her head, trying to clear it of the thoughts.

She had a lot to do to get ready for tonight. She had decided to fix Jesse his favorite meal for lunch and have Greg and Nancy over for a birthday party. So tonight, she would take him out for dinner and dancing. She'd already set up for Nancy to take Christian with her when they left. Since Jesse had never actually celebrated his birthday, she wanted this one to be perfect. So no disappointments were allowed today.

Greg had come to get Jesse to take him out so she could bake his cake and fix lunch. Nancy had stayed at the house with her. Jesse didn't care to go bowling and had protested when she'd mentioned it, but she'd finally told him it would be good to hang out with someone other than her. So, he had finally gone out with him. As soon as he'd left, Renee started taking everything out. While the cake was baking, she hung decorations in the kitchen. Nancy blew up balloons and hung them.

When Jesse and Greg returned, Renee was just finishing putting the plates on the table. She walked into the living room and got Christian just as they walked through the door. Renee walked up and kissed him. She smiled and took his hand, pulling him towards the kitchen.

When they entered the kitchen, everyone yelled surprise! Jesse's eyes widened as he looked around the kitchen. There were balloons, streamers, and a Happy Birthday sign hanging up. There were plates of food on the table. He noticed it was his favorite meal. He felt tears prick his eyes. He didn't even think Renee had remembered, let alone cared enough to do anything for him.

He cleared his throat and said, "Thank you. This is...this is great. I really appreciate it."

Renee blushed as he looked into her eyes while thanking her. He knew she saw the tears, but she smiled, trying to act nonchalantly about the whole surprise. He appreciated her not acting like this was his first celebration because she was the only one who knew that. They all sat down and ate. He couldn't help but smile as everyone chatted and had a good time. He reached under the table and placed his hand on Renee's thigh, squeezing it slightly. She put her hand over his and squeezed it to let him know she understood.

Renee stood up and cleared the plates. Then, she put candles on the cake and lit them. When she turned around, they all sang Happy Birthday to him. She set the cake down in front of him so he could blow out the candles. Once that was done, she cut the cake and handed it out. Christian immediately dug his hands into his, and everyone laughed. She got icing on her fingers, and she blushed when Jesse grabbed her hand and licked the icing off.

"Get a room," Nancy laughed.

"I have a room. Just didn't think it would be polite to leave our guests out here."

When Greg and Nancy left, Jesse was surprised to find that Christian was going with them. Renee had only let them keep him overnight a few times. Even on their date night, he was only there for a few hours. So why was Christian spending the night tonight? Was she doing this because it was his birthday? He smiled as he closed the door and turned toward Renee. He gathered her in his arms and kissed her deeply.

"Thank you for today. I've never had a good birthday. I'll always remember this one," Jesse said as he held her.

"Your birthday isn't over yet. That was just the first part of today. I have other plans for tonight. That's why I had Nancy keep Christian," Renee said as she smiled at him.

"Hm. Well, how about we get started on tonight, now?" Jesse asked as his hands squeezed her butt.

"Well, I guess if you don't want your present at the end of the night then we can get started now. I figure if we do that then we won't leave. But, it's fine," Renee said as she started walking towards the bedroom, stripping off clothing as she went.

Jesse started trailing behind her, watching her hips sway as she walked. Just watching her take off her clothes every few feet had him turned on, but he was also curious about the surprise. Renee started to get on the bed when Jesse wrapped his arms around her, pulling her against him. His hand moved down her side and slid across her hip and down over her folds. His lips kissed down her neck to her collarbone.

"So, I take this as you don't want the surprise I had planned for you?" Renee asked breathlessly.

"Does it involve me burying myself inside you?" Jesse whispered into her ear.

"I'm not going to tell you. It wouldn't be a surprise then. You either have to wait until later to find out what it is or we have sex now," Renee said as she ground herself into him.

She moaned as his fingers began to make slow circles over her clit. His other hand began caressing her breast. Jesse wanted to bury himself inside of her and just stay in bed the rest of the night, but if she had planned something out for him, he didn't want to disappoint her. He groaned as he stopped playing with her and just stood there for a moment to calm down. Renee turned in his arms and wrapped her arms around his neck, pressing her body against his. She had a massive smile on her face.

"Couldn't stand not knowing what that surprise was, could you?"

He smiled as he said, "No. If you planned it for me, I have to know. I love what you did for me today. No one has ever cared enough to do anything like that. But, just know, by the end of the night, you will have my dick buried deep inside you."

"Maybe," Renee said, laughing as she pulled out of his arms.

She walked over to the closet and pulled some things out. She lay the clothes bags on the bed and walked over to her dresser. She grabbed out some underclothes and came back. Then, she proceeded to undress him. When his dick sprung free of his boxers, she teased him with her hand.

"Keep that up and we definitely aren't going anywhere."

"I can relieve some of your...tension if you want me to."

"Unless that relief is in the form of you slamming your tight pussy onto my dick, no. I love it when you use your hand or mouth on me, but I'm craving you. I want to be inside of you. I'll wait."

"You'll like your surprise. I hope you think it's worth the wait," Renee said shyly.

"I'm sure I will since it's coming from you. So, what's all the stuff you have here?"

"Oh. Right. First part of the surprise. Put those clothes on, please. I'll get dressed so we can go."

"Where are we going?" Jesse asked as he walked towards the bed.

"Well, I'd like to drive if you don't mind. I've been studying a map so I'll know how to get there. I just hate that it's your money I'm spending."

"I've never cared if you used it before."

"I know, but you shouldn't have to pay for your own birthday."

Jesse smiled as he said, "Well, consider this money you've earned by taking care of everything in my life. How about that?"

"It's still not the same, but ok. Now, get dressed."

Renee picked up her clothes and went into the bathroom. Jesse picked up the clothes and saw a nice pair of black slacks and a dark blue, almost black, button-down shirt. He put the clothes on and found a pair of cufflinks on the bed. He put those on and looked in the mirror. He actually looked good in the clothes. He looked up as the bathroom door opened.

Renee came out, smoothing her dress down. Jesse felt himself grow hard again, and he knew he would have blue balls by the end of the night. The dark blue dress matched his shirt. It was bunched on the sides into a design that looked like mini waves going down her sides. The sleeves were actually over the upper part of her arms. The chest piece barely covered the tops of her breasts. It hugged her curves and stopped mid-thigh. If she bent over the wrong way, he was sure she would be showing her ass. The pantyhose were so thin that he could see through them. At least they were covering up her legs. The high heels she was wearing made her three inches taller.

Her hair had small clips pushing it back from her face. She had a few tendrils hanging on the sides of her face. The rest was up in two braids that connected in the back. Her makeup was simple but made her eyes look smoky. Her plump, red lips beckoned him to kiss her. He saw the back of her dress when she turned towards the dresser. It stopped right above her butt and hugged it.

He saw a glint on her hand when she went to put earrings in. He felt a smile cross his lips as he realized she was wearing her wedding ring set. She had never worn it before. He had mentioned it repeatedly, but she kept telling him she wasn't comfortable with it. Now, she was wearing it willingly, and he found he was extremely pleased with how it looked on her finger. It took all of his willpower not to rip those pantyhose and drive himself inside of her.

Renee walked up to him with a necklace in her hand. She smiled and held the necklace out to him. He took it, and she turned around, pushing her butt into him, taunting him. He groaned and grabbed her hips, grinding into her. His hand started to slip down her thigh and run under her dress. She grabbed his hand before he could get to the top of her pantyhose.

"Later, babe. I want to get tonight started."

"You are going to be the death of me," Jesse sighed and put the necklace on her.

Renee giggled and walked out of the room. They went outside, and she opened his door for him. She got in and held her hand out. He gave her the key. She started the car and revved the engine slightly, sighing with contentment.

Jesse realized she had missed driving. He would have to put some serious thought into letting her lead her everyday life, as she called it. She could have left by now, but she hadn't. She knew he would keep his promise to hunt her and Kevin down. But this time, he would not only have anger backing him but the pain of losing her and the betrayal of it all. He didn't think he could handle losing her. She was one of three people he had ever truly cared about.

He watched her as she drove down the road, looking at street signs to figure out where she was. She looked so cute, concentrating so hard on figuring out where to go. He smiled to himself as he knew he would do just about anything to make her happy. There was only one thing he wouldn't do: let her leave him. When they pulled into a parking lot, he saw a restaurant. It looked fancy.

Renee parked the car and put her hand on his arm as he went to open the door. He stopped and looked at her. She smiled and got out, coming around to his side. She opened the door for him and held out her hand. He raised an eyebrow but put his hand in hers. She giggled as he got out.

"Since I'm taking you on this date, I figure it's my job to pull out the chairs and open the doors for you," Renee laughed.

Jesse smiled and shook his head. She was something else. She opened the door to the restaurant for him, and they walked up to the hostess. He looked around and saw just how fancy the restaurant was. Crystal vases were on each table with a single rose in each. Lanterns were hanging along the walls as the only light, setting a romantic atmosphere.

"I have a reservation for two under Morgan," Jesse heard Renee say.

He smiled to himself as he heard the hostess say, "Of course, Mrs. Morgan. Right this way."

Renee grabbed his hand, and they walked over to the table. She smiled as she pulled his chair out. He slid it forward as he sat down. She pouted slightly but sat down across from him. He couldn't help but chuckle at her reaction.

He had to admit that he was enjoying tonight. Renee had ordered a bottle of red wine to go with the food. They drank a glass and talked while they waited for their food. When it showed up, Jesse felt his mouth water. The cordon bleu looked delicious. His steak and shrimp smelled so good that he was ready to dig in immediately. Renee tasted her food and let out a small moan.

Jesse's head snapped up at the sound. He watched her as she enjoyed the explosive taste in her mouth. Her reaction made him think of other sounds he wanted to hear from her. How would he keep himself under control all night with her doing things like that? Renee stabbed another piece with her fork and held it out to him.

"You have got to try this. It's delicious!"

Jesse decided to tease her a little bit. His tongue traced the piece of chicken before he slowly put his mouth over the fork and pulled back

187

slowly, so his mouth slid down her fork. He saw her eyes widen slightly and her breath quicken. He smiled as he chewed the piece she'd offered him. It was delicious.

"You're right. It's delicious. Not as delicious as something else I'm going to taste tonight, though. But, no worries. I always save room for dessert."

Renee blushed. He took a bite of his steak and offered her one. She took it and made that little moan again. Finally, she opened her eyes and looked at him.

"Damn. You even make eating food sexy."

"Or maybe you only think about one thing," Renee laughed.

"I think about more than that, but sometimes you make it hard for me. Well, make it hard to think about anything else," Jesse winked.

Renee blushed again. They continued to eat and talk. Jesse kept trying to get her to tell him his surprise, but she wouldn't. Finally, when it was time for dessert, Renee nodded at the waiter. He brought out a small slice of chocolate cake with a candle on it.

Jesse raised his eyebrows. He blew out the candle, and Renee picked up a fork. She put the fork in it and held it out to Jesse. He smiled as she fed him the cake and then took a bite herself. How in the hell did her eating cake and feeding it to him have such an effect on him?

Renee paid the bill once the cake was gone, and they left. He realized where they were going when they started getting close to work. Renee pulled into the bar and again opened his door for him. When they walked up to the door, Renee grabbed his hand. They walked into the bar hand in hand. Jesse was thrilled that she was claiming she was there with him in that way.

She went and got them a table and then got some drinks. After a couple of drinks, a table opened up. Renee went and grabbed it. She had Jesse break, and when she went to take her turn, he saw her dress start to ride up. He moved, so he was blocking anyone else from seeing anything. He pressed into her just as she stood up.

"I don't think this dress is a good thing to be wearing while playing pool. If you had to lean over the table, your ass would definitely be showing."

Renee turned around as she said, "And you don't want to see my ass? Or is it that you don't want anyone else seeing my ass?"

"No one else is allowed to see it. However, I'll look at it all I want."

Renee smiled and turned back around, leaning over the table and taking another shot. This time she bent over farther than she needed to, so her dress rode up enough that he could see she was wearing thigh highs. The dress had barely covered them, or the garter belt that he could now see clipped to them. The dress was right under her ass which he didn't even think was covered. He snaked his arm around her waist and jerked her back against him. She stood up.

"Are you even wearing any underwear?" Jesse whispered into her ear as his free hand slipped in between them.

"Uh-uh. You'll find out later," Renee said as she stopped his hand.

Jesse sighed, knowing that if another man looked at her, he would wind up killing him. They continued to play pool for a while, but Jesse was literally on her ass the whole time to keep anyone from seeing what belonged to him. After a couple of hours had gone by, Renee was pretty buzzed. Jesse was getting there, but he knew he could not drink too much, or his temper might get the best of him if another man approached Renee. She kept trying to get him to drink, but he wouldn't. He would wind up driving them home as she was too wasted to drive.

"Jesse, lighten up. I had all this planned out. We are going to take an Uber to our next destination," Renee said into his ear as she pulled him onto the dance floor.

"There's another destination after this?"

"Yep. I told you I had a surprise for you. All of tonight is part of your surprise. Now, can you loosen up and enjoy it?"

"You know I have a bad temper. Drinking enhances it. I'll lose control of it if someone hits on you. You know this."

"No, you won't. Everyone can see I'm here with you. And if someone does hit on me, so what? We both know I'm not leaving with anyone but you. Let them look and see what you and only you will have tonight while they can only sit and drool over it."

Jesse thought about it. She was his and only his. He was taking her home tonight, not the other guys. He downed the drink in his hand and pulled Renee against him. His hands trailed down her back and to her ass as he ground his hips into her. She smiled and wrapped her arms around his neck, beginning to grind back into him. He loved the smile on her face and the look in her eyes as she looked at him. He had almost screwed all of this up just a few days ago. Nevertheless, she was doing all of this for him regardless of his stupidity.

They danced and drank for a few more hours before Renee scheduled their Uber. He didn't particularly like leaving the car there, but he would have to deal with it as they were too intoxicated to drive. When her phone went off saying her Uber was there, she pulled him in the direction of the door. He was curious to know their next destination as she hadn't said home. Renee had put a lot of thought and time into his birthday. He loved her even more than he had before.

CHAPTER 18

When they pulled up in front of a hotel, he was surprised. How had she pulled all of this off without him knowing about it? He checked her phone often. It didn't have much data, but he always knew when she used it. He would look at her history, and he hadn't seen anything about a hotel. He got a little angry. So, she had gone behind his back and did things so he wouldn't know about it.

"You look angry. What's wrong?" Renee whispered into his ear.

"How did you do all this without me knowing about it? You told me you hadn't gone behind my back."

"I got Nancy to help me. I wanted to surprise you so I got her to look everything up for me. I booked the hotel on her computer. I also called the restaurant from her phone so you wouldn't ruin the surprise," Renee said as she fidgeted in her seat.

They got out, and she walked away from the car but didn't go into the office to check in. Instead, she waited until the driver had left to speak. Then, she put her hands in his and looked at him. He saw that hint of fear and hated it. Her hands were even trembling in his.

"I did all of this for you. So please, don't be mad. I just didn't want you to find out about it and ruin it. I wanted you to have a really memorable birthday since you never really celebrated it," Renee said as she looked at their hands.

Jesse pulled one hand out of hers and cupped her chin, making her look up at him. He kissed her lips, pulling her against him. She had taunted him all night, and he didn't want his anger to take over and make her afraid. Instead, he wanted her to continue the way she was now, being loving and affectionate. She was sexy, fun, and carefree. He broke the kiss, and Renee gave him a tentative smile. She pulled him along as they went into the hotel's office to check in.

Jesse was curious when the clerk just handed her the room key without checking them in. She waved the key at him and pulled him out the door to find their room. Once inside, Jesse pulled her against him. She kissed him and then pulled him into the middle of the room. She grabbed the chair from under the desk and set it down behind him. She gently pushed him into the chair.

"Wait here. I'm going to blindfold you. Don't take it off, ok?"

"Renee, I'm not sure I can keep the blindfold on. I don't really like surprises," Jesse admitted.

"Oh. I guess you don't want my final surprise for you then," Renee pouted as she walked over to the bed and picked up the blindfold.

"Fine," Jesse sighed. "Put the blindfold on me."

Renee got a massive grin on her face and walked over to him. She sat in his lap and pressed against him as she tied the blindfold behind his head. He reached up to touch her, but she stopped his hands.

"No, no. No touching until I say."

"I swear you are trying to make my balls explode."

He heard Renee laugh as she walked off. He waited and waited, but she didn't come back. Finally, he shifted in the seat, wondering if she had run away. He started to take the blindfold off, but he heard a door open. He listened intently but didn't hear it shut again. Then, finally, he heard movements behind him and started reaching up to take the blindfold off.

"Put your hand down, or I'm leaving," Renee whispered.

"I told you I don't like surprises. It's been a while since you put it on."

"Just a little bit longer. Good things take time," Renee said as the room suddenly got darker than it already was behind the blindfold.

Suddenly, music was playing, and he felt Renee's hands slide over his shoulders and down his chest as she pressed her body against the chair and his shoulders. She reached as far down as she could and pulled his shirt out of his pants. She slowly unbuttoned it and slid her hands back up over his shoulders and to the blindfold.

She untied it as she said, "Remember, no touching unless I say so."

Her hand trailed around his shoulder until she got beside him, and she danced her way to the front of him. Jesse grinned as he saw what she was wearing. She still had the garter belt, thigh-highs, and high heels on. In addition, she had on some material that made the shape of a bow over her pussy. The strings crisscrossed her stomach around her back and came back to make tiny bows over her nipples. The string then wrapped once around her neck.

Jesse sat back and watched her dance for him. When she turned around, he saw the string crisscrossed across her butt, but that was all that was covering it. Was that all she had been wearing earlier? He noticed the only light in the room came from candles throughout the room. She didn't have all of this stuff with her before.

Renee swayed her hips more than usual as she walked toward him. She sat in his lap and started grinding her body into his. Then she stood up and pressed his face into her breasts as she shook them. He started to reach up, but she stepped away and wagged a finger at him. He had to adjust in the seat as the pants were too tight now. He watched as Renee reached up and untied the string behind her neck so the bows came off, revealing her breasts.

"Would you like to open the rest of your present?" Renee said as she again straddled his lap.

Her fingertips ran over his stomach and up to his chest. She pressed her breasts into his chest as she ran her hands down his arms, pushing his shirt off. She undid the cuff links to finish taking it off his wrists. She dropped everything to the floor and undid his belt. His hands traced up her thighs and over her hips. He found the string that was tied on each side of her hips. He pulled them, and the cloth fell off her and into his lap.

Renee stood up and began caressing her body as her hips gyrated to the music. Jesse undid his pants and pulled them down along with his boxers. He kicked his shoes off and watched as Renee crawled on her hands and knees until she was in between his thighs. She finished taking his clothes off and ran her hands up his legs until they rested on the inside of his thighs. Then, she pushed them further apart so her whole body was between them.

Jesse watched as she kissed the inside of his thighs and her hands ran up to his hips, barely grazing his stiff dick. He groaned as he reached out to grab her and pull her up, but she quickly grabbed his hands, interlocking their fingers and holding them by his sides. Her tongue licked the tip of him, and his hips bucked. She slowly slid her mouth down the length of him. Her tongue curled around him as she moved back up his length. She sucked the tip of him and then released his dick.

She let go of his hands and moved hers up his stomach and over his chest as she stood up. She gripped his shoulders as she danced for him and then straddled his lap. She continued to dance, and when she leaned back, he reached up and began to fondle her breasts. She grabbed his hands to stop him from moving them.

"You were a bad boy. I said no touching unless I said so."

"Renee, I can't take this. I need to be inside of you."

"Not yet. My dance isn't over."

Renee put his hands down and came off his body, so she was rubbing against the tip of him. She swung her hips from side to side, and her breasts were in his face. Her hands were in his hair. He couldn't wait any longer. He grabbed her hips and slammed her down on his dick, thrusting his hips up simultaneously. Her hands tightened in his hair as she moaned.

She was so tight and wet. She was ready for him to fuck her and had been delaying it. He knew she had been trying to drive him crazy, but he wasn't waiting anymore. He buried himself as deep in her as he could with each thrust upward, holding her hips so she couldn't go anywhere as he drove his dick into her.

"You-you were supposed to wait," Renee panted.

"You can't tell me you didn't want this. You purposely drove me crazy all night taunting me, teasing me, and then doing a sexy ass dance all over my dick. No more waiting. I'm fucking you now and you are loving every minute of it. You may say no with your mouth, but your pussy says yes."

Jesse started pushing up on her hips and pulling back down on them, making her ride him as he thrust his hips up. Finally, Renee took over and started riding him hard and fast. She ground herself into him as hard as she could as her walls tightened around him. Jesse began sucking and biting her nipples, making them harden for him. He loved how her breasts bounced on his face as she moved up and down on his dick. He wasn't going to last long. She had taunted him for too long.

He pushed her up, so she was no longer riding him. He made her stand up, and she thought they would go to the bed, so she stepped back. He grabbed her hips and spun her around. He smacked her ass and pulled her back down onto his lap. He shoved himself back into her and began pushing and pulling her hips, making her ride him as fast as he wanted to go. When he stopped, Renee picked up the rhythm. His hand reached around and started playing with her clit as the other hand pushed on her back, so she was bent over slightly.

The angle his dick was going inside of her made it slide over her G-spot repeatedly. Renee moaned, and her hands grabbed his thighs, her fingernails digging in. Jesse felt his dick swelling inside of her as he got closer to his orgasm and took up every bit of space in her walls. Renee was panting and moaning as she rode him, driving him over the edge. His fingers applied more pressure to her clit as he rubbed faster, feeling his climax coming.

"Renee, I need you to cum. Now!"

"Cum for me, Jesse. I want you to," Renee said as she slammed back into him.

His fingers moved as fast as they could as he exploded inside her. He felt her get tight and then felt her orgasm slide over him as she moaned and her nails dug further into his thighs. She leaned back against his chest, and Jesse cupped her cheek, turning her face towards his. He kissed her as his arm wrapped around her waist.

After a few minutes, Renee stood up. She reached out her hand, and Jesse stood up, taking it. Renee led him over to the bed and waved for him to lay down. He did, and she signaled him to flip over onto his stomach. He obliged, and he heard her walk off. He put his arms under his head and turned it in the direction she had gone. He watched her pick something up from the nightstand and walk back to him.

"Put your arms by your sides, please."

Jesse did as asked and lay his head on the pillow. Renee crawled onto the bed and sat on his hips. He felt liquid on his back, and then Renee began to massage it into his shoulders and down his arms. He groaned with pleasure as the massage oil began to heat up as she massaged him. She worked the oil in from his neck down to his toes. When she had him flip over, he was ready to fuck her again. She smiled as she dripped some oil onto his chest and sat right below his dick, on his legs.

She again started on his neck and massaged his shoulders and down his arms. She moved back up the insides of his arms, down his chest, and over his stomach. Finally, she moved off of him, and when she got beside him, she was within reach for him to play with her. She massaged his legs as he slid his finger up her slit and pushed into her wet hole. He felt her body still as he inserted another finger and found her clit with his thumb.

Renee moaned as he played with her clit on the inside and the outside. She suddenly sat up and poured some of the oil on her breasts. Sitting sideways, he could see her rubbing the oil over her breasts, making them glisten. When she leaned back down to massage further down his legs, her breasts brushed over his dick, and she began to rub them back and forth over him as she rocked her body. This also caused her to fuck his fingers as he was still playing with her.

He reached between them and grabbed his dick, rubbing it on her breasts as he felt himself growing harder. When he knew Renee was ready to go again, he grabbed her hips and pulled slightly. She moved back, so she was sitting on her legs. He got up and pushed on her back, so she leaned forward. He kept pushing until her chest was on the bed and her ass was up in the air. He smacked her ass on both sides. Renee moaned for him.

He grabbed his dick again and slid it along her slit until he felt his juices wetting it. He pushed it inside her and moved one leg so his foot was on the bed, and he was straddling her ass. He started smacking her ass periodically as he pounded her tight pussy. He grabbed her hair and pulled it, causing her head to come back slightly.

He moved his free hand over her back, using just his fingertips, and he felt a shudder run through her body as her walls tightened around him. His own body shuddered in response to his dick being gripped so tight. He let go of her hair, and his hands trailed down to her breasts. He squeezed them hard, pinching and rolling her nipples between his fingers, causing her to moan and slam back into him.

Renee started driving her body backward onto his dick. His balls were hitting her clit as she jerked her body up while she pushed back onto him. His hands were clutching her breasts tight. She cried out as her climax hit.

"Fuck! Suck my dick with your pussy. I love it!" Jesse shouted as he lost control of his rhythm, grabbing her hips and slamming into her as he came for her.

Jesse pulled out of her and lay on the bed, feeling drained. Renee crawled up the bed and lay beside him. He wrapped her in his arms and began stroking her hair. She snuggled into him as she rested the side of her face on his chest.

"Best birthday ever. Thank you," Jesse whispered as he kissed the top of Renee's head.

"I hope the surprise was worth the wait."

"It was definitely worth it. But, I do have one question. Were you wearing that string under your dress?"

"Yep. I had it in my dresser. That was my "underclothes" tonight. Why?"

"Your ass is for me and only me to see. That dress is too short to not have real underwear on under it," Jesse said as his arms tightened around her.

"I didn't hear you complaining when it's all I had on during your lap dance," Renee said as she smiled.

"Oh, yeah. It's definitely sexy but I don't want anyone else seeing it."

"And no one else did. I knew you wouldn't let anyone else see because you'd be behind me all night if I bent over," Renee giggled.

"Tease," Jesse said as he smiled.

He stroked her hair and back until he felt her body relax against him. He lay there for a while, thinking about the whole night. Finally, he shifted and kicked something. He slowly moved away from Renee and found the bottle of massage oil she had used. It was made for foreplay.

He didn't know she had bought any of this stuff. He must be easing up somewhat on checking up on what she did. He shook his head and put it on the nightstand. He lay back down and pulled Renee against him again. He drifted off to sleep with a strange feeling he wasn't used to. He felt cared for.

*   *   *

Renee woke up still in Jesse's arms. Her stomach growled, and she slowly slid out of his arms. She was surprised he didn't wake up like he usually did when she moved. She grabbed some clothes and got dressed. There was a restaurant within walking distance.

She grabbed the hotel key, her wallet, and her phone. She walked to the restaurant and placed a to-go order. Once it was ready, she walked back to the hotel. She hoped the pancakes would still be hot when she got back.

Her phone started vibrating in her pocket when she got into the hotel's parking lot. Her hands were full, and she was having difficulty getting her phone. Finally, it stopped, and she just kept walking. When she got to the door, her phone started vibrating again. She sighed and set the stuff down, and grabbed the hotel key. Right before she went to push the door open, it jerked open.

Jesse was standing there with a pissed-off look on his face. Renee slowly bent down to get the bags, watching him to make sure he didn't do anything to hurt her. He watched her pick up the bags and juggle them to ensure she didn't drop them.

"Why didn't you answer your phone?"

"Can't you see my hands are full? I was trying to get back here so breakfast wouldn't get cold and when you called I was already in the parking lot."

"You should have woken me up before you left."

"Jesse, are you really going to do this right now? Or do you want to eat what I walked to get for you? And came back with no less. After last night, you still don't trust me. I'm done caring. Here," Renee said as she shoved his bag at him.

CHAPTER 19

Renee pushed past him and sat her bag down along with the drink carrier. She left her food and went to the bathroom, locking the door behind her. She was trying to hold back the tears. Why did she feel like crying? So what if Jesse was mad at her? It wouldn't be the first time. Maybe it was because he was still like this after everything she had done for him last night. The tears fell as a sob left her mouth.

Jesse sighed and sat at the table, waiting for Renee to return. He had been pissed that she had left and not woken him up. He always woke up when she got out of bed. This time he didn't. When she didn't answer the phone, he thought she had run. Of course, she would have had to get Christian first, but who knew how long she'd been gone? He should have checked the tracker on her phone before he got mad. He was always screwing things up with his temper. He got up and went to the bathroom. He knocked on the door.

"Renee, open up."

When she didn't answer, he tried again.

"Renee, please open the door. I really don't want to have to pay to fix the door because I broke it down."

Renee wiped her eyes and threw some water on her face. She opened the door after drying her face. Jesse reached for her, and she jerked back. He dropped his hand and moved back. Renee walked over to the table, sat down, and took the food out. Jesse came up behind her and wrapped his arms around her. She tensed, but all he did was kiss the top of her head and walk around to sit at the table.

"I'm sorry, Renee. I shouldn't have jumped to conclusions."

"Your apology won't be accepted this time. It's bullshit anyway. You aren't sorry if you keep repeating the behavior you apologized for. Let's just eat so we can get out of here. I want to see my son. At least he actually loves me with no conditions."

"I love you and there are no conditions."

"Yes, there is. Everything has to be your way or you're a total jerk. You couldn't even appreciate that I did all of this for you. You turned around and got pissy because I went and got breakfast. If I was truly able to have freedom, then it wouldn't matter what I do or where I go as long as I come home and don't cheat. Instead, it comes with conditions like being tracked and knowing every single thing I do. And the biggest one is I cant leave. And you wonder why I'll never love you," Renee said, her chest heaving.

"Fine. Don't accept my apology. I'll just have to prove to you that I'm sorry," Jesse said as he put his hand over hers, feeling pain in his heart at her words.

"I'll believe that when I see it," Renee snorted.

Jesse sighed and started eating his food. He was a dumbass. Renee had done something extraordinary for him last night, and it had taken a matter of minutes to fuck it all up just by thinking she had made a run for it. They ate in silence, with Renee picking at her food. Once they were finished, Renee called Nancy so she could come to pick them up. Renee packed everything up as they waited for Nancy to arrive.

Once they were back home, Renee jumped in the shower to let the hot water wash some of the stress away. Jesse was such an asshole. After everything she had done to make his birthday special, he had managed to ruin it. Why did she even bother? It's not like she loved him or had even given up hope on being with Kevin one day. For some reason that she still couldn't fathom, she cared about him, and his actions and anger hurt her. Why did she let it bother her? She sighed as she started washing her hair. Halfway through rinsing her hair, she felt hands on her hips, and she jumped.

"I didn't mean to scare you."

Renee didn't respond. She just kept rinsing her hair. When she moved forward out of the water, Jesse pulled her against him. She didn't respond to his touch or his kiss. He frowned as he pulled back.

"Guess you didn't believe me when I told you that I didn't care anymore."

"I know that's not true. If it was then you wouldn't be so upset or angry at me right now. Is taking sex away from me my punishment?"

"I guess that really is all you care about. I won't enjoy sex with you when I don't care about you, but you're going to do whatever you want anyway. I won't be willing but I won't stop you."

"So, you aren't even going to give me a chance to make this up to you, are you?"

"How many chances do you need to stop doing this shit in the first place? I didn't even want this life, so, why should I always have to forgive and forget? Why can't you be the one to compromise for once? Why can't you let me have a life? Why can't you just trust me? I've done everything you've asked me to and you still manage to ruin everything," Renee yelled.

"I have compromised. I've changed so much about myself for you, but you don't give me credit when I do good. You only ever see the bad. I wasn't trying to ruin everything. I told you that you terrify me. I'm scared you're going to leave me. Can't you see that?" Jesse pleaded.

"I have acknowledged when you've done good by being here with you. By being your wife in every sense of the word. However, when you do this, it makes me feel stupid. I feel like you've just pulled me into a false sense of security so you can hurt me worse with your cruelty. Why can't you see it from my perspective? And I can't leave, can I?"

"Ok. I can understand that my actions have upset you. I can even understand that it scares you when I threaten you, but can you at least give me a chance? At least allow me to be a human being and screw up? Can you find it in you to forgive me and stop being scared of me? Can you at least attempt to really be with me without allowing the past to define your future?"

"All of that depends on you. If you want me to move on from the past, then you have to stop doing things that you have always done, and making me relive it. Can you do it?"

"I'm going to do my best for you," Jesse said as he pulled her against him and kissed her.

"I've heard that before," Renee mumbled.

He would have to put his fears aside so that he didn't drive Renee away. The one thing he didn't want was what he was going to get if he kept going like this. He washed her body and let her get out of the shower while he took one. As much as he didn't want to, he would have to let her do what she wanted and stop worrying about her leaving him. It would be five years that she had been with him in just a few months. For half of that time, she had stayed willingly because she could have run at any time. He would make this up to her even if it killed him.

*   *   *

Tuesday came, and Renee got excited. She got Christian ready, and she headed to the library. She got there early to find a book for Christian to look at while she talked to Kevin. She looked at Christian. She pushed his hair back away from his face. He looked so much like Kevin when he was a little boy. She remembered the pictures that he had shown her. Christian's hair was almost a platinum blonde, slightly lighter than Kevin's in the pictures, but the bright green eyes were the same. Christian smiled at her and went back to his book.

Renee got on the computer and logged onto her account as Marie. She immediately pulled up the chatbox and saw Kevin's name wasn't lit up. She felt disappointed. Maybe he had forgotten? She decided since she was here that she would send him a message anyway.

"Hello, my new friend. How was your weekend? Mine was a mixture of good and bad. It went great Saturday because it was my boyfriend's birthday. He enjoyed everything we did, and then he went and ruined everything Sunday. I told you I would explain everything to you, so let me start at the beginning.

When I first lost the love of my life, I met my boyfriend. We moved in as roommates, and I found he was a controlling jerk. I hated him. It took me a long time to stop hating him and come to care for him. However, he would get what he wanted and what he wanted was me. We wound up hooking up, but that was it. He kept trying to get me to be in a relationship with him, but I couldn't see past everything he had already said and done. After a while, I found that he wasn't all bad. He started telling me about his past, and I realized he had let it define who he was. He truly needed someone to show him compassion, something he had never had before.

Now, he loves me, but I don't reciprocate those feelings. He knows it, but it still upsets him sometimes. Now, he shows me a side of himself that he never showed anyone else. He's loving and tries hard to be a good man for me. However, his possessiveness of me makes it hard sometimes. Certain things I do will set him off. He tries hard not to let it, but it happens anyway. Then, my temper gets the better of me, and we wind up ticked off at each other. One of these days, I'm hoping he'll realize that going backward in a relationship isn't good for anyone.

The best thing I have out of all of this is my son. He looks exactly like his father, with beautiful green eyes and almost platinum blonde hair. My boyfriend loves him unconditionally. I couldn't ask for him to be a better father to him. He's the one thing that keeps us together. I don't know what I'd do if he ever tried to take him from me, but I couldn't care for him financially if I left since I don't work. So, now you know a bit about me. Why don't you tell me a little about you?"

Renee sent the message. She noticed the tiny green dot beside Kevin's name was lit up. So he had gotten online after all. She felt her heart skip a beat. Would he respond? She waited with bated breath until the message came through.

"Hi, Marie. My weekend wasn't great. When I'm not working, I hang up "Have you seen me?" signs. I hit the whole town and then move on. I try to search close by towns on my days off so I can work at one job longer. Sometimes I have to work at a job longer than I want so I can save some money up. I live

out of motels. I haven't had a permanent home in so long that I'm not sure if I even could anymore. I get occasional calls or texts from my family and friends. Other than that, I'm not in a place long enough to make friends and go out.

My fiancée and I never had kids. It makes it easier to move around but I wish I had been able to have a family. I always wanted to have a family with Renee. I call her my fiancée but she really wasn't. I picked out a ring and planned to ask her to marry me the night she was taken. I loved her so much that I almost went crazy after she was taken. I still love her, and that's why I keep looking for her. I don't even know if she's still alive or not. But, every time I start to give up, vengeance takes over. I know it probably sounds wrong but I'm going to hunt the bastard that took her down even if it takes the rest of my life. Still want to talk after hearing that?"

Renee felt her heart break. Kevin had planned to propose to her. She noticed he had called her his fiancée before but hadn't thought about it until now. She had wanted that life with Kevin. If only she could tell him that he did have a son and she was still alive. Instead, all she could do was pretend to be Marie and show understanding of the loss.

"I'm sorry you didn't get to have your family. It's hard to lose the things you've dreamed of-the future you planned out for yourself. I know she would have said yes if you had been able to ask. I can't say as I blame you for wanting to hurt the one who shattered your dreams, but you are better than that. What would Renee think if you did that? Do you think she is dead?"

"Honestly, I don't know if she is or not. I think, or at least I had hoped, that if she was still alive, that she would reach out to me. If the guy that took her didn't kill her, I would think she would've found a way to escape and get help. Surely she wouldn't have stayed with him. Let me tell you how she was taken. The bastard broke into our home and knocked me out. While I was out, he tied me to a chair and beat on Renee. When I came to, he raped her right

in front of me! Then, he took her and left me tied to the chair. By the time I was finally able to get help, he was long gone with her. I can't think of any good reason she would stay with him and not get help. I mean, what would you do in that situation?"

"I would try to escape if it was just me. But, seeing as how he did all of that, I'm sure she was afraid. What if he threatened to go back and kill you if she ran? If that was me, I would have stayed for the simple fact that the man is obviously crazy and has already proven he has no problem doing some sick stuff. I wouldn't be able to live with myself if I got the man I loved killed. If she hasn't reached out to you, do you think he still has her?"

"I guess I could see that. Knowing Renee, if she did stay, it would be because of something like that. But she's always been so strong-willed that I don't know if she could have stayed with him. It would be against her nature to stay in that situation. I mean, he didn't take her to be with her. He took her to hurt me, and he all but said he would continue to rape her. How could she have let him continue to do that to her? Even if he had threatened to kill me, I would want her to escape; consequences be damned. You don't have to answer if you don't want to, but why are you with your boyfriend? You said you hated him but then "hooked up" with him. How can you do that with someone you don't like or who mistreats you? I can't understand it."

"I didn't have a choice. I had no way to take care of myself, and he was taking care of me. But, he wanted something in return. So, I imagined the love of my life and was able to give him what he wanted. I stayed so long for my son. I told you that my boyfriend was possessive. I fear what he may do if I try to leave. Plus, he tracks everything I do. This is the first time I've been able to talk to anyone about this because he can't track what I do at the library. And, he's always different around our friends. Over the past few years, he has opened up to me and showed me a side of himself that I didn't even think existed. That

part of him is so sweet and loving and what I care about. He was never shown compassion or love in his life, which breaks my heart.

Everyone deserves that in their life. I know I can't go back in time to be with my love, so I choose to make the best of the life I have now. As long as I'm a good girlfriend, he is good to my son and me. I know people don't understand, and that's ok, but sometimes people compromise to protect someone else or take care of themselves. Sometimes people feel like they don't deserve better or won't find anything better. Fear can do many things, Kevin."

"I'd rather die than be stuck in that situation. I'm sorry if that upsets you but I couldn't do it. And shouldn't he be good to his son without you being a good girlfriend? So, he treated you like crap and now he's sweet so you stay? Why didn't you leave immediately? I understand you had no way of taking care of yourself, but couldn't your family help you?"

"He treats my son well no matter what. I don't have to do anything for him to love him. He thinks that Christian is his, but I hide the fact that he isn't. He never liked Alexander, Christian's birth father. I chose to let him think this because I was scared that he wouldn't let me keep him otherwise. I didn't have anyone to help me. I was alone for a long time. I would have taken off if it had been just me, but I couldn't do that knowing I was pregnant. I would never put my child in danger like that. At first, he wouldn't let me out of the house, and that's why I didn't leave immediately. It was a long time before I was finally able to. Again, I don't expect you to understand, but I did what I felt was necessary at the time. Over time I guess I just realized that this is my life. It's not perfect, but it's better than it was."

Kevin read and reread the messages. Marie was Renee's middle name. Alexander was his. Was this Renee? Or was he seeing what he wanted to see? If it was Renee, why didn't she just tell him that it was her? Was the story she told about being afraid why she hadn't reached out? Her story

211

about running across his page just didn't add up. All the things this woman had told him made his blood boil. The things she had put forward about Renee being threatened with his life had him wondering.

This woman had said her son looked exactly like his father. He scrolled back through the messages and saw the description. Her son had blonde hair and green eyes, just like him. His heart started beating faster. He had to get this woman to open up to him. He had to know for sure this wasn't Renee.

"What do you mean by putting your child in danger? Was your boyfriend abusive? Did you think he would hurt you if you tried to leave? Why would he keep you in the house and not let you leave?"

"Kevin, I'm trying to be your friend and lend you an ear, but I don't want to go back through all the bad stuff that happened in the first part of my relationship. It's good now except for an occasional flare-up of a temper. Can we please change the subject?"

"I'll respect your privacy then. Maybe if we keep talking, you will decide you need an ear and open up. Until then, let's talk about something else. Let's see, you've probably seen my picture. I like horror movies. I haven't really watched many in the past few years because I feel like I'm in one. I like rock music. Red is my favorite color. How about you? What do you look like since you don't have a picture posted."

"Let's see. I like country music and some pop music. I'm into any kind of movie as long as it's good. Purple is my favorite color. I'm 5'5, with black hair and hazel eyes. Is this your way of changing the subject? Are we going to play 20 questions now?"

"Well, I figure if we get to know each other better, we can talk about the deeper stuff later. Your description is a lot like Renee, except she has reddish-blonde hair. I used to love running my fingers through it. It was always so soft and smelled like flowers. I can still close my eyes and see her beautiful smile, which always lit up my world. I fell in love with her so quickly. I just knew she was the one for me. I'm sorry. I've gotten back into the deep stuff again."

"It's quite all right. I told you I would lend an ear to listen. When I first met Alexander, it only took a glance across the room to know I wanted him. He didn't notice me at first. I watched him for a while before he did. I never thought someone as beautiful as him would want a plain Jane like me. He had this half-cocked smile that I used to love to see. That first night, he smiled at me and walked my way. When he introduced himself, I thought I was going to faint. His voice was deep and a little gruff, so sexy! I'd give anything to hear it again. I always loved to run my fingers through Alexander's hair, so I get it. His eyes were always what got me, though."

"So, what's your favorite thing to do? Changing the subject to get off the depressing stuff."

"I love to shoot pool. I think I'm pretty good at it. My boyfriend showed me how to play better. How about you?"

"I used to love four-wheeling. I don't do anything anymore. Every once in a while I might go out and have a drink or two. This is the most I've talked to someone other than my family. It's nice to just be able to sit and have a conversation, even if it is just through text."

"I agree. Well, Kevin, my time is almost up. And my son is getting hungry. I'll get on here again and shoot you a message just to check on you. Maybe we can chat again sometime. Take care."

"I hate to say goodbye so soon, but I know you have to go. Be careful out there, Marie."

CHAPTER 20

"Jesse, we need to talk about Christian."

"What about him?"

"He's four now and ready for pre-k. I found out what school he will be going to and I went to get the packet to sign him up. I thought you might want to take a look at it so we can decide together if we should send him now or wait until Kindergarten."

Renee handed him the packet as she sat down on the couch opposite him. It had been several weeks since they had talked to each other. She had utterly shut Jesse out after his little episode. He had tried to touch her, but she had just laid there, and he had backed away. She wasn't sure why he didn't just go ahead and take what he wanted as he had before, but she wasn't complaining. She no longer showed him any affection.

Jesse had tried again to apologize. He had brought her flowers and taken her out on a date. Nothing had worked, and he was frustrated, but Renee still wouldn't forgive him. Hell, he was surprised that she asked him about signing Christian up for school. He had stopped checking her phone to see what she was doing on it. The alerts still popped up for her Uber rides, but he had ignored them. He was trying hard to give her space and freedom. Why couldn't she just see that and forgive him?

He sighed and looked through the packet. He looked at Christian coloring in his book with Renee. She was smiling at him as he colored mostly inside the line. Guess it wouldn't be wrong to send him to school early to get a good start on it. Renee had been working with him to teach him the basics. Christian talked well for a four-year-old. Jesse put the folder down.

"Hey, Christian, come here for a minute, bud."

"Yes, Daddy?" Christian said as he crawled onto Jesse's lap.

"Would you like to go to school? You'd be learning a lot of new stuff and maybe even make some friends there. Does that sound like something you would like to do?"

"Yes!" Christian yelled, excited.

"Alright. Mommy will sign you up tomorrow. And this weekend, we can all go and get you some school stuff. How does that sound?"

"Ok, Daddy. Can I go back to coloring with Mommy now?"

"Sure, buddy, but I need to steal Mommy for a little bit."

"Ok," Christian said somewhat dejectedly.

Jesse smiled and looked at Renee. She smiled at Christian and kissed his forehead before she got up. She walked over to Jesse, and he gestured for her to go to the kitchen as he got up. They walked in, and he sat at the table with Renee following suit.

"What are you going to do while Christian is at school?"

"I guess I'll do what I'm doing now. Nothing. I go out every once in a while just to get out of the house. What else can I do?"

"What do you want to do?"

"Get a job. Have a life, have friends, and be able to have the life I've asked for a million times. However, it doesn't matter what I want because I never get it."

"Have you even noticed that I haven't been checking up on every little thing you've been doing?"

"No, I haven't noticed. I told you I just don't care anymore. I'm tired and can't do it anymore. You're nice one minute and a complete ass the next. You watch every little thing I do, and now you say you aren't. Why would you stop now?" Renee asked as she sat back, crossing her arms over her chest and staring at Jesse.

"I told you I would show you I was sorry. I'm just as flawed as the next person, but I'm trying to let go of my fear. I'm trying to let you have a normal life. I'm just, hell, I don't even know what I'm trying to do anymore. But, the point is, I'm trying to give you what you want. And you haven't even noticed. How ironic," Jesse said as he sighed.

"It will take a lot more than just you 'trying,' Jesse. You always say you will do this or that, and then you always backtrack. I did everything you asked of me. I tried to make this work. I gave it my all, but you never did. I honestly don't know what else I have to do to prove to you that I'm not going to run away. I would never allow you to harm Kevin, Christian, or me. I've seen how you truly are, and I couldn't live my life always looking over my shoulder and wondering when you would come after us. And as sick and twisted as it may be, I care about you. Not the monster in you, but the kid that never knew what it was like to truly have someone in his corner. You were right when you said I did care because it does hurt me when you do stupid crap like you pulled, but it never stops you. You always let your fear or anger take over in any situation."

"Don't you think I know that? I'm trying to let all that go for you. You could have run away a long time ago, but you didn't. I would love to hear you say it's because you love me, but how can I expect that when I'm just a monster. And who can love a monster, right?"

"Then, don't be a monster. It's that simple. I'm going back out there with Christian. Thank you for allowing me to sign Christian up for school. I think it would be good for him to interact with other kids his age."

"I didn't know you were asking permission to sign him up. I thought it was a mutual decision. Guess I was wrong in thinking you were trying to make things work between us."

"You don't give me anything to work for. Let me go. If you truly loved me like you say you do, then you would want me to be happy and this situation doesn't make me happy."

"I can't let you go because I do love you. If you gave me a chance, I could make you truly happy. There's only one thing I can't do for you, letting you leave me. But other than that, I'll do anything."

Renee sighed and stood up. She walked out of the kitchen and back into the living room with Christian. The one thing Jesse couldn't do was make her truly happy because she wanted Kevin. He would never understand that, however. He only wanted what he wanted, which wasn't good enough. So it wouldn't do any good to keep talking or arguing about it. It was always the same old thing over and over again.

*   *   *

Renee walked into the school and the office. She talked to the secretary and handed her the packet she had filled out for Christian. She then proceeded to take a tour of the school with Christian. He was excited to start school next month. Once they were done with the tour, Renee took Christian to the park. He got to play with other kids his age, and Renee got to have a breather.

"Hey, Tabitha!"

Renee turned around and saw Valerie coming toward her. She smiled and waved. Valerie had a three-year-old named David, whom Christian always played with. Valerie sat down beside her on the bench.

"Hey, Valerie. What have you been up to lately?"

"Not much. Just got engaged!"

"Oh my God! That isn't 'not much', Val! Let me see the ring."

Valerie lifted her hand and showed Renee the ring. It was a beautiful diamond. Valerie had been dating her current boyfriend for a little over a year. David's father was killed in a work accident when Valerie was still pregnant. She worked at a coffee shop just to make ends meet. That's where she had met Bobby.

"Bobby said he wants me to quit working once we get married. I don't know if I want to quit my job. I love the people I work with and I think it would be boring to be home all the time. I guess I could spend more time with David. What do you think?"

"I think you should do whatever makes you happy. If being a stay-at-home wife and mom makes you happy, go for it. If you want to continue working, then tell Bobby that. You shouldn't have to stop doing what you want just because you are getting married. Marriage is all about compromises, after all."

"I wouldn't mind staying at home for a while. I don't know if I would want it to be a permanent thing, but honestly, I have always wanted to go back to school. Plus, I could still go to the shop to get some coffee and just chit chat with everyone. Didn't you tell me that you were a stay at home mom and wife?"

"Yep, but Christian just got signed up for school today. So, my days are going to be a lot different. I would love to get a job but I don't know if Mark would go for that."

"Well, like you said, marriage is all about compromises. Make him compromise."

"Yeah, if only it was that easy. Mark feels like a woman shouldn't work because the man is the provider. I don't need to work but I want to. I just want to be able to get out and do something during the day and have my own money. It's not like Mark tells me I can't use his money, but I would prefer to have my own."

"I get that. Hey, I have an idea! If I decide to quit, I can put in a good word for you. Maybe you could take over my job. I'm not getting married until the end of the year, but if you are willing to wait, I'll talk to my boss for you."

"That would be great, Val. I've been out of the workforce so long that I don't even know if anyone would hire me. So, it couldn't hurt to have someone put in a good word for me," Renee said as she smiled.

"Well, great. That means you'll be free for a little while first. Would you like to earn some money now? I sure could use a wedding planner that won't charge me an arm and a leg."

"Are you asking me to plan your wedding?"

"Yeah, I am. Only if you'd be ok with doing it. Honestly, everyone I know works and I love my friends, I really do, but they throw the worst parties. Christian's birthday party was put together so well and everyone loved it. I would love to have you do it!"

"Can I have a few days to think about it?"

"Of course! We aren't getting married for another five months. And of course, you're invited. This is so exciting! You can bring Mark and Christian. Do you think you could let me know by the end of the week?"

"Yeah, sure."

Renee stopped at the library before she went home. She was excited about possibly getting paid to plan a wedding and a possible job. Her first thought had been to tell Kevin. She just hoped she could talk Jesse into letting her do it.

"Hey, Kevin! I just got offered a job planning a wedding. I'm super excited about it. I've never planned one, but I like planning birthday parties. My friend likes the way I plan them, too. I just registered Christian for school today. I'm hoping to get a job to have something to do while he's there. The girl getting married might be quitting her job at the end of the year. She said she would put in a good word for me. Since I haven't worked in so long, I'm not sure if anywhere will hire me. So I'll plan the wedding first and then see about getting an actual job. I'm sure all of this is boring to you, but I was so excited that I had to share the news with you since we have been talking lately."

Renee sent the message and was surprised when Kevin sent a message back saying hey. So she decided to stay on a little longer and see if he would talk.

"I'm happy you have found something exciting! If it works out, then maybe you could be a wedding planner. I'm glad you shared your news with me. For the first time in a really long time, I look forward to talking to someone. It's been nice getting to know you. And please, don't take this the wrong way, but you remind me of Renee. It was always so easy to talk to her. Some of the things you say sound like something she would say. Would it be wrong of me to ask you to send me a picture?"

"I like you, Kevin. You seem sweet, but you are also online. Maybe if we keep talking, I'll get more comfortable and send you one. Even though it doesn't really matter what I look like, does it?"

"No, it doesn't matter what you look like. Would just like to put a face with the person I'm talking to. So, do you have any ideas for the wedding you are planning?"

"Not really. Since I'm not really sure if I'll be able to do it until later, I don't want to get my hopes up."

"Why wouldn't you be able to do it?"

"My boyfriend doesn't want me to work."

"How are things going between you two? I know you said you had basically been ignoring him. Are you still mad at him?"

"No, I'm not mad anymore. Just tired of caring. I mean, I keep doing stuff for him, and he always finds a way to ruin it. I wish he would get it through his head that he is driving me away. He always tries to make up for it, but it's not enough anymore. I feel that if you are truly sorry for something you did, then you wouldn't continue with that behavior. You know what I mean?"

"I get it. Maybe you should break up with him and move on. Have you ever thought about being with someone else and seeing if it turns out better?"

"There's only one person I want to be with and I can't, so there is no point in wondering that."

"Why can't you be with them?"

"Because my love is lost. I can't get over him to even bring myself to love again. If I could, then life would be simpler, but I can't. He was everything I had ever wanted in a man."

"You never told me what happened to him."

"Well, it's complicated. Let's just say that he wasn't given a choice to leave me. That's all I can say as it isn't my story to tell, so I just can't bring myself to go there."

"So, the man you love is still alive?"

"Yes. He just can't be with me anymore. I know that, but it still hurts."

"Can't you go to wherever he is and be with him? If you love him so much, I would think that you would do everything you could to be with him. I guess it just doesn't make sense to me why you didn't go with him to wherever he went if you two loved each other so much."

"While he did not have a choice of leaving me, I also did not have a choice of staying with him. Believe me when I say if it was possible, that I would be there with him in a heartbeat, but it isn't. Have you thought about moving on and being with someone else?"

"No. My days have been consumed with finding Renee. I told you that you are the first person I have talked to. It's been nice getting to know you. If I could move on, and you could move on, do you think we might wind up together?"

"I don't know you well enough to say yes or no to that, but it doesn't really matter at this point as neither of us is moving on."

"Why did you initially message me? What made you do it?"

"I saw the posts about Renee, and I know what you are going through. So, I thought it would be nice to have someone to talk to that had been going through the same thing. But I guess it was my loneliness that made me do it. I thought it might make me feel better to talk to someone who understood my situation or at least part of it. So, what made you respond?"

"Do you want me to be honest?"

"Yes. I wouldn't have asked if I didn't."

"I thought you were Renee reaching out to me. But, I've tried to trick you into telling me the truth and you have stuck with your name, description, and everything, so I guess I was just wishful thinking."

"What would you have done if I had been Renee? Your reaction to someone like me wasn't exactly good. I mean, you all but called me stupid for sticking with Mark. So how would you have dealt with Renee sticking with the man who took her?"

"I honestly don't know. I have often wondered if she was still alive and would even be ok mentally. I often wonder if Jesse is still raping or beating on her. If she is still with him, why? Was it because he had her locked up or what? I just couldn't imagine him letting her do whatever she wanted. Moreover, why wouldn't she try to contact me if he did?"

"Let's role-play then. Let's say I'm Renee, and we will go through it. She was raped in front of you and taken. Jesse, the man who took her, kept her locked up so she couldn't contact you. Eventually, he started letting her leave the house with him, but he threatened to kill you if she tried anything. So, she stayed. Over time, she started being with him as she was always scared of what he would do if she ran. She already knows what he is capable of. Now, go with your first reaction since you have a 'backstory' to react to."

CHAPTER 21

Kevin read through the message. His heart ached at the backstory. He saw Marie was typing, and he wasn't sure if he could take seeing anymore. He felt like this was Renee reaching out and telling him what she truly wanted to say. He closed his eyes and took a deep breath as he saw the following message pop up. He opened his eyes and began to read the message.

"Kevin, this is Renee. I know you probably thought I was dead. I'm not. I have been living with Jesse because he threatened to torture and kill you in front of me. I wasn't allowed to leave the house unless he took me out at first. I can go where I want now, but I'm always worried about running away. I know if I did, I would live in fear for the rest of my life, wondering when he would find us.

I hate to admit this because of what you must have gone through, but I have to be honest. I have been living my life with Jesse as his wife. When he first took me, he continued to beat and rape me. Then, he started treating me better. Who knows why. But, we are in a relationship now, and I have come to care for him. I am contacting you today because I wanted you to know that I'm still alive and that I have always loved you. I just wanted you to know that you have been in my thoughts, and I'm sorry. Even though I didn't choose this life, I'm trying to live it the best I can. I hope one day you can forgive me. Please, move on with your life and be happy. You deserve it!"

Kevin sat back and stared at his phone. He didn't know what to think. His heart was breaking. Renee being in a relationship with Jesse and caring about him was not something he'd thought of. It saddened and angered him. How could she not reach out to him? He would gladly bear the consequences of Jesse possibly finding him. Hell, he had been looking for him so he could kill him. He was more convinced than ever that this was Renee under a false name. He had to keep trying to get a location out of her.

"Honestly, it angers me that you hid away due to a threat. I would gladly have dealt with Jesse. I have been searching for years and never lost hope. There were times when I almost did, and killing that bastard kept me going. I wondered if you were even still alive and what your mentality would be after years of abuse. How could you live a life with him after everything he did to you? To us? Do you love him? I've loved you the entire time. I've never moved on. You say you love me, but how can you when you choose to be with someone else? Did you ever stop to think that I may not want to live without you? That I'd rather die than know that you are living with him? Furthermore, you're living with him as his wife? That was supposed to be our life together!"

"I told you why I chose to stay. I couldn't let him come after you. You make sacrifices for the people you love, and giving up my life for yours was all I could do. I couldn't stand myself if you were killed because of me. I choose you every day that I stay. That is how much I love you. If I told you where I am, then you would show up and I don't know if you would survive. What am I supposed to do if that happens? I chose to act as his wife so that the rest of my life wasn't a living hell. But, it has always been you, Kevin. You have always been and will continue to be the one I love and want to be with. I'm sorry that my decision angers you. I'm sorry that I came to care for the one person I never wanted to be with. I'm sorry about being with him as his wife when it should be you. I love you and nothing will ever change that. And I hate that this is goodbye, but I know I can't risk contacting you again. Please, move on with your life and forget about me."

"As much as I want to move on with my life, I can't. I'll always choose you. You are my life. I won't stop until I find you. You may be able to move

*on, which hurts me more than anything else, but I just can't do that. I hope
one day you will come back to me."*

"Do you feel better now that you've 'talked' to Renee about how you feel?"

*"No. This has been emotionally draining. I have to go. Maybe we can talk
some other time."*

"Sure, if you still want to."

Kevin logged off. He couldn't take any more messages from Marie.
He felt like his heart had been ripped out. She couldn't possibly be some
random person. The way that 'conversation' had gone, it was like Renee
was telling him exactly what had happened. There was no way someone
could come up with that out of the blue and say so much emotional stuff.
But Marie had a child. Renee wasn't pregnant when she was taken. How
could she have a child that looked like him? He ran his hands across his
face and logged back on. A message was there from Marie.

*"I'm sorry if I upset you. I thought it might be therapeutic to say what you
had been wanting to say to Renee. I have to go now. I'm guessing by the way
that went that you don't want to talk to me anymore. I might come back later
to check, but most likely it will be a while. Peace and love, Kevin."*

Kevin stood up and went to the cabinet and took out the bottle of
whiskey. He usually didn't drink much, but today, he needed it. *It's five
o'clock somewhere*, he thought to himself. He turned the bottle up and
chugged a quarter of it, feeling it burn down to his stomach. He sat on the
bed and drank the whole bottle while rereading the messages between him
and Marie. It wasn't long after that when he passed out.

* * *

When Jesse got home, he sat beside Renee on the couch. She didn't react as she was deep in thought. He put his arm around her shoulders, and she didn't pull away as she had been. He leaned over and cupped her cheek, turning her face towards him. He lightly brushed his lips against hers.

"What's wrong, Renee? You seem far away. You didn't even pull away when I kissed you."

"I've just been thinking about some things that happened today. I guess I was far away."

"Do you want to talk about it or are you going to continue to ignore me like you have been?"

Renee sighed and said, "A lady I have become friends with is getting married. She invited us to the wedding. She also asked me to be her wedding planner and offered to pay me to do it."

"So, you are wondering if I'll let you? Or is there something else on your mind?"

"There's a lot of things I was thinking about. But, the main thing was the job I was offered. I want to do it, but I know I can't."

"You can do it. You're great at planning parties."

"That isn't why I said I can't do it and you know it."

"I know. But, I am also saying you can do it. I know you're still pissed at me, but I have been trying to do better about letting go. I haven't picked up your phone or paid attention to where you've gone. I've thought about it all night and I want you to live a normal life. I want you to be happy with me. So, if being a wedding planner for this girl is what you want to do, then go for it. I won't stop you."

"Are you serious?"

"Yes, I'm serious. You're right. I have to trust you. If I don't, then I'm definitely going to lose you. So, plan the wedding if you want. Or if you don't want to do that, then just go get a regular job. I won't say anything either way. I'll be here to support you."

"We'll see. You always say you'll do something and turn around and ruin it. I'll wait and if things actually improve, we'll go from there. Valerie invited us to the wedding. Do you want to go?"

"As your date? Or just to support you?"

"Does it matter? If you go as my date shouldn't you support me anyway?"

"Well, yes, but I wanted to know if you wanted me to go as your date. I've never met this Valerie person. Does she even know about me?"

"Yes. That's why I said she invited us to the wedding. I didn't just mean me and Christian. You would be going as my husband, Mark. So, are you going or not?"

"Of course, I'm going to go. I would love nothing more than to be on your arm and meet your friend."

"Ok. I'll let Valerie know we will be going and that I'll plan the wedding for her."

Renee was feeling good about this. She was finally going to be able to live normally. Or at least she hoped she was. She looked at Jesse, and he smiled and kissed her lips. She kissed him back, but she still held back, wondering if he would let her do this.

* * *

Renee met with Valerie to go over what she wanted out of her wedding. They were getting married on New Year's Eve, so they could always end the year on a high note. Renee liked the thought of that. She had always wanted to get married and have a big, fancy wedding. Of course, that would never happen now, but she could still dream.

Valerie gave her the budget for the wedding. Renee's eyes got wide at the 15,000-dollar allowance. What did her fiancé do for a living? That was on top of paying her $5000 for the job since she would be keeping everything updated for five months. They had even paid her half of it upfront.

Renee went home and started looking things up on her phone. She wished she had a computer and internet access. She sighed as she started writing down the names and numbers of bands. Then, she started looking for the perfect venue. It was essential to get that booked first thing. She got frustrated when her data ran out.

Since she couldn't do anything else internet-wise, she started writing down figures for Uber rides. It would be costly to take all those rides to look at venues and go to other places to use the internet. She needed to talk to Jesse. It was ridiculous that she was so limited. He said he was trying to do better. He needed to let her get a car, computer, and internet.

There was no way she could do this without the proper resources. Not only that, but she would be spending all the money she made just to set everything up. Furthermore, if she were going to get a job after this, it would be easier to get back and forth with a car. She thought about ways to bring it up without making Jesse mad. Maybe she could just leave her figures sitting around, so he found them. Yes, that's it. She smiled and wrote everything down that she would need, from the internet to a car and the cost of everything without them.

*   *   *

When Jesse got home, he found Renee looking at a bridal magazine while Christian watched cartoons. Renee had all sorts of things sitting around her. He wanted to sit beside her but didn't want to move anything and mess her up. He leaned down and kissed her cheek. She looked at him, and he pointed at the couch. She just nodded and started picking up some of the things. He picked up some things and sat down.

"Looks like you've been busy today."

"Yeah. I ran out of data. I'll have to start going to the library more."

Jesse looked down at the things in his lap. There were crude sketches of what looked like tables. He moved that aside and found a notebook underneath. It had figures on it. He skimmed over it, thinking that it was for the wedding, until he noticed a repeat of Uber. Then there was internet with a question mark and library beside it. Finally, he noticed the total at the bottom.

"I know I said I wasn't going to track you or anything, but I have a few questions about this wedding planner gig."

"Ok. What is it you want to know?"

"Are you going to actually make money from this?"

"Depends," Renee said as she shrugged.

"On what?"

"On how many places I have to go. I have to check everything out and then have Valerie and Bobby meet me at some places to try out food or check out the venues. If I can get locations near each other, I can walk to them instead of using Uber. I'll also need to go to the library more since I can't look anything else up. I don't have what I need to plan all of this out so I'm going to do what I can to try to cut costs."

"What do you need to make this work for you?"

"Internet for one. I think my biggest cost is going to be Uber."

"Is that what this is?" Jesse asked, holding up the notebook.

Renee nodded and went back to looking at the magazine. Jesse thought things over for a little bit. He didn't want to give her an even bigger chance to run, but he had agreed to let her plan this wedding. He sighed.

"Would you be willing to take me to work and pick me up on the days you need to go out? You'd have to get up early."

"Are you serious?"

"Yes, but you have to be up on time. I don't like being late. I get there early. And I don't want to be picked up late either."

"I'll do it!" Renee exclaimed as she threw her arms around him and kissed him.

Jesse kissed her back and pulled her into his lap. He wrapped his arms around her and held her tight. He felt his jeans grow tight and knew he had to back off before taking her straight to the bedroom. He broke the kiss when he heard Christian yell gross.

"Can we continue this later?" Jesse whispered in Renee's ear.

She reached between them and squeezed him through his jeans as she kissed him. He groaned into her mouth. He was going to take that as a yes. Renee broke the kiss and got up to fix dinner. Jesse was left with his thoughts going between sex and the problem of Renee taking the car. Could he get back in her good graces by getting her a car? He picked up the notebook and saw she had written computer and internet on the paper. She had also written down more internet on phone with a question mark beside it. He sighed. He didn't like the idea of a computer and internet in the house, but he could give her more internet on her phone. His fear tried to creep up on him, but he doused it with the thought of being able to be with Renee before he had messed it up. He smiled and made up his mind about what he needed to do.

CHAPTER 22

Renee started calling the venues she wanted to look at. After setting up appointments for the rest of the week, she started calling the bands. She texted Valerie. She needed to be there when the band was selected. Valerie texted her back and gave her dates and times that she could listen to the bands.

When it was time to go to see some churches, she left. Christian was bored with looking at places after an hour. She went to her appointments and then took Christian out for lunch. She let him play on the playground until it was time for her next appointment. Luckily, he went to sleep on the way.

Renee went to the library to do some investigating on the bands. She wanted to hear the way they played so they could tell if they wanted to audition them or not. It had been a few days since the episode with Kevin. She wondered if he had messaged her back. She wasn't planning on messaging him unless he contacted her first.

She checked on Stratus, but there wasn't a new message. So she pulled up another tab and started researching the bands. A couple were playing when Valerie was available since it was a weekend. She messaged Valerie about the dates and times. They were all playing at bars. Renee wasn't sure if Jesse would be ok with her going with just Valerie.

She smiled as she thought of his reaction when she told him that she was going out. She wouldn't dress up too much so he wouldn't think she was going on the prowl. She jumped as a ding pulled her out of her thoughts. She pulled up Stratus.

"Hi," was all Kevin said.

"Hi. Wasn't sure if you were going to talk to me again," Renee sent back.

"Honestly, I wasn't sure at first either. I thought about it and I don't want to lose our forming friendship. I'm still hoping one day you will let me call you. I'd love to hear your voice. Right now I'm just depressed after the conversation we had the other day. Been trying to get out of this funk for days."

"I'm sorry, Kevin. I should have never brought it up. I thought you might like to talk about it, but I should have waited until you were ready. Not that it matters, but it upset me, too. It's never my intention to hurt anyone. Your reaction made me think of how Alex would take my situation. It didn't make me feel good. I can't call you. I told you that Mark is a jealous man. It wouldn't end well if he found out we were talking like this."

"Do you think he would actually harm you for talking to someone?"

"Yes. He would see it as cheating. I have no doubt about it."

"You need to get out of that relationship. No one deserves to be with someone like that."

"I wish it was that simple. My situation is complicated and I've run through it a lot. I was planning on leaving him. I've thought about it for years, but I know I can't."

"It's not that complicated. Just leave. Pack your things and go. Take your son and leave. It's not his son, right?"

"No, but he thinks he is. I can't exactly leave and try to make sure he can't take Christian at the same time. I also know that he would hunt me down if I ever left. Have you ever heard the expression, 'I love you to death'? I believe he truly would do just that. I don't know if he would take it out on me or Christian, or find Alex and harm him. He knows if I ever left him it would be to find Alex. Mark knows people that can find anyone, so I know he would find me in no time."

"Why don't you just kill him? Then run."

"And be hunted down as a murderer? No way. No one would ever believe me about my situation. He has too many friends and he doesn't put his hands on me anymore so it's not like there's evidence of physical abuse."

"Mental abuse is enough. Especially if he's threatened to harm you if you ever left."

"It's not me that he's threatened to harm. That's why I stay. He would leave me alive to torture me because he had killed Alex and he knows it would kill me. Especially since it would be my fault for trying to run."

"Have you ever thought that Alex could take care of himself? It might not end up how you think it would."

"I just can't take that chance. He plans things out before he does them. He's meticulous about it. Can we change the subject?"

"Ok, Marie. Last thing and I'll leave it alone. If you ever need me, call me. If you ever want to get away from him, I'll help you. I wish someone would have done that for Renee."

Renee saw him post his phone number in the text message. He hadn't changed it. Had he been hoping she would call? She sighed. What could she say to that? He was so sweet to 'Marie' and offered to help her.

"I appreciate the offer. So, do you have to work today?"

"Yeah. I go in at five. So, did you take the job as a wedding planner?"

"Yes, I did. I've been looking into venues and bands the past few days. Mark is letting me keep the car, so I can look at some places. They paid me half upfront. So I'm thinking about getting a car with it."

"That's great! Then we can talk more often."

"I don't know about that, but it might be possible. We'll see."

"Ok, ok. If I stop pushing, maybe you'll take it upon yourself to call or text me."

"I almost feel like there's a reason you are being so pushy about that."

"Because I want to talk to the Angel that has helped me open up. And not through a computer screen."

"Whatever you say, Kevie."

Kevin was shocked. Kevie was Renee's nickname for him. He sat back in his chair and ran his hand over his face. The more he talked to Marie, the more he was convinced that this was Renee. When they had first met, he had told Renee his name. She had blushed and started stuttering. She had stuttered when she said his name and called him Kevie instead of Kevin. It had been a joke between them ever since. Yes, he was trying to get her to call him so he could hear if it sounded like Renee. He looked back at his phone as it dinged. He sighed when he saw her message.

"Well, I have to go now. My time is almost up. I hope to talk to you again soon."

"Ok, Marie. Take care and remember my offer."

"I will. Thanks, Kevin. Don't work too hard."

Renee logged off and pushed Christian's stroller out to the car. Once they were in the car, she drove to Jesse's job. She was singing along to the songs on the radio, in a good mood from talking to Kevin. However, she felt a tug at her heart when a love song came on. She was tempted to call Kevin just to hear his voice again. Renee pulled into the parking lot and waited for Jesse to get off work.

When Jesse got in the car, he asked, "So, how was your day?"

"Good. I checked out some venues today. Looked into some of the bands. I've booked appointments to see other venues for the rest of the week. It felt good to work."

"So, you'll need the car for the rest of the week?"

"Yeah, is that a problem?"

"No. I guess I'm like everyone else and don't like being left without a ride if something happens. Would you like to go check out some cars just for the heck of it? We could grab some dinner after."

"Sure, if that's what you want to do."

"Alright. I'll give you directions."

Renee followed Jesse's directions, and they wound up at a used car lot. She got out and put Christian in his stroller. He was wide awake and checking out the cars, too. She saw a couple that she liked. A car salesman came out and started talking to Jesse. Jesse asked her if she wanted to test drive any of them.

"I wouldn't mind taking a look at the SUV over there."

"Great choice. It's good on gas despite being an SUV. It's also spacious enough for a family with lots of cargo space. If you'd like to test drive it, I'll need your driver's license.

Renee handed him her license so he could make a copy of it. Jesse was checking out the vehicle. He had even popped the hood to check out the fluids and the engine.

"Jesse, why are we looking at vehicles? It's not like I can afford this thing anyway."

"It's only $5,000. Didn't you say Valerie was paying you $5,000 for planning her wedding?"

"Well, yes, but she hasn't paid me all of it yet and I spent some of it. Only about $50 of it but still."

"Ok. Then give him what you have and I'll give him the rest. You can pay me back later."

"I wouldn't be able to pay for insurance or gas, so again, what's the point?"

"Haven't I always provided for you?"

"Yes. But, this is a lot."

"I love you, and you need transportation. This SUV looks good. I'm trying to do better by you. You said it was all or nothing, right?"

Renee was shocked. Jesse was relinquishing the proverbial reins on her. She got ready to respond when the salesman walked back out. He handed her the keys and a slip to be able to drive the Pathfinder. Jesse put Christian's car seat in it, and they got in.

"We'll see you in a bit," the salesman said as Renee started the SUV.

Renee liked the sound of it. So she took it out and got on the highway to speed up. Once they hit 80, she found an exit and went back to the dealership.

"There aren't that many miles on this vehicle considering its age. It sounds good. It drives smoothly. I don't hear any odd noises that would signal something's wrong. What do you think? Do you like it?"

"I love it. But, I can't afford it. What do I have to do in return for getting it?" Renee asked, suspicious of Jesse.

"Stay with me. Be with me like you were before. It's all I want in return," Jesse replied with sincerity in his voice.

"So, all I have to do is what I was doing before you ruined it again? How do I know you won't do that again?"

"You give me absolutely no credit. You've had your freedom. I haven't said or done anything out of the way have I?"

"No, but that's generally how it starts."

"I know, but I've been trying really hard not to do that. You always come home to me. You've given me no reason to think you'll leave. I want us to be a happy family. If you want this vehicle, then get it. I'll take care of everything for you, and when the wedding is done, you can get a real job."

"Ok," Renee said as a huge smile lit up her face.

She pulled into the lot, and Jesse talked to the salesman. She had the money Valerie gave her in her purse. She'd been afraid to carry it, but she didn't want to put it into Jesse's account.

She went in with Christian and found Jesse going over the paperwork with the salesman. He was putting a loan onto the car for the remaining amount. She gave him $2000 of what she had since Jesse said to keep the rest if she needed it. Was he buying this car for her? He'd said she could pay him back, but she wouldn't have enough for that when Valerie paid her the rest. He had to know that, and she couldn't pay for the insurance, gas, or maintenance. He had said he had always taken care of her. To her, that meant he was buying this car for her and up-keeping it because he did love her.

Jesse had her sign the paperwork. Once everything was said and done, the salesman put 30-day tags on the car. They walked out, and Jesse handed her the keys. She felt giddy, threw her arms around Jesse's neck, and kissed him hard. He kissed her back and smiled as she went over to the SUV, lovingly looking it over as she got in.

"I'm going to put Christian's car seat in here until you get one tomorrow. He can ride with you to the restaurant."

"Ok," Renee said as she smiled at Jesse again.

CHAPTER 23

Renee got ready to go out with Valerie. The only jewelry she wore was the wedding band set that Jesse had given her. She nodded to her reflection and walked out of the room. Jesse was sitting on the couch as Christian had gone to sleep already.

Jesse looked up when she walked out of the room. He looked her over as she walked over and sat on his lap. Then, he put his arm around her waist, and his other hand crept up her dress. Renee blushed as his hand ran over the garter belt.

"Don't you have any regular pantyhose? And your underwear feels like they are too sexy to be wearing to a bar without me being there."

"Jesse, I'm wearing the clothes I have that cover me up the most. No one is going to see my underwear or garter belt so it doesn't matter if I have them on. Are you ever going to trust me?"

"I don't like other men looking at what's mine. They don't get to touch what's mine," Jesse said as his hand moved over the panties, making her hot and bothered.

"I'm the only one allowed to make you wet. Remember that when you're at the bar," Jesse said as he kissed her and pressed his thumb into her sweet spot.

Renee moaned into his mouth as she pushed her fingers into his hair. Jesse broke the kiss when he heard a knock on the door. He smiled at her as she got up and straightened her dress. It wasn't his usual smile, and Renee knew she might get in trouble later over this. However, she was going to do it anyway. She gave Jesse a quick peck on the lips and went to the door. Valerie smiled at her as she opened the door.

"You look beautiful, Tabitha."

"Thanks, Valerie. You too."

"Let's go. I haven't had a night out in forever! I'm so excited."

When they got to the bar, it was almost packed. Valerie drug her inside and immediately ordered a drink. Renee ordered one, too, but she was sipping on hers. Valerie was downing her drinks pretty fast. Thirty minutes later, Valerie was dragging her onto the dance floor. Renee danced with Valerie, and when the band came on, she made Valerie sit down so they could listen to the music. The band was excellent. Valerie got her back on the dance floor. She had drunk so much that she was stumbling. A couple of guys came up and danced with them. Renee was a little uncomfortable with the guy who was dancing behind her. Valerie was having a good time.

"Valerie, we need to call Bobby to come to take you home. You can't drive like this. And I definitely don't think it's a good idea for you to drive me home on top of it."

"Do I have to? We're having fun!"

"We can take you lovely ladies home," the man dancing with Valerie suggested.

"No thanks. I'm married and my friend is engaged. Valerie, let's go call Bobby," Renee said as she started dragging Valerie outside.

"Aw, Tabby, you're ruining our girl's night out!"

"You'll thank me later when you wake up with Bobby instead of some stranger. Now, give me your phone, unlocked, please."

Renee held out her hand as Valerie dug her phone out. She unlocked it and handed it to Renee. Unfortunately, she was so drunk that she dropped it instead of putting it in Renee's hand. Renee sighed and bent over to pick up the phone. She felt a hand slip over her hip as a body pressed against her butt. She grabbed the phone and stood up, feeling her body tense up.

Renee turned around and found the same guy dancing behind her standing there. She stepped away from him and grabbed Valerie, who was giggling about the whole thing. Then, she walked toward the bouncer. She dialed Bobby's number and waited for him to pick up.

"Hey, baby! Are you enjoying your night out?"

"Bobby, this is Tabitha, Valerie's friend. She's had too much to drink and it isn't safe for her to drive. Can you come to get her?"

"Yeah, I'll come to get her. I'm only ten minutes away."

"Ok. Thanks, Bobby."

Renee hung up and put Valerie's phone back in her purse. She took out her phone and dialed Jesse's number. The guy who grabbed her was hanging around close to her. She didn't like that at all. Jesse didn't answer the first time she called, so she hung up and immediately called back. He answered that time.

"Hello?" Jesse answered.

"Hey, baby. Can you come get me? Valerie has had a little too much to drink. Her fiancé is coming to get her."

"You never call me baby. Are you drunk?"

"No. I didn't have that many. How long before you can get here?"

"About twenty minutes. Is Valerie staying with you until I get there?"

"No. Her fiancé will be here any minute."

"That guy keeps following you," Valerie said in her ear.

Renee had hoped calling Jesse' baby' would get the man to stop stalking her, but it didn't work. He had come up and asked her to dance with him. She'd said no, but he still hadn't left. Finally, Bobby pulled up, and she helped him get Valerie in the car.

"Now that your friend doesn't need to be taken care of, you want to dance?"

Renee turned and looked at the man as she said, "No. I'm married. I told you that."

"What he doesn't know won't hurt him."

"No, thank you. I'm getting ready to leave anyway."

* * *

Jesse pulled into the parking lot and saw a man put his arm around Renee's waist as he pulled her back against him. Jesse was seeing red as he pulled up as close as he could. Renee went to step away from the man, but he pulled her back. Jesse got out of the car and walked up to Renee.

"What the hell are you doing?"

"Who the fuck are you?" the man asked.

"I'm her husband and she's leaving. Renee, get in the car."

Renee jerked out of the man's grip and moved in front of Jesse. He looked at her, and Renee shivered. She placed her hands on his arms and pushed slightly, trying to make him leave with her. He didn't budge.

"He isn't worth it, Jesse. Take me home, please?" Renee asked as she looked into his eyes.

"Get in the car. We'll talk about this at home," Jesse snapped as he walked back to the car.

Renee got in and buckled her seatbelt. Jesse didn't speak to her the whole way home. Once they arrived, Jesse got Christian out of the car while she went to their room. Jesse came into the room and saw her unzip her dress. He quickly jerked her body against his as his arms tightened around her.

"I told you before you left that no man was allowed to touch you but me. Why did that man have his hands on you?" Jesse asked as his hand pushed under her panties and moved over her folds.

"He just wanted to dance but I told him no."

"That's not what I saw. I saw his hands on you and he was pressed up against you. Did he make you wet?" Jesse asked as his fingers pushed inside of her. "Did that guy do it for you, Renee? You're getting wetter as I speak."

"Y-you're making me wet," Renee stuttered.

Jesse removed his hand and shoved her back, pushing her upper half onto the bed. He drew back and smacked her ass hard enough for it to echo. Renee screamed into the bed. He slipped his belt out of his pants.

"I guess I need to remind you whom you belong to," Jesse said as he yanked her panties, ripping them off and making her body jerk.

Jesse pulled his shirt off and grabbed Renee's hair. He jerked her head up as he leaned over her, rubbing his jeans against her. He grabbed the back of her bra and yanked. The material tore until it was entirely in half. He stood up but yanked her hair so her face was to the side so she could see his hand go up and come back down. He let go of her hair and rolled her over. Jesse jerked her off the bed, so she landed on her knees on the floor. She looked up at him.

"Suck my dick," Jesse demanded.

Renee unzipped his jeans. She unbuttoned them and pulled them down along with his boxers. She licked her lips and slowly moved towards him. Jesse grabbed her hair and pushed her face forward. She took him in her mouth and began to suck and lick him. Jesse groaned as his grip on her hair tightened. He started to shove his dick deeper into her mouth as he got more aroused.

"Stop," Jesse said as he jerked her head back.

Renee stood up, and Jesse pushed her back onto the bed. He moved between her legs, and his hands gripped her breasts hard. His mouth followed right behind as he bit her nipples hard. Renee whimpered. Jesse began to rub his dick against her.

"These belong to me," Jesse said as his hands squeezed her breasts again.

His hands trailed down to her hips. He stepped back and flipped her over. He slapped her ass again but not quite as hard this time. He rubbed the handprint on her ass as he smacked the other side.

"Your ass belongs to me."

Jesse trailed his fingers down her back to her hips and moved again. He flipped her back over and began to nip at her nipples. His hand trailed down her stomach and to her pussy. He slid his fingers inside of her and curled his fingers over that spot inside her. Renee moaned as he continued in slow-motion over that spot. His mouth trailed kisses down her stomach until his mouth found her clit. He sucked and licked it as his fingers quickened their pace. Just as Renee was about to cum, Jesse stopped. Renee groaned.

"Not yet," Jesse said as he stood up and rubbed his dick on her.

When he was satisfied she was frustrated, he slammed into her and said, "This pussy belongs to me."

He slammed his body into hers over and over, hard and fast. He built her back up to that point of cumming and stopped.

"You don't cum until I tell you to. Who's making you wet now, Renee?" Jesse asked as his hands gripped her hips.

"You are," Renee breathed.

Jesse pulled out of her and slammed back in. He stood there for a few seconds like that. Renee reached to grab his hips, but Jesse grabbed her wrists and pushed her arms onto the bed over her head.

"You belong to me. No other man is allowed to touch you. Say it."

"No other man is allowed to touch me. I'm sorry, Jesse. Please, let me cum," Renee begged.

"Why should I? You've obviously forgotten who your body belongs to. But, you're going to remember after tonight."

Jesse pulled out of her and slammed back in. He stayed like that for a few seconds and then repeated the action. He lost control for a minute as she tightened around him and began to pound her pussy again.

"Fuck, you're so damn tight and wet. Who does your body belong to?" Jesse asked as he slammed himself into her again.

"You. It belongs to you," Renee moaned.

"Remember that, Renee. I'll kill the next motherfucker that touches you," Jesse said as he retook possession of her body.

Jesse pulled out of her when he felt her about to cum. She cried out in frustration. Jesse let go of her wrists and grabbed her legs. He put them on his shoulders as he leaned down and pushed forward, so her knees were in her chest. He slammed back into her and ground his hips into hers.

"Who do you belong to, Renee?"

"You. I belong to you and only you!"

"I want to hear you say my name. I want to know that you know who you belong to," Jesse said as he pulled out of her and slammed back in.

"Jesse. I belong to Jesse. Please!" Renee begged again for release.

Jesse started pounding her body harder and faster. His mouth found her breasts and claimed them as his simultaneously. He felt her body quivering as she tried not to cum until the rush of hot fluid spilled over him and onto the bed as she squirted her orgasm. He groaned and lost all self-restraint. He punished her pussy with his dick for not waiting for permission. At the same time, his body reacted to her cumming like that as he got harder. Finally, he came hard, surprised that so much cum poured out of him. He let her legs down and lay on top of her.

After he caught his breath, he began to mess with Renee again. He was going to remind her all night long whom she belonged to. She'd make sure not to let another man touch her as that guy at the bar had ever again. She was his, and he would put his mark on her body so it would never crave anyone else's.

CHAPTER 24

Renee went out and looked at venues. Then, she stopped and got lunch. It was odd to sit and eat by herself. She took out her phone and went online when she remembered that she'd used all of her data. She was getting ready to put her phone up when she realized it had brought up the internet. Had Jesse added more data and not told her? She started looking up wedding dresses, and it was letting her. She smiled. Jesse was letting up, but it was slow. Now, if she could just get him to trust her, so she didn't have to go through the fear of him losing control again.

She had given up running away a long time ago. She could never bring herself to run and have Jesse hunt Kevin down. He was so damn sneaky that they wouldn't see it coming. She knew that Kevin thought she should let 'Alex' handle it, but she couldn't deal with it.

After lunch, she went and picked Christian up. She had to stop herself from crying again when he ran up and threw his arms around her. She placed him in the backseat. Then, she headed to the last venue of the day.

Renee loved the scenery on the drive. It was a beautiful countryside drive. The trees were in the stages of changing colors since fall was right around the corner. Maybe she could talk Jesse into going on a family drive one day. She'd have to text him and let him know she'd be home late. He was already going to be mad when she talked to him later.

She'd bought a computer with the remainder of her money. Now that she had data on her phone again, she could use the hotspot for the computer. It would make planning the wedding a lot simpler. She could also talk to Kevin while she was home. She knew Jesse wouldn't be happy about the computer, but she wouldn't ask him to install the internet, so he'd just have to get over it.

Renee pulled into the venue, and her eyes widened. Just the outside was gorgeous. An archway led to a huge building that could easily seat 150 people. The building had Victorian gothic architecture. She could just see it with snow on the ground. It would be beautiful with all of the trees surrounding it. She got out and took Christian out. She walked through the archway and envisioned flowers going around it. A red carpet would be rolled out from the archway to the building.

Renee walked into the building and found a hall leading to double doors. To her left were several rooms. There was a sign pointing to the right reading office. She walked that way and went into the office. The woman sitting at the desk stood up and smiled at her.

"Hi. Welcome to Le Blanc Cathedral. Are you Tabitha?"

"Yes, that's me. Are you Susan?"

"Yes. Nice to meet you, Tabitha. So, what are you looking for?"

"I'm planning a wedding and I'm looking at venues."

"Oh, congratulations!"

"It isn't for me. I'm the wedding planner. This is my first time doing anything like this."

"I see! Well, let's go have a look, shall we?"

"Yes, thank you."

Susan showed her around the small rooms first. You had a room for the bride and one for the groom. There was a full-length mirror in each room. There was a table and a couple of chairs, and a stool in front of the table. Susan took her to the double doors next. They were a heavy oak with a dark stain on them with a high polish. When she walked into the central part of the building, she gasped at its beauty.

It had a high, gothic vaulted ceiling. You could see the rafters made of old wood, giving it character. The windows were all stained glass and made beautiful hues where the sun shone through. There was a ring of roses on each window in different colors and little crosses embedded in each rose. There were doves in flight on some of the windows. The floors were old hardwood but had a beautiful, polished look. The floor could be for chairs or dancing. There was a platform at the end of the room.

It was made of the same wood as the floors, but it had a glossy stain that made it shine. There was plenty of room to have a band play on the stage. She pictured the wedding. There would be padded chairs on both sides of the platform, leaving plenty of room for the bride to walk down. The flower girl would throw rose petals from the door to the platform, where she would walk up the three steps to her groom. A small arch would be behind them with white peony flowers mixed with purple succulents. The bouquet would have peach roses, peonies, and baby's breath.

"Would you like to see the reception hall?"

"Yes. I got a little lost in my thoughts," Renee said as she blushed.

"It's quite alright. It's easier to envision something when you're actually in the place. Come this way."

Renee went through the door beside the platform and found a room as big as the previous one. It had another platform in it, just like the previous one. This place was perfect. The question was could she fit it into the budget? And would Valerie and Bobby like it?

"How much is it to rent the place for one day? Her wedding is on New Year's Eve."

"It's five thousand dollars. And our reservations fill up fast. We already have appointments out until Christmas."

"Would it be possible to bring her by to see it tomorrow?"

"That will be fine. I'm here until five every day."

"Great. I'll go call her now. Thank you for your time, Susan."

Renee went out to her car and called Valerie as she hooked Christian in. Valerie didn't answer at first. She hadn't talked to her since Saturday night when she'd called Bobby to come to get her. She hoped that Valerie wasn't mad at her. She left a message letting Valerie know that she had found the perfect venue. On the way back home, Valerie called her back.

"Hey, Val. How are you?"

"I'm good. I'm sorry I haven't called you. I was embarrassed after what I did Saturday. I haven't been out without David for a long time. I guess I should have held back."

"It's ok, Valerie. We all go a little crazy every once in a while."

"Mark didn't get mad that he had to come get you, did he?"

"No. He got jealous about the creep that was stalking me but we made up," Renee laughed.

"Oh, good. I was worried about that. So, you think you found the perfect place, huh?"

"Yes," Renee said excitedly. "You have to see it. The lady said that reservations were filling up fast though. They're already booked up until Christmas. So I was wondering if you were free to come see it tomorrow?"

"Sure. I don't have to go into work until five tomorrow. We can go around lunchtime. Maybe we can grab some lunch after?"

"Sounds good. I'll pick you up around 11."

"It's a date."

"By the way, I really liked the band we listened to Saturday. I'd like to hire them for your reception. What do you think?"

"Go for it. I loved that guy's voice. It was yummy."

Renee laughed and ended the call with Valerie. If she liked the venue, then Renee had two major obstacles out of the way. The band had a website, and they charged 500 dollars for a gig. That was pretty cheap, so she was happy about it. Most of her budget would be left so she could make sure to have enough for the dresses, flowers, and food. The tuxes were going to be rented, which was another $500. $9,000 should be enough for what she had left, or she hoped it would be.

*   *   *

Jesse got a text from Renee saying she would be home late. He didn't like this new freedom she had. He knew he had to get used to it, but it was hard. He had to do something to get his mind off of it. He'd cook. He hadn't done that in a while since Renee always took care of it. He sighed and took everything out. Maybe if he cooked dinner for Renee, he would score more brownie points with her.

Jesse heard the door open as he was finishing dinner, and Renee called out that they were home. He called out that he was in the kitchen. Christian came running in and hugged his legs.

"Daddy!" Christian yelled.

"Hey, bud! How was your first day at school?"

"It was great! Mommy picked me up and we went for a long ride," Christian said as Jesse picked him up.

"You did? Where did you go?"

"It was a big place. Mommy got a funny look on her face when she saw it."

"She did?" Jesse asked as he looked at Renee.

Renee walked up and kissed Jesse and said, "Whatever you're cooking smells good."

"I thought you might appreciate dinner since you got home late. It's ready if you and Christian want to wash up real quick."

"Ok. Come on, Christian," Renee said as she took Christian to wash his hands for dinner.

Jesse set the table and put everyone's plate on it. Then, he started filling their glasses as Renee returned and put Christian in his booster seat. They were halfway through dinner when Jesse decided to ask her about the building.

"So, what building did you go look at?"

"It's a venue for Valerie's wedding. It's beautiful. I'm taking her there tomorrow. I hope she likes it. It would be perfect for her wedding."

"Is that the look Mommy got earlier, Christian?"

"Yep!" Christian giggled.

"You look kind of wistful, Renee. Did you like the building that much?"

"It was beautiful, and I can just picture everything in my head. So I bought a computer today to help me put everything together."

"I took the block off of your phone."

"I know. I appreciate it. That's why I bought a laptop. I can use the hotspot to get on it. I can use excel for the bills. I can use other programs to put pictures together and show them to Valerie. It's really going to help me plan this wedding. And later on, I can use it for everyday things like games if I get bored or checking out things to read."

Jesse shifted. If he got mad about this, he knew he'd lose the progress they had made. Renee was really into planning this wedding. He could see her doing this full-time with how she had taken to it. Or was it that she wished she could have a wedding? They were married as Tabitha and Mark, but she'd never actually gotten married or had her dream wedding. So was she wistful for the wedding she'd never have?

"I'm glad it'll help you in your business."

"Really? You aren't mad?"

"No," Jesse sighed.

Renee smiled, and he couldn't help but smile back. They finished their dinner, and he got Christian ready for bed while Renee cleaned up. When Renee came to bed, he was surprised that she came onto him. Did not getting angry about the computer do that? He'd think about it later. Right at this moment, he wanted to enjoy being with Renee.

* * *

The next day, Renee took Valerie to see the Cathedral. They chatted most of the ride there. Valerie picked on her about the fading hickeys. Occasionally they belted out a tune or two when a song they liked came on. However, they both went silent when Renee pulled up to the Cathedral. Even though she'd already seen it, it still took Renee's breath away. Valerie was smiling, and she hadn't even seen the inside yet.

They got out, and Renee took Valerie inside, where they met up with Susan. Susan gave Valerie the grand tour. She also went over the history of the place with Valerie. Valerie fell in love with the building.

"I want it," Valerie said.

"Great. Let's go do some paperwork. I believe Tabitha told me you wanted New Year's Eve. It is still available so let's get you in there. Are you able to pay today?"

"Yes. I want to make sure it's booked. Tabitha, I can't believe you found this place!" Valerie said as she grabbed Renee's hands excitedly.

"I fell in love with it just from the outside."

They both laughed as they followed Susan to the office. Renee waited outside while Valerie conducted her business with Susan. Once they were done, they got back in Renee's SUV and headed to lunch.

"I'm going to call the band when we get back. I'll make sure to book them. Now, we have to discuss the dress, foods, and flowers."

"One of Bobby's friends is going to cater for us as a wedding present. We just have to buy the food. People will have a choice between chicken and steak. He's going to make baby greens, creamed potatoes, gravy, and rolls. There will also be a side salad. He's also making our cake for us. It's going to be three tiers. It's a marble cake with white fondant on top of it."

"So, maybe $2,500 for food and drinks?"

"Yeah, that should be enough."

"Great. I'm going to get some ideas together for the flowers. We can go over those later. Then, we need to go shopping for bridesmaid's dresses and your dress, of course."

"Great! I can't wait to go dress shopping."

"Me either. I know you're going to find the perfect dress."

Valerie and Renee finished eating and went home. Renee went to work on booking the band and searching for a photographer. Things were coming together nicely.

*   *   *

Over the next month, Renee had put together the flowers for the wedding. She had set up a program that allowed you to design a room.

She had put the archway on the platform. It was decorated along with the archway outside with white peonies and purple succulents. A red carpet was going from the archway to the door and another from the double doors to the platform. Padded chairs were on both sides of the carpet. The carpet had peach rose petals on it. Lights were strung up around the room that were white and blue. There were two vases on each side of the platform holding peach roses, red roses, white peonies, and ivy.

In the following picture, she had the bridal bouquet. It had peach roses, white peonies, and baby's breath. There was also a bouquet of silk flowers for Valerie to throw. The bridesmaid's bouquets were white peonies and purple succulents. The men's boutonnières consisted of one white rose and baby's breath. Renee felt her eyes water as she looked at the pictures. This was her dream wedding. The one she would never get to have. She sighed as she logged into Stratus. She hadn't talked to Kevin much lately as she'd been busy with the wedding. However, they had scheduled to talk today.

"Hi, Kevin. How have you been?"

"Just keeping busy with work. Sometimes I get to talk to an angel. How have you been?"

"Sometimes I get the feeling that you are hitting on me, but I know that can't be right since you are still in love with Renee. But anyway, I've been really good. I love planning this wedding. The only downside is I find myself planning MY wedding. It's everything I would want. The bride-to-be has loved all of my ideas, though. I guess that's a plus. It's just making me want something I know I'll never have."

"Well, I guess I'm trying to see if I can move on, but you're the only person I've found that I want to get to know better. I'm still searching for Renee, but I'm afraid I'll never find her. But, why can't you have your dream wedding?"

"Mark already considers us married. He'll never ask me to marry him. Hence, why I'll never have a wedding. I'm glad you are trying to move on. You deserve to be happy. You don't deserve to spend the rest of your life alone. But, I'm already taken."

"I know you are, but I can still try. That sucks about your boyfriend never proposing and giving you a wedding. Every woman deserves that. So, you want a big wedding then?"

"Actually, no, not anymore. I love the building I found. It's gorgeous, but I don't want a winter wedding. I would love to have mine in the fall. And I want a small, intimate wedding. Just the family and friends. I can't see inviting work associates and people I'm not close to. As far as the flowers and the lighting, yeah, I'm envisioning those for my wedding. What kind of wedding would you like?"

"I would also prefer a small wedding. I was planning on proposing to Renee as I told you before. The only thing I cared about was getting to marry the woman I loved and having her by my side the rest of my life. I could care less if we got married in a courthouse and she was wearing pajamas. She'd look beautiful to me no matter what."

"You are so sweet. I can see you in a suit and standing at the altar waiting for your bride. I bet she'd be crying happy tears down the aisle. I know I would be if I was marrying the love of my life."

"How are things going between you and Mark?"

"Really good. He's been doing so much better. He still has his off moments, but he's been trying really hard to show me he loves me. I've accepted this is my life, so I'm trying to make it as happy as I can. I know he wants me to love him, but I can't. I can't give him my heart when it belongs to someone else. But, I care about him a lot. Even though we'll never get married, I was thinking about getting him to take me on a vacation, kind of like a honeymoon. I was pregnant with Christian when we 'got together' so I'm hoping that the time away with just me might make him realize that I'm not going anywhere."

"How old did you say Christian was?"

"He's four. He'll be five in no time."

"How could your boyfriend not realize that your son is not his? Wouldn't the pregnancy have ended too soon?"

"I didn't even know I was pregnant when he took me. I found out from the doctor I was only a few weeks pregnant when everything happened. When I went into labor, I played it off like I was only a few weeks early."

Kevin reread the message. When he took her? Did she even realize she just said that? As far as he knew, Renee hadn't been pregnant when she was taken, but she wouldn't have known if she was only a few weeks. He had a son whose life he was missing out on if he was right. He shook his head. This couldn't be Renee. How could she think it was a good idea to make the best of her life with Jesse? How could she come to care for someone who had done so much to her?

"I just don't get it. How could you care about someone like that? Someone who hurt you and scares you? What about that situation made you say, 'Hey, I care about this guy'?"

"Honestly, I wish I could answer that myself. I feel like I'm crazy. I guess I just tried to do my best to be happy for my son. And there were moments when things were good between us that I just kind of forgot what happened. I guess my mind decided it was going to take those moments and run with them. Since I saw no way out, I just decided it was easier this way. I constantly had to trick my brain into thinking I liked him so I could have sex with him and enjoy it so it didn't hurt. I started looking at him as just a normal man. Over time, I guess I even tricked myself into believing my lies. This is so embarrassing. Can we change the subject?"

"Not yet. It sounds like you have Stockholm syndrome. You depend on that person for survival because you know they will harm you any other way. Eventually, your mind comes to think you can't live without them and you begin to live a normal life with them. I think if you really wanted to, that you could go find Alex and live a normal life with him. You need to put your fear behind you and try to remember what it was like before the situation you're in now."

"I've said before I wish it was that simple. I think Mark loves me because he saw something in me that he never had. A mother that loves her child. He told me he fell in love with me while I was pregnant. He said he wanted me to look at him that way, with that unwavering love. I think he could love someone else if he wanted, but he's always been such an asshole to everyone that he doesn't know how. The only love he's truly known is my love for Christian. He loved his brother but that kind of love is different. As crazy as he was in the beginning, I couldn't, or just don't want to, imagine what he'd do now that he thinks he loves me."

"He has a brother? What about the rest of his family? Do any of them know what he did to you?"

"He doesn't have any family. They are all gone. No, no one knows what he did, but you. The only reason I told you was that you can't say anything to anyone he knows because you don't know where we are."

"Marie, I truly wish you would let someone help you."

"Help me with what? Don't you see? Anyone looking into this is just going to see a loving husband who cares for his family. He doesn't beat on me. I willingly have sex with him, so no signs of rape, no bruises from beatings. And if anyone comes snooping around, I don't even begin to want to think about what he'd do. He would definitely see that as a betrayal. So, no, there's no help."

"What happened to his brother?"

"He was killed. That's all I really know."

"Ok. Let's change the subject. You obviously don't want to talk about this anymore."

They talked for a few hours before Renee finally told him that she had to go. She cleared Stratus from her history and logged off her computer.

*   *   *

"Alright, Valerie. We've been dress shopping every week for a month. October is almost over. And we are running out of places to look. You are going to have to find something you like. The tuxes are already rented. The boys have already been fitted for them. You've already approved the way I'm going to set up the actual wedding. And we haven't even started on the bridesmaid's dresses. You still haven't picked out a color for them."

"I know, I know. I just want the perfect dress. Plus, we've got two months left. No need to rush."

"What if your dress needs to be altered? You don't want to wait until the last minute to find that out."

"I know. I've been thinking of the bridesmaid's dresses. I want them to be peach or purple. The flower girl is Bobby's niece. I think a little white dress or maybe peach for her would be good. I'm just glad David is taking his duty as a ring bearer seriously. At his age, I didn't think he would. But, he loves Bobby and even calls him Daddy."

"That's great, Valerie. I'm so happy for you. Have you thought about your honeymoon? Do you guys have that all planned out?"

"Not really. Where did you go on your honeymoon?"

"I never had one."

"Well, that's not right. You should take one. Sort of a second chance honeymoon," Valerie suggested.

"I'd thought about taking one to Hawaii. I want to bring it up to Mark, but I'm not sure how he would take it."

"Just tell him how you're feeling. He loves you. He'll understand."

"Yeah, maybe."

Valerie kept looking over the dresses. Finally, after another hour, Valerie got excited. Renee looked at the dress. It was a beautiful ivory color. It flowed from the waist down to the floor with a train behind it. It had a sweetheart neckline with a beaded corset. The sleeves led down into lacy ruffles over the wrists.

"Are you going to try it on?"

"Yes."

Valerie went into the dressing room. Renee looked up when Valerie cleared her throat. Renee smiled. She had found her dress.

"Now we just need to put the veil on."

The veil was made in the cathedral style and was made out of tulle. It matched the dress with the design. It had flowers and vines leading down its edges where the dress had it on the bodice and going down the front of the skirt. Valerie had tears in her eyes as she looked at herself in the mirror.

"It's beautiful, Valerie, and you look beautiful in it."

"Yeah?"

"Yes. I think you have found your dress, and it fits you perfectly."

"I think so, too. And it's in our price range. It's $1,900."

"Great! Now we have a little leftover for a really good pair of heels."

Valerie laughed, and the sales clerk came over to help her change out of the dress. Afterward, Valerie continued to look around and decided that she didn't care for the bridesmaid's dresses at that shop.

They went home, and she decided to start all over at the shops they had already been to, trying to find the perfect bridesmaid dress. Two shops later and Valerie found a dress she liked. It was a peach dress with an illusion neckline, lace bodice, and a ribbon-defined waist. The sleeves were also made of lace. The skirt was a fluid mesh with a slit up to the thigh. There was a satin wrap that went around the shoulders. Renee didn't care for the color, but the dress was gorgeous.

"Are you sure this is the one you want?"

"I'm sure. It's gorgeous, don't you think?"

"I agree. I just want to make sure this is the one you truly want. We need to have your bridesmaids come try it on and make sure it fits right. If not, then we will need to have it altered, which means they will need to be measured."

"I'm going to have them put them on layaway and get the girls to come up here and try them on."

"Alright. I'll wait here for you."

When Valerie was done, Renee took her home. Renee was tired from all of the driving and walking around. Who knew that dress shopping was so tiring? She headed home and found Jesse and Christian playing outside. She sat down on the swing Jesse had put up for her and watched them.

She didn't realize she had dozed off on the swing until she felt someone lifting her. Jesse had picked her up and was carrying her into the house. She snuggled into his chest and felt him kiss her forehead. Instead of taking her to the bedroom, he sat down on the couch so she was on his lap. Christian climbed onto the couch and got behind her legs, so he was snuggled up to Jesse's side and her legs.

Renee smiled and ruffled Christian's hair as she snuggled deeper into Jesse's chest. Jesse turned the TV on for him and Christian to watch, but he kept it low. Jesse's body heat was soothing as her body pressed into his. She fell back asleep almost instantly. She never even realized it when Jesse picked her up and put her in bed for the night.

CHAPTER 25

"Jesse, can we talk for a minute?"

"That doesn't sound good."

"It's nothing bad. I was just, um, well, you know I've been planning Valerie's wedding for a few months now. Planning it has gotten me to thinking. I'll never get to have a wedding of my own or a honeymoon. But, I still want one. Since we are technically married on paper, I was wondering if you might like to go on a honeymoon type vacation with me?"

Jesse was shocked by her question. He watched as she wrung her hands. She wanted to go on a 'honeymoon' with him? Was this a ploy to take him out where no one would know them and do something to him? After all this time, was this how she planned to get away?

"You want to go on a honeymoon with me?"

"Yes. I thought that maybe Nancy could watch Christian for a week and we could go somewhere. I was kind of thinking about Hawaii. It's always warm there. So, we could go out and swim or just enjoy the beach. There is a nightlife there that we could go and enjoy as well. What do you think?" Renee asked as she bit her lip and peeked at his face.

"You won't even wear your wedding band unless you are going out to a club or something. You don't want to say you are married to me if you don't have to. I wear my wedding band all of the time, but you won't. If you hate the idea of being married to me, then why would you want to go on a honeymoon with me?"

Renee shrugged as she said, "I guess I just wanted something normal for a change. Something most women if not all want. It's ok. Forget it."

Renee stood up and turned to leave when Jesse grabbed her wrist. He pulled her down into his lap, and she didn't move. He cupped her chin and lifted her face. She didn't lift her eyes to meet his. He pressed his lips against hers.

"I'll think about it," Jesse said as he broke the kiss.

"You will?"

"Yeah, let me think about it. Was this wedding planning really what brought this on?"

"Well, I guess I got kind of wistful with all of this. Valerie asked me where I went for my honeymoon and I told her I didn't have one. I always wanted to get married and have a normal honeymoon. Our 'relationship' isn't normal so our 'marriage' isn't normal either. I guess I just want a little piece of a normal 'married' life."

Jesse ran his hand across her cheek, and she closed her eyes. He would love to marry her for real. If only they could come out of hiding, he would marry her in a heartbeat. Renee leaned into Jesse, laying her head on his shoulder. He wrapped his arms around her and held her for a while. Would giving her a 'honeymoon' prove that he loved her and wanted her to be happy? That he wanted her to be happy with him? Would she finally see them as 'married' after that?

*   *   *

Renee had convinced Jesse to go on a countryside drive. They had spent hours as a family. Then, on the way back home, Valerie called Renee in a panic.

"Hey, Val! What's up?"

"Tabitha, I need your help! The tailor has altered Kristy's dress, but Kristy is sick. She isn't able to come and try it on. Who knows when she will be better? You are about her size, can you help me out? This tailor is booked up for weeks. If she doesn't finish this dress now then I don't know if it will be done before the wedding. The fitting is in thirty minutes. Kristy just called me and I'm in panic mode."

"Calm down, Valerie. It's going to be ok. Hold on a minute."

Renee put Valerie on mute and looked at Jesse. He had heard the whole conversation through the speakers of the car. He just looked at her and raised an eyebrow. He wasn't sure what she wanted from him. Did she want his permission to go?

"Are you ok with me going to try the dress on? You would have to bring Christian in and keep an eye on him."

"It's fine. How long could it possibly take to try a dress on?"

"It shouldn't be too long. I appreciate this."

Renee took Valerie off of mute and said, "Valerie, I'll be there. I might be a few minutes late as we were out on a drive, but I'll be there as soon as I can."

"Thank you so much, Tabitha! I'll let the tailor know that you are coming. I so appreciate this!"

"No problem. See you in a bit."

"So, you are going to try on a bridesmaid's dress? Are you going to be one of the bridesmaids?"

"No. I'm about the same size as one of her bridesmaids, so they will try the dress on me to make sure it's altered to the right specifications. Of course, it still might not be right since she may be a little bit smaller than me in the chest and thighs. But, of course, I'm not exactly as small as her, but it shouldn't be much of a difference."

"Do you have to wear a particular dress for the wedding?"

"No. I'm just the wedding planner. I can wear whatever I want. I think it would be inappropriate to not wear a dress, though."

"Ah. Do I have to dress up for the wedding?"

"Yes. It would be nice if you wore a nice shirt and dress slacks. You have something you can wear in your closet. It's not like you don't dress up when we go out. That's really all that's expected of you."

"Ok. I can do that."

Thirty minutes later, Renee pulled into the parking lot of the dress shop. She went ahead in while Jesse got Christian out. He sat on a bench outside the dressing rooms while waiting on Renee. Valerie sat beside him.

"So, I was talking to Tabitha about honeymoon ideas. She said you guys never took one. She seems to really want one. Oh, I'm Valerie by the way. Nice to meet you, Mark," Valerie said as she held out her hand to Jesse.

Jesse shook it and said, "Hi, Valerie. Nice to meet you, too. Tabitha has mentioned the honeymoon to me. I was thinking about it."

"Don't think too long on it. Every woman wants that dream wedding and honeymoon. Tabitha is no different. I've seen the way she looks at the dresses and the way she looks when she talks about how the wedding will be set up. She wants that. I take it that you guys never had a real wedding?"

"No. It was just a courthouse wedding," Jesse lied.

"Oh. Do you love her?"

Jesse looked at Valerie and said, "Yes. She's my wife."

"Then show her. Take her on that honeymoon and ask her to marry you all over again. Even if it's just a show, take her somewhere on that honeymoon and have a small ceremony to renew your love for her. It will mean more to her than you will ever know."

"Do you really think so?" Jesse asked as he studied Valerie's face.

"I don't think, Mark, I know it will," Valerie said as she saw the thoughtful look on Mark's face.

Jesse looked at the dressing room as the tailor came out. Renee came out behind her, and his eyes went wide. She looked gorgeous in the dress. Valerie was right. She deserved a wedding and honeymoon. He wished he could marry her as Jesse, not Mark. However, he could at least give her the wedding she wanted. He had to let go of his mistrust completely. Renee had asked him for something she had apparently always wanted. He wanted to show her he loved her. He was going to take her on the honeymoon.

Christian reached out for Valerie, and she took him as she nudged Jesse and nodded toward Renee. He stood up and walked up to Renee as the tailor made a few quick adjustments to where the dress needed to be redone.

"You look beautiful," Jesse whispered in her ear.

"Thank you," Renee said as she looked at him in the mirror.

"Why don't you pick out a dress while we are here?"

"This isn't a regular dress shop. It only has dresses for weddings."

"Oh, Tabitha, some of these dresses can be for any occasion. We can find you one," Valerie said as she winked at Jesse.

Jesse smiled at her as she was getting what he wanted to do. He stepped back and took Christian from Valerie as Renee went and changed out of the dress. She came back out with Valerie in tow, and they went dress shopping. Valerie picked up a dress and had her try it on. It was an actual wedding dress, and Renee protested.

"Just try it on for fun! What can it hurt? It's not like you are buying it!"

"Fine," Renee sighed and went to try it on.

When she came out, Jesse's heart stopped. She was breathtaking as a bride. Valerie put the veil on her, and Renee looked at herself in the mirror. Jesse saw a small, sad smile on Renee's face as she looked at herself in the gown.

"Daddy, look at Mommy. She's pretty!"

"Yes, she is, buddy. That she definitely is," Jesse said, not even looking at Christian.

Renee looked at them in the mirror and gave him a shy smile. He couldn't help but grin back. He wanted to see that gorgeous smile looking at him as they were married. Yes, he was going to take Valerie's advice. Renee went in and changed out of the wedding dress and went looking for another dress.

She tried on another one that she fell in love with. It was a cream-colored dress with vintage lace going over the shoulders and down the sides. Crystals were attached to the breast that went to the sides and hooked the lace pieces over the breast. It trailed down the back and sides of the dress to the ankles. The rest of the dress was made of soft satin material and was plain. It was backless and sleeveless. There was a slit going up the left side to mid-thigh.

"That's gorgeous on you, Tabitha. I think you should get it."

"I don't have anywhere to wear it."

"You could wear it to my wedding."

"Don't you think it's a bit much to wear to a wedding?"

"No. I think you could wear that dress anywhere."

"I do love it, but I don't need it. I have a lot of dresses."

Renee went and took the dress off. The sales clerk took the dress and went to put it up. Valerie started talking to Renee, so Jesse went over to the sales clerk before she could put the dress up. Renee had looked stunning in it, and he knew she liked it.

"Excuse me, miss?"

"Yes, sir, how can I help you?"

"Can I buy that dress and have you hold it for me? I want to surprise my wife with it, but I don't want her to see it."

The clerk smiled as she said, "Yes, sir, we can do that for you. When do you want to come pick it up?"

"Monday at 5 pm."

"Alright. We will see you Monday then. Let's get you rung up and put this away for you."

Jesse followed the sales clerk and paid for the dress. She gave him a receipt and a pickup ticket. He walked around for a minute, so Renee didn't think anything. Then, she found him looking at a dress and raised an eyebrow. He smiled sheepishly.

"Are you ready to go home now?"

"Yeah, sure. I was just trying to kill some time until you and Valerie were done talking."

"Well, we are all done here. Let's go home."

Jesse put Christian down and took his hand. He used his other hand to lace his fingers through Renee's. She smiled at him. He smiled back at her as his plan was formulated in his mind. He rather liked Valerie's suggestion. She obviously knew something he didn't. He would take it to heart and hope that Renee had a good reaction to it.

*   *   *

"I have a surprise for you."

"Yeah?" Renee asked without looking up from what she was doing.

"I thought about the 'honeymoon' you asked me to go on with you. It's booked. We leave in two weeks."

"Really?" Renee asked as she turned in her chair to look at him.

"Yep. Are you happy?"

"You're serious!" Renee squealed.

She jumped up and hugged him.

"Is that why you were late coming home today?"

"You got me. Yes, I was late because I was booking everything. I want you to have everything in life, Renee. I love you. I realize you will never actually get 'married', but I still think of us as married. I want you to have this as a great memory of us. So, I have something special planned out for you. I hope you'll like it."

"I'm sure I'll love it."

CHAPTER 26

Renee logged on to her page so she could talk to Kevin. Since Jesse had announced to her last night that they were going on a honeymoon, she felt guilty. She should've been going on a honeymoon with Kevin.

She needed to stop talking to Kevin. She knew that she couldn't keep this up and put her past behind her and live the life she had now. She had to stay strong, so she wouldn't run away to be with Kevin and put all of their lives in danger. Even though Kevin had told her in his own way that he would and could handle Jesse if he came for him, she knew that he couldn't. He would never even see Jesse coming, and they couldn't run the rest of their lives. She had Christian to think about, and he deserved a normal life.

She resolved herself to be with Jesse and put the thoughts of being with Kevin out of her mind for good. She had to do what was best for all of them. Furthermore, always thinking about Kevin wasn't good for her. It broke her heart to think about letting go of Kevin, but she just had to. She'd talk to him until the honeymoon and then stop. With determination in her heart, she sent him a message.

"Hey, Kevin. Just wanted to pop in and see how you were doing. I got some news last night. Mark told me that he is going to take me on an actual honeymoon in two weeks. I'm excited but sad at the same time. I always thought I would be getting married to Alex, and living my life with him. Isn't it funny how things turn out? I've resolved to be happy with my life since I can never truly have what I want. I'm hoping that doing this will make Mark realize that the way we have been isn't good. Maybe he will change for

the better and life will be simple from now on. I still can't say I love him, but maybe one day. Who knows? Christian and Mark are happy. Why shouldn't I be? I've never been able to admit my feelings to anyone, but I still feel guilty. I feel like I'm cheating on Alex even though we aren't together. It still doesn't change how I feel though. I also want to say thank you for being a friend and always being there. You're the only person I have been able to talk to like this. The only person who truly knows what is going on."

Renee sent the message and sat back in her chair. Kevin wasn't online right now, so she knew he wouldn't respond. So she logged off and started playing her music.

*   *   *

Kevin logged on after his shift to see if Marie had messaged him since it had been days since he got on. Sure enough, there was a message from her. Looking at the date, she had sent it a few days ago. He pulled it up and couldn't believe what he was reading. 'Marie' was going on a damn honeymoon.

Moreover, with the 'boyfriend' who had been cruel to her and made her feel bad about herself. He had to stop this, but how? He couldn't shake the feeling that this was Renee, and she had reached out to him as Marie because she was too scared to tell him that it was her. She just had too many similarities to Renee. He sent a message back.

"Hey, Marie. I just got your message. It blew my mind to read what you wrote. Mark is a bad guy. You shouldn't settle for being with him. I know you feel like there is no way out of your situation, but there is. I will help you out of it. Please, don't do this. If you feel that guilty about being with this man, then you know it isn't right. Leave him and find Alex. You helped me by making me think about things I wanted to say to Renee. Let me do the same for you.

What would you want to say to Alex? I'll take over his side of the conversation. Once we have done that, really think about what you are doing, ok? I'm off tomorrow so I will stay logged on and we can chat if you do get online."

Kevin sent the message and logged off. He knew Marie wouldn't get back to him tonight. She only talked to him during the day. If this was Renee, then Jesse was out of the house during certain hours, and that was when she talked to him. Was there some way for him to find her? Was the name she was using listed anywhere? If this was Renee, then were all the names she used fake? He would have to start investigating this possibility. Maybe he could find 'Marie' that way.

*   *   *

Renee woke up and went through her daily routine. At lunch, she sat down with her computer in her lap. She had checked for a message from Kevin for the past couple of days, but he hadn't responded. When she logged on, she noticed Kevin was online, and there was a message from him. She read it and sighed.

"Kevin, I have told you that my situation isn't as simple as leaving. Don't you think I would have left by now if it was that simple? I never imagined my life would turn out like this, but it has. If I could go back in time and change it, I would, but that isn't possible. There is so much I want to say to Alex, but I can't go there. I have to let those thoughts and feelings go. I need to get over them."

"Then talk to me. Tell me everything you feel and want to say to Alex. And I mean EVERYTHING. Let it all out and see how you feel. Can you do that for me?"

"Ok, but I don't even know where to start."

"*Start from the beginning. Tell Alex how you felt when he left. Start from there up until now.*"

"*Alex, I have so much I want to say to you, but I'm sure it will come out as rambling. I don't really know how to process my feelings into a message. It's been a long time. When I was first separated from you, I was scared and lonely. I hated everything about what was happening to me. All I wanted was for you to come get me and hold me. I wanted you to take away the pain of what I was going through. Mark, the guy you hated, forced himself on me. He kept me locked up in the house all of the time. I was under so much stress that all I wanted to do was die. I was tired of being forced into sex. When I realized that I may be pregnant, I was scared. I couldn't face the fact that the monster I was with had impregnated me. He was actually happy about the baby. That was something I wasn't expecting. For some reason, the baby made him change somewhat, but I hated him. I couldn't move past that. He wanted me to be with him, but I never wanted that. I wanted you. It hurt me to know that I wouldn't have been in this situation if it weren't for you. For so long, I felt rage, hatred, depression, sadness, and love.*"

"*I found out that the baby didn't belong to Mark. You have a son, Alex, and he looks just like you. His middle name is even Alexander. I'm always scared that Mark will one day realize that he isn't his son, but yours. I fear what he will do to him because he hates you so much. I didn't have a choice but to stay with Mark because I was scared of what he would do if I left. He's vindictive as I'm sure you are well aware. But the fact that I was pregnant made me choose to stay. There was no way I could run away while being pregnant. I had no money, no car, no phone, nothing. He made sure of it. I couldn't let him hunt me down and harm our baby. After a while, Mark started acting like he liked me. It took me off guard and I didn't know how to react to that.*"

"I had to pretend he was you to be with him. After a while, I think I just got over it and tried to live my life the best I could. I had to compromise a lot of myself to be where I am today. If it hadn't been for Christian, I think I would have taken my own life, but I couldn't do that to our son. Over the past few years, Mark really opened up to me. He showed me a side of him that I didn't think could exist, a loving side. If he hadn't had such a messed up past, I think he would have been a normal person and wouldn't have done what he did. But since he hated you, he wanted to destroy everything you had, which, unfortunately, included us, me. He succeeded. You are no longer here with me. I'll never see you again. And that alone hurts me more than you will ever know."

"I have been living with him as a normal couple would for years now. I care about him, and that makes me feel like an idiot. Who cares about someone who tormented them? It makes me feel guilty because I feel like I betrayed you. How can you say you love someone and choose to be with a different person? What kind of sick person cares about someone who is abusive to them?"

"I wanted you to know that not a day has gone by that I haven't thought about you. I always wonder what you would think of me. I wonder if you would hate me for choosing this life. Would you think I was as sick as he is? I must be sick to stay with someone like him, right? I often wonder if you would even still want me since I have been with him all of this time. Who could love someone who chose not to reach out to them and try to get them back in their life? Do you still love me? Or did you forget about me? I don't expect you to want me, and I can understand if you don't. But know this, I will always love you. However, I have to do what is best for everyone. Keeping you and our son safe is my main priority. I will always choose you two over myself. So, if being with Mark permanently does that, then so be it."

Kevin read everything that was sent. Tears welled in his eyes. Every word stabbed his heart a little more. He knew this was Renee in his heart, and she'd reached out to him. It had been so long that he had honestly thought she was dead. He knew there was no way Jesse had kept her alive, not even to torture him. In a way, this was worse than thinking Renee was dead. She was alive and living a life with Jesse, a life that should have been his. And on top of that, she cared about Jesse. She had described Christian and said he looked like his father. Him. He was Christian's father. That realization stunned him. Renee had been pregnant when she had been taken.

He thought back to their conversation when she had 'pretended' to be Renee. She had been describing what her life had been like. He had reacted badly to that. Now, it was showing what she thought about his reaction. It made her feel like he didn't want her. How could he get her to tell him it was her? How could he make her see that he still loved her and wanted her? She had to know that by now, right? They had been talking for five months, and most of that time had been him talking about how he still loved Renee.

"Marie, I'm glad you reached out to me. Reading what you wrote to me tore my heart to shreds. I felt a stabbing pain with each line. I never would have chosen to leave you. I never wanted to be apart from you. You were my whole world and still are. I love you, always have. I would never choose for you to live with someone else. I wish you would have reached out to me as soon as you were able. I would have come to get you if I had known what was happening. I know everything that has happened is my fault. I'm sorry just doesn't cut it and I know that. I would spend the rest of my life making it up to you if you would let me."

"I have a son. God, I hate that I have missed his life and yours. I want us to be a family. I understand that you have done what you needed to do to survive. I understand that you have chosen to protect our son. All great mothers choose their children over themselves. However, please don't choose to stay because of

me. I can protect myself. I would NEVER want you to live in hell because you were scared something would happen to me. I choose you, baby, every day. Let me help you. I will fix this. You don't have to be afraid anymore. I will come and protect you. All you have to do is tell me where you are and I will come for you. You never have to worry about me not loving you."

"I can't say that I wasn't angry when I first read that you cared about this man after he abused you. But, I realize now that is just who you are. No matter what, you are always the one who cares too much. It's one of the best things about you and why I love you so much. No, I don't think you are sick because of it. I think you have come to think this is all life holds for you, but that isn't true. It holds so much more for you if you will just let it."

"You don't understand, Alex, that I can't tell you where I am. I could never put you or Christian at risk like that. Mark acts normal now, but I know his true nature. When someone hurts him, he snaps. You never see him coming. He will wait and then strike when you least expect it. I would live in constant fear of what he may do. I will be honest. He has threatened to track you down and torture you right before my eyes. I believe he would. I'm no longer being abused. Christian is safe, and so are you, so I choose to continue living the way it is. I know you don't understand that. I know you think you can handle the situation, but I don't think you can. I'm sorry if that hurts you, but I can't live with myself if you get hurt."

"Neither of us was prepared for this, but it is what it is. I have been Mark's 'wife' in every sense of the word for years. In order for me to stay and be happy, I have to let you go. God, it hurts to even write that. I feel like I am being ripped apart. This is so much harder than I thought it would be. But, I have decided to be happy, even if it is only a little bit. Goodbye, my love."

Renee wiped her eyes, trying to see as she hit the send button. This was so hard. Kevin had written out that message from 'Alex' like he knew it was her. She often wondered about some of the things he said. Did he suspect it was her? It doesn't matter now. She had said everything she wanted to say, so it was done. If he did suspect it was her and was telling her what he truly felt, at least she knew he still loved her. She would hold on to that in a small place in her heart forever. She logged off, not even waiting for Kevin to finish typing.

Kevin sent his message. Marie wasn't typing, and it wasn't showing the message as read. He looked at her name, and it wasn't lit up anymore. He threw his phone and paced around the room. She'd told him goodbye. What was he supposed to do now? He punched the wall, leaving a hole in it. He was angry that she had given up on him. He was angry that she didn't believe he could protect her. He was angry that she had chosen Jesse and told him goodbye.

"You might not believe I can take him out and protect you, Renee, but I can. I will find you and I will kill that motherfucker," Kevin said as he punched another hole in the wall.

CHAPTER 27

The week flew by, and Jesse and Renee wound up at the airport. Hours of flying later, they arrived in Hawaii. Jesse took her to the luggage pickup. They had a while before dinner. He was going to suggest she got some rest when they got to the hotel. That would give him time to set everything up. They waited until the luggage came out, and he grabbed it. Then, they proceeded to get the car rental.

Arriving at the hotel, Renee got into bed with him right behind her. He snuggled up to her back and waited until he knew she was asleep. He got out of bed slowly, so he didn't wake her up. He unpacked the suitcase, so he could hang her dress up and remove any wrinkles from it. He took out his dress clothes and hung those up as well.

He checked to make sure Renee was still asleep and went down to the front desk. He looked at their menu and placed an order for room service to arrive at 4 pm. The ceremony was to take place at 7. That should give them plenty of time to eat and get ready. He went back upstairs and took a shower. He set the alarm to wake Renee up at 3. That would give her a few hours of sleep.

He called the venue to confirm the ceremony and make sure everything was ready. He'd set up the vacation like he did because Tabitha and Mark had a marriage license stating they got married on December 5th. So he wanted to renew their vows officially. Although he couldn't marry Renee as himself, he was still excited about this plan.

At 3 o'clock, the alarm went off. Jesse came into the room and shut the alarm off as Renee got up. Jesse sat in the suite watching TV. Renee sat beside him, snuggling into his side.

"Why don't you go hop in the shower? I made plans for tonight. Dinner will be here in less than an hour."

"Why are we eating so early?"

"Because I have a surprise for you later. And I don't want to be late. As much as I'm enjoying you pressing into me, I really want to show you my surprise."

"Ok. I'm going," Renee whined.

Renee grabbed her toiletries. The shower helped wake her up. It always took her about an hour to shower and get ready because her hair was so long, but Jesse said dinner was in less than an hour. She'd tried to be quicker, but it hadn't worked. She'd just throw a shirt on with her boy shorts. It's not like they were going out for dinner. Her hair was still drying, so if the shirt got a little wet, it wouldn't matter. She opened the bedroom door to find Jesse waiting on her.

He was all dressed up. Renee looked him over, starting with the crisp white shirt under a black vest. It was short-sleeved, so it showed off the tattoos on his forearms. Damn, he even had on a tie! The black dress pants hugged his hips and were somewhat loose on his legs. He'd even shined his black dress shoes. His hair was slicked back, so it was away from his face and had a shine to it. He looked good.

And here she was in underwear and a shirt. She felt underdressed, but he just smiled at her and held out his hand. Renee took it, and he led her out to the balcony, where there was a table with covered dishes, two wine glasses, and a bottle of wine being chilled. There was a single rose in a vase in the middle of the table. The view of the beach and the ocean was a fantastic backdrop.

"Wow. This is gorgeous."

"It could never be more beautiful than the woman sitting in front of me."

"Thanks, but I am totally underdressed compared to you," Renee said as she looked him over again.

He was mouthwatering in what he was wearing. The sun was shining on him, making his black hair have purple streaks in it. Jesse didn't really plan romantic dinners. Especially not ones where he dressed up. He usually only did that at Renee's request. So the fact that he said he'd planned out a surprise for her and this was part of it had taken her completely off guard.

Jesse took the covers off the food and poured the wine. They ate and talked, but he seemed nervous. After dinner, he took Renee's hand in his. He had a slight shake of his hands. Renee raised an eyebrow at him.

"Renee, I know I haven't been a good man for you. I've screwed up so many times that we've both lost count. I want things to work between us because you've already said you aren't going anywhere. I don't want you to be sad or fearful. I want you to feel loved because I do love you. I've been thinking about things a lot lately."

"I know you don't love me, but I know you do care about me. More than you want to admit, but you show it with the things you do for me. It's time I start showing you I love you. No more threats, no more empty promises, no more lack of trust. On paper we are married as Mark and Tabitha Morgan, but you never got to have a wedding or a honeymoon.

I scheduled this honeymoon like I did because today is technically their anniversary. They've been together for six years but you've been with me for five. I want to give you everything you deserve. If I could marry you as myself I would in a heartbeat. I also realized when I sprung your wedding bands on you that I could have done better."

"So, Renee, will you marry me?" Jesse said as he got down on one knee and held up the engagement ring he had initially given her.

Renee was shocked. Not only had Jesse planned out a beautiful dinner, but he had proposed to her. Furthermore, what he'd said was so sweet. He'd put so much thought into this vacation. However, she still felt guilty because it wasn't Kevin proposing to her.

Renee felt tears spring to her eyes as she thought about what this meant if she said yes. She bit her lip. Jesse just sat there on one knee, patiently waiting. She was never going to be with Kevin, and she knew it. Would this make things better if she 'married' Jesse as Mark?

"Yes," Renee breathed out.

Jesse put the ring on her finger and pulled her out of the chair. He kissed her long and hard. He leaned back so her feet were off the ground, and she jumped, wrapping her legs around him. He carried her into the bedroom and kissed her again before setting her down on the bed. Renee was surprised when he walked off. She figured he'd take her. Instead, he walked over to the closet and opened it. He grabbed out a dress bag and brought it over to her.

"I'd like for you to get dressed and do your hair and makeup, please."

He lay a pair of white sandals with straps on the bed. Little jewels were decorating the top strap. They looked fancy. Renee unzipped the bag and saw the dress she'd fallen in love with at the shop. Her head jerked up as she looked at Jesse. Was that why he was so dressed up?

"What am I missing?"

"You'll see. Will you please get dressed? I really don't want to be late for the surprise."

"Ok," Renee said as she walked over to her luggage.

She grabbed out some nice lingerie and walked over to the bed. She stripped down as Jesse walked out of the room. She noticed he had a small bag with him. Her curiosity was up.

She put her underclothes on and then slid the dress on. Once the sandals were on, she took a look at herself in the mirror. She sighed. Her eyes widened as she realized she looked like a bride. Was Jesse planning on them getting married? Was this what all of this was about? If so, there was nothing she could do anyway.

She applied her makeup and curled her hair. She pinned the sides back but left the rest to flow down her back in loose curls. When she was ready, she stepped out of the suite. She didn't see Jesse. She opened the door to the room. Instead of Jesse, a man was standing there.

"Are you ready, miss?"

"Um, I'm looking for my husband."

"Yes. I'm Lelo. I'm going to take you to Mr. Morgan. Please, come with me," Lelo said as he held his arm out.

Renee was a little nervous as she didn't know this man, but she put her hand on his arm, and he walked her out of the hotel. There was a car waiting outside. He opened the back door for her, and she got in. Her nervousness really kicked in when they drove for over thirty minutes and still hadn't stopped. Finally, they came to one of the most beautiful places she had ever seen. There was lush greenery and trees. The sun had set, so tiki torches were lighting up a pathway.

Lelo helped her out of the car and put a veil on her that was cathedral style. It was white lace and went all the way down to her ankles. He handed her a bouquet that contained hibiscus and plumeria. He held out his arm again, and she took it. He walked her down the pathway. The earthy trail turned into sand.

She looked up and saw the sand leading to the beach. There was an archway covered in Hawaiian Lilies and Naupaka. In front of that archway were Jesse and an older gentleman. Off to the side were several men who started playing the ukulele and a one hand ihu, which looked like a flute. The music was almost haunting but so beautiful.

Renee felt her eyes fill with tears. The wedding was beautiful, but Kevin wasn't the one standing there waiting for her. Instead, she walked this path to Jesse, to a man she didn't love. She never would have dreamed she was getting married like this, with a fake name, no family, and without the man she loved. She closed her eyes, trying to stop the tears from falling. Lelo smiled at her as she sniffled. He thought she was holding in happy tears. She gave him a weak smile.

He walked her down to Jesse. The officiant asked who gave her away, and Lelo said he did. He then placed her hand in Jesse's. Jesse was grinning from ear to ear. Renee gave him a half-hearted smile. She had to give Jesse credit; he surprised her with this one. Never in a million years would she have guessed that he not only planned out a honeymoon but also the proposal and marriage. Now, they really would be on a honeymoon-Mark and Tabitha's.

Lelo went to stand by Jesse. A woman that was standing behind her took her bouquet. Renee had to admit that it was a beautiful 'wedding' the way Jesse had set it up. The tiki torches on either side of the archway provided just enough light. It left the full moon reflecting on the ocean as they had a nighttime wedding. The officiant said his part and had them repeat their vows after him. They exchanged rings.

"By the power invested in me by the state of Hawaii, I now pronounce you man and wife. You may kiss the bride."

Jesse put his hands on the sides of her face and kissed her. Renee burst into tears, no longer able to contain them. Jesse pulled back and ran his thumbs across her cheeks, wiping away the tears.

"I can't tell if those are happy tears or sad tears," Jesse whispered.

"A little bit of both," Renee whispered back.

The woman behind Renee handed her the bouquet back, and Jesse took her other hand, lacing his fingers through hers. He walked her over to a nearby table with a small cake on it. He sat her down as everyone left but a photographer. He took pictures of them cutting the cake and feeding each other a piece. She was waiting for Jesse's temper to come out, but she knew it wouldn't happen while people were around. Once the photographer left, Jesse turned to her.

Here it comes, she thought to herself.

"Why would you be crying sad tears? I thought this would make you happy."

"It was a beautiful ceremony, Jesse. You put so much thought and effort into this. I appreciate every bit of it, but you know why this makes me sad. I don't want to ruin tonight, ok? Can we just forget about it?"

Jesse took a deep breath and let it out slowly. She was sad because he wasn't whom she wanted to marry. He wanted to feel anger, but all he felt was pain. She might as well have stabbed him in the heart. He had done all of this just for her, hoping it would change things. He'd hoped that she would finally accept her life with him as her husband. Finally, he stood up and walked down to the beach, shoving his hands in his pockets. After a few minutes, Jesse felt Renee wrap her arms around him, pressing her body into his back.

"I'm sorry. I've decided to let go of the past and move forward. I guess everything just hit me all at once. I didn't mean to hurt you."

Jesse stood there for a while with her pressed against him. He didn't know what to say. He'd never felt like this before. He had to let go of his fear of losing her. He loved her. And that love was killing him. Even though she was here with him physically, mentally and emotionally, she would always be with Kevin. And that shattered him more than he could have ever imagined. He wasn't a good man. He indeed was a monster as he wanted to kill her love for Kevin like she was killing him. It was taking everything in him not to go back to his old ways and hunt Kevin down because he was again taking something away from him.

Rationally, he knew that Renee had never been his in the first place. But the irrational part of him only saw that she belonged to him now, not Kevin. And Kevin was taking someone he loved away from him all over again. He hated that motherfucker with a passion that even scared him. He sighed and turned in Renee's arms. She ran her hand across his cheek and stood up on her toes to kiss him.

"I realize now that no matter what I do, it will never be good enough. I love you, Renee, I really do. When you're ready to leave, let me know," Jesse said as he pulled out of her arms and walked away.

Renee felt confused. Why did it hurt her heart to see Jesse like this? She stood there for a long time, trying to sort out her feelings. She liked that Jesse had put this together for her. Even when she had cried because she wasn't marrying Kevin, he hadn't gotten mad. Had he truly changed? She had hurt him deeply. She turned back to the trail leading up to the table. Jesse was just sitting there.

She walked up to the table. Jesse didn't look at her until she stepped right in front of him. Once he was looking at her, she held out her hand. She had to make things right. It wasn't fair of her to expect him to change and be better for her when she couldn't even appreciate what he had done for her tonight.

"Will you dance with me as my husband?"

Jesse stared at her hand for a minute, but he eventually took it. She put one hand on his chest and the other on his shoulder. He wrapped his arms around her.

"We don't even have any music."

"That's ok. I'll sing to you."

"Why would you even want to dance with me? It's obvious you don't want me."

"How do you feel right now, Jesse?"

"You already know."

"I want to hear you tell me."

"I'm upset and sad. I did all of this for you and all you can do is think about someone else. It kills me that I love you so much and you don't give a damn about me."

"So, you feel sad because you can't have the one you love, right?"

"I guess. I don't know. I guess I just thought this would change things between us. I thought if I showed you how much I truly loved you, that you could finally be happy with me."

"Jesse, think about what you just told me. It upsets you that you can't have the one you love. I feel the same way and have for a long time. I have resolved to be happy with my life, but it isn't the life I chose. But, before tonight, I didn't think you truly loved me because you didn't know what love was. But after all of this, I believe you do love me. I didn't even think you were capable of doing something like this. It was a beautiful, grand gesture. I love it. I don't know what tomorrow holds, but for tonight, I'm all yours. No thinking about anyone else or what might have been. It's just you and me, ok? We start our lives together right here, right now, at this moment."

Jesse let out the breath he'd been holding and pulled her close. She sang I'll Stand By You as they danced their first dance. He felt the pain ease a little as she rested her head on his shoulder and pressed into him. He could feel her voice in his chest, and it made his heart beat faster as he listened to the song she had chosen to sing for him. For tonight at least, she was choosing him. He would have to deal with his feelings later.

CHAPTER 28

Renee pulled back from Jesse after she finished the song. She pecked his lips and took his hand, dragging him to the beach. She took off her sandals and her veil. She lay them on the ground and reached under her dress. She took her panties off and slipped the garter belt off. She quickly slid her panties back on. She began to take her dress off.

"What are you doing?"

"I'm going to get in the water. Care to join me?" Renee asked as she put the thigh highs and garter belt in her pile.

"Right now? You don't even have a bathing suit on."

"Neither do you."

Renee stepped out of her dress, leaving it where it was. She turned to look at Jesse, and he looked her over. He went to reach for her so she would put her clothes back on, but she sidestepped him and ran towards the water. Jesse quickly stripped to his boxers, chasing after her.

Renee was standing in the water up to her knees. When Jesse came toward her, she ran up the beach. He ran after her, and she laughed. As he got close, she veered into the water. She splashed water at him as he picked her up and spun her around. He took her deeper into the water as he shifted her, so she was against his chest. He got an evil grin as he stopped waist-deep in the water.

"What are you planning?"

Renee knew what he was doing when she felt him lift her and push his arms out. He'd thrown her in the water! She quickly plugged her nose. She stayed under the water and swam until she felt his body. He reached down for her, but she quickly swam behind him. She came up and jumped on him. He stood firm. He didn't budge a bit when she tried to dunk him. He just laughed at her.

"I can't believe you threw me!" Renee cried.

She let go of him and started to get out of the water. Jesse followed her and pulled her back, turning her towards him as he did.

"I thought it was funny. But, damn, if you don't look sexy as hell all wet," Jesse said as he kissed her.

"I probably look like a wet mop with my makeup running and hair all over the place," Renee pouted.

Jesse pulled her against him and ground his hips into her. She wrapped her legs around his waist and her arms around his neck as she pressed further into him. He walked out of the water, carrying her to the beach. Renee let go of him, and Jesse started to pick up his clothes to get dressed. Renee wasn't having that. She wanted to stay on the beach a little bit longer. She smiled as she started running off.

"Renee! Come back here! We're leaving!"

"Catch me if you can!"

She ran down the beach and veered left and right as Jesse started to catch up with her. Jesse felt his fingertips touch her skin as he almost caught her. Her hair was floating out behind her as the wind had caught it. He heard a throaty laugh drift back towards him, and he groaned. He'd only heard that laugh out of Renee a handful of times. It was music to his ears.

Renee ran into a small grouping of trees near the end of the beach. Jesse didn't see her after that. Where had she gone? He saw a grouping of rocks with an outlook point and what almost looked like a cave entrance. He slowly walked up there, thinking she was hiding there.

"If you can catch me, you can have me," he heard Renee call behind him.

Jesse turned and saw her standing in the trees, waving at him, topless. Jesse's eyebrows shot up as she started pushing her panties down. He was even more turned on than before, but he also didn't like the idea of her running around naked where someone might see her. He started walking towards her, and she waited until he was halfway there and took off running.

So, she wanted to be chased? He'd chase her and fuck the shit out of her when he caught her. He took off running at full speed. He broke through the trees and saw Renee by the water. She grinned and took off running as he got close.

She hollered behind her, "I guess you don't want me since you haven't caught me!"

Jesse heard that throaty laugh again as she taunted him. He kicked up the pace and got very close to her. She squealed as he again brushed his fingertips across her back. Finally, he gave it everything he had and caught her, pulling her back against him, so her body wound up slamming into his. It took his breath away, but he pushed through it and turned her towards him. She was grinning from ear to ear.

"Caught you," Jesse said with a low, menacing growl as he kissed her hard and yanked her against him.

He let go of her long enough to push his boxers down without breaking the kiss. He grabbed her ass and pulled up on her so she would wrap her legs around him. When she did, he lowered them down to the sand. He shoved himself deep inside of her, taking her hard and fast. He kissed down her neck, sucking and licking as he went. Renee moaned in his ear as he pounded into her body.

"You like being chased and fucked, Renee? You were already so wet for me," Jesse said as he pulled out of her and slammed back in.

"Yes," Renee breathed out as he again pulled out and slammed back into her.

Jesse looked into her eyes as he grabbed her shoulders, holding her body tight to his as he moved harder and faster. He watched as her facial expressions changed, and he knew she was getting close. She was so fucking tight that he had to fuck her harder just to get deeper inside of her. He kissed her, and she kissed him back as he thrust his tongue in her mouth, their tongues battling. It was the most passionate kiss they'd ever had.

Renee pushed her fingers through his hair. Her grip tightened as she screamed her pleasure into his mouth as she came. Jesse broke the kiss and put his face in her neck. He groaned as he came, but he didn't stop. He kept going until she was starting to build back up, and so was he. So they went for round two without ever stopping from round one.

Jesse reached in between them and started rubbing her clit. Renee's hips bucked off the sand. She pulled him down and kissed him again, sucking on his bottom lip. She let go of his lip and started kissing and licking his neck. His body spasmed in response, and she grinned. She moved back up and started nibbling on his ear. His fingers started moving faster.

"You like that, Jesse? You like my mouth and tongue on you while my pussy is wrapped all around you?" Renee said, breathing in his ear.

Jesse felt a shiver go through him at her words. She'd never talked dirty to him without him making her do it. And even then, it was just to make her beg for what she wanted. He felt her pussy clench around him and knew she was doing that on purpose, not just reacting to the sex. It felt so damn good.

"I love everything you do, Renee. I can never get enough of you."

"I've never had sex on a beach before. I find it makes me hornier to know we could get caught. You going to put that fire out for me? If so, you need to fuck me harder and make me cum hard," Renee said as she licked her way back down his neck to his chest.

"You are going to be the death of me," Jesse growled and gave her what she wanted.

Renee continued to kiss his chest as her hands moved over his back and down to his ass. She squeezed it and pushed forward, pushing him deeper into her. He groaned. He was not used to Renee being this aggressive. He wasn't sure what had changed, but he liked it. His fingers quickened as he was drawing close to cumming again. Renee was thrusting her hips up into him with each thrust. Her breasts were rubbing his chest as she kissed his mouth.

She broke the kiss, and her hands were on his back, gripping him as her body pressed entirely against him. He lost it when she screamed his name as she came hard. He shoved himself in deep and came for her. He lay his head on her shoulder, trying to catch his breath. Renee was still wrapped all around him, and he loved it. When he finally caught his breath, he kissed her lips softly and got off her. She stayed on the sand with her eyes closed.

"I'm going to get your underclothes," Jesse said as he grabbed his boxers and put them back on.

"Ok. I'm going to lay here a little bit longer."

Jesse stood there for just a minute, looking at her. The moonlight was hitting her, making her skin glow. She had a slight smile on her face. He almost wanted to retake her, but he knew he would need a few minutes before he could do that. Plus, he needed to get her back to the hotel. He sighed and walked back to the grove of trees and searched for her underclothes. He found them and headed back to where she was.

He didn't see her lying on the beach anymore. He looked up and down it but didn't see her anywhere. Then, when he got close to where he thought they had been, he saw footprints. His eyes followed them right down to where they stopped at the water's edge. He searched the water and found her floating on top of it. Surrounded by the water, her skin was pale, and her hair blended in with it. He dropped her underclothes and stripped his boxers back off. He walked into the water and stopped where she was floating.

She had her ankles crossed and her arms out wide. She was just staring up at the night sky with a beautiful smile. She looked satisfied. He moved next to her side and put his hands under her. He began to turn in little circles, so she was spinning in the water. Her eyes turned towards him, and he smiled. She smiled back. He stopped after a few minutes, letting her settle back into floating. She wrapped one arm around his waist, staying against his side.

"Are you happy, Renee?" Jesse asked, his curiosity getting to him.

Renee looked at him and said, "Yes, I'm happy."

"Are you just happy because of where you are? Or are you actually happy with everything?"

"Do you want to know if I'm happy with you, Jesse?"

"I'm not sure if I really want to hear your answer."

Renee stood up in the water and put her hands on the sides of his face as she said, "I'm happy. You did something beautiful for me tonight. Something I never would have expected from you. Instead of treating me like your prisoner, or your possession, and expecting me to marry you, you asked me to marry you. You got the dress that I loved because you knew I loved it. You gave me a proposal, a wedding, and a honeymoon because you knew it was something I wanted. I can't give you what you want and say I love you, but yes, I'm happy, Jesse. I'm happy with you."

Jesse felt a thrill go through him. She was right, he did want her to love him, but the fact that she was happy with him was a significant improvement. When he had asked her if she was happy with him on her birthday, she hadn't been able to say yes. She'd been happy with the changes he had made, but not with him. She had not only agreed to marry him but had married him. His fear of losing her dissipated as he knew she wouldn't leave him. Renee agreeing to be his wife and putting her past behind her for good changed something inside of him. He felt different.

"Thank you. It makes me happy to know that you are happy with me. I've been trying so hard to make you happy, to hold my temper, and not screw up. I wasn't sure if it was making a difference or not."

"It's made a difference. I honestly thought you were going to lose it earlier, but you didn't. When we were at the airport, I know you thought I had taken off. You still don't trust me. I was hoping after all this time that I could have left but didn't, that would change, but it hasn't. But, I'm not scared that you are going to hurt me physically anymore. I'm not afraid to say what I think or feel anymore. Just as you were hoping this honeymoon changed things between us, so was I. I've officially accepted being your wife. Does that make you happy, Jesse?"

"More than you will ever know," Jesse said as he leaned his forehead against hers.

Renee took his hand and led him out of the water. She started to sit on the beach, but he stopped her. He sat down and tugged on her hand to get her to sit in his lap, which she did. He wrapped his arms around her. They sat for a while, watching the water as it went in and out. There was a slight breeze. The moon and the stars were beautiful. Renee snuggled into Jesse's chest. His hands began to wander up to her breasts.

He lazily played with her nipples as they sat there. Renee shifted on his lap. Jesse groaned as she reached behind her and began to play with him. She took his hands off her breasts and turned around, facing him on his lap. She reached in between them and began to play with him again until he was ready to go.

Jesse moved back slightly so he could take her breast in his mouth. He sucked and licked her nipple until it was hard. His other hand went down and played with her clit. Renee moaned as she arched her back, pushing her breast further into his mouth. She suddenly moved, so she had his dick positioned at her entrance. She shoved down on him, so he was inside of her.

"I love it when you come on to me."

"Yeah? Do you like it when I grind my pussy all over your dick like this?" Renee said as she rolled her hips and slid back and forth on him.

"Hell, yeah," Jesse said as he cupped her butt, thrusting his hips.

"I think instead of talking, you need to put that mouth to better use," Renee said as she pulled his head towards her breasts.

Jesse greedily took her breast in his mouth as he played with the other one. He switched over to the other breast with his mouth as he switched hands to play with the one he had just left. Renee was riding him slowly at first, but then she pushed on his chest. He let go of her breast and looked at her. She pushed on his chest again, leaning her body forward simultaneously. He lay back on the sand, and she leaned over him, grinding her body even faster on top of his. Occasionally, she would move up his shaft and come back down before coming entirely off him.

She kept her hands on his chest for leverage but threw her head back as she got close to her orgasm. Jesse grabbed her breasts and played with them as she rode him faster and faster. Then, he started thrusting his hips up and holding them up as she ground into him.

"Oh yes!" Renee cried out as she tightened around him.

Jesse started rocking his hips which were, in turn, bouncing Renee. Her nails dug into his chest as cries of pleasure escaped her. Just the sounds she was making were driving him crazy. He watched her face as she orgasmed but kept going to make sure he got off. He grabbed her hips and slammed himself into her repeatedly as she ground into him as hard as possible. She bit her lip to keep from screaming as the waves of pleasure hit her. Finally, when he came, she slowed her grinding down but kept going.

"Feel better?" Jesse asked.

"Mmhm," Renee moaned.

"I'd better get you back to the hotel or we are going to be here all night having sex."

"I guess you're right," Renee sighed as she got up.

Jesse stood up and grabbed his boxers. He put them on while Renee pulled her panties on. She walked by him, still topless. She stepped into her dress without putting her bra back on. Guess she wanted to get back to the hotel quickly, too. She didn't even bother to put her sandals back on. Instead, she gathered everything up and walked up the trail towards the table.

Jesse walked beside her, taking her to the car. Renee stopped at the top of the trail and looked back at the arch where they had gotten married as Mark and Tabitha Morgan. A small smile played on her lips as she turned back towards him. Jesse couldn't help but smile. She'd hurt him earlier by crying over him not being Kevin, but she had told him she was letting go of the past. She was going to move on with him, which made him extremely happy.

CHAPTER 29

Jesse woke up and felt the empty bed beside him. He sat up and looked around the room. It had to be mid-afternoon, judging by the sun. Then, he saw a note with his name on it. He opened it and smiled.

"Jesse,

I went out to the beach. I wanted to let you sleep in but didn't want you to worry when you found I was gone. Come find me if you want. We can have lunch.

XOXOXOXOXO

Renee"

She'd even kissed the letter. He liked that she'd left the letter for him. Their honeymoon officially started last night, and things had improved drastically. Since he'd fallen for Renee, he felt that they would work out for the first time.

He went out to the beach. He found Renee walking up the beach, her feet on the water's edge. She had on a sundress that stopped at her knees. Her hair was put up in a clip. He watched as she walked back up the beach and sat on a towel. She turned her face to the sun, and he couldn't help but lose his breath. She was so beautiful, and she was all his. He walked up and sat behind her, putting his arms around her.

"Good afternoon, hubby," Renee said as she leaned back into him.

Jesse felt thrilled that she had called him hubby. He kissed the top of her head and pulled her back against him.

"Good morning, wife. How did you know it was me?"

"Your soap has a certain scent. I love the way it smells. Plus, I know the way your body feels against mine."

Jesse held her tighter. Everything she said made him want her more. They sat for a while, enjoying the sun, the breeze, and each other's company. Jesse laughed as he heard Renee's stomach growl. She looked over her shoulder, trying to glare at him. That just made him laugh even harder.

"Keep that up, mister, and you won't be getting any tonight," Renee said as she turned forward.

"I'm not worried about that. All I have to do is create the problem and eventually you'll come to me to fix it."

"Or I can just take care of myself while you have to sit and watch, and not participate."

"Keep teasing me and you won't get lunch. Your mouth will be full of something else," Jesse teased as he played with her breasts.

"I think it's you who will have a mouth full. You have to eat your food before you get dessert. But I think dessert might be too much for you," Renee teased him back.

Damn, she had a way of turning him on without even touching him. He liked that she was going back and forth with him, teasing each other with no fear of repercussions. He stood up and pulled her up. He took the towel off the ground as she raised an eyebrow at him.

"What are you doing?" Renee asked.

"I'm taking my lunch to go," Jesse said as he threw her over his shoulder.

"Jesse! I can walk," Renee squealed as she grabbed the back of his shirt.

Renee was struggling to get him to put her down. He smacked her ass, and she moaned for him. Jesse strolled through the hotel without caring that some of the other guests were looking at them. Some of the guys grinned as they knew what he was doing. When the elevator stopped on their floor, he opened their door and went to the bedroom.

He threw her on the bed, crawling on top of her. The look on her face was one of lust, not fear. It made him want her even more that she was no longer afraid. Instead, he worshiped her body from head to toe before claiming it with his own. They wound up ordering room service hours later.

*　　*　　*

The day before they left, Jesse sprung another surprise on her. He made sure she wore shorts, a tank top, and sneakers. Then, they walked down to the lobby and out to the car. Renee wasn't sure what was going on. Jesse refused to tell her where they were going.

They drove for an hour to a completely different part of the island. Finally, Jesse opened her door for her as they pulled up in front of a hut. Renee got out, and her attention immediately fell on the four-wheelers sitting there. She got all excited just seeing them and hoping this was her surprise.

Jesse walked up to the man sitting in the hut and told him his name. The man started discussing something with him, but all Renee could do was go check out the four-wheelers. There was stuff packed on them.

"You ready to go?" Jesse asked as he walked up.

"Where are we going?" Renee asked as she looked around.

"You'll see," Jesse grinned.

He walked over to the four-wheelers and cranked them. Renee was confused as there was stuff on the four-wheelers.

"Alright. Hop on."

"What's all the stuff tied to the four-wheelers?"

"You'll see. Stop worrying about it and hop on. I told you I had a surprise for you. This is part of it. You'll see the rest later."

Renee got on the four-wheeler and closed her eyes. She felt it idling under her and grinned as she revved the engine. She opened her eyes and saw Jesse watching her. He got on the other four-wheeler. She popped the four-wheeler in gear and did a U-turn on it, speeding off. She didn't know the terrain, so she kept a constant eye out for any danger. She enjoyed the feeling of freedom and the wind blowing through her hair. She'd missed this. Jesse caught up to her, and they rode for an hour before he told her to stop.

"We are going somewhere specific. The guy gave me a map. Judging by the way we have been riding around, we need to go right and find this path."

Renee studied the map so she knew where to go. Once she thought she had it figured out, she took off. They rode for another hour, just playing around on the four-wheelers. When they finally got to a specific spot, they pulled over and had lunch. She took pictures of the island as they went along. There was a waterfall in the middle of a lush forest.

Once they were done eating, Jesse took a bag off the four-wheeler and brought it over to her. It had a bathing suit for her and a pair of trunks for him. There were also two towels in it. They went to an overgrowth of rock and moss and went behind it. He started stripping down, so Renee did too. The bathing suit was a skimpy two-piece.

"Jesse, there isn't much material to this bathing suit. Where did it come from?"

"I arranged all of this before we came. I gave them your size and mine and they put everything together. I like the way it looks," Jesse said as he turned her around to check it out.

The bottom part came halfway down her butt and had strings on the sides. The top had a small strap tied behind her back and around her neck. Jesse took her down to the water, and they went swimming for a while. Renee went over to the waterfall and put her hand through it. She found there was a cave behind it.

She grabbed Jesse and pulled him into the cave. It was just big enough to hide behind the waterfall. Jesse wrapped her up in his arms and kissed her. She felt his fingers slide under the bottom of her suit and inside her. He moved them so she was pressed up against the cave wall. Renee reached down and pushed his trunks down enough to free him of them.

Jesse held her bottoms to the side and slid inside her folds, thrusting into her as his free hand gripped the rock, giving him leverage. Renee wrapped her legs around him, pushing her heels into his butt. Jesse took his time and moved slow and steady, building her up at a slow pace. It was sensual and pleasing, not rushed in any way. When they got close, he picked up the pace. Renee gripped his shoulders as her cry of pleasure was muffled by the sound of the waterfall. Jesse kissed her as he released inside her.

He pulled out of her and moved her bathing suit back in place. He pulled his trunks up, and they came out of the waterfall. They floated around for a while before they got out. They packed everything up, and Jesse looked at the map to find their next destination.

They arrived at a little ranch. A man showed Jesse over to an area, and he started grabbing stuff off his four-wheeler. Renee realized it was a tent big enough for two. Jesse got a blanket out of the bag and took it into the tent. While he was setting everything up, a woman approached her.

"Would you like to hula dance with us tonight?"

"I don't know how to do that."

"We will teach you. Come with us. Mr. Morgan can go on the boar hunt with the men."

Renee walked up to Jesse and said, "Mark, do you want to go on a boar hunt? This lady is going to hang out with me while you go if you want to."

Jesse thought about it. He agreed to go on the boar hunt, and Renee pecked his lips. She walked off with the woman as Jesse left with the group of men.

A few hours later, they returned with a boar. They set the boar on spokes in the ground and left it to cook over the hot coals. Then, they sat around and started drinking. When they were ready to get the party started, they took Jesse into the house, making him remove his shoes.

They wrapped him in a traditional loincloth over his trunks. When they came back out, there was a table laden with food and a fire burning. The men gathered around and got the boar off the spit. They placed it on the table as the women came out of another house.

Jesse's eyes widened as he saw Renee come out of the house with the women. She had on a grass skirt and a lei over her bare breasts. Her hair flowed down her back and had a crown of flowers wrapped in it. There were flower bracelets on her wrists and ankles. She was gorgeous. How could the men allow their women to go topless like that? Renee's face was flushed.

The men started dancing and singing as he sat and watched. The women stood by and waited for the men to finish. Once they were done, the women danced, including Renee. He couldn't take his eyes off of her graceful movements. He watched as her hips swayed to the music being played by the men. He knew that the dance was probably their way of giving thanks or some other tradition, but to him, it was erotic because of the way Renee looked and moved.

Once the dances were over, they all ate. The women served their men first and then fixed their food. Renee came over and put his plate in front of him. He smiled and thanked her, unable to keep his eyes off her. She blushed at the way he was looking at her. She'd felt awkward coming out half-naked, but Jesse hadn't taken it out of the way, which had surprised her. The women had told her that she was allowed to keep the grass skirt and lei. Perhaps she could dress up like this for him again.

Once the party wound down, Renee helped clean up while the men sat and talked and drank the night away. Finally, they all sat around a big bonfire, and Renee felt content. She had missed this. It wasn't the traditional bonfire she was used to, but it was still good. Jesse had planned an amazing surprise for her today. He was sitting on the ground behind her with his arms wrapped around her.

"Did you have fun today?" Jesse asked.

"I did. Today was amazing. I even learned how to hula dance."

"I'm glad you enjoyed it. I wanted you to have good memories of us. I hope I've accomplished that since we have to get ready to leave tomorrow," Jesse said as he nibbled on her ear.

"You accomplished everything you set out to do this week. I have good memories of us," Renee said as she turned her head to look at him over her shoulder.

She felt a shiver run down her spine as she saw the primal look in his eyes. He moved forward and kissed her. His fingertips slid up her sides, grazing the sides of her breasts. He moved them over her shoulders and down her arms. They lazily came back up her arms, over her shoulders, and down the sides of her back. He broke the kiss, and she knew by the look on his face that he had other things in mind.

Jesse stood up and held out his hand. She took it, and he pulled her up. They walked over to their tent, and he opened the door for her. The tent wasn't huge, but Jesse managed to get them undressed and lay on top of her. He kissed and licked her body until she was panting from need. He kissed her lips, covering any sound she made and thrust into her. They made love most of the night until they were both tired.

CHAPTER 30

"Hello?"

"Hey, Tabitha."

"Hey, Valerie! Getting nervous? Your wedding isn't too far away."

"Not really. I'm excited. Anyway, I called to invite you to my bachelorette party. It's going to be the Saturday before my wedding."

"You're having a bachelorette party the day after Christmas?"

"Yeah, why not?"

"Well, ok. What time is it and where is it going to be?" Renee asked.

"Just be at my house by seven. Kristy said we're all going to leave from there. And bring Christian. He can stay over with David. Also, what are you guys doing for Christmas Eve?"

"We don't have any plans."

"You do now. You guys come to our house. We are throwing a big party."

"Ok. I'll let Mark know."

"Speaking of Mark, how was the honeymoon?"

"It was wonderful. I never would've thought he could've planned something like that out. And he had several surprises set up for me when we got there and throughout the week."

"How did you like renewing your vows before your honeymoon?"

"It was a beautiful ceremony. Wait. How did you know about that when I didn't say anything?"

"Well, Mark may have run a few ideas by me. I talked to him at the dress shop. He told me you two got married at the courthouse. You told me that you had never had a honeymoon. I found it sad. So, I slipped him my number so he could talk to me about it."

"I should've known those ideas weren't his."

"Oh no, they were his. All of it was his idea. I just gave my opinion on the things he picked out. He said he wanted to give you the wedding and honeymoon you deserved. I tried to tell him the whole four-wheeler thing should be cut out. He insisted that you would love it. Did you?"

"I loved it. We camped out at this little ranch and the men took Mark hunting. The women taught me how to hula dance. It was an amazing ending to the week," Renee said.

"Well, I'll be damned. See. He had all good ideas. I even fell in love with him a little seeing what he had planned."

Renee laughed with her. They talked a bit longer and said their goodbyes. Renee began to think about Kevin. She hadn't tried to talk to him since she had told 'Alex' goodbye. She logged onto Stratus and saw a lot of messages from Kevin. The first one was where they had been talking last. He'd been talking as Alex asking her not to give up on him. He'd practically begged her to tell him where she was.

Other messages asked her if she was all right. Some stated he hadn't heard from her in a while and just wanted to check in on her. Another asked if she was back from her honeymoon yet. She was surprised when she saw one where he said he missed her. One had asked her to call him. One asked her was she mad at him and if that was why she hadn't answered him. The final one said he wouldn't bother her again as he was sure she didn't want to talk to him again. Renee sighed. She should have told Kevin goodbye. Instead, she typed out a message and sent it.

"Kevin, I went on vacation with Mark. We got married. He decided to surprise me with a small ceremony that was just us and a couple of locals as our witnesses. That's one reason I haven't talked to you in a while. I'm sorry. I couldn't handle the last conversation we had. I'm not mad at you. That wasn't why I didn't respond. It's hard talking to you. I love our friendship. I appreciate all the support, laughs, and just general conversations you've given me the past six months. But, you remind me of something I will never have. I can't keep going like this."

Renee sent the message and logged off. Kevin wasn't online right now anyway.

*   *   *

Renee logged onto Stratus. It was the last chance she would have to talk to Kevin for a while. Jesse's job always shut down the week of Christmas through New Year's. She had gone out and parked in the visitor center. If Jesse happened to get off early today, he wouldn't catch her. Once she logged in, she saw a message from Kevin.

"Hi, Marie. I'm glad to hear back from you. I'm sorry about our misunderstanding. I know how you feel as I felt the same way when we talked like you were Renee. We didn't talk for a while then either. I get it. I want to say congratulations on your marriage but it would be false so I can't. I can't believe you married him after all the things you have gone through. I guess I can't understand because I'm not in your situation. If you truly want to be with Alex, I just know he would come running if you told him where you were. So, you saying I remind you of something you can't have, is beyond me, because I know I would be there in a heartbeat if Renee reached out to me. I've come to care for you and hate to see you unhappy. I've enjoyed our friendship, too, but it sounds like you are telling me goodbye. If that's the case, do me a favor first. Call me just once. I'm only asking for a couple of minutes and then I'll never bother you again, ok? Please just think about it."

Renee reached under the seat and found the phone she'd bought just for this. She was telling Kevin goodbye. It was ripping her apart, but she had to hear his voice one last time. She had to move forward with Jesse and be happy. She had to protect Kevin at all costs, even if he didn't understand it. So she messaged him back since his name was lit up.

"Kevin, I care about you, too, but I can't keep this constant reminder going. I know you don't understand, and as I've said before, I don't expect you to. I am telling you goodbye. So, I'll call you and say a proper goodbye."

She sent the message and picked up the phone. She put the number in and hesitated. Could she tell Kevin goodbye? Did he remember what her voice sounded like? She still remembered what his voice sounded like. Her computer dinged and made her jump. She looked down at her laptop and saw Kevin had messaged her back.

"Marie, I'm ready. Please, call me. I hate that you are telling me goodbye, but I need to hear your voice. Just once."

Renee hit the send button on the phone as her heart started racing. Kevin picked up on the first ring and said hello. Renee's eyes filled with tears as she heard his voice.

"Hello? Marie, is this you?"

"Kevin," Renee breathed out his name.

"Renee, I'd know your voice anywhere. God, baby, please tell me where you are! I love you and will protect you. You don't have to worry about me. I'll end this if you just tell me where you are."

"No. I told you I can't. I love you so much it hurts. But, please, stop looking for me. Goodbye, Kevin," Renee said as a sob escaped her.

She hung up the phone and burst into tears. The phone rang, and she saw Kevin's number and cried harder. She turned the phone off. She went onto Stratus and deleted the account as Marie. She couldn't do this anymore. It was so good to hear Kevin's voice. To hear him say he loved her one last time.

When she finally calmed down, she started the car. As she drove down the road, she threw the phone out of the window onto the interstate. There was no way she could let Kevin know where she was. And she couldn't let Jesse know she'd been talking to Kevin.

*　　*　　*

Kevin felt his phone vibrate in his pocket. He secretly took it out and saw Marie had messaged him. He got another cook to take over and went to the bathroom. No sooner had he gotten in there, his phone rang. He answered it and said hello. At first, he didn't hear anything, so he tried again.

"Hello? Marie, is this you?"

"Kevin," was all he heard, but he knew that voice. He'd been dreaming about that voice for five years but never thought he'd hear it again. He was right. Marie was Renee.

"Renee. I'd know your voice anywhere. God, baby, please tell me where you are! I love you. I will protect you. You don't have to worry about me. I'll end this if you just tell me where you are," Kevin pleaded.

"No. I told you I can't. I love you so much it hurts. But, please, stop looking for me. Goodbye, Kevin."

Kevin heard her sob but then heard a click. No! She'd hung up on him. He immediately dialed the number back. No answer. He hung up and called it again. This time he got a message saying the wireless customer was unavailable. He looked at his phone in disbelief. Renee was alive, and she married that bastard! He had a son! And she'd just told him goodbye forever. He slid down the bathroom wall, breaking down.

This could not be happening. He didn't know how long he'd been there when his manager came to find him. Then, when he saw his state, he sent him home. Kevin wasn't even sure how he got back to his motel room.

He pulled up the number and called it again. Again, he got the same message. He pulled up Stratus and looked at the messages between him and Marie. Her side was now showing user instead of Marie. She'd even deleted her account! He'd never be able to find her now that she was no longer communicating with him.

An idea finally popped into his head. He reverse-searched the number and found it was from Washington state. She had to be living there. She'd used their middle names to represent her and her love. She'd mentioned that Christian even had the same middle name. The question was about the last name. He knew Marie Morgan wasn't the name she was using. How did he search for her if he didn't know her information? His head and heart were hurting. He'd figure it out tomorrow.

*   *   *

The days flew by, and before Renee knew it, it was Christmas Eve. They were going to Valerie's tonight for a Christmas party. Jesse had never really interacted with her friends before. They had hung out with his friends from work, but that was it. She wondered how this was going to go. She got Christian dressed first before she started getting ready.

When she went into the bedroom, Jesse was getting dressed. He was mumbling about the tie she was making him wear. She smiled. He looked good in his white shirt, black vest, black slacks, and tie. The only difference between this and what he wore in Hawaii was that the shirt was long-sleeved. She went over and straightened his tie.

"I don't know why you're complaining. You wore the exact same thing in Hawaii."

"That was a special occasion."

"This is a special occasion. And you look sexy in it."

Renee looked into his eyes and saw the lust there. She smiled at him, and he pulled her against him. He kissed her long and hard.

"If you like it, I'll wear it. You rarely ever compliment me. I like it."

"Things have been different since Hawaii. That trip changed a lot of things, don't you think?"

319

"I do. And I'm glad it did. Now, let's get you ready so we won't be late."

Renee got her dress out while Jesse picked out her underclothes. She grabbed her garter belt and put it on. She slid one thigh-high up and hooked it as she noticed Jesse was standing there watching her. She slid the other one on and hooked it. She slowly slid the panties up as her fingers slid over her skin, teasing him. He'd picked out the skimpiest lingerie she owned. She slid the bra on and adjusted it. Her breasts were almost popping out. She put her hands on her hips as she looked at him.

"Is this really what you want me to wear?"

"No. I don't want you to wear anything but I don't have time to fuck you senseless right now. So, for now, yes, this is what I want you to wear."

Renee put the dress on and walked over to Jesse for him to zip it. His hands went inside the dress and around to her breasts. He kissed her neck as he played with them. Then, after a few minutes, he stopped and zipped her dress. Renee's breathing was fast, and she hated that he affected her. Jesse slid her cross necklace on next. She turned towards him, and his hands ran under the dress and cupped her bare butt.

"I'm not sure if a thong is the right thing to be wearing."

"Ok. Then go bare. Easy access," Jesse grinned.

"You are insatiable."

"Only for you, baby," Jesse said as he pecked her lips.

Upon arriving at Valerie's, Renee saw a bunch of cars. She felt nervous around this many people, especially ones she didn't know. Valerie greeted them as they came in, taking their coats. She introduced Jesse to Bobby.

Jesse shook his hand and took off with him to talk. Renee found that odd. It was almost like they already knew each other.

Renee shook it off and followed Valerie. She took her into the formal room where everyone was. Christian immediately ran up to David, who was with a small group of children. Renee smiled. She loved that Christian was happy and had friends. Valerie introduced her around to everyone. She saw Jesse and Bobby sitting in a corner, and it looked like they were planning something.

"Valerie, has Bobby ever met Mark before?"

"Not that I'm aware of. Bobby asked me who Mark was one day when I was texting him. I explained that he was your husband and was planning a surprise for you and wanted my help. That was the last I heard about that. But, Bobby has been acting suspiciously for a week now. He's planning something, I think. Maybe he wanted another guy's opinion? Someone he knows that won't tell me?"

"Hmmm....that does sound suspicious. Maybe he's getting pointers for your honeymoon?"

Both women laughed at that. Then, Valerie got pulled away by another guest, and Renee decided to walk around and check out the rest of the house. She stood near the double doors that led out to the yard when arms wrapped around her.

"You owe me a kiss," Jesse whispered in her ear.

Renee turned in his arms and raised an eyebrow. Jesse pointed up to the ceiling. Renee looked up and saw the mistletoe hanging above them. She smiled and kissed him. His hands were running over her body as she kissed him. It was a good thing they were alone. She felt him pressing into her and knew what he wanted. Jesse broke the kiss and grabbed her hand, pulling her along. He looked around and made sure no one was watching them as he pulled her into the bathroom.

"What are you doing?" Renee asked as he locked the door behind them.

"I can't wait anymore. You've been driving me crazy since I watched you get dressed at the house."

Renee's eyes widened, and she said, "No. We are so not doing that in Valerie's bathroom."

"I'll be quick," Jesse said as he turned her towards the sink.

She heard him unzip his pants. Before she could react, he had pulled her panties down. His wet fingers found her clit and rubbed it as he kissed her neck. She closed her eyes as she saw his face in the mirror. His eyes were dark and full of lust as he pressed into her. His fingers slid into her.

"You tell me no, but the thrill of this has you wet for me already."

Renee hated to admit he was right. He spread her legs just enough to thrust into her. Renee gripped the counter and bit her lip to keep herself from moaning. He was slamming into her and rubbing her clit as fast as he could as his other arm held her tight to his body. She looked into the mirror, and their eyes met. It was erotic to watch him as he fucked her. She was tight in this position, and he hit her G-spot with every thrust.

He watched her face as she was building up as quickly as he was. Her lips parted, and he put his hand over her mouth, so she didn't make any noise. She moved her head to suck his fingers to stop herself from making noises. Jesse slammed into her, thrusting up until he was on his toes. He took his fingers out of her mouth and covered it again as she came all around him. He buried his face in her neck to stifle his groans of pleasure as he came inside of her.

"I'll let you get cleaned up. I'll leave first so no one suspects anything," Jesse said as he pulled his pants back up.

Renee moved behind the door and shut it behind him, locking it. She leaned against the door, trying to catch her breath. She looked in the mirror and saw her face was flushed. She cleaned herself up and put her panties back on. She waited a couple more minutes to let her face calm down. When she walked out, she looked around and found Jesse talking to Valerie and Bobby like nothing had happened.

When he saw her and smiled, she blushed again. How would she get through the rest of the night without blushing when she couldn't stop thinking about how hot that was?

Jesse slid his hand up her leg at dinner and stopped on her thigh. He squeezed it as he winked at her. He was keeping her turned on, on purpose. She moved her hand up his leg and squeezed him. When he looked at her, she winked and squeezed him again.

Jesse leaned over and whispered, "Do I need to take you back to the bathroom?"

"Only if you don't want a longer session when we get home."

Jesse moved back and studied her face. She was flirting with him. Her lips parted, and her breathing quickened as he jerked against her hand. He leaned over as his hand slid over hers, squeezing him again.

"I hope you'll be ready when we get home because I will thoroughly enjoy fucking you in every way I can."

"Promises, promises," Renee said, smiling, as she knew Jesse would do as he said.

CHAPTER 31

"Jesse, are you sure you don't want to hang out with Greg tonight? I'll be with Valerie and Christian is spending the night with David. You'll be here alone."

"I'm good. I'll be waiting for you when you get home," Jesse replied as he packed an overnight bag for Christian.

Renee wasn't sure how tonight would go. It was a bachelorette party, after all. What if there were strippers there? How much trouble would she get into with Jesse? He'd been doing so well, trusting her and not worrying about her leaving. He hadn't even made a big deal about it when she'd told him about the party. He also hadn't said anything when he'd seen her dress. It was short, stopping right above her knee. The plunge line stopped right between her breasts, yet, he'd said nothing.

"Are you sure you're ok with this?" Renee asked.

"I trust you. You married me. You're wearing your wedding ring, and you always come home to me. You like the things I do to you, so I know you'll come to me to fix it if you have a problem. Stop worrying so much," Jesse said as he cupped her face and kissed her lightly.

Renee knew what happened when Jesse got jealous. Although she wanted to believe he'd changed, she couldn't be sure. Jesse drove her and Christian to Valerie's house. Bobby opened the door and looked at Jesse like he was his savior. Renee heard many women laughing in the background and knew why Bobby looked like that. She patted his arm as she walked in with Christian.

"I'll see you later, baby," Jesse called out.

"You aren't coming in with me?" Renee teased.

"Uh, no. I think I'll stay here with Bobby," Jesse said.

Renee laughed at both of them. She couldn't blame them. She was even afraid to get around a group of women she didn't know. She knew Kristy and Laurie as they were the bridesmaids. She walked into the room, and Valerie squealed as she saw her, hugging her.

"You made it! Let's take Christian up to David's room, and we can go. Tiffany will spend the night, so we are free to stay out late," Valerie said as they walked up the stairs to David's room.

"Isn't Bobby staying with them?"

"Unfortunately, no. He has a late meeting with the manager of his restaurant. He won't be home until late so Tiffany is staying the night."

"Ok. As long as you're sure."

They left Christian with David and Tiffany and headed back downstairs. Valerie gathered everyone to leave when her phone dinged. They went outside, and two limos were waiting. Half the women got in one, and then Valerie and her group got in the other. Renee was glad that Valerie pulled her over to her limo.

They barhopped for the next three hours. Renee decided not to drink because Kristy was getting sloppy drunk and not watching out for Valerie, who was also getting drunk. She drank a glass at the first two bars so Valerie wouldn't think anything was wrong but got virgin margaritas. She wouldn't let Valerie do anything stupid to ruin her relationship. Everyone danced and had a good time. When they came to the final bar, it looked deserted.

"Kristy, I don't think this place is open," Valerie said.

"Oh, it's open," she giggled.

Men started pouring out of the bar. They stood beside the limos, and each one took one of the women inside. Renee took the hand that was offered, but the guy had a mask on. He didn't speak to her as he took her inside. His profile looked familiar, but she didn't know any men that worked at bars. He sat her in one of the chairs facing the stage. Renee looked around, and quite a few men were wearing masks.

"Thank you," Renee said as the man sat her down.

He smiled at her, and she again thought he looked familiar, but he kept his face down slightly. Finally, he nodded and kissed her hand before leaving. Kristy had a round of drinks ordered. Once she had hers, she got on the stage, grabbing a microphone.

"Ladies, it's time to kick this night up a notch. I rented this bar out for the night. Valerie, congratulations, girl! I wish you all the best with your marriage. But, let's have a little fun before you get married and turn into an old woman."

The women started laughing. Kristy came and sat on the other side of Valerie. The lights suddenly went out, and music started playing. When the lights came back on, a group of men who'd escorted the women into the bar was on stage dancing. They danced and stripped down to

G-strings. The women were going crazy and throwing money at them. The men started dancing with the women off the stage as another stripper came on. This one was wearing a mask.

He danced on the stage but then came onto the floor. He stopped in front of Valerie and started dancing. Valerie started cheering as she watched the dancer gyrate in front of her. She began to touch him, and the dancer started smiling. He gave her a lap dance and stayed with her. He must be her stripper since she was the bride to be. The other men were dancing with all the women. One tried to dance with her, but she said no. This was such a bad idea. Valerie was all over the dancer, but it would be fine if she didn't leave with him.

They started having single dancers come out. Some had masks on, and some didn't. They were all introduced as they came out. All the ones with masks on chose a different woman to incorporate into their dances. Renee had to admit that it was erotic.

The next dancer was introduced as Romeo. The lights dimmed, and the spotlight came on, pointing right at him as 'What's Your Fantasy?' started playing. His head was down, and a hat shadowed his face. He wore a black suit, white shirt, tie, and nice dress shoes. He began to move his body, so it was like he was making waves with it. His hand slid down his body, grabbed his dick, and thrust his hips forward. The women started going crazy as he danced while slowly taking his jacket off. Renee felt her face flush as he threw it her way, looking up slightly and at her. She caught sight of the mask covering his face. It left his mouth, and the bottom of his jaw uncovered, but he was definitely smiling at her. She realized that the dancer had walked her into the bar.

She watched as his hips rolled and bucked as he danced around the stage, stopping long enough for the women to look but not touch. Then, he slowly unbuttoned his shirt and came down the steps heading toward her. Renee felt like this was going to cause trouble for her later.

He stopped in front of her, took her hands, and placed them on his chest. He again moved his body, so a wave was going down him from head to toe. He moved her hands down his chest and to his belt. She unbuckled it and pulled it out of his pants as her face flushed. She watched as he loosened his tie but left it on and removed his shirt. He moved close enough to where her head was directly in front of his crotch as he rolled his hips. She looked up at him, and the eyes looking back at her were familiar. *Jesse?* She thought. No, it couldn't be. Jesse had tattoos where this man had none.

He sat in her lap and continued rolling his hips and grinding into her as he again took her hands and put them on his pants. Renee unbuttoned and unzipped them with trembling hands. Renee grabbed his pants and pulled them down enough to show off his tight, black satin shorts. He stood up and shoved the pants down while kicking off his shoes. He stepped out of them as he pulled her up out of the chair.

His hands grabbed her ass, yanking her up. She wrapped her legs around him as he started thrusting his hips into her like they were having sex. Renee's face was so hot that she felt like she would pass out. She had to admit that this man was affecting her. She kept looking into his eyes and thinking they looked like Jesse's. The body was right to be Jesse's, except for the tattoos. He smiled at her as he sat her down and turned her. He bent her over the chair and again thrust his hips forward, so he was shoving his front into her ass. His hands stroked down her back and down to her hips, where he thrust forward hard enough to push her body forward.

Renee bit her lip to cover up the moan that came out of her. This was very reminiscent of how Jesse fucked her. He suddenly stood her up and turned her back around, sitting her back in the chair. He took his hat off and put it on her head. He danced his way backward and ran slightly as he went down on his knees, sliding to a stop in front of her chair. He thrust his hips up towards her a few times. His head went between her legs as he moved his head, rubbing his hair on her panties.

The women started cheering when he did that. He slid his body up hers until his face was right in front of hers. He took her hand and moved it down his body until it was over his dick, where he squeezed her hand on him. She looked at the eyes staring into hers and again thought this was Jesse, but how? When in the hell did he learn to dance like that? Her face was flushed with desire and embarrassment. She tried to get rid of the thoughts. This man turned her on. She was trying to make him into Jesse, so she didn't feel bad about it. That's all this was. But damn, if he didn't have a sexy body and what he was doing with it was driving her crazy.

He stood up and put his hand on her neck, pushing her face forward as he rolled his hips in front of her. Her face was so close that she looked at how big he was as he was hard. He suddenly let go of her neck and bent so his arms went around her. He picked her up and sat on the chair with her on top of him. He shimmied his body under her and then pushed his hips up and down, bouncing her on him. When the song ended, he grabbed her hand and kissed it. Then, he stood up and set her back on the chair, grabbing his hat off her head and putting it back on.

Several women came over to her and were gushing about the dance she'd gotten. She was embarrassed that it had her all hot and bothered. Even Valerie's dancer hadn't done as much as Romeo had. She felt eyes on her, and she looked around, finding Romeo standing in the corner of the bar, watching her. He was still in just those satin shorts, mask, tie, and hat. Her eyes traveled over him, trying to figure out why he reminded her of Jesse.

Her eyes traveled back up his body and to his face. Her eyes locked with his, and he grinned. Even his grin reminded her of Jesse's. He walked towards her as 'All Over Your Body' came on and pulled her out of her seat. He began to dance with her. She didn't think the dancers were supposed to touch the woman so much. However, his hands were everywhere on her body, skimming over her. When the song was over, she stepped back.

"Thanks for the dance. I think I should go to the bar now."

The dancer let her go with a grin. She started fanning herself as she walked over to the bar and ordered a drink. She downed it and used the glass to roll over her face, trying to cool down. She was practically panting from her interaction with that guy. Jesse was a jealous guy, and even though he'd been doing better, he would not like the fact that someone else affected her. She turned, looked at the floor, and saw one of the women coming on to the dancer. However, his attention was on her only.

She didn't like that he was dancing with the other woman even though his gaze was on her. He wasn't dancing sensually with her even though she was trying to. She had to get that mask off him and determine if it was Jesse.

Renee grinned as she heard 'Your Body's Callin' come on. She walked up to where the dancer was with the other woman. She swayed her hips as she walked toward him. She tapped the woman on the shoulder, and she looked at her.

"This one's mine for the night," Renee said as she grabbed the tie he had on and dragged him away with it.

It might get her killed if she was wrong about this, but she had this nagging feeling that she couldn't get rid of. Logically, she knew it wasn't Jesse. Jesse had tattoos over a good portion of his body; this man had none. Also, Jesse had scars on some parts of his body that this man didn't. Furthermore, she didn't smell Jesse's soap. It was a different scent. Jesse could dance since they had been going out dancing, but he couldn't move as this guy could. Nevertheless, she still felt like she was right because of his eyes.

She turned towards him and began to dance with him. She ran her hands over his chest and down to his hips. He grabbed her hips and pulled her into him, grinding into her. Her hands went up, and she stopped at his face.

"Damn, you have got a great body and know exactly what to do with it to get a woman all hot and bothered," Renee whispered as she moved her face close to his, their lips almost touching, and started to push up on the mask.

The voice that came out was deep and gruff but reminded her of Jesse's if he had thrown his voice when he said, "I can show you exactly what I can do with this body if you want," as he took her hands away from his face before she could lift the mask.

"If only I weren't married. I would take you up on that in a heartbeat because you are sexy and got me all hot and bothered. My husband doesn't know how to dance like this, but you remind me a lot of him," Renee said as she stifled a moan because he grabbed her ass as he rubbed himself on her.

Romeo took her hand and moved it down his body as he danced with her. Suddenly, he shoved her hand under his shorts and gripped his hard dick. Her face flushed as she found Romeo was clean-shaven under those shorts. She jerked her hand out. Jesse was not clean-shaven. She looked at him, but he just grinned as he moved closer to her face.

He whispered, "What your husband doesn't know won't hurt him," and kissed her.

They had wound up dancing themselves into a dark corner of the bar where no one was paying attention. Renee turned her head to break the kiss. He started kissing down her neck, not giving up. His hand moved up her thigh to her panties.

"Romeo, stop. I'm married and I'm not a cheater."

"You can't tell me you don't like this. You're so wet that I can feel it through your panties," he said as his fingers slid under them, feeling exactly how wet she was.

"No. Get off. I honestly thought you were my husband trying to trick me somehow."

"I know you want me. I can feel it, but if you insist, I'll stop. No worries. Your husband will thank me later when you go home and fuck his brains out because I got you all wet. Just try not to call out my name when you cum thinking about me."

Romeo kissed her hand and winked at her before walking off. Renee's heart was racing but not from fear. Her panties were soaked. Damn, he'd had a significant effect on her body. She'd never had someone dance like that for or with her before. The bastard was confident. She thought he was Jesse, but Jesse would never shave down there, would he? Romeo's intense gaze followed her wherever she went the rest of the night. He told other women no over and over as they tried to get him to dance. He removed their hands as they tried to get touchy-feely.

She noticed several of the men had kept their masks on. Several of the women left with them. What the fuck? Strippers weren't supposed to leave with the customers. Valerie came bouncing up, drunk and excited.

"We're taking off. I'll see you next week," Valerie said as she hugged her.

"What? You can't possibly be leaving with the dancer! You're going to cheat on your fiancé a week before your wedding?"

"Actually, she's going to a hotel with her fiancé since the kids are at the house," the dancer said as he took off his mask.

Renee's eyes widened as she saw Bobby. Valerie was grinning from ear to ear. Renee started looking around for Romeo. He was gone along with the other dancers. Shit. Was that Jesse? Why wasn't he still here and waiting on her if it was? Moreover, how much trouble was she in if it had been him?

"How did you know it was Bobby?"

"I'd know that body anywhere. But, he told me that Kristy had planned this out with him so I wouldn't get myself into trouble tonight."

"I see. Why were the other dancers wearing masks?"

"Well, he couldn't be the only one. That would look suspicious, wouldn't it?"

"I guess so," Renee replied, still looking for Romeo.

"Looking for the hot guy you were dancing with? Girl, he was working his body on you," Valerie laughed.

Renee blushed. She had been thinking about it all night.

"I wondered if it was Mark since your dancer was Bobby, but he didn't have Mark's tattoos, so that can't be right. So I guess I need to call Mark and have him come get me."

"Nonsense. The limo will take you home. It's taking several other women home. I'm not sure if it was Mark or not. Seems odd that he didn't take you home if it was, especially after that dance. It was hot. Anyway, don't worry about Christian. He's still spending the night with David. So, you can go straight home to Mark."

"Thanks."

CHAPTER 32

An hour later, Renee finally got home. She'd been thinking about Romeo the whole way home. She would've jumped him in the bar if it'd been Jesse. She wouldn't even have cared if anyone saw them. Valerie was right about that dance being hot. She felt herself get wet again thinking about it. She was hoping Jesse was asleep so she could shower and try to go to bed. She knew she wouldn't be able to sleep as horny as she was, but she couldn't come onto Jesse. He'd know what had happened or at least suspect it.

When she went in, the house was dark, but she heard music playing. She walked into the living room and found Jesse sitting on the couch with his head lying back like he was asleep. There was a small lamp on. He had on a pair of jeans, and that was it. So, it hadn't been him earlier. His tattoos were visible. Before she could move further into the living room, Jesse turned his head towards her.

"Hey, baby. Did you have fun tonight?"

"I did. I think I'm going to go to bed," Renee said as she moved toward the bedroom.

"Why don't you come here and spend some time with me first?"

Renee closed her eyes for a minute and let out the breath she took in. She walked over to the couch, and Jesse pulled her onto his lap. He kissed her as he wrapped his arms around her. Renee was so horny that her sense of touch was heightened. Having Jesse kiss her and run his fingers over her back made her moan into his mouth. Jesse broke the kiss as his hand slid up her thigh.

Renee tried to stop his hand from reaching in between her thighs. She was practically panting, and he hadn't even touched her pussy. Jesse quickly moved his other hand between her thighs and felt her panties. They were so wet that they were sticking to her.

"Damn, baby. How much did you drink?"

"Three drinks. That's it," Renee said as she tried not to squirm.

"If you're not drunk, then what's got you so hot and bothered?"

"N-nothing," Renee stammered as she squeezed her thighs together.

"Were there strippers there?" Jesse asked.

Renee swallowed and said, "Yes."

"Did they turn you on, baby? Did you like what you saw? Don't lie to me either because your pussy is telling me everything anyway," Jesse said as he plunged his fingers inside her.

"No. They didn't turn me on."

"So, just one of them, then? What did he do to you, baby? What made your pussy so fucking wet? Did he touch you? Did he kiss you? Tell me what he did to make you so horny that I can't even touch you without you moaning."

Renee was losing her mind with Jesse's slow movements in and out of her. She wanted to ride his hand and get off. But was it fair to do that to Jesse when it was someone else she was thinking about? She figured he'd be angry and flipping out on her by now. But instead, he was touching and kissing her.

"Some of the strippers picked out different women to dance with. I got chosen for one of the dances. Jesse, please stop," Renee begged.

"Why? You can't tell me you don't want to fuck. Your pussy is so wet that your panties are stuck to you. I'm going to have to peel them off. Tell me what the dancer did. Tell me everything."

"Why? You're just going to punish me anyway."

"No punishments. Maybe I'd just like to know what has my wife so turned on. And why she won't let me fuck her senseless to release some of the pressure."

Renee thought about what Romeo had said. She was so not going there. Jesse took his fingers out of her and moved her off his lap. He looked at her, and she looked into his eyes. How had he done it? His eyes and Romeo's were identical. She couldn't believe she would tell Jesse what happened, but she had to know that she wasn't crazy.

"The dancer, Romeo, danced with and on me. It was extremely sensual, and a lot of the movements mimicked sex. Then, during another dance, he kissed me and tried to put his fingers inside me. He knew he got me all hot and bothered. He also put my hand on his dick, twice. And he told me not to scream out his name when I came while fucking my husband."

"And what did you do while he was doing all of this?" Jesse asked, his eyes dark.

"I told him I wasn't a cheater. And that's why I'm going to bed now," Renee said as she stood up.

"Wait," Jesse said as he pulled her towards him. "So, I don't get a chance to prove that I'm just as good? Let me get you wet and fuck you until you can't take it anymore."

Renee was confused. Jesse hadn't gotten mad. Instead, he wanted a chance at getting her horny. Jesse didn't wait for her to answer. He left the room and came back with a kitchen chair. He made her sit in it and picked up the remote to the stereo. He turned on 'Anywhere'. He began to sway his hips from side to side as he ran his hands over his chest and stomach. Renee saw Romeo dancing, blinking her eyes, and seeing Jesse. Jesse did particular spins as his hips rolled and thrust at her. Those tight jeans he had on looked terrific on his ass as he shook it for her. Jesse danced his way to her and sat in her lap. He started moving the top of his body in waves.

"Could you touch your dancer, baby?"

"Y-yes. Somewhat."

"Then, touch me. The only difference is you can touch me as much as you want."

Renee's hands moved over Jesse's chest and stomach as she did with Romeo. She closed her eyes. She was conflicted as she knew this was Jesse, but her thoughts were still running towards Romeo and what happened earlier tonight. Jesse took her hand and put it on his crotch as he started grinding on her lap. Renee unbuttoned and unzipped his jeans, wanting to free his dick from its confinement.

Jesse stood up so she couldn't dive her hand into his boxers. He grabbed the chair as he was still standing over top of her. He started rolling his hips in her face. Renee grabbed the jeans and pulled them down to his knees. She kissed his stomach. Jesse grabbed her hair and shoved his hips forward, so his crotch was in her face as she grabbed his ass. She again reached out to free his dick, but he moved away.

Jesse took his jeans off, slinging them. He got on his knees and spread her legs, pushing her dress up and exposing her panties. Jesse's hands moved up her thighs and to her hips, where he grabbed her panties. She lifted slightly and pulled them off. He pushed her dress up, so she was completely exposed to him.

"Mmmm.... you're dripping you're so wet," Jesse said, putting his head between her thighs and licking her folds.

He suddenly stopped and stood up, grabbing her off the chair. He ground his hips into her, and she moaned.

"Did he make you pant like this, baby?"

"Y-yes," Renee stammered.

Jesse put her down and leaned her over the chair. He smacked her ass and started grinding against her. Renee felt so hot and flustered. No sooner had Jesse shoved his fingers in her than she orgasmed. She bit her lip, so she didn't call out the wrong name. Jesse immediately pulled his fingers out of her and leaned over her, still dancing against her.

"Did he make you do that, baby?"

"No," Renee whispered.

"Good. That's my job."

Renee was still frustrated. The orgasm hadn't been enough to satisfy her. Between Romeo and Jesse, she was ready to go. However, Jesse stepped back from her, went over to the couch, and sat down.

"That's it?"

"That depends on you. You want more? You've told me no several times tonight."

"No, I didn't. I just...." Renee trailed off.

She was trying to get herself together and finding it hard to do. Finally, she slowly lowered down onto the chair. She had only told Romeo no. She looked over at Jesse. He was watching her with the same intensity as Romeo had earlier.

"I didn't think you could dance like that."

"I've been practicing. You want more?"

"I won't say no."

"Come here," Jesse said as his gaze became more intense and lust-filled.

Renee walked over to him. Jesse pulled her down in his lap and kissed her as his fingers pushed inside her. He kissed down her neck, licking and nibbling it. When she started getting close, Jesse pulled his fingers out of her and stood her up. He stood up and danced with her, grinding into her and moving back from her so he could roll his hips. All the while, he was walking forward, causing her to back up without even realizing it. He took her hands and ran them down his chest and stomach as he rolled his whole body.

Renee moaned as he made her grab his dick. He left her hand there as he thrust his hips forward. He reached behind her and unzipped her dress. He pushed it off her shoulders and unhooked her bra. Renee pushed his boxers down, but he grabbed her hands before she could grab his dick. He pushed the dress down, and Renee kicked it away. He pulled the bra off and slung it, too. He took her hands and put them above her head as she felt her body hit the wall.

"Are you still insisting I leave you alone?" Jesse asked as he kept his body far enough back not to touch her.

"I never told you to leave me alone."

"But you did. Now, remember, don't scream my name out while your husband is fucking you," Jesse said as he thrust into her.

Renee closed her eyes, crying out with the intense pleasure she felt as Jesse filled her up. He lifted her, and she wrapped her legs around him. This time felt different than the others. The words that Jesse said finally hit her as she opened her eyes. She gasped as she saw the mask Romeo had on. It was Jesse! Fuck, she was shocked and turned on all at the same time. She didn't know Jesse could dance like that. He'd never done that when they went out.

"You like this, baby? You still think this is a great body?" Jesse said as he ran her hand over his chest.

"Yes. You have a very sexy body and you know exactly what to do with it to get a woman all hot and bothered."

"I'm going to show you exactly what I can do with this body."

"I'm ready," Renee said as she wrapped her arms around his neck and kissed him.

Jesse rolled his hips and thrust into her. He danced for her while he took possession of her body. His hands and mouth were all over her breasts, neck, and lips. He walked them to the bedroom and lay on the bed, so she was on top of him. She started riding him, feeling the friction from him being clean-shaven. It was a fantastic feeling. She looked at him with the mask still on, and she wanted it off. She wanted to see Jesse's face, not someone else's. He was the one who had gotten her all riled up, and she wanted him to be the one to finish her off, not some fantasy. She reached down and pulled the mask off.

"There's the real Romeo," she whispered as she felt an intense orgasm building.

"I'll always be your Romeo, baby," Jesse said as he bounced his hips under her.

"Jesse!" Renee cried out as wave after wave of pleasure crashed over her.

"That's right. You know whose fucking you and bringing you to new heights of pleasure," Jesse said as he rolled her to be on top of her.

He rammed into her over and over until he came. Renee was feeling minor aftershocks of pleasure with each thrust. She didn't want him to stop as it felt so good. But, it wasn't enough. He'd turned her on so much that she was ready to go again. So, she started rubbing herself against him as he lay on top of her.

"Still not satisfied?" Jesse laughed.

"It's your fault. You got me so turned on that I can't get completely satisfied. When did you learn to dance like that?"

"I've been practicing when you weren't around. Bobby told me about the idea Kristy had for Valerie. So, he turned it into the husbands being the strippers if they were willing. We all had to wear masks. I didn't want you to know it was me. I wanted to see your reaction."

"How did you cover up your tattoos and scars?"

"They make a special makeup to cover scars and tattoos. It worked well. But I feel you knew it was me, especially when you jerked my tie and led me away from that other woman. That was hot, by the way. I didn't think you would get jealous over me."

"You're mine just like I'm yours. No other man is allowed to touch me and I'll be damned if another woman gets to touch you."

"You're the only woman I want to touch me. It was a major turn-on when you said you were married and not a cheater. What made you change your mind about it being me?"

Renee blushed as she said, "I knew you didn't shave down there. I couldn't figure out how you hid the tattoos and stuff, but I knew you well enough to know that wasn't something you did. Or at least I thought I did."

"I was told most strippers do that. So I thought I'd give it a try and see how you liked it. I didn't know just how turned on you would get by a dance. I like your reaction."

"The dancing was hot. I'm not even going to attempt to lie because I know you know otherwise."

"I'll have to dance for you more often then. Have your hormones calmed down any?" Jesse asked.

"No. Talking about it is making me think about it. Unfortunately, it's making matters worse."

"I'm here all night, baby," Jesse said as he kissed her.

He stood up, walked over to the closet, and got the tie out he'd worn earlier. Then, he walked over to the bed and climbed on it, sitting on her hips. Renee wondered what he was doing until he grabbed her hands and tied them above her head, then to the headboard with the rest of the tie. Once that was done, he left the room. Then, she heard him turn on Nobody. Renee was panicking as he had thrown her back into the beginning stages of being with him when he tied her up, raped her, and left her there.

She started struggling against the tie as she called out for him. She started panting when he didn't answer, trying not to hyperventilate. By the time Jesse came back, Renee's face was flushed, and her chest was heaving. Jesse saw the panic in her eyes and ran over to the bed, putting the stuff he had in his hands down.

"Hey, what's wrong?" Jesse said as he pushed her hair out of her face and ran his hand across her cheek.

"Untie me. Untie me now!"

Jesse quickly realized why she was panicking. Instead of untying her, he picked up the ice cream he'd gone to get. He scooped some out and trailed it over her breasts. He didn't want her to panic if he tied her up. He bent down, licked the ice cream off, and trailed more over her breasts and down her stomach.

"Untie me, Jesse, please," Renee breathed out as his tongue licked from her stomach to her breasts.

"Ok, I'll stop," Jesse groaned as he sucked her nipple.

"Don't stop. Just untie me."

"If I untie you, then I stop."

"Don't stop," Renee whispered.

Jesse trailed more ice cream over her body and slid it down over her folds. He sucked and licked her breasts longer than need be to get the ice cream off. Next, he moved over her legs and licked down her stomach to her folds. He sucked her folds and opened them enough to put ice cream directly on her clit. She jerked from the cold and then moaned as he licked the ice cream until it was gone. Her hips bucked at the sensation. Jesse pushed his fingers inside of her as he continued to suck and lick her clit. She felt a warm sensation as Jesse backed off and came back to start licking her again. It got a little overwhelming as it got hotter.

"What are you doing to me?" Renee whimpered.

Jesse came up and kissed her. She tasted herself and peppermint. He thrust his tongue into her mouth as he thrust into her. She pulled on the tie, wanting to stop the overwhelming sensations in her body. Jesse didn't stop or untie her, however. Instead, he sat up and thrust into her as he moved up and down, causing friction between them as he rubbed her clit. Finally, he moved his legs to the outside of hers and pushed them together while still inside her. He began thrusting into her as hard as possible before pulling back some and ramming back in.

"Oh my God!" Renee yelled, her eyes rolling back as an intense orgasm hit her.

"That's right, baby. You cum so good for me, and you take this dick so well," Jesse said as he kept his rhythm the same.

Renee squirmed under him as her sensitivity was too much for what he was doing. Her body began to buck. Her breathing was harsh, causing her chest to heave. He'd tied her up so he could torture her. But it was so good. Her body was in overdrive as she built back up quickly, never fully recovering from her orgasm.

When Jesse felt her drawing close again, he pulled out of her. He pushed her legs up and onto one of his shoulders. He thrust into her and pushed her legs back into her chest, which caused her to become extremely tight. He put his hands beside her to get leverage and fucked her hard and fast. She screamed as her orgasm hit, and her hips bucked off the bed. Jesse was right behind her calling her name as he came.

"Satisfied now, baby?" Jesse panted as he untied her hands.

"Very," Renee said as she curled against his side and instantly fell asleep, feeling extremely satisfied and spent.

CHAPTER 33

Renee drove to the Cathedral to make sure everything was set up the way she wanted. The wedding started at 4 pm. So there was plenty of time to make sure everything was right. When she pulled up, the workers were wrapping the flowers around the arch outside. It was just as pretty as she'd pictured it, with snow on the ground and the trees. They had cleared the walkway for the carpet and had hauled it off, so the snow was flat on both sides of the walkway. She walked into the building and saw the men decorating the arch inside.

Men were on tall ladders putting the lights around the ceiling. She walked into the second room and found the caterers setting up the tables. She went back out and started setting up the chairs. An hour later, she looked around and saw everything was almost done. Then, two men rolled out the carpet to the door. She closed the doors behind her, not wanting anyone to see anything yet.

Valerie showed up with Kristy and Laurie in tow. Renee greeted them and showed them to the bride's room. Bobby showed up ten minutes later. His best man and groomsman walked in a few minutes later. She showed them to the room they would be in.

She went outside and saw everything was finished. She was highly pleased with the way it looked. She went back in and checked everything out. The workers turned on the lights, and they made the room sparkle. She smiled. The band had come in through the back door and set up in the dining room.

The photographer came in, and she got them to take pictures of the archway outside and then come back in. They took pictures of the wedding hall. She sent them to take the before pictures of the bride and groom. Valerie had her come in and take pictures with them.

Jesse came in with Christian in tow. She sat them in the middle where she could quickly get to them without interrupting the wedding. When it was time, she went and got Bobby. He took his place under the arch. The guitarist started playing the wedding march after the preacher took his place. The flower girl came out and began throwing peach rose petals on the carpet.

David was next. He looked so cute in his tux. His face was scrunched up with concentration, trying not to drop the pillow with the rings on it. He went and stood beside Bobby. Bobby's best man came next, walking the maid of honor down the aisle. They took their places on the stage. The best man was standing on the top step across from the maid of honor. The other groomsman came next with the last bridesmaid. The last bridesmaid and groomsmen were on the second step.

Valerie came next. She looked breathtaking in her dress. Renee had added ivy to Valerie's bouquet, so it trailed down Valerie's hands. She had her hair up in a half bun, with her hair being curled as it traveled down to her shoulders.

Valerie came down the aisle, her train trailing behind her. Renee smiled as she saw the grin on Bobby's face and how Valerie was trying not to cry. This is how a wedding was supposed to be, beautiful and full of love. Renee felt eyes on her, and she looked at Jesse. He was watching her reaction. She liked what he had done for her, but she missed having her family there. Valerie's father walked her down the aisle and put her hand in Bobby's. Renee watched as Valerie married the love of her life.

Once the wedding was over, Renee ensured everything was set up as the photographer took photos of the bridal party. Jean had his people setting the plates out. There were name cards for everyone so they would get what they ordered. Renee was pleased with how Jean handled his staff.

When everything was ready, she brought Valerie and Bobby in. She sat them first and then the rest of the guests. She had put Jesse and Christian in the back with her. While she had been invited to the wedding, she was still the wedding planner.

Jean's staff began to uncover the plates, placing the tops on a cart. Once that was done, they poured everyone a glass of wine. The children received grape juice. Anyone who didn't want either received water. Everyone dug in and started talking. The place was alive with a buzz of excitement.

The reception lasted for hours. The toasts were made. Then, Valerie placed her hand on the knife to cut the cake, and Bobby put his on top. They cut the cake together. Valerie wiped the cake on Bobby's face. He smiled and kissed her, rubbing his face on hers. She laughed, and Bobby put a piece of cake in her mouth. He took a napkin and wiped her face and then his. The look of love in their eyes said it all. The music started and the bride and groom had their first dance. Once that was over, everyone danced. Renee danced with Christian before he ran off to play with David.

"May I have this dance?" Jesse asked as he held out his hand to her.

"Yes, you may," Renee said as she took his hand.

"It looked like you were sad during the wedding."

"I miss my family. I always thought my father would give me away. I miss having my crazy best friend around. She definitely would have done something like Kristy did. I wonder if they ever think about me and miss me as I miss them."

"I'm sure they do. If I took you back, they would arrest me so I can't."

"I know I can't go back and I can never contact them. They wouldn't understand why I disappeared and never returned. They probably think I'm dead. But, I'm sure they've grieved for my loss and moved on."

Jesse felt guilt grip his heart as he saw the tears in her eyes. He loved her and wanted her to be happy. But, he knew not seeing her family saddened her. Renee put her head on his shoulder and closed her eyes, fighting back the tears. He kissed her as the song ended. She smiled at him, but it was her fake smile, the one he hated to see on her face. He had become a better dancer in the past few weeks of practice. So, he kept her on the floor for a fast-paced song. When she finally let go of him, she looked a little happier.

Renee danced with Bobby, then Valerie. She danced with Valerie, Kristy, and Laurie as they all laughed at each other. She had a wonderful time after she got over her initial sadness. Before she knew it, it was nine o'clock.

"Alright, ladies and gentlemen, the bride and groom need to get going. So, we are going to do the tradition of throwing the bouquet and garter belt," Renee called out.

Once that was done, Bobby and Valerie headed to the dressing rooms to change. Renee started seeing the guests out. Once all the guests were gone, Jean and his crew began to clean the area. Jesse came up to her with a sleeping Christian in his arms. She smiled at Christian's angelic face. He'd played himself out.

"Are you leaving after you see Valerie and Bobby off?"

"No. I have to stay and make sure everything is cleaned up."

"I'll stay with you then."

"No, it's ok. Take Christian home and get him into bed."

"Alright. If you're sure. Be careful going home," Jesse said as he kissed her goodbye.

"You too," Renee said as she broke the kiss.

Renee kissed the top of Christian's head and said, "I love you."

Jesse left as Valerie and Bobby came into the wedding hall. Valerie's parents took their wedding attire and left with David in tow. Valerie came over and hugged Renee goodbye.

"Thank you, Tabitha. It was a beautiful wedding. It was better than I imagined it would be. And thank you for overseeing the cleanup."

"It was my pleasure. I really enjoyed planning your wedding. And it made Mark do something I never thought he would. Especially the whole dancer thing," Renee laughed.

"I still can't believe that was him. Maybe I should get him to show Bobby some moves."

"Hey! I wasn't that bad!" Bobby said, acting offended.

"No, you did a great job, baby," Valerie laughed.

"Alright, you two. Time to get going so you don't miss your flight."

Renee ushered them out and watched them drive away in Bobby's car. She went back in and oversaw the cleanup. She checked the entire building to make sure everything was gone. Once she was done checking, she turned off all the lights and locked the doors. She got into her SUV and hooked her seatbelt. She took one last look at the Cathedral and backed out. She turned up her radio and jammed to her music on the way home. It started to snow when she was halfway home. She drove a little slower just in case it was icy anywhere. Finally, she came to a red light and stopped.

When it turned green, she started to go. Halfway through the light, she heard screeching tires. She looked to her left just as a car smashed into her side of the car. Her body jerked to the right and back to the left. Her head smashed into the driver's window hard enough to shatter it as the car hit the door. The car flipped over as the other car kept coming out of control. As the car skidded down the road, Renee's last thoughts were on Kevin and Christian and how she would never see them again. They would never get the chance to meet.

*   *   *

Jesse looked at his watch. It was midnight, and Renee still wasn't home. He went to the front door and opened it. He was worried as it had started snowing and sticking to the ground. Maybe she was just driving slower due to the weather. He closed the door and went back into the living room. He picked up his phone and called her. It just rang until her voicemail picked up. Why wasn't she picking up the phone?

He kept trying to call her, but it just rang and went to voicemail every time. He knew she wouldn't run away. He had Christian. He was pacing the living room, calling her number over and over. After thirty minutes, someone finally picked up. Jesse got angry when he heard a man say hello. He hung the phone up, feeling rage going through his veins. His phone rang, and he saw Renee's number. Had she really called him back after a man had answered her phone?

"Are you seriously calling me back after a damn man picked up your phone?" Jesse yelled.

"I'm sorry, sir, but this is not who you thought was calling. We weren't able to get to the phone until now. My name is Ryan. I'm with Unit 19, the EMS crew. How do you know the woman who owns this phone?"

Jesse felt the blood drain from his face. EMS crew? Where was Renee? He couldn't think straight. What was happening? His grip on the phone tightened as the guy said hello.

"My name is Mark Morgan. This is my wife's number, Tabitha Morgan," Jesse whispered.

"Mr. Morgan, I'm sorry to inform you this way, but your wife has been in an accident. We had to use the jaws of life to get her out. She was struck on the driver's side by another vehicle. She's unresponsive and lost a lot of blood from multiple injuries. We won't know the extent of those injuries until she gets to the hospital. She's on the way there now. You need to get there, but be careful. The roads are icy."

Jesse just stared at his phone. He heard the man calling his name, but it sounded like he was talking through a tin can. He finally put the phone back up to his ear and told him thank you as he told him what hospital she was being taken to. He hung up the phone and grabbed his keys. He had to get to the hospital. Right before he got in the car, he thought about Christian. He shook his head, trying to clear it. He couldn't take Christian to the hospital with him.

He went back into the house, calling Greg on the way to Christian's room. Greg didn't answer, so he hung up and called right back as he grabbed Christian's shoes and coat. He put on the jacket and hung up the phone. Then, he redialed Greg's number as he put Christian's shoes on.

"Hello?" Greg's sleepy voice said.

"Greg, it's Mark. I'm sorry to wake you up so late, but Tabitha's been in an accident. I need to get to the hospital immediately. I can't take Christian with me. Can you guys watch him for me?"

"Yeah, man, we'll watch Christian. Do you need me to come get him?" Greg asked.

"No. I'll bring him there on the way to the hospital. I have to go so I can get there."

"Ok, be careful."

Thirty minutes later, Jesse was knocking on Greg's door. Greg took Christian out of Jesse's arms, and Jesse immediately ran back to his car. He had to get to the hospital. He had to get to Renee. He couldn't lose her; he just couldn't. He wanted to fly like a bat out of hell, but the roads were too icy. He feared he'd be too late if he didn't get there. However, he wouldn't do Renee any good if he wound up in the hospital. So he had to force himself to slow down.

"Hang on, baby. I'm coming," Jesse mumbled.

He pulled into the parking lot and found a spot. He rushed into the ER and ran to the nurse's station. The woman was on the phone, and he was growing impatient. He finally lost his patience.

"Lady, I need to know where my wife is! She was in a bad wreck and brought in almost an hour ago!"

"Sir, I need you to calm down. What's your wife's name?"

"Tabitha Morgan!" Jesse yelled.

He was trying his best not to strangle this woman when she raised an eyebrow at him. His knuckles turned white as he gripped the counter. Finally, she looked at her computer screen, and her face softened.

"Mr. Morgan, please have a seat. I'll let the doctors know you're here. They'll need to come to talk with you."

Jesse's heart felt like it would beat out of his chest. Was Renee dead? He paced around the waiting room for what seemed like hours. A nurse finally came out and started asking him for information about Renee. His fear was turning into anger as he wasn't getting any answers. Finally, he sat in a chair and put his head in his hands, trying to calm down.

"Stay with me, Renee. Things were finally good between us. I need you with me," Jesse whispered as he started to cry.

Printed in the United States
by Baker & Taylor Publisher Services